NORTHBROOK PUBLIC LIBRARY
1201 CEDAR LANE
NORTHBROOK, IL 60062

AUG 1 4 2008

Northbrook Public Library

3 1123 00856 5783

MURDER IN THE
RUE DE PARADIS

W9-COJ-705

NORTHBROOK PUBLIC LIBRARY   AUG 1 4 2008
1201 CEDAR LANE
NORTHBROOK, IL 60062

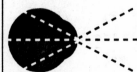

This Large Print Book carries the
Seal of Approval of N.A.V.H.

AN AIMÉE LEDUC INVESTIGATION

MURDER IN THE RUE DE PARADIS

CARA BLACK

WHEELER PUBLISHING
A part of Gale, Cengage Learning

GALE
CENGAGE Learning

Detroit • New York • San Francisco • New Haven, Conn • Waterville, Maine • London

GALE
CENGAGE Learning

Copyright © 2008 by Cara Black.
An Aimée Leduc Investigation Series.
Wheeler Publishing, a part of Gale, Cengage Learning.

ALL RIGHTS RESERVED
Wheeler Publishing Large Print Softcover.
The text of this Large Print edition is unabridged.
Other aspects of the book may vary from the original edition.
Set in 16 pt. Plantin.
Printed on permanent paper.

LIBRARY OF CONGRESS CATALOGING-IN-PUBLICATION DATA

Black, Cara, 1951–
    Murder in the rue de Paradis / by Cara Black.
        p. cm. — (An Aimée Leduc investigation series)
    ISBN-13: 978-1-59722-786-5 (softcover : alk. paper)
    ISBN-10: 1-59722-786-2 (softcover : alk. paper)
    1. Leduc, Aimée (Fictitious character) — Fiction. 2. Women
private investigators — France — Paris — Fiction. 3. Paris
(France) — Fiction. 4. Large type books. I. Title.
PS3552.L297M865 2008b
813'.6—dc22   2008015566

Published in 2008 by arrangement with Writer's House, LLC.

Printed in the United States of America
1 2 3 4 5 6 7 12 11 10 09 08

To Leyla Zana
and all the ghosts

"Getting history wrong is an essential part of being a nation."
— Ernest Renan, French historian

■ ■ ■ ■

PARIS
AUGUST 1995

■ ■ ■ ■

Monday Evening

Pigeons scattered and fluttered under the rue de Rivoli's nineteenth century arcade as Aimée Leduc shut the taxi door. She fanned herself in the dense humid heat that clung blanket-like over the street which was deserted except for a bedraggled group of Japanese tourists. Across from her, the street lamp's glow was reflected as gold from the tall windows of the Louvre's Cour Carrée.

"*Au revoir,* Jean-Paul," Aimée said, eager to leave her blind date.

"You sure you won't come for an aperitif?" Jean-Paul asked from the taxi's back seat. A fortyish ministry *fonctionnaire* with a red tie, blue shirt, and thinning hair, Jean-Paul had discussed his stamp collection over espresso.

"*Desolée,* too much work," she said.

He waved away the francs she held out to him through the open taxi window and grasped her hand. "Then the theater tomor-

11

row," he said, "I'll call you when I get home."

Aimée hurried past the corner café on rue du Louvre into the deepening twilight shadows mottling her office building. As she mounted the staircase to Leduc Detective's third-floor office she vowed, no blind dates. Never again. No matter how desperate she felt.

She switched on the office light, her eyes resting briefly on the chipped carved ceiling moldings, the dim chandelier, the pile of bills on her desk. A faint breath of air from the window stirred, pierced by the insistent whine of a siren from the Seine. Another long evening stretched ahead of her: balancing accounts and drafting more computer IT proposals to potential clients. But there was no man in her thoughts.

The office phone rang. Jean-Paul already? She dreaded having to come up with more excuses not to see him again.

"Leduc Detective," she said.

"My partner likes your IT proposal, Aimée," said Michel, the head of Microimages.

She almost dropped the phone. Only yesterday she'd left a proposal at his video post-production company.

"Michel, you want me to consult?"

"Bring a contract, Aimée. We're having a blowout party for our big project!"

The thump of a bass guitar vibrated over the phone.

"So we can celebrate?"

"You and a few others."

A plum consulting job!

"I'm on my way."

She grabbed a standard contract from the desk drawer, stuck it in her laptop bag, and opened the office armoire. Her trusty little black dress and pearls wouldn't do. Not for Michel's. She searched through the hangers, past the blue work jacket, the electricians' overalls, finding a leather halter dress, then a strapless Louis Feraud chiffon more suited for the runway. But she ended up in a '60s minidress composed of tiny black mirror-like sequin rectangles. Vintage Carnaby Street. She outlined her eyes with kohl and knotted a scarf around her neck. After all, it was business.

Back on rue du Louvre, she caught a taxi, then turned off her phone to avoid Jean-Paul's call. Approaching Michel's district on the wide shop-lined boulevard leading to Gare du Nord, the taxi turned left at a soot-stained old convent wall. Here the streets narrowed. A couple emerged, laughing, from a dimly lit bistro. The taxi passed a dark warehouse, the side of an old building still bearing a faded blue Dubonnet advertisement, and let her off in front of an arched stone passage between shadowy buildings.

Aimée choked in the haze of blue smoke as she stood wedged among the bodies dancing to a pounding techno beat at Microimage's party. Microimage's sandblasted stone walls vibrated; half-filled glasses of *rouge-limonade* rippled as they stood on the concrete slabs serving as tables. Red velvet drapery swags hung from the arching iron metal struts in the former leather factory.

Perspiration dampened her bare shoulder blades. Fresh air, she craved fresh air. She thanked God she'd chosen vintage, considering the eclectic crowd around her. Her laptop-bag strap dug into her bare shoulder, but she shot a grin at Michel, the savvy red-headed twenty-something Microimage founder who had the attention span of a gnat. His arm draped a tall Goth type, clad head-to-toe in black lace, and he gave Aimée a thumbs-up.

"Nice outfit," he said. "I like consultants who complement the decor. We'll sign the contract; pick it up day after tomorrow."

She reached out to shake his hand.

"My way of doing business," he said, or at least that's what she thought she heard as he handed her a tangerine from his pocket. She was thrilled to snag the consulting job. The retainer would cover her office rent and more. Dry-mouthed, she peeled the thin skin away from the pulp as she worked her way toward the door. The citrus essence clung to her fingers. She scanned the crowd.

She popped a tangerine segment into her mouth, enjoying the sweet burst of flavor. She avoided a karate chop from a gesticulating, long-haired journalist in black leather pants attempting to drive home a point. His audience was composed of a *télé* exec, a sweater knotted around his shoulders, and a rail-thin model in a belted T-shirt passing for a minidress. Just. A crowd interested in racking up business connections and on the prowl for an *adventure,* the one-night kind. Not her type. Forget meeting a man here, she thought. Conversation was next to impossible against the blasting beat.

She edged her way out the door, inhaled the warm air, and gazed around her. The warehouse at the end of the cobbled courtyard housed a recording studio. Lining one side of the yard was an old glass-windowed workshop, now an architect's office; and beside it stood the wooden storefront of a shuttered lute-repair shop.

Behind her, the Turkish concierge swept up leaves and scooped them into a bin. She'd left the consulting proposal with him yesterday to be hand-delivered to Michel upon his return.

"*Bonsoir.*" She smiled and nodded to the concierge.

"*Bonsoir,* Mademoiselle," he said.

The dense August evening air lay still and heavy. A figure was leaning against the cream-colored stone walls under the glass-awninged *marquise* canopy.

No trains ran this late after the terrorist Metro bombing a few days ago in Saint-Michel that had claimed eight lives. She stuck a stop-smoking patch under her arm and wondered what her chances were of catching a taxi this time of night.

A voice came from the shadows. "So you're still trying to quit."

That familiar voice. The tilt of the head . . . she froze. But it couldn't be . . . he was a continent away!

Yves, her former boyfriend, stepped into the light. And her breath caught. His dark eyes were more deepset, but he had the same long black hair and snaking sideburns; this was a more tanned, gaunter version of the man she'd maintained an on-again, off-

16

again relationship with.

"Cairo not hot enough for you, Yves? But . . . how did you find me?" she said, trying to cover her confusion.

"Investigative journalists have their ways, Aimée." He stepped closer, a softness in his eyes. His fingers traced her bare shoulders. "Nice outfit. I just flew in, wanted to see you first."

His musky scent drew her again. Still her bad-boy type. But she remembered that the last time they'd said good-bye, on a street corner on the Left Bank, she'd told herself never again.

"So you appear and expect —"

"To have a drink, Aimée," he said, the back of his hand brushing her cheek. "You didn't answer my e-mails."

This would go nowhere. Just another pit stop for him. Whenever their paths crossed, the next morning he'd say good-bye on the street corner, step into a taxi and out of her life.

"Give me some warning next time," she said, backing away. "We'll try for that drink."

The Turkish concierge's twig broom raked the stones. A glimmer of yellow light from the party behind them swept Yves's face. She saw an expression she couldn't identify.

"I'm catching a taxi," she said.

"But I've already got one waiting out front," he said with his lopsided smile. That wonderful smile. "Let me drop you."

So sure of himself.

"Forget it, Yves. You're not coming to my place."

"Did I say I was? I'm stationed in Paris now. Let's have a drink to celebrate, that's all."

Outside of the dark passage, the taxi idled forlornly on the deserted street. The Metro was closed and she'd have a long walk in her three inch Louboutin heels to her empty apartment where not even her dog Miles Davis waited.

Relenting, she said, "One drink."

She repressed a quiver of unease and got into the back seat.

The taxi took off. It passed a "for sale" sign in the broken windows of a dilapidated 18th-century *hôtel particulier.* Then it turned onto rue de Paradis, a street of shuttered crystal and porcelain shops, the only sign of life a stray cat on the cracked pavement. On the building walls hung peeling posters announcing an iKK — Kurdish Workers Party — protest.

She watched Yves, wondering what lay behind his sudden appearance in Paris. The taxi edged along rue du Château d'Eau filled with African hair-supply shops and crowded hairdressing salons, open late. Multicolored wigs, dreadlocks, and extensions hung in the windows like confetti. Here the street teemed with life. Another world. Young African men gathered, laughing and talking, on the packed corner.

"Stop a moment," Yves said to the taxi driver.

He disappeared inside Afro Coiffeur, a small shop filled with women having their hair braided. The warm air from the open window brushed her knees and the bubbling syllables of Tongolaise dialect teased her ears.

Yves emerged a moment later, a bag in his hand.

"What about that drink, Yves?"

"You'll see."

A few blocks later at the Canal Saint-Martin, a dark stain of water running to the Seine, Yves paid the taxi driver. The canal's surface was pockmarked with the reflections of streetlights like so many diamonds, framed by the leafy plane trees that lined the banks. An arched metal footbridge spanned the narrow canal. No barges were cruising at this time of night.

Yves patted the slatted wooden seat of a bench near a squat bollard meant to block

19

parking. He pulled a bottle of Veuve Cliquot from the bag, worked his thumbs on
the cork, and popped it. Not a drop spilled.

"Still your favorite, Aimée?" he asked,
handing her the bottle.

"Since when do you get champagne from
a beauty parlor?"

"Pays to have connections when the shops
are closed." He grinned. *"Salut."* She heard
the rumble of a truck along the narrow
street on the opposite bank. A dog barked
in the distance.

"I almost forgot how big your eyes are,"
Yves said, his voice the same, the reasoned
tone and familiar warmth as well as the bad-
boy glint in his eye.

She ran her fingers through her spiky hair,
then took a swig from the bottle. The chilled
champagne slid smoothly down her throat.
"That may have worked last time, Yves."

Last time and every time.

"You're a force of nature, Aimée. My
nature," Yves said. "Stay with me."

She blinked. Just like that?

"You just appear. . . ."

"Without warning." He gave that little
lopsided smile, that same wonderful lopsided smile. "Selfish, I know," he said. "But
now I'm based here and I've put in an offer
to buy my friend's loft. Right there." He

gestured to the renovated warehouse behind them. It had been a printing works. There was a light in one of the rectangular window slits. "I can't forget you," he said. "That's the problem."

"Correction: *your* problem."

And then his mouth was on hers, searching, moving on to nibble her neck. In the evening warmth, a frisson flared up her spine.

"Let's try again, Aimée," he begged.

She averted her eyes from his dark searching ones. She'd thought of him, more times than she'd like to admit.

"We've tried this before, remember? It doesn't work," she said, one hand clutching the bench.

No matter how much she'd wanted it to. A lone pigeon pecked at the cobblestones by her feet. The still water of the canal was like a ribbon of dark-green silk.

"This time it's different," he said. "No more quick visits, no more good-byes on street corners."

"And pigs may fly, Yves."

He grinned. "You never used to mix passion with practicality."

She wished she didn't want him to kiss her again.

"So I'll prove it to you," he said, standing

up and reaching for her hand.

Common sense dictated that she hail a taxi and leave trouble behind. She stood. But when had she listened to common sense?

The luminous digital clock read 1 a.m. when she woke up. The champagne was now a dull thud in her head. She felt a cold space beside her. She rubbed her eyes, in a strange unknown room, her dress in a heap on the floor. Then she remembered his arms around her, his mouth running down her shoulder blades. Once inside the dark industrial loft, they hadn't even made it to the bed.

She elbowed herself up. Yves sat on the floor, a sheet around his shoulders, silhouetted against the floor-to-ceiling window overlooking the blackness of the Canal Saint-Martin. Quiet and dark, like the canal.

In her bare feet she padded past metal rungs in the wall. "I'm chilly," she said, snuggling beside him.

The moon shone above the filigreed shadows of the trees. The glow from the canal streetlight illuminated a copy of *Le Monde* beside him. He simmered with some emotion she couldn't put her finger on. A quiet sadness mixed with anger? He wrapped his arms around her, pulled her close. Part of her knew she should let him wrestle with his private demons alone, but another part wanted to offer consolation or comfort.

She'd first met him in the Marais, disguised as a skinhead, involved in an exposé of the neo-Nazi movement. "You're undercover again, aren't you?" she asked.

"I can't talk about it." He pulled her closer. The stubble on his chin brushed her cheek.

More secrets. "You want a relationship, yet you won't talk about what you do?"

"It's complicated." He averted his eyes.

"This can't work, Yves."

"Look, I had to go there," Yves said. "And find out."

"Find out that you could only expose a percentage of the world's corruption?"

She could have told him that.

"Turkey's incredible," he said. "So beautiful. You'd love the indigo and aquamarine sky over Mount Ararat, Aimée."

Surprised, she sat back. "You know I'm a city girl."

His gaze was far away. "Nothing prepares you for the vastness, the monumental scale of the landscape. Breathtaking and harsh. Everything is bigger than life there." He looked down. "Red dust, baking heat . . .

23

and the refugees. The children are the worst."

A wren winged over the canal, the soft flapping of its wings and ruffle of leaves as it settled on a branch across from them just audible.

"What do you mean, Yves?"

"I mean it's useless to fight how I feel about you."

"Quit changing the subject."

Aimée clutched the sheet around her. Was he lonely, overworked, or. . . .

"I haven't been here for you, Aimée."

She wondered where that came from.

"That's trite, Yves."

He took a deep breath. "You know, I've never said this to anyone . . . I want to spend my life with you."

Her breath caught in her throat. He'd changed, something felt different.

His dark eyes searched hers, then he took her hand. She felt something smooth and cool. In her palm lay a bright embroidered patch, a coin amulet on a frayed woven string. Tribal by the look of it. Unique.

"An Anatolian Sufi gave me this amulet at a Kurdish Dervish ceremony."

In the slant of moonlight, she stared at the gleaming worn Ottoman coin.

"A talisman for vision, to help you to see

your way. It prevents you from being blinded by obstacles and false paths. Betrothed girls wear this before the wedding ceremony. And a ring like this."

He held out a beaten copper Turkish puzzle ring.

"Will you accept this?"

Dumbfounded, she stared at him.

"Close your mouth, Aimée," he said. "You can nod yes or no."

She stared at him. "You're serious?"

"That's not an answer," he said. His eyes crinkled in sadness. "Or maybe it is."

"For real, Yves?"

He nodded.

Something shifted inside her. A warm feeling welled up . . . happiness, security, or the knowledge that he was the one . . . the words didn't matter. Now it was all so simple. Her doubts were gone in a flutter of air. She wanted him. Had wanted him for a long time.

"And we can make some babies," he said. He reached for her cheek and her hands caught his.

"That takes work."

"So you'll have me?" A slow smile spread on his lips as she guided the ring onto her ring finger.

She edged her leg around his waist,

gripped his neck, eased him flat on the floor, straddling his hips.

" 'Have you,' Yves? Yes, yes, yes."

He pulled her down on top of him, and smothered her words with kisses.

Aimée blinked at the pink-apricot rays filtering through the half circle of the loft window. The clock read 10 a.m. Late! She reached out and felt an empty space beside her.

"Yves?"

No answer. No welcoming aroma of coffee. She stood and pulled a sheet around her. She looked in the bathroom and spotless kitchen. No note. No Yves.

She didn't see his briefcase, and wondered for a moment if she'd dreamed last night. But his musky scent still clung to her.

He'd asked her to marry him. The beaten copper ring encircled her finger. Why shouldn't she trust him? She knew he was undercover. But old doubts invaded her. He'd left without even waking her to say good-bye. She was ready to kick herself for her stupidity. Again. She slipped into her clothes and shouldered her laptop case.

Blinking back angry tears, she walked through the narrow courtyard lined with bamboo trees in planters of the former printing works. Wind chimes tinkled and sun glinted on the tall, wood-framed loft windows. At the door, she knotted her scarf around her shoulders. Outside, by the canal, whose waters shimmered in the sun, she caught the stares of truck drivers driving past. Luck was on her side; she caught a taxi.

Outside her office she nodded to Maurice, the one-armed Algerian-veteran news vendor whose kiosk was near the café. With an adroit maneuver of his stump, Maurice stacked yesterday's *Le Monde,* the same edition she'd noticed lying on Yves's briefcase last night.

"Business good, Maurice?" she asked.

"These headlines increase sales," he said. "Sad to say."

The article in the paper on the Metro bombing cited a police source indicating that new leads to suspects ranged from Bosnian Serbs angry at the French accords, members of Hamas angry at Arafat's projected visit, the iKK Kurdish party that had demonstrated last week at the Turkish Embassy and to militant GIA Algerians suspected of murdering a moderate imam two weeks earlier.

In short, the police had nothing to go on,

and so had fallen back on the usual suspects.

"The Metro's running on a limited schedule," he said. "You know how that goes."

With half the city taking part in the annual vacation exodus, the museums closed, bus schedules reduced to the minimum, and heightened security, the streets lay quiet. She slipped Maurice two francs, took a paper, and headed to her office.

The sun filled the air; another hot August day. A few cotton puff clouds hovered over the Louvre's Cour Carrée façade. For a moment the image of Yves, the stubble on his chin and the feel of his warm legs enfolding hers, filled her. But when she fingered the Turkish puzzle ring she was tempted to toss it into the sewer drain.

When he called she'd demand an explanation. She pushed Yves out of her mind.

In the cool foyer of her office building she sighed. There was an "out of order" sign posted on the elevator. Great! That meant no repair until September.

Inside Leduc Detective, she set her laptop on the desk, headed for the armoire, changed into a top and black pencil skirt, then switched on the espresso machine. In five minutes thick brown-black liquid with a decent tan foam dripped into the demitasse cup. She stirred in brown sugar cubes, sipped, and welcomed the jolt of caffeine.

The office door unlocked and she turned, cup in hand, to see the flushed face of her partner, René Friant. A dwarf, he wore an off-white double-breasted linen suit tailored to his four-foot-tall frame. And matching tasseled loafers.

"The elevator repairman on his way, Aimée?"

The concierge was no doubt sitting on a shale beach in Brittany with his family as they spoke.

She shook her head.

He took out a handkerchief, wiped his wide brow and set a printout on her desk. "It's only one of many things that don't work here. The heating's more temperamental than my Italian printer, working full blast now instead of in December." René gestured around the high-ceilinged wood-paneled office which was filled by a period recamier, marble fireplace, directoire desks, and computer ware. "And we've outgrown this place."

True. But her grandfather had founded Leduc Detective at the very desk she now used.

"Check this out, Aimée," he said. "It's for sale."

On the printout she saw price comparisons

of building footage. "A factory floor in Passage du Desir, René? You're kidding, right?"

"The mortgage payments will be less than our rent," he said. "And we'd own it. Instead of scrambling every month to pay off our *landlord's* mortgage."

What had gotten into him?

"And if we didn't make it, René," she said, "there'd be no extension from the landlord, and we'd be out on the cobblestones."

"Look at the figures, Aimée. Our payments would go for space we'd own," he said, a child-like excitement in his eyes. "We'd build equity, instead of throwing money at a landlord every month and having nothing to show for it. It makes financial sense." He pointed to the peeling wainscoting and the dim, wavering chandelier suspended from the high ceiling.

Talk about being able to get the peasant out of the country, but not the country out of the peasant. At heart, like most, René believed that only land was secure, the only guarantee against famine in wartime. A misconception proved during every famine and war.

"The star pupil in my hacking class referred me to this real estate broker," he said, sitting down on his orthopedic chair and booting up his computer. "The property's

30

in probate; the estate will make a deal. Aimée, we can't go wrong, the quartier's up and coming."

"A hip investment in old proletarian Paris, René?" she said. "I was there, in that very neighborhood, last night."

She handed him a demitasse of espresso. René raised his eyebrow.

"Partying?"

She kept Yves's visit to herself; no use telling René, or he'd say she'd fallen for Yves's line yet again.

"Working. I netted the Microimage contract last night."

René inhaled and whistled. "Not bad. Should take care of those, eh?" He pointed to the bills on her desk. Then an expression she couldn't read crossed René's face. "Why didn't you answer your phone?"

She thumbed on her cell phone. Nothing.

"Try charging the battery."

A voice said, "Mademoiselle Aimée Leduc? I'm from the Commissariat."

Aimée looked up see a blue-uniformed *flic* standing at the open office door. Short cropped brown hair, muscles under his shirt, and no expression on his face. Goosebumps ran up her arms despite the heat.

"Permettez?" he said, entering the room. "I agree with the gentleman." His thick

black shoes creaked over the wood floor.

"What do you mean?"

"You might want to keep your phone charged," he said. "Will you accompany me, please?"

"Since when is it against the law —" she caught herself. "What's this about?"

"Routine. We need to ask you some questions."

"But I don't understand."

"My vehicle's outside," he said.

René set down his cup hard. Little brown drops spattered over the real estate comparisons. "Does this have to do with her cell phone, officer?"

He shrugged. "Her number was the last one dialed from a victim's phone."

"A victim?" René asked. "Are you saying she's a suspect?"

"Pure routine, as I've said. We'd appreciate your cooperation. Now."

"But that was me. . . ." René eased off his orthopedic chair and stood.

"I'm afraid not, Monsieur," he said. His gaze held for a moment, taking in René's stature. Like many did.

Aimée said, alarmed, "I'm not going anywhere until you explain."

"Take it up with the Commandant, Mademoiselle; he's waiting. That's all I can say."

René looked at her and then handed her his cell phone. "Mine's charged. Call me afterward."

The *flic* gestured toward the door.

"After you."

Each time the Commissariat's double doors swung open, Aimée heard the blare of car horns layered over the sound of the rushing water of Canal Saint-Martin.

The bad feeling she'd had in the police car heightened. The *flic* had responded to her questions in monosyllables, refused to reveal any more information, and escorted her inside the station. He'd disappeared once she'd seated herself on a contoured plastic chair. She tried to think who had been the last person to call her. And then it hit her . . . Jean-Paul, her disastrous blind date.

"He'll see you now," said the receptionist. "Room 12."

Aimée strode inside an office. Metal file cabinets lined the walls, anonymous, standard issue, like those in any other commissariat except for the map of the tenth arrondissement taking up half the wall. Another map sectioned the arrondissement into quartiers: Saint Vincent de Paul, the working-class section with hospitals and Gare du Nord and Gare de l'Est; Porte Saint-Denis, Michel's district of renovated warehouses, 18th-century *hôtels particuliers* and covered passages; Porte Saint-Martin, old convents and theatres; and l'Hôpital Saint-Louis, bordering the Canal: an arrondissement notable for hospitals, train stations, and old prisons.

A middle-aged man with sparse brown hair, a broad forehead, and rolled-up shirtsleeves swiveled around in his chair. Behind him, floor to ceiling windows overlooked the dirt-encrusted metal-and-glass canopy roof of a workshop. His smooth-shaven face, the lines more pronounced around the close-set eyes, was familiar.

"Maillol?"

"It's Commander Maillol now," he said, thumbing open a file on the otherwise clear desk. She remembered him; one of the recruits her father had worked with before Maillol had been assigned to the statistics bureau. A numbers man. And a backstabber, rumor went. Soon after working with Maillol, her father had left the force and joined her grandfather at Leduc Detective.

No doubt he still won at belote, she thought, recalling the smoke drifting from the off-duty *flics* around the card table in their kitchen. She remembered the late nights, empty bottles of pastis, and Maillol counting his winnings with a smug look. Maillol, her father had said, was a frustrated academic who'd failed his baccalaureate exams several times.

"Is this about Jean-Paul Orcut?" she asked, concerned.

"Mademoiselle Leduc," he said, "what's your relationship to Yves Robert?" He consulted a file, answering her question with his own.

She was taken by surprise. She sat without being asked. "Problematic at best. But perhaps you should explain why I'm here and what this has to do with —"

"Your number showed on his cell phone," he said consulting the file.

"Why shouldn't it? Is that illegal?"

"If you'd kept yours on, this formality could have been averted. We could have just called you."

This didn't make sense. Neither did his businesslike tone or his distancing himself from their shared past.

"I work with absolutes." He pointed to a chart on the door. Cases solved, cases pending, all arranged in neat columns in black marker.

"I don't understand," she said. She leaned forward. "I'm more than acquainted with procedure. . . ."

"We found the victim's cell phone in the suspect's possession." He looked up. "Your number was the last one dialed."

Her hands gripped the armchair. "A victim? The Brigade Criminelle handles homicides."

"You're right, it's in the Brigade Criminelle's hands. They would appreciate your assistance. Formal identification is needed at the morgue."

Her world spun and crashed. Nausea rose in the pit of her stomach.

"*Non* . . . you've got the wrong . . . person." Her voice rose. "There's some mistake."

"A sanitation worker discovered a corpse at 7 a.m. on rue de Paradis," he said, his tone removed and businesslike. "So far, a wallet and a cell phone have been found in the suspect's possession."

A body; a suspect. Her mind whirled. This was moving too fast.

"It appears to have been robbery and murder during a sexual assignation gone wrong."

"Sexual assignation?"

"The suspect, a male prostitute, has as good as admitted it."

"But that's impossible!"

Of course, they'd gotten the wrong person. A mistake. She could breathe again.

"In what way?" Maillol's close set eyes narrowed into slits.

"Yves was with *me* last night."

Maillol pushed the file to the side and leaned back, tenting his fingers. "Why don't you tell me about it, Mademoiselle Leduc?"

The white-coated morgue attendant pointed to the logbook. "Sign in and date it, please, Mademoiselle Leduc."

The attendant looked no more than twenty-five. Blue ink stained his palms. He was probably a pre-med student, Aimée thought. Her hands shook as she clutched the pen. Then it fell from her fingers and clattered on the white-tiled floor.

"Use mine." He pulled one from his lapel. "Sign right here, next to Number 48."

Her stomach churned. She'd visited the bowels of the morgue to identify the charred remains of her father after the Place Vendôme explosion, had later been to the viewing cubicle in the basement to try to identify a drowned woman, but she had never been to what was known as "the freezer." Her signature came out a blotted scribble.

37

The attendant took her arm. "*Bon,* we'll just pull him out and then you can —"

"I know there's a mistake. That's why I'm here," she interrupted. There had to have been some error. A horrible one. "I'm cooperating so the real victim's loved ones can be found."

He cocked an eyebrow. "Can you handle this, Mademoiselle?"

The last thing in the world she wanted to do was walk into the freezer.

"Of course," she said, taking a deep breath. In the few minutes she'd stood here, the combined odors of formaldehyde and pine disinfectant had overwhelmed her. She wanted to get this over, get out of here, and get the smell off her clothes. Then she'd find Yves and give him a piece of her mind. A big piece of her mind. What business did he have just appearing, asking her to spend her life with him, leaving without a good-bye. . . .

"Mademoiselle?"

She followed him through the swinging doors, through the strips of clear plastic that enclosed the frigid air. Their footsteps echoed off the glazed white tile. Built-in stainless steel drawers lined the chilly room, numbers handlettered on index cards inserted in slots above the drawer handles.

She closed her eyes. Heard the creaking of

the wheels as rollers slid out, the stiff crackling as the plastic sheet was folded back, and smelled the cloying sickly-sweet smell of death.

"Ready, Mademoiselle?"

Please God, she prayed, don't let it be him. Like she had prayed for her father. Made all those little promises that she'd be good, do the right thing — whatever that was — if it just wasn't him. Get a grip, she told herself. She'd met Yves when he was undercover. He was an investigative journalist, he knew how to handle himself. Of course, he'd been following a tip, meeting a contact . . . this whole thing was a terrible mistake, some bizarre fluke.

A buzzer sounded, startling her, and she jumped.

"Mademoiselle, we're busy. I need to answer the door."

Her eyes opened and her gaze fell on Yves's face, the charcoal stubble on his chin, the milky white crescents just visible in his three-quarter-closed eyes. A sheet covered his mouth and chin.

She stumbled against the cold drawer and grabbed the handle to steady herself. And yet he looked almost as if he were sleeping. She peered closer.

"Yves?" she called.

He was sleeping the vacant sleep of the dead.

"He can't answer, Mademoiselle."

"But . . ." she reached out, and the attendant caught her hand.

"I can assure you —"

"Let me see him," she interrupted. "All of him."

"The identification procedure doesn't permit me to do this."

"You mean you don't want me to see —"

"I want to spare you the. . . ." He paused, hesitation laced with irritation in his voice, "details unnecessary for an identification."

Before he could stop her, she pulled down the blue plastic sheet with shaking hands. She gasped at the sight of the uneven black thread stitches closing the wide incision running down his chest. Autopsied . . . already? His head slumped, but not enough to hide the red slits in the skin of his neck, nor the red swirl under his ear.

Pain wrenched her. She took Yves's cold white hand in hers and tried to rub it warm. Dirt rimmed his fingernails. He'd put up a fight. She leaned down and raised his hand to her face. The hand he'd brushed across her cheek in the warm dark of the previous night.

Non, this wasn't real, this wasn't happening.

She touched the face that had pressed against hers, now stiff and cold. This was the man who'd wanted to spend the rest of his life with her.

"The commander didn't tell me how he died," she said.

"I don't know what you mean," the attendant said.

"They slit his throat."

She fought waves of pain, a rippling anger. "I'll find out who did this, Yves," she whispered to him. She placed a black tendril of hair behind his ear. Her thumb came back sticky, smeared with a tan streak. She held it up to her nose, smelled it: the floral scent of makeup. She noted a thin tan line behind his earlobe, a smudge in the cleft of his cheek.

The buzzer sounded again.

The attendant pulled a small clipboard from his white jacket pocket. "You've seen enough to identify him. Yves . . . ?"

"Yves Robert, an investigative journalist for Agence France Press," she said, her words coming from far away, mechanically. She made her feet move. One in front of the other.

"Mademoiselle!" the attendant called after her.

She ignored him. Out in the hallway she ran to the WC, made it to the bowl, and threw up. Threw up until nothing came out. Her stomach wrenched with dry heaves; there was an acid taste in her mouth. Her body shook; tears ran down her face. Who would slit Yves's throat? But that red swirl. . . . And why had Yves worn makeup?

Someone pounded on the door.

"Eh, you don't own the facilities!" said a woman's voice. "My bladder's bursting."

She let go of the bowl and, shaking, got to her feet, washed her face, and rinsed her mouth.

"About time!" said an old woman who glared at her.

Aimée leaned against the cold tiled wall, trembling. She had to find some answers. A reason. Something.

But when she reached the second floor office of her pathologist friend, Serge, the receptionist looked up with heavy-lidded eyes.

"Serge's *en vacances*," she said, fanning herself with the thin morgue-personnel directory. "He'll be back at the end of August."

"Can I speak with . . ." She paused and

took a breath, made herself say it. "The attending autopsy pathologist?"

"They autopsy in the morning," the woman said, glancing at the wall clock. "We're on vacation schedule, half days. Everyone's gone now."

No help there. No answers. Just a potted palm withering in the dense office heat.

"Merci."

Hollowness gnawed inside her. Emptiness. She walked down the wide staircase, past the bust of Pasteur, out the doors of the red-brick morgue to the quai. But she couldn't make sense of Yves in that closed steel drawer, rough stitches sewn down his chest.

She pictured him in the middle of the night sitting at the window, his face flushed. Details came back to her: the musky scent of him on the duvet, the coarse sheet, the hot air clinging in the loft corners. He'd said he couldn't talk about what he did. Stupid. Why hadn't she pressed him, why hadn't she insisted?

Under the now-threatening charcoal clouds, *bateaux mouches* glided by, making silver ripples in the green Seine. Humid heat baked the cobbles under her feet. Not a breath of air stirred the plane trees lining the embankment. René's phone vibrated in her pocket. She didn't know how long it was before she answered. In the particle-charged air, her hand brushed her shirt and it shocked her, crackling and clinging with static electricity.

"Did you clear things up?" René asked.

"René . . ." she couldn't say the words. If she did, it would make it more real.

The cell phone reception wavered. "Can you pick me up, René?"

A few reluctant, soft drops of rain fell, darkening the cobblestones.

"I've got this last report printing," he said, exasperation in his voice. "Can you grab a taxi? 10, Passage du Desir." His words broke up. ". . . the real estate agent can squeeze us in right now . . . you know I'm catching a train for the country."

A male pigeon, its violet-purple feathered breast puffed out, strutted toward a drab female.

"Aimée?"

The drops fell, leaving a pattern of wet spots on her shoulder. "Something wrong?" Before she could summon the words, the line cut out. A crack of thunder, then a jagged bolt of lightning illuminated everything. And the sky opened.

Aimée felt as if she were underwater, submerged in memories. Yves's lopsided smile, the bubbling champagne, the red slit across his throat; everything swirled through her mind. From somewhere, a horn honked in an insistent rhythm. Sheets of warm rain pelted her face.

Shivering, she looked up through wet eyelashes to see a taxi, its windshield wipers scraping in futile attempts against successive waves of beating rain.

Tuesday Noon

"All praise to Allah," Nadira breathed, finishing her prayers. She rolled up her prayer rug and hid it in the niche she'd made between the wood slats under the bed in her room. An attic room that Balzac, in the novel she'd attempted, would have described as a garret. Her window overlooked the statue that stood in the center of the circle in the middle of chic Place Saint Georges. Exclusive, tree-lined, and encircled by nineteenth-century townhouses.

Nadira's cell phone vibrated right on schedule.

"Oui?"

"The swallow flies over the stones," said a voice in Farsi. The line clicked off. The jihad had started. She swallowed hard, hoping that in her two years as a nanny, she'd prepared sufficiently for this new mission.

A devout Shi'a, she'd followed Allah's will, disclosed to her by the mullah behind the grande mosque in Tehran. Nadira had been orphaned when she was only nine — an age at which she was considered to be a woman and eligible for marriage — and been one of those lucky to be chosen for study in the mosque's orphanage. Later, handpicked by Ruhal, an Iranian Sorbonne-educated teacher, now a hardline cleric in the post-Ayatollah regime, she'd been enrolled in French classes. More grooming and training ensued until she'd been selected for the mullah's overseas division for further jihad activity. That day, pride and gratitude had swelled Nadira's heart.

"*Tiens,* Nadira." Madame Delbard, her employer, the wife of a French pharmaceutical firm manager, called from the stairwell. "Paul's waiting."

"I'm coming, Madame!"

She took a deep breath, checked the wide-mouth thermos, and tucked it into four-year-old Paul's Lego backpack. She picked up the infidel's symbol, a gold crucifix, clasped it and hung it around her neck, before she shut the door. Downstairs, she grinned at the waiting mother and little Paul.

"The rain's stopped and we're all ready.

Goodies, too." Nadira smiled and helped Paul slip his pack over his shoulders.

"Which park today, Nadira?" Madame Delbard asked, flicking specks from her peach-colored Chanel suit and adjusting her pearl earrings in the mirror of the entryway. An expensive floral scent rose from Madame, competing with the sprays of flowers she insisted that the florist deliver fresh every day. Their apartment encompassed two floors in the former townhouse of the mistress to the Duc de Grammont, as Madame never tired of telling her.

"The Buttes Chaumont, Paul's favorite, of course." Nadira kneeled and slipped a sun hat onto little Paul's blond hair. "And *a treat* if he listens well to Nadira!"

Adoration and excitement battled in Paul's eyes.

"I loved that park, too," Madame Delbard said, with an indulgent smile. "Off you go, take your time. Don't worry about packing Paul's clothes later, Nadira. We're not going to the country house after all. We're stuck in town a bit longer."

"But Maman . . ." Paul pouted.

"*Desolée, cheri,* but we'll do something special instead," she said. A small sigh escaped her. "Nadira, tonight my husband's got a dinner engagement and my appoint-

47

ment might run late."

Perfect, thought Nadira. No added chores; she could feed Paul and put him to bed early, then prepare for her mission. She took Paul's hand in hers, gripping the stroller handle with her other.

"*D'accord,* Madame," she said and curtsied. Madame liked that.

In the playground of Buttes Chaumont, a former gypsum quarry with a superb view, turned into a park by Baron Haussman, Nadira rubbed sunscreen on Paul's nose, then on her own skin. With her topaz eyes and light complexion, she could pass for European. The Shah's era had spawned many like her, once members of the educated elite, now in prison or exile.

She adjusted her pink sun visor, matching skirt, and large white sunglasses, trying to ignore the nakedness of exposed knees and uncovered hair. She longed for the security of the veil. But she'd studied the other nannies' outfits and knew she must blend in with them on the park bench. Not to look out of place was most important, Ruhal had said over and over. Her mission demanded it.

"Thirsty?" Nadira asked.

"*Non,*" Paul said, his eyes on the slide.

"Ah, but I am," she said, pulling out the extra wide thermos and winking at the other nanny, then averting her eyes from the big-boned Swede in a halter top who fanned herself on the playground bench near the sandbox.

"Can I go slide?"

She took the thermos and, as if as an afterthought, reached down into the backpack, then handed a caramel to Paul. "Go ahead."

She pushed the Lego backpack with her sandal-shod foot, and it lodged under the bench. A few minutes later, she stood and joined Paul, glancing back. The man in the blue track suit whom she'd seen by the trees was gone. And so was the backpack.

By the time Paul tired of the slide and the teeter-totter, it was time for more sunscreen and a drink.

Back at the bench, she reached down and felt underneath. The Lego backpack was back. Fuller and heavier. "Like an Orangina?"

Paul's eyes gleamed. A favorite, forbidden by the dentist.

"Let's wash your hands first."

In one restroom cubicle, with Paul in the next, she unzipped the Lego backpack and unscrewed the thermos top, looking for instructions. Inside she found a ticket for a symposium on Women in the Arab World to be held at the Kurdish Center, featuring Jalenka Malat, member of the Turkish parliament, as a speaker. The first Muslim woman, and a Kurd, the ticket read, to be elected to parliament. From under the thermos in the backpack, she pulled out the dull gray metal barrel, forearm, scope, mount, and silencer of a disassembled high-powered rifle. The model she'd been trained on. But she figured her assignment would be like her last job, which had been to drop the rifle off in her local café's cleaning closet.

"I can't reach the paper," Paul said.

"Okay, Paul," she said, about to screw the thermos top on. Her fingers froze. A message in Farsi was glued to the underside. It read "This is your target. Prove yourself worthy of Allah."

Tuesday Afternoon

Aimée left the taxi at Passage du Desir. This part of the passage, straddling two boulevards, narrowed into a lane lined with three-story brick and cut-stone buildings, now damp and dripping with rain. Two centuries earlier, the passage had been the haunt of prostitutes. Later, artisans had filled the

50

small shopfronts. Now gentrification had brought upscale trendy designers.

She stood in the high arched entry to the alley until she grew aware of René, beckoning from his vintage DS Citroën, pulling up at the curb.

"You're sopping wet," he said. "Get in." He leaned over and opened the door, his engine idling. His car radio was tuned to a scratchy Mozart concerto to which the windshield wipers kept time. "A bus skidded, big accident, sorry. Why didn't you wait inside?" He paused. "*Mon Dieu,* you're white . . . what's the matter?"

"I just identified Yves's body at the morgue."

"What?" René's mouth dropped open. "Yves . . . but he's in Cairo."

"Not any more."

"I'm sorry, Aimée."

Her wet hand shook as she pulled his phone from her pocket.

"But what happened?"

"*Un moment,* René."

Information connected her to the Commissariat.

"Maillol," he answered.

"Commandant, who's this homicide suspect in Yves . . . the case —"

René blinked and reached for Aimée's

other hand.

"Why?" Maillol asked.

"I need to speak with him."

She heard a sigh.

"He's in custody, of course," said Maillol. "According to procedure, we can't have the public involved."

"I'm not the public," she said. His attitude spurred her on.

"For starters, did this suspect admit slitting Yves's throat?"

She felt René shift on the damp leather upholstery.

"Maillol, please, it's important. Give me five minutes to talk to him."

"A suspect in custody charged with a homicide and *you*'re asking to interrogate him?" She heard him suck in a breath. "May I remind you, it's the Brigade Criminelle's business now."

"But you know me . . . can't you tell me something?" For God's sake, he'd bounced her on his knee when she was little. Lightning was just visible now over the arch. Condensation formed on the windows. She felt too hot in the stifling, steamed-up car. She would grovel, pull any threads in the old-boy network. She had to do this.

"You worked with Papa . . . my father. Bend the regulations a little, for his sake."

"I wanted to spare you the more sordid details," he said. "*Bon.* The suspect's a known junkie and male hustler with numerous convictions, one of the men who cruise the area at night," he said. "Seems your boyfriend went both ways."

"But I told you, Yves was an investigative journalist. Maybe he was working undercover, interviewing a source. No doubt this *mec* attacked him." And then she looked at her fingers, smelled again the trace of makeup that had been washed off by the rain. Doubt crept into her mind. But the way Yves had acted last night. . . .

"In respect to your father, well, I told you myself. The Brigade's handling it. I'm sorry," he said. His voice softened for a moment. "I appreciate your making the identification. But now I've got a meeting," he said, his voice again businesslike, and hung up.

She leaned forward, cradling her dripping head in her hands.

René sat, not saying a word.

"None of this makes sense, René."

Yves appearing, disappearing, and now in the morgue.

"Yves showed up last night. . . ." She couldn't finish.

"What happened, Aimée?"

53

"That's just it," she said. "I don't know."

"It might help if you start at the beginning," he said.

She took a deep breath and told him what she knew.

René listened, then set her phone in her lap. "I charged your phone battery. Maybe you should listen to your messages."

The red light blinked. Two messages. With trembling hands, she hit her voicemail button.

A low cough, muffled, as if a hand was being held over the receiver. "Aimée." Yves's voice, deep and modulated. "Pick up . . . please." A little breathless, a catch at the end. She wanted to bang her head on the windshield. Stupid, not recharging her phone. More coughing, waiting for her to answer and she hadn't. "If you don't know by now how I feel . . ." She heard a low, rich chuckle. He'd certainly shown her last night. These were not the words of a man en route to a sexual assignation. Then there was a pause and the sound of footsteps echoing, coming closer. "Call me back . . . *salaam aliekoum . . .* what the — ?"

Then the buzz of a broken connection.

Salaam aliekoum, the Arab greeting. She hit the voicemail again. One more message. Static, no words . . . clanging, and what

54

sounded like the phone dropping. No more messages.

If only . . . if only he hadn't left her, if only. . . .

She replayed it. Straining to hear more, another sound, another nuance, another detail.

What she heard in his voice was his caring, and his need for her to respond. She wanted to yell "Say what you mean, Yves, say it . . . who's there?"

"It's my fault, René," she said, rubbing her wet eyes. "I didn't —"

"Save him?" René shook his head. "Check the time."

"What?"

René hit the voicemail function. "Notice the time, 6:47 a.m. The next message is at 6:52 a.m."

She tried to pull herself together in the fog of pain. "What do you mean? He tried to call again?"

She stared at René.

"Or his killer did, Aimée, and hit the redial button," he said, his brows furrowed with worry.

A shiver of fear shot up her spine.

She thought of Yves's underlying tension despite his *tendresse,* and his wish to spend his life with her. Nothing indicated that he

55

had gone out to seek a rendezvous with a male hustler in a doorway. Her gut feeling said he had been working undercover.

"The street cleaner found him at 7 a.m., according to Maillol," she told René.

"Instead of blaming yourself, Aimée, share your information with the authorities."

Right, of course, René was right. More important than wallowing in pain, she had to piece this together. "True. René, Yves was telling me something. His last words before. . . ." She gripped the door handle. Squeezed it until her fingers hurt. Couldn't say it.

A man knocked on the steamed-up car windows. "Monsieur Friant?"

"What bad timing . . . the realtor!" René said and rolled the window down.

A middle-aged man's smiling expectant face leaned in. He had a receding hairline and carried his suit jacket over his arm in the damp heat. "Quick. Both of you, please, not a moment to spare."

"I'm not sure this is a good time —" René said. But the realtor had already opened the car door.

"There's another offer coming in this afternoon. You must see the place, Monsieur Friant. The perfect location, footage. . . ."

The last thing Aimée wanted to do was

look at real estate.

"Something's come up," René said.

"Go ahead, René," she told him.

The realtor sprang to the other side of the car. "Let me help you out, Mademoiselle. The puddles!"

"I don't think —"

He handed her his oversized card with a smile, *P. Boutarel — Immobilier* imprinted on it. "Monsieur Friant told me he won't make a decision without you."

"Not right now, Monsieur."

Exasperated, Monsieur Boutarel stepped back. "*Tiens,* but I canceled another appointment to squeeze you in. I might even lose a sale."

Ready to shut the car door on the annoying real estate agent, she registered the disappointment on René's face. Such bad timing. Yet he'd come through for her on countless occasions. She pushed her reluctance aside. "We'll have a quick look."

Aimée followed René up the winding stairs bordered by a chipped curlicue ironwork banister. From the first floor she heard sewing machines and voices in a Slavic dialect and she smelled cooking oil.

The third-floor double doors stood open; pewter light streamed onto a scuffed wooden plank floor. She stepped inside into a high-ceilinged series of rooms with carved woodwork, yellowed, turn-of-the-century floral wallpaper still visible in peeling tatters. Even with the period detail and grimy charm, the place looked like squatters had just vacated.

"Imagine the possibilities. . . ." Monsieur Boutarel was saying.

"I like the fiber optic lines installed next door," René said.

Aimée's heels clicked on the wooden floor. She wished she hadn't agreed to enter this abandoned place with the tang of leather hides emanating from it. Yves's murder . . . right now she should. . . .

"Aimée, are you all right?" René asked.

She nodded, swallowing hard.

"We'll go in a minute. I'm sorry."

"What do you think, Mademoiselle?" Boutarel asked.

"It's large."

Too large. And dirty, and needed tons of work, if not total gutting, and new electrical wiring and plumbing.

"Little happens in August, Monsieur Friant, as I mentioned on the phone. However, we've had two offers since yesterday," he said, with a shrug. "I expect another this afternoon."

Typical real estate pressure . . . if you don't

make an offer. . . .

"Serious offers?" René asked, his large green eyes gleaming even larger in the glow of the one hanging electric bulb. He was an astute businessman; she recalled the acumen he demonstrated dealing with clients who neglected to pay up. But she'd never seen him like this . . . displaying all the classic telltale signs of a *coup de foudre,* love at first sight.

"It's hard to say. But not many places come up for sale in this passage. The quartier's booming, I don't need to tell you that," Boutarel said, his words echoing off the walls. "The 'bones' are good." He gestured to the flaking plaster pillars. "Steel behind, eh, you can see that, a sound structure."

René was drinking it up. She imagined the wheels turning, calculating figures in his head.

"You must excuse me. Now I must run or I'll be late for my next appointment. Monsieur Friant, you come recommended." He nudged René with an insider's smile on his face.

"Show Mademoiselle around, then leave the keys with the concierge. I know you've got a train to catch, but Mademoiselle Leduc . . . isn't it?"

59

She nodded.

"Please revisit tomorrow, spend more time. Though I wouldn't wait too long."

As he put on his suit jacket she noticed that he had a withered arm. And then he'd tucked the sleeve in his pocket and taken off down the stairs.

"Just look out the back, Aimée. A quiet courtyard, room for a garden, think of the old stable for a garage," René said.

She stepped through the rooms with peeling wallpaper, single bulbs hanging from wires in the ceiling, doors leaning from broken hinges. Below spread a vast weed-choked cobbled courtyard littered with a rusted bicycle and piles of rotted wood. A lifetime project, as far she could see. Bordering the courtyard wall stood soot-stained sculpted lions' heads adorning the front of the adjoining *hôtel particulier.* A jewel in a state of exquisite decay.

"We could carve out several work areas, there's so much room."

True. To the right was a wing with more dilapidated rooms holding the scent of mold. She had to choose her words with care. Extreme care. Living in a one-room studio, René dreamed of space. But she lived in a cavernous 17th-century *hôtel particulier* and faced the daily headache of ancient plumbing.

"Full of charm and possiblities, I agree," she said.

He rocked on the heels of his handmade Italian loafers. "You don't like it."

"Liking it doesn't matter, René," she said. "It's my bank balance that counts. I still owe my own contractor."

When last heard from, her contractor was on vacation in St. Bart's.

"How can I commit to another contractor?"

"That's the reason for my trip," he said. "My mother's sold property, she wants to help me buy something in Paris."

Another bill, another commitment she couldn't deal with. Or did René envision going off on his own? Someday, with his talent and skill, she feared he would. Yet she couldn't face throwing obstacles in his way.

"Think about it. I did a little groundwork." He handed her a sheaf of papers with calculations and contractors', plumbers', and electricians' estimates.

Aimée shrugged.

In the narrow passage below, puddled with rain, bright sun rays parted the clouds.

René took a large step to avoid a puddle. He almost made it. A chocolate-gray spray splashed his cream-colored linen-clad calf.

"*Merde!* Just had them dry-cleaned."

A late model Jaguar pulled up, the strain of Senegalese hip-hop vibrating from its open window. A woman climbed out of the car, her head shaved except for the strip of rainbow dreadlocks arranged in a mohawk descending to her shoulders. She flicked a thin brown cigarillo onto the pavement, ground it out with the heel of her red platform boot, and gave them a sidelong glance before clomping through the doorway.

"Interesting neighbors, René."

"I'll change my tickets, Aimée, and go later. . . ." René said. "You need some support."

"And miss your trip?" She managed a smile. René had planned this for months. "*Non,* René, I won't let you do that."

René idled the Citroën in front of the Gare du Nord's columned front near the taxi rank. In the era of split vacations, half in July, half in August, those Parisians who'd left were returning and those who hadn't were now leaving. In the crosswalk, couples pulled roller suitcases and dragged protesting small toddlers.

"Hurry, René, or you'll miss your train," she said. Somehow she'd manage.

He hesitated. "Will you talk to the Brigade?"

She nodded. "Something's way off, wrong."

"I'm sorry, Aimée . . . you're in shock. Promise me you'll go home and rest."

As if she could. Yet after the disbelief, the shock, a drifting numbness was taking over. Maybe René was right.

"How well did you know him?" René said.

"I slept with him last night, René, for God's sake," she said. "He asked me to marry him."

René blinked.

"I mean *really* know him, Aimée."

She knew his scent, the tan birthmark behind his knee, the way his lopsided smile erupted into a grin.

"He'd been in Cairo more than a year . . . I don't know how to say this any way but the wrong way." René averted his eyes, tongue tied. "What if Yves had another life?"

"And went both ways?" Her voice rose.

"Did I say that?" René's eyes clouded.

"You don't have to," she said, and hit the steering wheel. "You sound like Maillol, implying —"

"I'm saying if Yves was working undercover, there's more to this than we know. It's dangerous," Rene interrupted, wiping his brow, then glancing at his watch. "Think of that cryptic message he left."

That stopped her in her tracks.

"You're right. But the suspect would know."

"Aimée, that's the Brigade Criminelle's job. Go home, change, and take a rest."

"Hurry, or you'll miss your train."

René paused, his hand on the handle of the rain-beaded door.

"Promise me, Aimée, take care of yourself. I'll call you tonight."

She nodded, reprogrammed the Citroën's seat adjustment, and extended the pedal for her five-foot-eight height, instead of René's four-foot reach. As she pulled away, she glanced in the rear-view mirror and saw René's troubled look as he hailed a porter.

She gunned the engine and headed to the Canal Saint-Martin. All she could do was hope Maillol hadn't transferred the suspect to the Brigade yet.

Back in the Commissariat for the second time, Aimée's eyes swept the front reception counter. No one sat behind the desk. As she leaned over the counter, her damp skirt molded to her thighs. Forms and binders marked *proces verbal* were slotted in dividers by the phone console. She saw no files on the desk or in the box labeled "in transit."

"He's not responding!"

She turned to see a cluster of uniformed *flics* and white-coated medics near the wire cage of the holding cells. She walked toward the group. No one was paying her any attention; their focus was on the last cell. Peering over a blue-uniformed shoulder, Aimée saw a stretcher with a clear plastic portable drip and tubes hanging from hooks attached to a pole.

"Second junkie this week," said a *flic* with a knowing look. "Bad stuff going around."

The medic, a woman with a blond ponytail, pulled the stethoscope from her neck. "An asthma attack," she said, straightening up. "Romeo needed air in his lungs, not stuff in his veins."

Aimée stared at the chalk-white-faced figure curled in a fetal position on the stretcher. Platinum spiked hair, tight red Levis and turquoise earrings.

He didn't look like a killer — but then, he was dead. He looked more like one of the surplus store mannequins tossed out on the street after the January sales. Concave chest, chiseled defined cheeks and pale open lips . . . almost pouting, but then he'd been desperate to get air to his constricted lungs.

Yves, and now this *mec* . . . she tried to still her shaking hands. Gave up and stuck them in her skirt pockets.

"The homicide suspect . . . ?"

"*Oui*, and now he won't talk. I'll have to inform the Brigade. . . ." The *flic* frowned before he could finish. "*Et alors*," he said, "no public allowed." He herded her to the reception area. "What are you doing here? That area's off limits."

She saw that it said Sergeant Theroux on the name tag above his pocket.

"Commander Maillol questioned me this morning concerning Yves Robert's . . ." she paused, then forced herself to go on. ". . . murder. Was this man the suspect?"

"Are you family?"

She reached in her bag for her card. Her fingers touched a worn, smooth rounded coin. The coin from the betrothal amulet Yves had given her.

"I identified Yves's body at the morgue," she said.

"I'm sorry." He read her card and stroked his chin. "We responded to the call concerning an attack and discovered a homicide. It took time for the Police Judiciare to arrive. The Brigade instructed us to send the victim's body over to the morgue, and the suspect to the Brigade. But now, well, the case looks open and shut."

"Open and shut?" That was the easy way, but she bit her remark back, determined to hold herself in check. If she flew off the handle, demanded . . . well, by the look of Theroux she'd get more out of him with tact.

"That's the Brigade Criminelle's call," she said. "Did this man confess?"

"I'm the one to ask questions, Mademoiselle," he said, glancing at the wall clock.

"But of course, Sergeant," she said. "Such a shock, everything's happened so fast. Why would this man . . . ?"

He shrugged. "Look, we see it all the time. I shouldn't say this, but we figure it's a lover's quarrel or pimp payback time."

"But —"

"Even the decent ones sell their bodies when their veins need it. It's a disease."

She gritted her teeth. He assumed too much.

"How does that explain slitting Yves's throat?"

"The victim's cell phone and wallet were in this *mec*'s possession."

Circumstantial evidence at best, she thought. "Did he admit it?"

"I'm not privy to the report, Mademoiselle," he said, closing down. "As I said, it's the Brigade Criminelle's domain. Talk to them."

Prying information from them was hard. Despite the sergeant's simple take on Yves's murder, she counted on the Brigade to perform a thorough investigation. Yet the sergeant indicated that there had been a time lapse before they realized it was homicide and the Police Judiciare responded. Evidence might have fallen between the cracks. She was determined not to leave without discovering *something*.

"May I claim Yves's belongings?"

"Not my department."

She tapped her foot. "Officer. . . ."

"Go through the proper channels, Mademoiselle," he said. "Fill out the proper forms."

One of the medics covered up the junkie with a sheet. The other snapped the medic kit closed with a sigh.

René's question circled in her head, "How well did you *really* know Yves?"

"*Ne quittez pas,* hold on," the uniformed receptionist said, putting her hand over the phone receiver and staring at Aimée. *"Oui?"*

Several perspiring *flics* burst through the station doors holding a wild-eyed man, his tie undone and suit jacket falling off his

68

shoulders, shouting "I'd do it again; the *mec* stole my wife."

"Intake!" one of the *flics* said. "We need a free cell. Now."

"I'm requesting a victim's belongings," Aimée said, hoping to grab the receptionist's attention long enough to get the proper paperwork. It had taken a year and a half to obtain the charred contents of her father's pockets and his melted eyeglasses.

"Fill out Form 405, back and front." The receptionist slid a stapled sheaf of papers over the counter, then gestured with a thumb behind her at the *flics*. "Escort monsieur to intake room one. Our first cell, *the* premier accommodation, will free up in a moment."

By the time Aimée came to the end of the form under "relation to the deceased," she stopped. Her chest tightened and she wrote fiancée. Confronted by a blank under "next of kin," she realized she didn't even know if Yves had family.

"Takes ten to fifteen working days," said the receptionist, stamping a time-date on the application.

"But —"

"That's for family members," she said, not looking up. "Otherwise it's up to the com- mander." She paused. "*Non,* I'm wrong, the

69

Brigade will handle this."

Aimée nodded, knowing it useless to argue. Meanwhile, the blond medic who seemed to have been acquainted with the junkie might prove more helpful.

Outside the station at the end of the street, a black barge floated in the canal's dark green water, waiting to enter the next lock. Leaves on the plane trees lining the canal glittered with raindrops in the now-bright sun. Muggy dense heat filled the air and sunbeams danced on the puddles between cobblestones. A bucolic scene except for the *panier à salad,* the "dead van," pulling up behind the ambulance.

"Renaud V-o-r-n-e-r aka Romeo Void, spell it right, Jean," said the medic to her partner who was filling out a form on his clipboard.

Aimée paused by the ambulance as the two medics shut the back door.

"You're more acquainted with his medical history than he is . . . was, Giséle."

As Giséle, the blond medic, pulled off her latex gloves and headed to the driver's door, Aimée reached for her damp sleeve. She had to seize her chance before they drove away, no matter how awkward it felt.

"*Excusez-moi,* I overheard that you knew Renaud Vorner. You're leaving now?"

"I wish," Gisèle said. "They have to catalogue his belongings. Who knows how long that will take?"

"Do you have a moment for a coffee?" Aimée said, pointing to the café awning behind them.

Gisèle's eyes swept over Aimée: the black pencil skirt, sandals, damp tank top sticking to her chest, and laptop bag slung over her arm. "Nice offer, but we're on call, we never know when we'll get —"

"How about the counter?" Aimée interrupted. "I've only got a few minutes myself."

Gisèle hesitated, checking her pager.

Aimée motioned to the other medic. "Bet you both could use one."

Gisèle stifled a yawn and nodded. "Two more hours on shift; caffeine's a good idea."

They passed the rattan café chairs bunched behind small circular marble tables on the terrace. Inside the café, the whooshing from the milk steamer and the clatter of saucers being stacked greeted them. A ceiling fan, circa 1930, sputtered overhead suspended from a ceiling patinaed yellow by years of cigarette smoke.

"Three expressos, *s'il vous plait.*"

"*Serre* for me," said Gisèle. Half the water.

"Me, too," Aimée said to the man behind the counter. Any other time, she'd relish a seat in a café overlooking the canal, imagining Yves joining her. Not now, she needed answers.

"How well did you know Renaud Vorner?" Aimée said.

"You're a reporter?" Gisèle asked.

Aimée handed her the card reading *detective privé* she kept for moments like this. "Aimée Leduc."

"A detective?" Her partner joined them at the counter and stared at her card. His eyes narrowed. "We provide services to the community, not to vultures like you."

A nice attitude, this one.

"Yet the *flics* let this man die," she said, turning to the blond medic. "He had an asthma attack, but the *flics* didn't respond in time. Right, Giséle?"

"Forget the coffee," Jean said. "I don't like types like you."

This Jean had a chip of concrete on his shoulder.

"Like me . . . what do you mean?"

"Nice act." Jean shook his head. "Snooping around. You're paid to report to the ministry and close down even more services to the homeless."

Giséle shot Jean a look as if to remind him of his manners.

"Not at all," Aimée said. "I just have a

hard time buying him as a murder suspect."

Giséle's eyes narrowed. "A suspect?" She thought for a moment, a flicker of doubt in her eyes. "The *flics* don't deal well with *habitués* like Romeo. But he had charm. If only he'd gone to the clinic," she said and shrugged. "Last week, I gave him an inhaler, prescriptions. Usually he stayed on top of his condition."

"What happened?"

A look of hopelessness crossed her face, then disappeared. "Some of them come round, attend the clinic, get into rehab. Better talk with the sergeant."

The sergeant who'd insisted she fill out forms.

"I imagine you know more than anyone else. Do you think Romeo would kill for a fix?"

The waiter set the small white demitasse cups on the zinc counter. Steam curled in a thin wisp and evaporated. Her fingers tensed on the small handle.

"In our job, we save people. Try to," Giséle said. "The rest I don't think about."

"He was the main suspect in my . . ." she paused, ". . . friend's murder."

Aimée felt their stares burn into her. Then tears welled in her eyes, and she blinked, willing them back.

"Are you kidding me?" Giséle said, leaning forward. "Not Romeo. I know the ones who'd slit your throat rather than shake your hand. But not Romeo. A romantic, we called him. Sure, he hustled, got by on his looks. But murder . . . never."

"I can't believe it either . . . you see, we'd just. . . ." The words tumbled out before she could stop herself. Her face reddened. How could she reveal herself to strangers like this . . . why couldn't she behave professionally? All her investigating skills were failing her.

Giséle laid a hand on her arm. "I'm sorry."

She blinked again. She didn't need pity. She needed answers.

"Heart attack . . . 84, rue Magenta," spit from the radio on Giséle's hip.

Giséle downed the espresso and her partner strode out of the café, speaking into the microphone clipped to his lapel.

Aimée tossed some francs onto the counter and followed, desperate to prise information about Romeo out of them. Something. Her heel caught between two street cobbles, cracked off, and she lurched forward, grabbing the ambulance for support.

"Here are Romeo's belongings," said a *flic,* handing Giséle a plastic bag through the

74

ambulance window.

"Who did Romeo hang with?"

From inside the ambulance, Gisèle shrugged. "A type who dyes his hair and sports a 'glam punk look'."

Aimée put her face to the half-open window.

"His name?"

"I don't know."

Giselle turned the ignition.

"Can you tell me where Romeo lived?"

"No place and everyplace."

If Aimée wasn't mistaken, Gisèle had a soft spot for Romeo. Aimée couldn't let her go. "What about last week, where did you see him?"

The red light flashed on the roof; Gisèle hit the siren.

"Up the canal, where rue Varlin crosses Quai Valmy."

The siren whined in Aimée's ears and the ambulance took off. She opened the car door, sat down, and wedged off her broken sandal with her big toe: a good pair of Manolos ruined.

Time to go home, change, rest, and follow René's advice. Then her phone vibrated in her pocket.

"Mademoiselle Leduc?"

In the background she heard footsteps.

75

"Oui?"

"Inspector Rouffillac, Brigade Criminelle," a voice said. "You're late!"

Startled, she sat up. *"Pardon?"*

"Do you mind explaining not showing up here an hour ago?"

"An hour ago?"

"Playing dumb doesn't cut it with me, Mademoiselle."

She heard what sounded like the slam of a car door, then a motor car starting up. "I left instructions at the Institut Medico Legal, Mademoiselle. Instructions you ignored."

"No one told me." And then she remembered that before she threw up, the morgue attendant had called something after her. "Does this concern Yves Robert?"

"Do I need to take you into custody, Mademoiselle?"

"Officer Rouffillac, I'm sure you realize Yves's murder . . ." she hestitated, caught her breath, and continued, ". . . didn't involve the male prostitute Renaud Vorner, aka Romeo Void. There's information I need to tell you. I'm en route."

She heard muffled voices. Static from a police radio. The metallic ratchet she could swear came from the snick of a gun.

"Later. Three p.m. My office, fifth floor."

76

Not even a request, a demand. The phone clicked off.

Unnerved, she realized that alarms must have rung in the Brigade after she ID'd Yves. But it appeared that Rouffillac had something else on his plate at the moment. She thought of the headlines in *Le Monde* about the bombings and turned on the car radio.

The nasal voice of the RT1 news announcer droned, ". . . authorities discovered an explosive device at Metro Louis Blanc. Expect disruption of Metro lines 7 and 7b and heightened security at Gare de l'Est."

Her fingers shook. And René's words came back to her. The last, blank message on her cell phone could have come from the murderer hitting Yves's redial button. If Romeo hadn't murdered Yves, the murderer was still out there. And knew her number.

Quai Valmy's embankment on the Canal Saint-Martin ended near the Bassin Villette, a known nighttime gay cruising area backing onto Place Stalingrad. Clairfontaine, the paper factory, still operated, but the packing houses and sand and charcoal depots dependent on the barges were gone. Now the quai lay deserted except for a group of starlings fluttering over the narrow green canal. Several blue plastic bags hung from the tree branches, the "baggage area" of the *clochards* and homeless who slept here at night. No use checking it out until tonight when it came alive, she thought.

At midday, in this summer heat, most Parisians wished to escape to a darkened bedroom and sleep. But she dreaded her empty apartment, knowing she would obsess over Yves, then about the office without René. She needed to keep her gnawing grief at bay and occupy herself until 3:00. She'd investigate what she figured the Brigade were ignoring.

She took out her cell phone and called Yves's job.

"Agence France-Presse," a voice answered. "How may I direct your call?"

And it hit her that she'd never called Yves here before or known which branch he worked out of.

"Foreign correspondent section, please," she guessed.

"Which bureau?"

Cairo? But he'd left. From what she'd gathered, he'd obtained a new posting in Paris.

"I'd like to speak with the liaison to the Cairo post."

"I can transfer you to the foreign bureau

chief's voicemail. He's in New York until the end of the month."

She couldn't wait that long. "Anyone else in that office?"

"I'll connect you."

A voicemail. She left her number, in case he checked in, then clicked back to the reception. "May I speak with the general foreign bureau . . . I'm looking for the correspondent who worked with Yves Robert." She went on, trying for some connection, "I lost his cell phone number."

"We don't give those out, Mademoiselle."

"May I have his extension?"

"Of course. You want Gerard, right?"

Now we seem to be getting somewhere, she thought.

"Oui."

"There are two Gerards. Which one?"

She took both numbers, got voicemail and left her name and number, indicating only that she knew Yves. She tried to ignore the chills racking her. Time mattered in an investigation; clues evaporated. Witnesses' memories, her father always said, grew hazy the longer the time between crime and questioning. She needed to visit rue de Paradis, where Yves had been murdered, now.

She started up the car again and took off

through "Little India," the area flanking the Gare du Nord's tracks. Opposite the second Empire-era Hôpital Widal, now a poison control center, she saw Tamil jewelry shops with gold bangles in their windows, video stores advertising Bollywood movies, dhoti wearing men running barber shops. The area even boasted a Krishna temple and autumn Diwali festival of lights that jammed the street filled with the aroma of turmeric as floats borne by participants passed by.

She cut over narrow rue Jarry, passing the unprepossessing hotels always found clustering in the vicinity of train stations. Once bordellos servicing the German Wehrmacht during the Occupation, they now catered to budget-minded salesmen.

In a quartier with street names like Passage du Desir and Cité Paradis, she'd figured stories of ministers' mistresses and even a king's favorite installed in the now decaying mansions had once been true, until her history teacher insisted that the names related to the devotion of the sixteenth-century cloistered nuns and that the quartier once had been filled with convents. Traffic slowed to a crawl on narrow rue Bleu, formerly rue d'Enfer, the Street of Hell, intersecting rue de Paradis . . . paradise and hell, she thought. Like her experiences in the past twelve hours.

Her lips pursed at the traffic jam on rue du Faubourg Poissonnière, the ancient fishmongers' route to the Les Halles market. So she parked on rue de Paradis opposite the pillared, imposing entrance of the "Depot des Cristalleries," Baccarat's crystal complex. The street, renowned for the *arts de table* since the monarchy's Restoration, showcased china and crystal shops. Their clientele were the types who registered for Baccarat crystal and Limoges china table settings for twelve as wedding gifts. Martine, her best friend since the *lycée,* insisted she was going to buy her wedding china here. But if so, Martine had better get married soon, Aimée thought, since of the sixty shops that had once lined this street, fewer than half remained.

She pulled her emergency footwear from her bag and changed into red high-tops. And then her stomach knotted as she spotted the yellow crime-scene tape dangling from a doorway. She leaned forward, her hands gripping the keys, about to gun the car to get away. Away from the spot where Yves had breathed his last. But the feeling that she owed it to him to investigate wouldn't go away.

For a moment, she thought of what could

have been, visiting the shops with Yves, and her lip trembled. She reached for her cell phone, about to call Martine and tell her the story. But Martine was in Curaçao — or the Antilles — she didn't remember which. There was no shoulder to cry on.

Many of the shops were closed for August. A perspiring man unloaded crates of Badoit mineral water from his truck parked by the corner café on the otherwise deserted pavement. Further down stood the old Choisy-le-Roi pottery building — the source of the Metro's white-bevelled ceramic tiles — now a designer's headquarters. Its mullioned windows were shaded by a stone arch bearing the *belle époque* tile scene of a beckoning draped maiden.

Water sluiced the gutter and rose up over the pavement carrying debris, leaves and paper wrappers. She took a deep breath and left the car.

The rank odor of heated garbage clung in the corners. Something crackled under her foot, her shoe caught on something sticky. She leaned against the stone façade of one of the porcelain stores, using a pencil to pick off the gum.

Rivulets of water coursed from the sewer spout near the garbage cans tied with yellow crime-scene tape.

She took another big breath, willing her apprehension to subside, and parted the tape.

Inside the dark recessed portal, a dried black-red stain on the stone wall tapered into a thin network. She stood there, shaking. Pain struck her stomach and her throat as she realized that she was standing on the spot where Yves had been murdered, asking herself again why he would leave her arms and a warm bed, to be knifed by a junkie hustler.

He wouldn't. She knew it in her bones.

She hit voicemail on her cell phone and replayed Yves's last message. Her throat caught. If only . . . but "if only" wouldn't get her anywhere.

Across rue de Paradis, a security guard stood between the pillars of a porcelain and crystal showroom complex, smoking. Behind him she saw vaulted windows reflecting the gleaming crystal and china place settings. If the security guard had been on duty, he might have seen Yves.

"My shift starts at 7 a.m., but the showroom doesn't open until 10:00," said Nohant, the security guard. He wiped his arm across his flushed brow. "Hotter than an old man's spit, eh?"

He had a Languedoc slur to his words, with a phrase to match.

"Like I said, I arrive early," he said, "to coordinate, you know, so everything's in order."

She'd flashed her PI license and he'd taken it at face value. Not the inquisitive type.

"Did you see a man at that doorway before the street cleaners came?"

He gave a big sigh. "But I told all this to the officers."

She nodded. "I'm sorry. But for my report, I need to ask you again. Did you see anyone?"

He shook his head. The dark blue lines of a tattoo on his arm showed at the edge of his sleeve. A stale scent of Paco Rabanne cologne clung to him.

"No reason to," he said. "Our work entrance faces Cité Paradis. I passed the hall, made sure the duty guard got his ass in gear to disarm the alarm, opened the doors."

"The police report indicated that the call to them originated here."

"Foreigners take it for granted, eh. Get a job and shoot flies when they're bored."

She wondered what that meant. This Nohant had an attitude. She sensed he'd dispense his world view before giving up any information.

"Shoot flies?"

"The night guard's a champion with a rubber band; disgusting."

She had to get him back on track.

"But he'd have surveillance duties, rounds to make."

"My cousin married one. Reads the papers all day and moans about the old country, how good it was there. Let me tell you, I've asked him why he doesn't go back to the pashas and Kurdistan if life there was so good."

"This guard's Kurdish?"

"He acts French, well he would, eh, wouldn't he, after serving in the Legion? Still farts higher than his ass."

He read her look before she could ask more. "We're all ex-Legionnaires here," he said proudly.

She wondered about the reputed "brotherhood" of the Legionnaires that Nohant seemed to lack. And the paunch he'd accumulated since his service.

"His name?"

"You're a curious one, eh?"

"I'm following up and need to contact him."

"That's the *flics'* job."

But with many of the shops closed for

August, there was a dearth of eyewitnesses. She needed to coax his cooperation. So far, no patrons had entered the showrooms except for shop staff. She had to get Nohant to talk.

"You've been so helpful," she said, managing a smile. "This would save me time. Everyone's overworked, short-staffed because of vacation."

He rocked on his splayed brown oxford shoes. "A funny one, that Vatel." He paused as if in deep thought, then lit another cigarette, flicking the match into the gutter. "But no more funny than most I served with. You don't ask them about their past, but they carry it like a weight on their chest. Like a badge."

"And Vatel's past?"

"Keeps him company in his nightmares, like all of us."

Nohant's brow furrowed; a dark look crossed his face, and then it was gone.

Maybe this Vatel was a Kurdish political refugee. "Help me here. Did Vatel call the *flics?*"

"He reported an attack. That's all I know."

"So he's off shift at seven and leaves by the back entrance?"

"He exits whichever way he likes when he leaves. But the Metro's closer on this side."

"So Vatel could have left this way to check out the attack?"

Nohant shrugged. "My break's over." He ground his cigarette out on the hot tarmac. "But I don't think so."

"What do you mean?"

He shrugged. "He said he'd seen an Arab woman."

"How could he tell from this distance?"

Nohant shrugged again. "They dress different, don't they?"

"Specifics would help."

"Like that." Nohant pointed to a woman in an enveloping black chador turning the corner.

She paused again at the the yellow tape. A sheen of sweat beaded her brow. *Let the scene speak to you,* her father had always said. *Observe the rhythm of the street, the passersby.* But right now rue de Paradis, lined with nineteenth-century buildings with ground-level shuttered windows, was empty, apart from the delivery man unloading crates from his truck and a woman leaning out a balconied office window, smoking.

She pictured the dawn scene: a street cleaner spraying the pavement, shocked to discover Yves's body. . . . The *flics* responding to a reported attack on a woman, then discovering his corpse, calling in the Police Judiciare, concentrating on this Romeo with his wallet. . . .

A child's laughter echoed off the walls. "Can't catch me," interrupted her thoughts. A woman wearing a head-to-toe black chador scurried around the corner behind a girl of eight or so in a yellow sundress. The little girl dropped a straw shopping bag on the wet pavement. Admonitions in what might be Arabic came from the chador-clad figure, a black head scarf covering all but her eyes. Aimée could only imagine how bulky and restricting the heavy robe and scarf must feel. And in this heat! Like a walking jail cell.

Aimée bent and picked up the bag before it got wet. The heavy black chador's hem was trailing along the wet pavement. Her mind clicked into gear.

"Merci," said the little girl, all big brown eyes, twisting her hands in embarrassment.

"No problem," Aimée said. "Excuse me, but I'd like to ask your mother something."

"She's my sister," said the little girl.

Aimée hesitated. "Your sister . . . ?"

"She speaks Farsi."

"Aaah," Aimée said. "But you look like a smart girl. Could you translate?"

The little girl nodded.

"Someone bad tried to hurt a woman here. And a man was killed. Right here this morning." Aimée pointed to the yellow crime-scene tape. "Can you ask her if she saw anything?"

A flurry of Farsi erupted. A pair of dark eyes in the rectangular scarf opening stared at her.

"She says we're late for the market."

"That's all?" Aimée rooted for a paper-wrapped Carambar, found one in the bottom of her bag and showed it to the sister. "Can she have this?"

The little girl's eyes brightened.

A short expletive in Farsi, then the little girl averted her eyes. "I'm naughty, she says."

Aimée leaned down close to the little girl. "I'm sorry to make you late." Aimée didn't know what else to say.

"I'm not allowed candy, but you're nice for a French lady," said the little girl, her fingers twisting her sundress.

Stupid. Of course, candy from strangers in any culture was forbidden.

"That's a pretty dress." Aimée straightened up and smiled again at the woman.

"My sister made it."

"For your birthday?"

The little girl shook her head. "She sews

at work and at night. She just got home and she says we're late."

"Didn't your sister notice anything this morning . . . did the neighbors talk?"

"How would my sister know? She's always working at the atelier."

One last try before they left.

"But this morning at 7 a.m., a woman wearing a chador was attacked here. Please, can you ask her if . . . ?"

Aimée didn't need a translation to understand the little cluck and shake of the head.

"Non."

"Thank you."

"You ask funny questions."

A hand reached out from the black folds for the little girl's. Aimée saw a flash of a red T-shirt inside; a whiff of Chantilly perfume drifted out. Then she stood aside and they walked by. Persistence had gotten her nowhere, and she still had gum remants stuck to her shoe. She unlocked the car. Nowhere.

"Mademoiselle," the little girl called back, "my sister says that's prayer time."

Aimée turned. "Prayer time, you mean 7 a.m.?"

"No one goes out. They pray at home or in the mosque. Like in our country."

"Your country?"

"All the big girls wear chadors there."

"Where's that?"

"There's a big blue mosque. I saw it, it's far away."

Speaking Farsi, and a blue mosque. That might mean Tehran.

The little girl's hands twisted again. "My uncle lives there. We send him money but I'm not supposed to know that."

And then she skipped away beside the black chador.

Tuesday Evening

Vatel sat bolt upright, his chest heaving. Loud ringing had startled him. It was the phone; Ursana was calling him. Of course, this was all a nightmare, a terrible nightmare. Ursana was picking apricots in the grove or embroidering their baby's clothes.

"*Roj baş,* Ursana," he said, lapsing into Kurdish.

"*Allô . . .* Vatel?"

The words jolted him awake. Jolted him into awareness of the hot room lit by sparse evening light and the beeping of horns from the traffic on rue Saint-Laurent below his window. And the emptiness. She was gone. They were all gone.

Glass shards twinkling like crystal were sprinkled over his security guard overalls

91

that lay on the floor.

"You there, Vatel?" asked Deranger, his boss.

"*Oui,* Monsieur Deranger," he said, recovering.

He'd knocked the lamp over in his nightmare. Always the same nightmare. The white light, his father twirling, wearing the conical hat and flowing skirt, spinning in the old Dervish way. The *dede,* the Kurdish village seer of their outlawed Alevi sect, rocking on the red Kilim rug to the strains of the mandolin-like *saz* and beating a goat-skin drum. His mother, her eyes closed, spinning near his father in the ritual *cem,* following the Alevi way of light. Their centuries-old worship of the sun and nature that stemmed from ancient Zoroastrian roots.

And then the thuds of Turkish artillery pounding the village. The beaten-earth floor shaking. Vatel reaching out for his mother as she spun away. His warning shouts, which no one heard. The drum beating louder, rushing water surging everywhere. Rising up the whitewashed stone walls of their farmhouse. Ursana, his wife, holding the telephone, a smile on her face above the red slash of her slit throat, floating by, her belly ripped open and their unborn baby —

". . . rotating shifts, the duty guard *en va-cances*," Deranger was saying. "*Alors,* did you hear me?"

Vatel caught his breath.

"Of course, Monsieur Deranger," he said.

This wasn't his village, no Turkish military was lobbing grenades, forcing Kurds to evacuate. This was not a damp prison cell, there was no knife under his fingernails nor electric cattle prod searing his flesh until he furnished names.

"So you can work the early rue de Paradis security shift tonight?"

Vatel gripped the sheets tighter. Rue de Paradis . . . and this morning's discovery came back to him. The man's body lying in the tiled doorway, his throat slit with the distinctive curling slash under his ear, a mark the Yellow Crescent left on "inform-ers." Informers like him.

And he was a wanted man.

"Much as I want to help, Monsieur De-ranger, I'm feverish, I woke up with the flu," he said, putting the sheet over the receiver, coughing. "I'm too sick even to work my shift tonight."

"That puts us in a difficult situation," De-ranger said, his thick voice low and raspy from the pack a day he smoked.

"I'm sorry. Why don't you ask Nohant?"

"Nohant do a double shift? But that's overtime."

"He always says he could use the money." Vatel paused. He'd bring it up now. "I know the Cour des Petites Ecuries building needs staff, saw it on the board. I worked overtime there last month and I liked the hours. . . . Can you put in for a transfer for me?"

"Something wrong? Someone was asking about you."

Already? He gripped the phone. Did the Yellow Crescent's tentacles extend here? Killing here, like they killed back home?

"*Non.* Who?"

"That's all I heard from Nohant," Deranger said. Papers rustled in the background. "I'm checking." More rustling of papers. "Cour des Petites Ecuries lost two staff, the manager requested help," he said, decisive now. "Report there tomorrow night. I'll do the paperwork."

Deranger hung up. The transfer seemed too easy. Vatel figured Nohant had complained. Or Deranger had sniffed the scent of trouble. Right now he couldn't worry about that.

The damp sheets twisted around his legs, sweat dampened his forehead; he envisioned dawn breaking over the arched doorway on rue de Paradis, the body in the shadows.

He had to calm down, reason this out. No one intent on murder would have noticed him inside the double thick glass building doors, or counted on him observing them from his guard post inside the showroom. Yet he couldn't be sure.

A loud *"Merde!"* came from his open window, then the opening strains of *Navarro,* the police drama following the TF1 evening news. The sound of his next-door neighbor's loud temperamental *télé* filled the court-yard. The smell of garlic wafted up from a kitchen below.

Vatel rubbed the scars on his chest left by the cattle prods. Three days of the Turkish Yellow Crescent's torture, and he'd revealed the location of the iKK Kurd guerillas' camp in the mountains. During a prison riot, he'd escaped and stowed away on a Black Sea tanker. He knew he could never return to Turkey. But then, he had nothing to return to.

In the Vieux Port of Marseilles with the last of his money, he bought a fake ID. Hungry, he hitchhiked to Aubagne, the Foreign Legion recruitment center where they never asked about your past. He passed the rigorous physical and mental screen-ings. After four months of basic training, he shipped out. A misfit, like everyone in his troop, he survived a tour of duty in Angola that caused him to relive the flooding of his village every night. He only slept in the day, when he could.

Five years later, the end of his contract found him in Paris, fluent in French and with a new identity. Still he feared a glance of recognition on the street. Even though he was twenty-three, not the eighteen-year-old bearded rebel who'd brought destruction on his fellow Kurds, his village, his family. The fear of a hand around his throat as he entered his dark foyer never left him.

He lived in this quartier, anonymous, moving between worlds. The best way to hide, an old Legionnaire had once told him, was like a blade of grass on the lawn among other blades of grass. Kurds and Turks coexisted here, working as concierges, sewing in the sweatshops, worshiping in courtyard mosques, and filling the cafés. He had a job; there was money in his bank account. With his pale green eyes, light skin, and dark brown hair, he could pass for European — and, using his French name, often did.

He took off the T-shirt sticking to his chest and pulled on a clean one. He had to keep busy, yet try to think. He swept up the filament and broken light-bulb shards from the floor, then boiled Turkish coffee in the long-handled copper pot. The tan foam rose until he added a *soupçon* of cold water to settle the grounds. Dark, strong, and intense, like at home.

His hands steady now, he sipped the coffee.

He had to prepare. One never knew. He put a tape in the player. Nilufer, the Kurdish singer, his one extravagance. Then he sharpened the kitchen knife on a whetstone until it felt razor-sharp. He strapped it to his calf.

If the Yellow Crescent operated here, that crazy Mehmet would know.

He heard a loud double knock on the door. Not the birdlike pecking of his eighty-year-old concierge.

No one ever visited him. No one knew he lived here except his employers. Shaken, he imagined it was the iKK, bent on revenge, or the Yellow Crescent. Looking out his back window, he saw a panorama of jagged, broken-tiled rooftops, a steep four-story drop. Escape meant at the least a broken ankle. And that was if he was lucky.

"Monsieur Vatel?" Another knock.

Stupid. He should have turned off the tape player. He pulled on his pants over the knife strapped to his ankle, then peered out the peephole. He saw a blue uniform and shuddered. Even worse.

"Brigade Criminelle," said the voice. "Open up."

Tuesday Afternoon

Aimée touched the Citroën's burning-hot steering wheel and flinched. The little girl's last words echoed in her head: "Prayer time . . . no one goes out." Yet the guard's report said an Arab woman had been attacked. She wondered how this fit, or if it did.

Could the woman have been Yves's contact? Had he tried to protect her? She filed that idea away, wishing she could file the ache in her heart with it. She stepped on the gas pedal, her last view of rue de Paradis the crime-scene tape rippling in the faint breeze.

The Canal Saint-Martin loft might hold answers. Yves must have left something, some trace. Until she searched it, she could only speculate. She'd have to speak with his colleague at Agence France-Presse, too.

The tang of paint blew through the car window. Red potted geraniums on window ledges adorned freshly painted buildings. More evidence of the new face of the tenth, wrought by the urban gentry: *bobos — bourgeois bohèmes* — the young, affluent and casually dressed, leftist-leaning sophisti-cates, like Michel. Eager for this central, cheap quartier bordered by the *grand boule-vards* in the south, the canal to the east, the train stations in the north, and the upscale Place Saint-Georges to the west. Buying property, as René intended, when small gar-ment sweat shops and old leather ware-houses and varied manufacturers vacated, was in vogue. Still, pockets of decaying *hô-tel particuliers* remained, and the members of the traditional working class. Only now the working class and immigrants were Pakistani, Turkish, African, and *bobos* whereas at the turn of the century they'd been Poles and Russians.

Rue Jean Poulmarch curved below the level of the canal in front of the loft she'd left this morning. She parked at the curb before an old wine merchant's shop. Its black 18th-century grillework featured a sculpted gold lion, clusters of grapes, and the smiling god Bacchus.

Inside the loft courtyard complex, she hiked up the stairs of the old printing works, hearing the tinkling of wind chimes. There was no answer to her knock on the loft door. She rapped again and waited.

Still no answer. She scanned the other doorways, but the closed shutters and bulging mailboxes below indicated that many tenants were away. Snipping sounds came from behind tall bamboo trees on the ground floor. She looked down. Just visible on a small terrace, a figure wearing a loose-tied floral kimono and wide-brimmed straw hat was trimming yellow leaves off the trees.

The figure paused but didn't look up. "That's Charlotte Vaudier's place. She's not here," came a man's voice.

Charlotte. . . . A green pang of jealousy hit her. Of course, she could be Yves's colleague . . . could have been.

"Pardon?"

"I saw you this morning," said the figure, the voice low-pitched.

"I forgot something —" her throat caught. Yves's warm arms and his lopsided smile came back to her. He had been here, with her, not even twelve hours ago. Now it felt like another life.

"I don't keep track of her friends."

Yet he'd been observant enough to spot her.

She walked downstairs to the terrace.

"Can you help me?"

"So you can tell the junkies and they'll break in again?" A young man pulled off the sun hat, revealing narrow cheekbones, widespread eyes, and tweezed eyebrows. He reached for his cell phone as if it were a weapon. "I don't think so, Mademoiselle. You'd better leave. Now."

She pulled out her card and showed it to him through the stalks of bamboo.

He reached for it with clear-polished fingernails. A better manicure than hers! "You need more ID than this little detective card anyone can print up."

She stifled her frustration. He might be able to put her in touch with the owner . . . this Charlotte. She rooted in her worn Vuitton wallet and then flashed her detective license.

He stared. "It says computer security here on this card," he pointed out.

"Correct. That's my job now, but I was trained in criminal investigation. Now, Monsieur . . . ?"

"Lolo," he said, folding his arms over his chest. "We don't let just anyone in."

"But I'm not just anyone. I stayed with Yves; ask Charlotte. Where can I reach her?"

"I forward Charlotte's mail to Ulan Bator," he interrupted. "She's researching the Uighar tribe."

Outer Mongolia. Not much hope of information here. She'd struck out again.

"Did you see Yves leave early this morning?" she asked.

He shook his head. "If you're checking up on behalf of his wife, some kind of spousal surveillance, forget it. We mind our own business here."

Her patience vanished.

"Nothing like that, Lolo. He was murdered this morning. If you saw or heard anything. . . ."

"*Nom de dieu* . . . where?"

She shook her head. "Nearby. I'm sorry to insist, but anything you can tell me may be vital." She waited.

"Such a good-looking man." He sighed.

So he knew Yves.

"What time did you last see him?"

Lolo leaned back against a trellis of ivy. "Your boyfriend?"

She nodded.

Lolo expelled a gust of air from his lips. "Love's a bitch, don't I know it. Charlotte's friends stay here all the time. He picked up her keys yesterday." He rolled his eyes.

Aimée tried not to think of what he meant by "friends." She shivered, feeling chilled despite the heat. She had to get inside.

"I'm late for an appointment," she said, improvising. "You must have an extra set of keys."

He waited.

She pulled out a hundred francs, slipped

it into his palm.

He looked around, set down his shears, and smoothed back his hair. "Just a minute."

She started in the loft's stainless steel kitchen, determined to view it as if for the first time. She checked the cupboards. A nice set of blue-and-white Dansk dinnerware, the requisite pots and saucepans. A silver Alesio espresso maker, apparently unused. The designer kitchen was sterile and impersonal. She found a plastic bag and emptied the contents of the garbage can into it.

Last week's *Le Monde,* a circular from an electronics shop. It told her nothing. And then, beside the garbage bag she saw a piece of blue paper. She picked it up. A one way London–Paris Eurostar ticket stub, dated yesterday, arrival time 18:35, Gare du Nord.

Alarms sounded in her head. Yves told her he'd flown in. For the second time she felt stabs of doubt. The Gare du Nord's men's room was well known as a male prostitute haunt; René's words about a secret life came back to her. But a man who made her feel the way Yves had wouldn't go right to Romeo, a hustler. After the messages he'd left on her cell phone, she couldn't believe it.

Romeo might have been his informer. Yet Romeo had stolen Yves's wallet and cell phone, according to the *flics.*

In the sleeping area, she fell to her knees by the duvet. Pain choked her. She couldn't hold back her sobs. She fell onto the sheets smelling of Yves's musky scent.

There was no way she could envision him meeting a junkie male prostitute for sex. She lay there watching dust motes spiral in the sun's rays glinting through the window, until her tears subsided. Spent, she took a deep breath and opened the closets containing women's clothes, the linen chest with sheets and towels. No bag, no newspaper, just his black suit and white shirt with empty pockets. And the empty green bottle of Veuve Cliquot.

She turned over the mattress and a newspaper fell onto the wood floor. Her eye rested on the front page, on the article Yves had circled concerning various groups suspected by the *flics* of the Metro bombing.

He'd drawn a box around the phrase "an insidious network."

Her hands trembled. What did it mean?

She shoved it in her bag, put everything back as she'd found it, and closed the loft door.

Downstairs, near the bamboo, Lolo stood with his arms tucked into the kimono sleeves and folded across his chest. He had to know more than he'd told her, Aimée hoped.

"Lolo, what time did Yves pick up the keys last night?"

"I'd just tossed the endive salad." Lolo thought. "Say nine thirty."

The Gare du Nord was fifteen minutes away. What had Yves done, who had he seen before he met her in the Microimages courtyard? Or did this ticket stub belong to someone else? But he'd connected for the champagne from the African coiffeur in the quartier. Did that mean he'd stayed in the neighborhood before?

"My partner, Philippe, can't sleep in the heat. He's restless, but that's a whole other story. At least we get the breeze from the Canal. This is a ghost compound; everyone has left for vacation," he said gesturing around the building.

Her chance of questioning other tenants crumbled. Battling her deepening disappointment, she scanned the shuttered windows. "You're sure?"

"Tout le monde," he said. Lolo waved his hand to encompass them all.

"If anything strikes you later or Philippe

can add anything, I'd appreciate a call."

A useless conversation. She turned to leave and then paused in mid-step. "Do your windows face the quai?"

"Of course; that's why the loft costs so much!"

They faced in the same direction as the loft windows Yves had looked from last night.

He yawned. "The noise woke me up before dawn."

"What noise?" Her ears perked up. Exhausted, she hadn't heard a thing.

"Like a hailstorm in August. On the windows."

"Did either of you see what made the noise?"

"It stopped and we went back to sleep."

She'd learned something. And if she wasn't mistaken, she'd find out more on the quai.

She stood by the Canal as it shimmered in the heat. Napoleon's "gift to the people of Paris" was completed after his death on Saint Helena. And like his code of law, the little tyrant's gift kept on giving. Even now.

Gravel popped under her sandals as she walked along the quai. The nineteenth-century *Hôtel des Douanes,* the customs house, loomed further down. She was trying to figure out what could have made that noise.

And then she stood under the loft windows. On the pavement lay some leaves curled in the heat and a few pebbles scattered on the light beige dust. "Like a hailstorm," Lolo had said.

Her first boyfriend had tossed pebbles at her window at night as a signal that he was there. She'd creep past her father's room, listening for his snores, then meet her boyfriend outside on the quai. They'd spend hours necking on the embankment.

Scenarios ran through her mind. Say Yves's contact tried to reach him. If Yves had turned off his cell phone, this could have been the only way to signal him. Or maybe it had been a pre-arranged signal from a contact too scared to phone him. . . . Her thoughts spun. Suppose this contact had thrown pebbles at the window to get his attention, to signal a meeting, or to summon him to the rue de Paradis for a rendez-vous. All plausible; but, again, why?

Further on by the gutter, she barely avoided a clump of dried dog droppings, a St. Bernard by the size of it. Nice calling card. And in the heat it gave off a pungent aroma. A scuffle of green leaves blew over the stone. So far all she had were pebbles, the Eurostar ticket stub, and Yves's marked-up copy of *Le Monde*.

She walked downwind, opened the Citroën's door, and sat, the hot leather burning her thighs. In the glove compartment she found René's oversize blue Plan de Paris, the taxi driver's street bible, and opened to the tenth arrondissement. With a pencil she marked the canal loft location; Microimage, where she'd met Yves; the Gare du Nord; and then the rue de Paradis. She drew lines connecting them. Two lines intersected, making a right angle. Almost a triangle. Yet it told her nothing. She wished his colleagues from Agence France-Presse would call; they had to know what Yves was working on.

She turned the key in the ignition and drove along the canal. The silver rippling V of a duck's progress marred the green-brown water's surface. It was the only progress she saw.

Tuesday Afternoon

A mess, René thought. The hum and clack of the rails, the shunt of steam from the old locomotive accompanied his thoughts. It took three hours and three trains to reach the nodding, cypress-lined Loire river valley where he could just make out a glint from a château's blue-tiled roof on the horizon.

Looking out the window at the light brown dappled herds of Charolais cows grazing on wheat and the purple-hued grasses, he berated himself. He felt guilty for leaving Aimée.

He hadn't seen her so shaken since her father's death. He couldn't understand how Yves, a fling when he breezed into town, a bad-boy type who wouldn't commit, could affect her so. She wasted her time on those types. But who was he to think ill of the dead. He'd only seen a corpse once, never hoped to again. Was he jealous of Yves? *Non,* he knew his place. That didn't mean he liked it or didn't hope deep down in some little corner of his heart that it would change.

More cows now dotted the green fields. *Eh, ça va la vache,* the palindrome with letters the same back to front, wound through his head. That second message on Aimée's phone — what if he'd guessed right and the killer had hit Yves's redial and knew Aimée's number? She wasn't safe.

He punched in her number and got a busy signal. He called Saj, his former student, a hacker, who'd taken over for him while he was away. He needed to check in; he had to attend to the business.

"*Allô*, Saj?"

"René, you're on vacation, *non?*" He heard something in Saj's voice. Seagulls squalled in the background.

"Where are you?"

"La Rochelle," said Saj. "But don't worry, I'm monitoring the systems."

"Everything okay?"

There was a pause. The seagulls' cries were louder.

"I guess you should know, the Fountain-bleu account's compromised," said Saj. "Sorry. I traced it to loose lips."

Only gone a few hours and already trouble! René's shoulders sagged. He planned all he could; set up appropriate fire-walls, barriers, password encryption; but it only took one savvy caller requesting confirmation of account data and a newbie to take the bait and give away sensitive information. He saw it all the time.

"I'm on it," Saj said. "I've already installed new protections on the firewall. But I guess it's best that you're not surprised on your return."

These attackers did their homework; culled names and e-mail addresses from company directories, contract service suppliers, and social-engineered information.

Often they called at lunchtime when only a single harried analyst manned the fort who would succumb to the line "I'm about to place your departments' order but Lynette's gone, and I'm out of the office. Shoot me the password."

It worked more often than not. And it just took one mistake to reveal sensitive account data. Education, René thought, you had to educate them.

"We can't stop attacks, but we can insist that no one confirms data online without permission. Thanks for letting me know, Saj."

"I'm on it, don't worry," he said.

"Meantime Saj, keep me updated, okay?"

He tried Aimée again, got her voicemail, and left a message cautioning her to change her number and call back with her new one.

By the time he hung up, the train was pulling into Amboise station where his mother stood on the platform with an eager smile.

Tuesday Afternoon

Nadira checked her watch, then Paul's rapt expression as he watched the darkened Theatre Gymnase's children's performance. In this 1820 jewel of a theater, under a dome whose interior was decorated with murals, they sat upon red plush seats, sur-

111

rounded by gilt-edged curlicues like cake decorations. Paul's attention focused only on the hip-booted pirate onstage brandishing a sword.

Perfect. On plan.

She nudged Paul. "I'm going to call your *maman*."

Paul nodded, his eyes never leaving the stage.

She leaned over to Carla, who organized the four-year-old playgroup's events. Carla's skintight V-neck shirt plunged. Nadira recalled the Koran's words: *Women are to lower their gazes . . . be modest, and draw their veils over their bosoms.* Nadira was glad that the darkness covered her momentary expression of disgust.

"Must make an important phone call," she whispered. "I'll meet you in the lobby."

"But I'll need your help if one of the children needs to go to the bathroom," Carla said. "Remember, they drank so much juice."

"Of course," Nadira smiled. "But Madame Delbard had some last-minute changes in her schedule."

"Shhh." Several of the children put their fingers over their lips.

Before Carla could respond, Nadira pointed to her cell phone and rolled her eyes mouthing "Madame Delbard." If Madame Delbard ever phoned, it was to ask her to run an errand to the drycleaners. But Carla didn't know that.

Out in the lobby lined with plaques commemorating the pantheon of former performers — Sarah Bernhardt, Cocteau, and Yves Montand — Nadira checked the exit, then the time again. Twenty-nine minutes until the end of the act. Another seven to ten for the children to assemble in the lobby. To accomplish her mission, she would have to hurry.

She went through the arched glass doors and, walking at a fast pace, covered the seven blocks of rue du Faubourg Poissonnière. It was time for prayers, but she couldn't perform the ablutions of washing her face, feet, and hands, rinsing her mouth, and running a wet hand through her hair. She'd make do. She pulled out a moist towelette, wiped her hands, bent as if she'd dropped something and ran it across her sandalled feet. Passersby jostled her.

As she walked, she inclined her head. To those on the street, it looked like she was window-shopping. But she'd calculated the direction of Mecca, and in her heart, she prayed. She prayed to strengthen her resolve in following Allah's way, enlightened by her mullah. Say the prayers in your heart, the mullah instructed, and accomplish your mission.

She entered the courtyard on rue Lafayette. In a doorway she donned a gray scarf and long sleeved blouse, and felt more comfortably clothed. She opened the door of the Institut Kurd.

"I'd like to join the center," she said, gazing to the side in respect to the woman behind the reception desk.

"Welcome! You'd like a student membership?" asked the woman. Leyla, Resource Manager, it said on her name tag. She wore a summery flower-print dress with no scarf. She grasped Nadira's hand.

Startled, Nadira recoiled.

Leyla might have been the twin of the nurse who'd discovered her, a shell-shocked nine-year-old, in tattered rags, searching the rubble for her parents' bodies. The past opened up for Nadira. Leyla's open smile, that same cinammon tinge to her complexion, her plump cheeks, those brown warm eyes crinkling in the corners. Nadira bit her lip, remembering the nurse's calm voice as she removed the shrapnel from Nadira's leg and daubed her wounds with antiseptic to prevent infection, which nevertheless spread. The Western-trained doctors saved her from the gangrene that threatened her life.

Nadira hadn't thought of that in years. Nor of the little charm the nurse had given her, an enameled blue horse. The one thing she still had.

"You bit your lip; here's a tissue," Leyla said.

Such kind eyes.

Flustered, Nadira felt rooted to the floor. Somehow she managed to speak. "Does membership entitle me use of the library?" she said, handing over a Sorbonne student ID with the name Shareen Labout.

Leyla smiled. "Of course. But we offer many cultural programs and events as well. Tomorrow Jalenka Malat's speech is titled 'To veil or not to veil: Muslim women's modern role in today's society.' "

Nadira averted her eyes, then managed a grin. "But I know of her work. How lucky."

"The Kurdish Woman's group asked Jalenka to address them earlier," Leyla said, leaning forward. "We're hoping she'll find time to speak to this smaller group too, so there will be a chance to meet her. Do check back. We're not publicizing it."

Nadira nodded, her training kicking in. Even better. *"Merci."*

She marshaled her thoughts. Leyla, with

her direct gaze, French clothing, and perfume, wasn't at all like that nurse, she
decided. After Nadira's leg healed, the nurse
had brought her to the mosque's orphanage
school for girls and introduced her to the
mullah. The nurse was dedicated to jihad
and had helped her understand the mullah's teachings.

Nadira completed the application form.
They were alone in the bright reception
area. While Leyla typed up her card, Nadira
looked around at the photos of Kurdistan
on the wall.

"Will Jalenka speak in here?"

Leyla gestured toward a pair of closed
doors. "It's the largest space we have, only a
little theater, but . . ." Leyla smiled. "We'll
fit in as many as we can."

"Would you mind if I look at the library?"
Nadira asked. "I have to hurry to babysit,
but I'd like to check on a book."

"Upstairs and to the right."

Nadira climbed the stairs and paused. She
heard Leyla's voice on the phone. Instead
of entering the library, she followed a narrow dark wood-paneled hallway to the left,
glad she'd worn sneakers that made no
sound on the carpet. She passed a man
working in an office but she kept going,
winding to the left. She found the door

labelled WC. Inside the cubicle was a porcelain chain toilet, toilet brush, and extra roll of pink toilet paper. She reached into her bag for a knife. At first, the metal-framed window resisted. After several tries, and a generous application of WD40, she pried it open. She pulled the toilet chain so the sound of the flush would cover the creaking of the window.

She stood on the seat. On the floor below, she saw a bank of three windows, all open, facing the small courtyard. The farthest window had a clear view of the stage and podium. Perfect.

She studied the angle then took out her tape measure, calculated the distance from the window ledge to the door, then peered up to the roof. Always have an alternate plan. She closed the window, brushed off the window ledge, swept the old paint chips into her palm and stuffed the chips in her pocket.

At the desk downstairs, Leyla handed her a membership card, now printed and laminated.

Nadira said, "They didn't have the volume I need. But tomorrow I'll try again. *Merci.*"

Twenty-nine minutes later, Nadira stood in the theater lobby again, in her hand a bag from the nearby boulangerie. "Who's hungry?"

A swarm of four-year-olds with open hands engulfed her.

Nadira held out the bag of still warm *pain au chocolats.*

"You're a lifesaver," said Carla.

Nadira just smiled.

Tuesday Afternoon

The police helicopter hovering overhead whipped up a vortex of leaves at the Metro Louis Blanc. Aimée tasted hot dust, dry grit stung her ankles. People in the crowd spilling onto the pavement shielded their faces. It was 3:00 p.m., and she was here to meet Rouffillac. Citing an emergency, he'd called and changed their meeting place.

Ambulances blocked the street. The helicopter dipped, then its *thupts* trailed off. A reek of burnt rubber and smoke clung in the oppressive heat. Horrified, her eyes were transfixed by the bloodstains smearing the green metal art nouveau Metro posts.

Another Metro bombing, the second since July. Low moans and mumbling in Arabic came from an old woman with a torn head scarf. Her face contorted in fear, her gnarled brown hands gripped a shopping bag to her chest as she hunched by the Metro kiosk. A female *flic* put her hand on the woman's shoulder, spoke in her ear, and then gently took her arm and led her to an ambulance.

From the look of things — black powder burns on the pavement and scurrying bomb-squad technicians — much of the scene had been secured.

A man stood by an unmarked Peugeot staring at her. A short, wiry man with brown-gray hair curling around his ears, who emitted a tensile energy.

"Mademoiselle Leduc?"

She nodded.

"We'll talk there," he said, motioning toward a florist shop behind her.

She followed him, stepping over the pink and orange rose petals fallen in the entry, and past a gigantic arrangement of blue delphiniums.

"Monsieur?" The florist looked up, setting down her clippers. She wore a smock; sprays of roses sat next to strips of gauze bandage on her work table. "Do the last roses of summer interest you?"

"Brigade Criminelle business. May I use your shop, Madame?"

"Bien sur," she said, her look expectant. "The medics needed some bandages cut. . . ."

"In privacy, if you don't mind?"

Without a word, she picked up the bandage strips and left the shop. The mingling of floral scents and damp earth filled Aimée's nose.

"What happened?" Aimée asked.

Instead of answering, Rouffillac leaned into the microphone clipped to his lapel. *"Oui?"* he listened, his expression hardening. "Sodium chlorate . . . weed burner and sulfur . . . *explosif* . . . you're sure?"

Sulfur or *drogene,* she knew, was the yellow powder sprinkled on the pavement by her neighbor to discourage pooping dogs. And weedburner was available at Vilmorin or any garden supply store. Common everyday ingredients, but combined they made a big bang. A lethal one.

"It should have been worse, thank God they did a half-assed job. . . ." Rouffillac said, shaking his head and turning away.

Aimée didn't catch the rest. The multicolored rose arrangements in the shop window framed the scene of now-diminishing horror outside. The last ambulance pulled away. Metro workers in blue-green vests hosed down the steps.

"Recount for me your movements and your last conversation with Yves Robert," Rouffillac said, consulting a small notepad that had materialized from his shirt pocket.

Caught off-guard, she cleared her dry, sore

throat. She felt hot and cold; her neck was flushed; the unmistakable signs of a fever.

"I didn't expect to see Yves," she said. "This on-again, off-again thing we had . . . well . . . always saying good-bye at street corners." She twisted the Turkish puzzle ring on her finger. "But this time he asked me to marry him."

Rouffillac looked up from his notes. "Mademoiselle, do me a favor and make this day a little better than it's going, eh? Start at the beginning."

And she did. He looked up only once, when she faltered describing the blood at rue de Paradis and the little girl's words.

"So the last time you saw the victim, Yves Robert, was before 2 a.m. in the morning?"

"I woke up then and he'd gone." She handed him the *Le Monde* she'd found behind the mattress. "Look, when I went back to search the loft, I found this article he'd underlined, it could bear on —"

"Not a smart thing, to take a victim's items or to search the loft, Mademoiselle. You've tainted evidence and made my boys' day harder." His mouth soured and he stepped so close she could smell the old-fashioned pomade on his hair. Didn't do much good to his curls, she noticed. For a small man, he moved with surprising speed and energy.

"But, of course, you realize that Yves was working undercover on a story."

" 'Realize,' Mademoiselle?" His voice lowered. "I investigate and gather evidence following procedure and the regulations prescribed by the Judiciare."

"But you have informants in the quartier, *non?* Ask them. . . ." she paused. "No doubt you've consulted with his colleagues at Agence France-Presse —"

"That's not your concern."

Of course they had informants and had contacted the AFP. Why wouldn't he confirm it to her?

"The Brigade has an 87% case solution rate, higher than any other European capital," he said.

She could almost see his chest puff with pride.

"I intend to better that, Mademoiselle, I don't need your theories or interference."

The typical swagger, the elitism notorious in the Brigade. And Rouffillac embodied it. Granted, only the *crème de la crème* were accepted in its ranks, but it didn't make them easy to deal with.

"You've got a lot going on, I know. . . ."

"We're on high alert," he told her, leaning over to speak into his lapel-microphone again, but all she caught was the word Alpha.

"Commissaire Morbier, my godfather, works at Groupe R in the Brigade," she said. He only worked there once a week, but maybe that would soften Rouffillac up. "I'm familiar with —"

"And I'm aware of your background, Mademoiselle," he interrupted. "Your cell phone, please."

Sharp; he'd caught the reference to the last message from Yves's number on her cell phone.

A plainclothes man appeared at the door, and Rouffillac snapped his fingers, like a overbearing patron to a waiter in a resto. The man took her cell phone and disappeared into a blue van outside.

"But, of course, you're pursuing other suspects besides Romeo?"

"That's all for now, Mademoiselle," he said. "I may have more questions. If so, I'll call you."

In true Brigade fashion, he revealed nothing.

"But you've got my phone."

"The officer will return it when you leave."

He strode to the door. He wanted to brush her away, as if she were an irritating fly.

"So you're bugging my phone?" She followed, her heels crushing the rose petals on the floor.

He gave her a tight smile. "Mademoiselle, we're recovering the evidence necessary to our investigation which you're required to furnish."

So far, she'd learned nothing.

"But how can I reach you?"

He slipped a card into her waiting hand. JEAN-MICHEL ROUFFILLAC, TERRORIST DIVISION, BRIGADE CRIMINELLE 06 42 78 09. "Leave the investigating to us, Mademoiselle Leduc. You understand, don't you?"

And then he got into a waiting car which drove off. The plainclothes officer stepped from the van and handed her cell phone to her. She opened the back cover and checked the SIM card. In place, no obvious bug. But maybe they'd cloned it.

Great. A hostile Brigade Criminelle investigator who made it clear that he brooked no "interference" and Yves's body cold in the morgue. She walked past the florist from whose shop came the scent of the last roses of summer.

Chills racked Aimée as she stood on the black-and-white tiled landing of her 17th-century apartment on Ile Saint-Louis. In spite of the heat, her nose dripped and all she craved was a hot bath. She prayed the antique boiler would cooperate.

She opened the door to her stale, empty apartment. No welcoming lick from Miles Davis, her bichon frise who'd spent the night at the vet's for shots and teeth-cleaning.

In the bedroom, redolent of the day's heat, she kicked off her shoes and scattered her clothes on the parquet floor, then made her way to the bathroom.

Every bone ached and she couldn't think straight. She tossed in eucalyptus salts and dried lavender, then turned on the cracked porcelain faucet. A shudder from the pipes, then a stream of hot water and fragrant steam wafted from the claw-footed tub. She couldn't get sick now. There was so much to do.

She drank bottled Volvic water, swallowing several pain- and fever-reducing Dolip-rane. From the medicine cabinet she took, and cut the edges off a brown glass ampoule — a homeopathic cold remedy her grand-mother had sworn by. She poured the golden liquid into the tub, slid into the hot water, and put a towel over her head so she could inhale the vapors. Her mind whirled; Yves's unease sitting at the window, Romeo the dead junkie hustler found with Yves's belongings, the woman in the chador. She lay there she didn't how long. The water had cooled when she heard her cell phone ringing from the other room.

She ran to it with the thick towel wrapped around her and reached it on the sixth ring. Evening light filled her bedroom.

"Allô?"

"Gerard Drieu with Agence France-Presse," said a deep voice. "Mademoiselle Leduc?"

Her hand shook. If only she could rewind the past twelve hours. She stood dripping on the wood floor, toweling off.

"Thank you for returning my call. I'm afraid. . . ." she hesitated. First she had to find out if he knew Yves. "I need to speak with Yves Robert's colleague and found there are two Gerards. Did you work with him?"

"Of course. I'm his admin boss. Sorry for the delay; I just picked up my messages."

"That's okay. When did you last see Yves?"

" 'See' him? But he's supposed to be attending a meeting that started half an hour ago." Pause. "Is there something wrong?"

"A meeting?"

"What's going on, Mademoiselle?"

"Hasn't the Brigade Criminelle informed

you of his murder?" she said.

Something dropped in the background. There was a muffled sound, as if a hand had been placed over the phone.

"Murder?" She heard the crinkling of papers. "*Mon Dieu!* But who are you and how do you know this, Mademoiselle?"

She took a deep breath. "I identified him at the morgue."

She heard papers shuffling.

"I've got so many messages, I haven't had time to check them. Here . . . yes, a message from Brigade Criminelle."

"I need to speak with you in person."

Her duvet beckoned and she wanted to curl up and sleep, but the Doliprane had taken effect. She could function. She had to. She needed face time with this Gerard and the news bureau staff to discover what Yves had been investigating; especially if he hadn't yet spoken to Rouffillac. . . . Who knew what leads they weren't following? Forget Rouffillac's warning, she told herself.

"This . . . you're sure?"

"As I said, I identified Yves's body at the morgue," she repeated, "since no one responded from your office. Place de la Bourse, right?"

"I'm shocked, at a loss what to say. . . . Do they have a suspect?"

"Past tense. And the wrong one," she said. "Please, can we meet? Say in thirty minutes?"

"*Mais oui*, in the lobby," he said and hung up.

She had to get herself together. She toweled her hair dry, did a quick kohl outline of her eyes, swiped Chanel Red across her lips, and pinched her cheeks for color. She stepped into the nearest thing hanging in her armoire, a black linen V-neck Givenchy with a gathered waist; the torn-off label hadn't hidden its pedigree from her at the flea market. She grabbed her jean jacket. Dust motes caught in the evening slants of twilight drifting onto the floor. She stuck a bottle of Volvic, more Doliprane, and a scarf into her bag.

As she turned to leave, the red light of the fax machine on the secretaire blinked, then a whirr signaled transmission. She hesitated, debating whether to stop and read it. If it came from Saj concerning the Fontainbleu account she could deal with that later. But when she glanced over, she noticed the header on the sheet grinding out: OFFICE OF THE STATE DEPARTMENT OF THE UNITED STATES OF AMERICA.

Surprised, she leaned forward and checked the time. Three a.m. in Washington,

D.C., early for the State Department; but then her contact there worked odd hours. No cover letter, but a smudged photocopy of an old passport application bearing the name Sydney Leduc, her American mother who'd left when Aimée was eight years old. She gripped the edge of the secretaire.

Six months ago, she'd asked her contact to check, but she'd never heard back. She'd figured he'd found nothing and put it out of her mind. Her hands holding the fax shook.

Persona non grata — ON WORLD SECURITY WATCH LIST — was stamped on the top. Over the subsequent blacked-out lines another stamp "Pursuant to the Official Secrecy Act, contents sealed for fifty years." Underneath this was a UNESCO Paris headquarters badge dated 1968. The year Aimée's mother had left her and her father. And that rainy March afternoon came back to her, the empty apartment she had returned to after school. No note, the armoire empty of her mother's clothes, only a chopstick on the floor. The one her mother used to wind back her long hair. More than twenty years ago. Knowledge of whatever was under the blacked-out line would have to wait another twenty-two years. Aching disappointment flooded her.

The whirring ceased: end of transmission. The fax machine lay silent. The one lead to her mother had ended on this paper.

That little breath of hope that went nowhere. Aimée ran her fingers over the smudged words. Now she'd never know what had happened to her. *Persona non grata*, on the world security watch list. Her American mother was still wanted — that is, if she was still alive.

She crumpled the paper, about to throw it in the trash, then smoothed it out and opened her bottom drawer. The drawer that held her father's death certificate, the one photo of her mother — carmine red lips holding Aimée as a baby at the baptismal font — the drawer of the past. She had to put this away. Forget and move on. But she didn't know if she could. Then she glanced at the time; Drieu was waiting. She put the crumpled paper in the drawer and closed it.

René's car . . . thank God. She'd take that, faster than a taxi. On quai d'Anjou she unlocked the car, turned the key in the ignition, and gunned the engine.

She crossed Pont Louis Philippe at the tip of the island, passing over the sluggish green currents of the Seine, drove up to rue de Rivoli, and turned left.

The sun, which shone to almost 11 p.m.

in July, set earlier now each day. She hated, as she had as a child, to climb in bed while vanilla light painted her room. And she loathed being sick.

Her mother's voice came back to her, the lilting singsong voice making up stories about Emil, the Royal mouse in the Louvre, illustrating them on old postcards in the bright splashed evening, dabbing Aimée's fevered brow. . . . Why think of that now? Useless.

She shook off memories, wedged the Citroën next to a sleek Mercedes, set the parking brake, and hurried out.

Inside the seventies-era steel-and-smudged-glass Agence France-Presse, video monitors showed sweeps of the interior. A blond man in his early thirties, his white shirtsleeves rolled up over pressed khaki pants, leaned over in earnest conversation with the reception guard.

He straightened up. Tall, wide brow in a tanned face with a jagged nose, handsome in a prizefighter sort of way. He extended his hand. "Mademoiselle Leduc?"

She nodded and reached for his.

Strong dry grip, a white untanned thread of skin where a wedding band would have been. "Gerard Drieu. I just got off the phone with the Brigade Criminelle. It's ter-

131

rible." He seemed shaken. "Words fail me to . . . well, to explain it."

He'd spoken with Rouffillac, as anyone — not just the smart, accomplished type she figured him for if he worked here — would do. Gotten the lowdown. She wondered if Rouffillac had warned him against her.

"Monsieur Drieu, I'd appreciate speaking with the members of the staff who worked with Yves." She shifted on her heels. "Could you provide me with an introduction?"

"I am sorry, but everyone's left. There seemed to be no point to the meeting," he said. "It's so hard to believe. Yves's work is up for the Renadot journalism award for that incredible piece he wrote on the Cairo poor dwelling in the cemetery. Like all his articles, incisive and based on solid reporting. Such a waste." Drieu shook his head. "We're stunned, we'll have to reorganize priorities and assignments tomorrow. It's a blow!"

More than a blow.

"A real maverick; he did it his own way. But then Yves got the stories no one else did. A stellar journalist."

Aimée clutched her bag. An award . . . she'd had no idea.

"There's breaking news, bureaus all over the globe, constant streams of data to coordinate. But as I told the Brigade, we'll furnish anything pertinent they need."

She aimed for tact. "Look, wouldn't the Cairo branch know —"

"But Yves worked out of Turkey for the last six months."

Why hadn't he told her? But then she remembered his words about the indigo sky over Mount Ararat. If only she'd insisted that Yves explain instead of interrupting with her stupid excitement over his assignment in Paris.

"Yves was involved in an investigation; I'm sure it had to do with —"

"But the Brigade indicated a man with his wallet and cell phone was suspected," Drieu said, his words slower.

Her anger rose to a slow boil. How could Rouffillac stick to that theory . . . unless it was only for public consumption.

"Somehow you were involved with this . . . ?" Drieu hesitated.

"Sordid mess?" she said. "We'd just gotten engaged."

Drieu's brow knit with concern; then he took both her hands in his. "Forgive me, I had no idea."

He seemed to be a company man thrust into an awkward position. There was no reason to attack him.

"Of course you wouldn't know, but I disagree with the authorities. An Arab woman was seen at the crime scene. Did they mention that?"

"The details he gave me were about a thief. You're sure?" He didn't wait for her answer. "But what does that mean?"

She shrugged. "Yves had circled an article in *Le Monde* about the Metro attacks, that's all I know." And saying that, she realized how insignificant her words sounded.

"Let's go outside." He opened the glass door and ushered her into the hot evening air. Across from them stood the pillared Bourse, the former Brogninart mansion, now the stock exchange, dead and deserted in the fading light.

"Excuse me, but I'm late for a meeting with my boss," he said. "You look pale. Are you all right?" Again, he took her hand.

She wanted to beat her head against the glass window, to make Drieu understand there was more to Yves's murder. To question him about Yves.

"I'm fine, but I feel Yves's work was key to his . . ." she took a deep breath, ". . . murder."

"Let me look into this more thoroughly," Drieu said. "I'll get back to you. That's the best I can do right now."

"Merci," she said.

The lines on the brow of his tanned face crinkled. "My condolences; it's hard to lose someone, I know," he said, his voice thick with what seemed like pain. He checked his watch. And with a quick nod he left for a waiting taxi.

She didn't want to leave. But without an introduction and with all the staff members who knew Yves gone, what more could she discover? A cigarette; she needed a cigarette. Too bad she'd left the pack in her desk drawer.

She stuck on a Nicorette patch. Another taxi pulled up. A young man with camera bags slung over his shoulder got out. An Agence France-Presse pass dangled from his neck.

She followed him, re-entering the reception area. The man flashed his photo ID press card, and she saw his name: Gerard Langois. Took a chance.

"01 32 55 78 23?" she asked him.

He paused and turned around. About her height, thick longish brown hair parted on the side, and deepset brown eyes in a long face. "You know my office number."

At least she'd found the other Gerard.

"And you know Yves Robert," she said.

He nodded, watching her. "Big eyes, long

legs. You're Aimée, the one he goes on about."

Her stomach knotted. Yves had talked about her and Gerard didn't know yet. His black camera case held stickers saying "Marriott Hotel–Sarajevo."

"A joke," he said, grinning and noticing her gaze. "Yves insists I —"

"Please, we need to talk," she said. "Upstairs?"

Gerard Langois signed in. She furnished ID to the reception guard and signed her name under his. Once through the automatic door, he took a quick left up a switchback of concrete stairs and then through a swinging door to a large low-ceilinged area with ten or so vacant desks and terminals. In a large cubicle at the corner, several men and women worked at desks. Banks of monitors showing breaking newsfeed perched on the walls. Fluorescent light panels flickered in the ceiling.

"So you've let Yves come up for air, eh? I'm already late for the meeting," he said, setting his bags on a desk, pulling out rolls of Agfa film. Amusement shone in his deep-set eyes. "But since I'm a freelance clicker, just contracted to Agence France Press, I can afford to arrive stylishly late. Besides, the good stuff comes at the end."

Fancied himself Robert Capa, did he?

"We'll talk after the meeting, Yves's waiting."

She shook her head. "There's no easy way to say this. Sit down."

His hand stopped on the roll of film. His smile froze and his gaze never left her face. "What happened?"

Her nose dripped as she sat. She wiped it with her sleeve. Tears threatened, but she willed them down.

"The meeting's cancelled. They should have informed you."

"Eh?"

She took a breath and gave him the bald facts.

For a full minute, shock painted Langois's face, then hardened into anger mixed with hurt. "Damn fool. I told him."

"Told him what?"

"When I met him at the Gare du Nord." Langois shook his head. "I said leave it alone."

She pulled out the Eurostar ticket stub with her shaking hands. The stub she'd forgotten to give to Rouffillac. "Yours?"

He glanced at it, nodded, then sat down on the edge of the desk.

"Leave what alone, Gerard?"

"His contact didn't show."

She leaned forward.

"What contact?"

"That's what I asked." Langois sighed. "But Yves knows everyone, has contacts everywhere. Getting to his sources is like peeling the layers of an onion. 'Better you see it when it happens, keeps your photos fresh,' he always says . . . said."

Langois averted his eyes.

He wasn't telling her something.

"So, like the *flics,* you think his contact was a junkie hustler? That's what you're saying?"

"Eh? You mean that asthmatic, the suspect you mentioned?"

She stared at him.

"I doubt it," he said. "When Yves met me arriving on the Eurostar at Gare du Nord, we waited thirty minutes at the gate for his contact."

"Any idea who the contact could be?"

He shook his head. "No clue. But instead of leaving by the main exit, grabbing a taxi, and having dinner, as we'd planned, he insisted we take the tunnel."

"A tunnel in the Gare du Nord?" she said. "You mean to the Metro?"

"I thought so," Langois said. "But after a ten-minute walk underground we ended up by some construction. A spooky place. Yves kept looking around, glancing at his watch; he said this was their backup meeting point."

She had a thought. "Did he get any calls on his cell phone?"

"No reception down there. Anyway, he said the contact didn't trust cell phones. Wouldn't use one."

She thought of the pebbles outside the loft window. Made sense.

"So the contact didn't show there or at the backup location . . . didn't he give you some idea what it concerned?"

"He asked one of the workers something. But I don't speak Turkish."

Surprised, she leaned forward.

"Yves spoke Turkish?"

"He's been stationed in Ankara as chief correspondent for the last six months until this. . . ." He stopped.

The Anatolian sufi amulet, the Turkish puzzle ring, of course. Like he said, peeling the layers of an onion. She had to construct the events of Yves's life before he met her at Microimage, so she could understand the events afterward.

"And then?"

"He got the keys to a great loft on the canal."

"Did he make calls on his cell phone?"

Langois thought. "Can't remember."

"What about his bags?"

He shrugged. "Instead of dinner, he said he had to go, he would call me later. Otherwise, to meet up here tonight."

She thought about *Le Monde,* the front page on the floor with the Metro bombing headlines.

"Does 'a homegrown insidious network' mean anything to you?"

"We photographers just capture an image; the journalists don't tell us much."

She had an idea. "How about the stories he worked on in Ankara?"

Langois pulled out a small large-format camera, switched on the power. "Yves went native, got inside the militant Kurd organization, the iKK party. Fancied himself a Lawrence of Anatolia for a while, until the Agence reined him in."

Now the dark makeup she'd discovered on Yves's face made some sense. . . . Suppose he'd applied it to make himself appear Kurdish?

"Yves wrote incredible stuff. But he always played it close to the wire." Langois's voice deepened in sadness. "Too close. He hated Ankara, but the countryside captured his heart."

Langois clicked on his state-of-the-art

140

digital camera. "Look."

Astounded, she stared at the photos displayed: an aquamarine sky over a purple blue mountain rising from desolate red earth plains, men in skullcaps, ragged suit jackets, and embroidered vests brandishing machine guns, old Kalashnikovs by the look of them.

"This camera's only available to the trade right now, but in ten years everyone will have one. Small enough for your pocket."

A little spark of hope flared up.

"Do you have any photos of Yves?"

"See." He pointed to a tanned man dressed like the others amid what looked like the smoldering ruins of a village, chunks of breeze blocks, upturned scorched trees and blackened stones. A solitary doorway without a house — a doorway to nowhere — stood framing Yves.

"He gave me this," she said, showing him the amulet.

Langois stared. "I remember how he bartered with the old Sufi. The Sufi insisted that it go to his betrothed, or bad luck would follow."

It already had.

"Can you make me a copy of this photo?"

Langois hooked up a cable to the printer. Within minutes, she had a damp photo of

Yves gone native. Achingly handsome, his eyes lit by an inner fire. The only one she had to remember him by . . . better than her last view of him.

"What if he dressed up again, played a part, and met with foul play . . . the junkie hustler might have been involved. Or not, and took advantage of the chance to grab Yves's wallet and cell phone."

He shrugged. "Ask him."

"Too late, asthma attack; he's dead. But his crony might know."

"Crony?"

"When I find him," she said.

"Let me come with you," Langois said.

Aimée glanced at the time. "Are you ready?"

"Hold on; I'll check in with Georges, the attending."

Langois's words raised more questions; she had to get access to Yves's belongings, see what clothes or disguise he wore. Maybe his bag and papers were still at the Commissariat if the Brigade hadn't requested them. Stupid; she couldn't assume anything. Right now Rouffillac had a lot on his plate.

In the cubicle, Langois held a long discussion with a gray-haired man in a long-sleeved shirt. Headphones hanging on his chest like a stethoscope made him resemble a doctor. By the time he returned, she'd trimmed Yves's photo with scissors she'd found on the desk and stuck it in her wallet.

"I've got a press shoot tomorrow, then an evening shoot at a women's conference, some female Turkish MP, a *cause célèbre* and darling of the *bobo* set. Boring stuff. At least Yves —"

He stopped his mouth pursed.

"Made it interesting?" She turned away. Controlled her shaking hands. "You up for this or not?"

"Never miss an opportunity," he said, shouldering his bags. "That's my creed. And I do want to help you."

At this time of the evening, the hustlers were working the Canal; the time was right to find Romeo's crony if he hadn't scattered and gone to ground. Only one way to find out.

Aimée parked by Cristallerie Schweitzer, the last crystal restorer in Paris. The hospital for broken beautiful things, she used to call it. As a little girl, she'd clung to her grandfather's coat pocket, trying to keep up with his fast pace over the cobbled Canal Saint-Martin quai as he carried his auction-find chandeliers here for repair. The workroom shelves, she remembered, were filled with etched Lalique vases, crystal globule pendants bigger than her fist refracting a rainbow dance of light onto the high walls. A place that smelled of turpentine and a special glue composed of sheep bone marrow, her grandfather had told her. Now, Schweitzer loomed, a dark turn-of-the-century hulk, the roof eaves a haven for pigeons with their soft bubbling coos.

She opened the car trunk and — true to his Boy Scout nature — found René's set of car tools, oil, toll receipts, a flashlight, and binoculars. Score one for René.

"Great night shots," Langois said, checking the adjustments on his camera. "Old metal drawbridge, the Hôtel du Nord, beret-wearing barge captains: Inspector Maigret country, eh?"

"We'll check out the action on the quai," she said. "You'll get the 'real' pulse up around the curve."

"I could use a drink," Langois said.

Two bridges up the canal, they stopped in a late-night café. From a table under the outdoor awning, they had a perfect vantage point for observation of the canal opposite on quai Valmy. And a clear view of the action on the embankment.

Her cell phone rang as Langois ordered a

Stella Artois.

"*Allô?*"

"You haven't changed your number, Aimée!" René scolded.

"I think the Brigade's taken care of that, René," she said. "They took my SIM card, probably cloned it, and are enjoying our conversation right now."

"I doubt it," René said. "That's illegal."

"That's never stopped them before."

She explained her "conversation" with Rouffillac.

"Buy a new phone, Aimée."

"I will," she promised.

So far the killer hadn't called her, either because he *was* Romeo, and was dead, or more likely the killer was someone else who hadn't noted her number.

"Look, Aimée, I can't begin to understand your grief," said René. "But I know Yves wouldn't have wanted you compromised."

Compromised . . . that didn't enter the equation. Justice, meted out to whoever murdered Yves, did.

"If he'd wanted you to know more —"

"Nothing makes sense. But I gave all the information I had to Rouffillac at the Brigade Criminelle."

"*Bon.*" He sounded relieved.

"And I filled out a form to claim Yves's

belongings."

"What will they show?"

"They mean something to me, René," she said, lowering her voice.

There was a pause before René said, "Of course."

She debated telling him more. Why worry him further?

"On top of all of this, Saj called," he said. "The Fountainbleu firm's computer network had a leak so I'm coming back early."

"René, we'll handle it. You're on vacation."

"I can't take my mother's rich food," he said. "I've gained a kilo in the last few hours!"

"Give her the chance to spoil you for another day."

"Only if you enlighten Microimage. No security by obscurity, I say."

Too bad she and René hadn't insisted on a security-lesson clause for all front-line staff prior to contract approvals.

"Can you raise the subject of a Security 101 course?" René asked. "No reason to knit the sweater if an untutored staff is going to unravel the yarn." She heard splashing, like a fountain, in the background.

If that would ease his mind, she'd do it. "Makes sense. Deal. How's château life?"

"The moat's pea-green with algae. Otherwise, *Maman's* busy with the comte's new acquisitions, *comme habitude.*"

The comte, a circus aficionado, had met René's mother at the Cirque d'Hiver and offered her a job running his *musée de mécanique* — mechanized toys — at his château. She'd raised René there, and Aimée suspected she was more to the comte than just his museum keeper. René never spoke about it, only said that growing up in the drafty château, attending the village school, had opened his eyes. Opened them, she'd guessed, to ridicule as a little person.

"*Maman* and the comte grew excited when I told them about the Passage du Desir," René said. "Just think of Leduc Detective's expansion . . . we'd give Saj an office and hire some of my student hackers."

She suppressed a groan. All that took money. Money she didn't have.

Langois claimed her attention, pointing to figures moving on the opposite embankment.

"I'll talk to you tomorrow, René."

"I hope you're at home. In bed," he said.

What he didn't know wouldn't bother him.

"Don't worry, René," she said. *"A demain."*

"To Yves." Langois clinked his glass against hers.

She nodded. "To finding Yves's killer." She drank water and popped two more Doliprane. With luck, she'd sweat this cold out. Feed a fever, starve a cold . . . or was it the other way round?

Langois set some francs on the table. "Looks busy over there."

Time to find Romeo's crony.

An algae smell drifted from the narrow ribbon of the dark inky canal. Langois gestured toward the shadows. The sound of shuffling and voices came from dark slanted shadows on the stone embankment. The leaves rippled. Two men stood engaged in a close conversation. She shivered, knowing that S & M types frequented the riverbanks.

"He look like the one?" Langois asked.

She saw a man poking a long-handled broom at the branches. He hooked a plastic bag and lowered it, his hands trembling. He wore tight red jeans and a skin-tight red long-sleeved shirt, and had gold-tipped short hair, sporting a young look at odds with his ravaged wrinkled face. Rail-thin and jumpy; the "glam" punk type Giselle had described.

She nodded, her heels catching in the cobblecracks as she approached him.

"Where's Romeo tonight?" she asked the man.

He looked her over. "You weren't his sort, *ma chére.*"

He used the past tense. Word traveled. He knew.

Then he shot an appraising look at Langois.

"Neither was Yves, the *mec* murdered on rue de Paradis," she said.

She pulled out Yves's photo. Stepped forward and held it up so he could see.

"Know him?"

"Why should I?"

She saw his concave chest heaving, shoulder blades sticking out. Pathetic. The man needed a fix. More than that, he needed a good meal. And rehab.

His hands gripped the handles of the blue plastic bag. She noticed the scratch on his neck.

"Was Romeo an informer?"

"For the Brigade?" The man snorted. "You're kidding, right?"

"Sorry, I mean was he helping an investigative reporter?"

He shook his head. "Not his style." His voice rose. "Romeo didn't kill that *mec.*"

"I agree," she said. From his comment, she realized that this man knew more than he let on.

He pointed at Langois. "What's he want?"

"How about a photo?" Langois asked.

"Forget it."

"He's a friend," Aimée said. "Tell me what happened, then we go our way."

"Why do you care about Romeo?"

"I'm Aimée, you're . . ."

"Berto's my work name."

But Berto had no takers. She noticed a thin sleeping roll on the stones, a pair of scuffed sandals. He didn't have much.

"Business looks slow tonight," she said.

"*Eh ma chére,* do you think anything I say matters to the Brigade?"

"Do I look like the law?" She paused.

"Not unless they're wearing designer clothes as an undercover disguise these days," he said, with a sneer.

"*Et alors,* we'll keep it just between us." She reached forward, a wad of francs in her hand.

He eyed the money.

"Interested?" she asked, her tone coaxing. "Tell me what you saw on rue de Paradis."

His long skeletal fingers darted out, and she jumped back just in time. As fast as a fox, this Berto.

"Talk first," she said. "Then the money."

"Over there. Your friend stays here. No photos, understand?"

Langois nodded and backed away. She

150

joined Berto under the shadowy hanging branches. She wondered if Berto used the hospitals in winter, as some of the homeless did to survive. They'd enter a hospital coughing, the main thing being to look like they belonged there, heat food in the staff kitchen, get boiling water, and sleep near the hospital incinerator, of course, timing the dump schedule. And with three hospitals in the quartier, they'd survive the winter. But she doubted Berto would last until the next one.

Berto leaned forward, his words coming fast. "Romeo and I would take rue de Paradis en route to Gare du Nord."

"Gare du Nord?"

"Well, for our early-morning commuter clientele."

She controlled her shudder.

"I heard the street cleaner shouting." He scratched his arms.

"And when did you take Yves's wallet and cell phone?"

He froze.

"Look, I don't care. It's over. Just tell me what happened."

"The street cleaner pointed. He was excited, jabbering in some kind of African," he said. "And then we saw a *mec* sprawled in the doorway. Nobody I knew, but Romeo

151

saw the wallet and phone next to him. Well, Romeo needed a fix. Then we took off."

"You just *left . . . ?*"

"We couldn't help him any more. Look, I live on the street. I know when someone is dead."

She was horrified; she couldn't imagine finding a dead body and stealing from it. But to Berto, it meant a fix and survival. This sounded like the truth.

"Who else did you see, besides the garbage man?"

He shrugged and held out his hand.

"Think. What else did you see down the street?"

"It was deserted. We heard sirens."

"How'd you get that scratch?"

He touched his neck. "We speeded up and turned into Cité Paradis. That's when I barrelled right into some *mec* and got this."

"Sounds convenient," she said.

"And we would have got away, too! Romeo didn't kill the guy. Maybe it was that *mec.* He was crouching, trying to catch his breath. . . ."

Her ears perked up. "What do you mean?"

"The *mec* was running away, like we were. . . ."

Her shoulders tensed.

"Was he the killer?"

Berto shook his head. "I doubt it. He was a little guy. Crying, too. 'Supposed to meet him. I couldn't help him,' he says, 'all that blood.' "

She leaned closer, smelled the acrid odor of something chemical from him. Junkies didn't sweat like other people.

"What else?"

"The *mec* was scared and then he took off."

"Describe him, Berto. Give me more."

Berto's shoulders twitched. "Little. Works at the train station."

Her hope soared. Yves's contact who worked at the Gare du Nord?

"You knew him?"

"You see them all the time at the station in their blue work jackets."

"A Turk?"

His head bobbed, anxious for the money.

"You're sure? Did he have a beard or a moustache?"

"I told you. A little man, a little moustache. Only Turks do the dirty jobs at Gare du Nord and Gare de l'Est. He took off, and then a *flic* caught Romeo at the corner."

"That's all?"

"If we hadn't run into the Turk, Romeo would have got away."

"But *you* did, Berto. How?"

153

"I hid behind a truck. Romeo bolted like a fool and got caught red-handed."

She handed him the cash, and he spun away. "Wait." She pulled out another twenty. "Go eat first, eh?"

Langois waited for her farther down the quai.

"You heard?"

"Most of it," he said. "And I got some photos, if you need them." He took Aimée's arm. "His story makes sense if this little Turkish *mec* was Yves's contact from Gare du Nord."

She nodded.

"You should speak with Gerard," Langois said. "He was Yves's Ankara admin chief."

"Gerard Drieu?"

Langois nodded. "Sad story. His wife left him a month ago. She walked out the door and got hit by a lorry as she was getting into her car."

That explained his aura of sadness. Poor man.

"But I just spoke with him before you turned up at the AFP. He knew little, but he said he'd search for Yves's articles."

Langois exhaled. "Yves got the trust of the iKK, the radical Kurd group, and traveled with them in the mountains. He insisted that they weren't the violent cut-throats the Turkish military termed them."

"Cutthroats?"

She stopped and thought for a moment. "Hadn't he given up all that? He told me he was buying the loft and would be stationed in Paris with a new job."

"Yves was the best, bar none. He was up for an award. AFP wanted to keep him, at least according to rumor."

She took out her phone and punched in a number.

"Rouffillac," a man's voice said after the first ring.

"Aimée Leduc," she said, summoning her courage. "Yves Robert had a contact he was supposed to meet at Gare du Nord, perhaps a worker, Turkish —"

"And your source for this, Mademoiselle?"

She hesitated.

"If you can't give me the source, then it's hearsay. Didn't I indicate that we're conducting this investigation and your help's not required?"

"His photographer . . . the man he worked with, told me. He's right here; why don't you speak with him?"

She handed her phone to Langois, who took it eagerly. As he spoke to Rouffillac, she had an idea. But before she could get the phone back, Langois turned to her. Rouffillac had rung off.

"Nice *mec,* thanks. Now I've got to appear at the Brigade. Says to tell you he's already canvassed the railroad station and to butt out."

"He said that?"

"In so many words."

"At least he won't say I'm obstructing his investigation."

If Rouffilac's men had canvassed the Gare du Nord, turned up suspects, and were following another line of investigation, she wanted to know what it was. But he'd never tell her.

Time to use a police connection and pull in a favor, which she hated to do. But the chance existed that a busy Rouffillac hadn't tied up all the loose ends.

Langois walked ahead of her on the cobbled bank, taking night shots of a confused squawking seagull.

No time like the present. She punched in another number. At this time of night, she hoped to reach the access machine, hoped it was still on.

The phone picked up. She heard clicks, then a long pause.

"Laure, *ça va?* You awake and feel like talking?"

She waited until the voice-activated, halting computer-generated voice answered. "Keep your skirt on Aimée, I'm checking e-mail. One moment."

Aimée's friend Laure, a *flic* and daughter of her father's first partner, had suffered a stroke eight months earlier as the result of an attack in which her partner was killed. Laure's slurred speech was slower than the typing fingers on her right hand. So she used a special program to allow her to respond over the phone. Her rehabilitation, a long, frustrating process, edged one step forward and two steps back. Laure did data-entry work for the Commissariat now. "My mind's lightning fast, it's the rest that's slow," she'd insisted to Aimée.

"Back on the old desk job two months, right?"

"And you know how I love it," said Laure's computer voice. "Give me a beat to walk any day. But it keeps me current until these legs get moving."

"I need a homicide report," Aimée said, "and a catalogue of the victim's belongings."

"Cut right to the chase, don't you? What about 'How're you doing, Laure, done your exercises today, lifted those weights?' "

"And sound like your therapist?"

"Right now, I'm pissing mad. I did all my exercises and feel like crap after lifting weights, thank you." Pause. "You don't want much, do you?"

"Matter of fact, I want the homicide victim's belongings. And I need them tonight."

"LOL."

"Does that mean you're laughing out loud?"

"Computers can't laugh, but you're perceptive."

"It's Yves, Laure."

"You've got more trouble with men than —"

"I ID'd him in the morgue this morning," Aimée interrupted.

"Yves, the on-again, off-again? Wait, start from the beginning."

And she did.

"I'm sorry," Laure finally said.

"Right now, I'm near the Commissariat," Aimée said. "And if you can approve my request for Yves's belongings with that *flic* voodoo you do, I can pick them up in a few minutes."

"A homicide gets routed to the Brigade, you know that."

"They're a little busy right now."

"I heard."

"Maybe Yves's briefcase or his laptop's still sitting in the Commissariat."

"I'm good. But not that good."

"You won't know till you try."

"If, and I said *if,* I can access the homicide report, I'd have to do some fancy footwork and e-mail it to you later. There's no other way, or they'll know."

"And Yves's belongings?" Aimée said.

"I've never tried that," she said. "Depends if someone has entered them in the system."

"Isn't that what *you* do?"

"More or less. Accessing files, inputting from the hard copy. They love me, everyone hates doing this."

"You thrive on challenges, Laure."

"No chance you know the case number?"

"I've got the receipt . . . somewhere." She rooted in her wallet, found it. "Form 405, citation request #092."

"At least someone's doing their job," Laure said a moment later. "It's been routed by a Commander Maillol to the Brigade for morning pickup tomorrow. It's all still here. But right away I can see you won't get approval. They never relinquish belongings to non-family. Even to fiancées. . . . Why didn't you tell me?"

Aimée chewed her lip. "Looking back, it feels unreal. Yves back in Paris to stay

159

and . . . telling me he wanted . . . then. . . ."

She couldn't finish.

"You're approved. Hurry up before Maillol realizes how accommodating he's been."

"And the report?"

"If I can access it, I'll e-mail it tonight or tomorrow. But don't hold your breath; it's probably in the Brigade's hands."

"Thanks, Laure."

"Take care, Aimée. Listen, I never did this and I can't ever try it again, *comprends?*"

Langois waited outside while Aimée entered the Commissariat for the third time in twelve hours. She strode up to the receptionist, now a male officer. Good, the night shift wouldn't recognize her. His eyes drifted up from his computer. "Lost your keys, Mademoiselle?"

"*Non,* why?"

"That's the usual problem with your type this time of night."

Her type? She thrust the receipt across the counter. "I'm here to claim these belongings. My taxi's waiting."

"And in a hurry, too. Let me check the status of this request. Strange. This ignores the usual procedure."

She hoped her luck held and Maillol

wouldn't walk in. She chewed her lip.

"Then with all that's going on . . ." He shrugged.

"Sorry, officer, but if you could . . ."

The desk officer whistled. "Applied for and approved the same day. You must rate."

A new respect shone in his eyes. Probably figured her for a judge's daughter. The old-boy network opened many doors.

"Where do I go?"

"Downstairs. Window 14. But I don't know if anyone's there. We're stretched thin tonight."

The Commissariat had once been a lingerie factory. Vestiges of the wooden support beams were visible at the subterranean level. The flaking plaster smelled moldy. The place needed a good airing.

After several minutes of repeated knocking, a yawning *flic* appeared. "Come back tomorrow. Notice our new hours. We're closed."

True enough. A hand-lettered sign read 9 a.m.–8 p.m.

"But I'm catching a midnight flight at Roissy Charles de Gaulle," she said, glancing at her Tintin watch. "Please, my taxi's waiting, I'm going to the funeral." She rubbed her eyes. "Those are my fiancé's things, his parents begged me, I have to bring the little there is left."

"I told you," he said, "look at the sign. Besides, it's not my department; I'm in Lost and Found."

"Not so different, is it? Look, here's the citation number, can't you just check?"

He scratched his head. Numbered wire baskets filled the shelves behind him.

"His mother's had a nervous breakdown, I can't go the funeral empty-handed . . . please. Otherwise she'll never forgive me."

He reached through the space under the window for the form. "No promises. They've got their own system; it's like reading hieroglyphics."

She heard him muttering as he walked away with the form. Please find it, she prayed. She doubted she could get away with this tomorrow.

She tapped her feet on the worn linoleum. She heard more muttering from the back and his halting footsteps. The linen dress clung between her damp shoulder blades.

Three minutes later, he returned with a creased Printemps shopping bag. "Sign here."

She grabbed the pen and scribbled her name.

"And here."

That done, he opened the window and

pushed the shopping bag across to her. "It arrived two hours ago from the morgue."

"*Merci,* Monsieur," she said.

"I'm bending the rules here. Don't make this a regular occurrence."

He needn't worry. She wouldn't.

Tuesday Early Evening

Warily, Vatel watched Florand, the Brigade Criminelle officer sitting at his wooden kitchen table. Medium height, shaved head, and work-out physique. Nothing to make him stand out from any *mec* on the street. Except for Florand's eyes, the clouded gray of dirty melting snow. Wolves' eyes. Like the wolves Vatel had once hunted in the Dersin mountains with his father.

"Coffee?" Vatel asked.

"*Non, merci.*" Florand pulled out a small notebook. "I didn't find you at work, so I'm here to ask you a few questions."

"Of course." Vatel coughed. "I've got a summer cold, the worst."

Vatel's knife was strapped to his calf under his trousers. He kept his face a mask, inwardly berating himself. By reporting the attack, he'd brought on this visit, questions, and the last thing he wanted: attention. In Turkey, he was on the Yellow Crescent's wanted list.

"Your papers, please."

Vatel opened his wallet, handed Florand his *carte de séjour* and *carte d'identité.*

"Monsieur Vatel, you've lived in France a while, yet I notice your accent."

His papers had held up. But even with his story prepared, perspiration dampened his collar. "French father, Yugoslav mother, born in Trieste."

Florand slid his papers back over the table. His gaze locked on Vatel's. "Nice job. But then the Legion works with us on this."

Startled, Vatel's hand shook. "I don't understand."

"We know you're ex-Legion. And I want to make it easy, so your past works for you."

"But —"

Florand gestured around Vatel's room, pointed to the long-handled copper coffee pot, the Nilufer CD on the table. "You're Turkish."

To the French, people from Turkey were Turks.

"A Kurd. Big difference. But I'm a resident and work here now."

Florand's face remained without expression. "We'll talk about that later. Now according to your call at . . ." Florand thumbed back through some pages in his notebook. ". . . 6:48 this morning, you

164

indicated a person had been attacked on rue de Paradis." He looked up, intelligence behind his gray eyes. "Give me more specifics."

Smart. Florand had worded his question without revealing the gender of the murder victim or the presence of the street cleaner. Vatel couldn't reveal that he'd discovered the body without inviting questions as to why he'd run away.

"You see, your colleague," Florand looked down consulting the notebook, "Nohant. Yes, Monsieur Nohant, observed nothing and couldn't offer much information other than that you indicated an Arab woman was attacked."

He handed Vatel notepaper and a pencil.

"Why don't you diagram the scene for me?" He gestured to the paper. "Explain your movements while you do so."

Vatel willed himself to control the shaking of his hands. In broad strokes, he sketched the rue de Paradis building where he worked security, the door and the street, the arches opposite. If the street cleaner, who they would have questioned, mentioned him running away, and could identify him in his jumpsuit, he was stuck. He should have stayed for the arrival of the police once he'd discovered this body. Not fled like a coward . . . like someone guilty.

"You see, Officer, after my rounds at 6:45, as usual, I checked the galleries, then paused here." Vatel made an X in the foyer by the door. "We're instructed to survey the street, to notice if any *clochards* or homeless have slept in the doorway. Just as a precaution, you understand."

Florand nodded.

So far, so good — and the truth.

"A few men, maybe two, clustered a few doorways down. Here. The usual types rousted from Square Albert Satragne. They don't bother anyone. Then, from the corner of my eye, I saw movement, bright clothes here."

He looked up. Florand's eyes had never left his face. Damp wet circles radiated from his T-shirt sleeves. "Under this arched doorway, I saw a robe, like a chador, black and long; then it was gone. I heard screaming, yes, even through the glass door, then a sound like a garbage can overturned. No . . . first the garbage can, then the scream. That's right."

Florand hadn't said a word. Vatel's palms were wet.

"A woman's scream?" Florand asked, breaking his silence.

Vatel blinked. No air stirred in the dense

166

hot room. "I . . . I assumed so."

"And then?"

"Nohant hadn't disarmed the alarm system from the upper floor yet. So I couldn't open the door. I punched in our direct police line and reported an attack. Nohant came downstairs, concerned, and I told him about the woman. Then at seven o'clock my shift ended."

He waited, knowing if he said another word, it would all come out in a babble of lies. So far he'd told the truth. Never lie if you don't have to, and if you do, keep it simple. An unwritten Legion motto.

"What about those men in the doorway?"

"Gone."

"And you, Monsieur, left your work from which exit?"

Here was the tipping point.

"Why, here . . . that's the staff exit." He lied for the first time. It would be his word against the street cleaner's. With luck, other security workers in the quartier would have gotten off at that time, he wouldn't necessarily be the only one in a jumpsuit. Or he could argue that . . . the man had made a mistake.

"This door's closest if you're going to the Metro," Florand said, pointing to the door on rue de Paradis and leaning forward. "But you live only a stop away. Isn't walking faster for you?"

"Not if I'm tired. That short ride makes the difference."

"But wouldn't the incident raise your professional interest, so to speak? Weren't you curious?"

"I reported the attack, that's my duty. I didn't feel well."

"Describe this woman for me again."

"A tall black-robed figure."

"Would you say tall for a woman?"

He nodded.

"And the face?"

Vatel shook his head.

"But you're the only one who saw her, Monsieur Vatel. How do you explain that?"

"Look, I did my duty. I reported it. You mean she got away?"

Florand pulled out a photo. The *mec* with the slit throat. And again it all came back.

"Do you recognize this man?"

Vatel kept his voice calm. "I don't understand."

"Didn't you see him in the doorway down the street?"

"It's hard to say."

"Look at his orange pants . . . didn't you see these, that flash of color?"

Vatel battled his confusion. Coughed. "It's

168

all in the report I called in."

"Think, Monsieur."

Static crackled from the police receiver clipped to Florand's collar. "Unit 813, backup needed."

Florand leaned forward, his eyes on Vatel, and spoke into the receiver. "Copy." That seemed to be the end of the radio conversation.

"I don't want to say the wrong thing, I'm not sure. It's terrible, but why show me this . . . what does it have to do with anything?"

Florand uncrossed his feet; the chair scraped back.

"This victim was found where you reported seeing the woman." Florand closed his notebook. "Had you seen that black-robed figure before?"

"Many women wear chadors in the quartier."

"You recognized the mark on the man's neck, didn't you, Vatel?"

Vatel drew back.

"You saw the body and ran away in fear because you recognized the mark on the neck."

"Look . . . I . . ." Vatel stammered.

"It's distinctive. It reminded you, didn't it?"

He was bluffing, Florand didn't know. No outsider knew.

"Reminded me? Look I'm not a part of anything like —"

"The terrorist iKK who go under the guise of the Kurdish Workers Party?" Florand finished for him. "I can pull your papers, deny your *carte de séjour*. That's just the beginning, Monsieur."

Vatel flinched. This Florand was too close to the mark. No Kurd talked to the authorities. And if they did, they didn't live long.

"But I've done nothing wrong. I reported an attack. You're just targeting the Kurds, as usual. Where's the proof?"

"Well, here's your opportunity" — Florand's chair scraped across the floor — "to prove me wrong. I need an ear in the quartier."

Vatel backed up in his chair, his T-shirt drenched. "I live a quiet life, don't mix with anyone, keep to myself."

"We know. Your dossier's specific on that."

The hair stood up on Vatel's neck.

"I suggest it's time to change, Vatel, to broaden your 'social horizons.' To get out more."

"You want me to inform?"

Florand pulled a cell phone from his pocket and set it on the table. "My number's programmed on your new phone. If you'd like to continue working and have your *carte de séjour* renewed, Vatel, do you have a choice?"

Tuesday Night

Aimée clutched the creased Printemps shopping bag to her chest as she joined Langois on the quai. He stood by the metal arched bridge in a pool of yellow streetlight. The laughter of a couple, walking arm in arm, echoed from the opposite bank.

"Did you shop in the Commissariat?"

"These belong to Yves."

Langois averted his deepset eyes. Scared, or apprehensive? She couldn't tell.

"Tell me if there's anything you recognize."

"You lied to obtain that, didn't you, Aimée?"

"Stretched the truth, more like it." She stared at him. "But why does it bother you?"

"You're dealing with big guys like Rouffillac. He used words like jurisdiction, evidence-tampering . . . he's playing on his home field, he knows the rules."

"Big guys like him don't play by the rules, trust me. Don't you want to know what happened to Yves?"

He nodded.

"Rouffillac's more concerned with Metro bombings and terrorism. He didn't know about Romeo, hadn't even questioned anyone at Agence France-Presse. I'm not waiting until he catches up."

A nagging suspicion deepened. Langois, someone so obvious . . . had he made up a story? Had he killed Yves?

"Or maybe there's a reason you didn't talk to him before?"

"My fault," he said. "You're going to blame me, right?" He gestured, his hands slicing the air. "But I only worked with Yves for three weeks. My first field assignment. Yves taught me the ropes. Told me to follow his lead and keep my mouth closed; I'd get better pictures that way." Langois wiped his brow. "I should have urged him to coordinate with AFP instead of playing the lone wolf." He expelled a long breath of air. "I'll tell you the truth. I was in awe of him. And you're right. I should have insisted."

Guilty. But a little too late. He seemed like a kid who was in over his head.

She looked in the sack, took the plastic bag labeled "Morgue," and opened it. There was a typed sheet listing clothing: a bloody yellow World Cup T-shirt, blood-spattered orange pants, boxers, scuffed Adidas had been forwarded to the lab at Brigade

Criminelle. Other than that, it held his worn brown wallet and the cell phone recovered from the suspect Renaud Vorner, aka Romeo Void. Yves's cell phone battery was dead. The ache of disappointment filled her.

"No briefcase, no laptop."

"Yves used Internet cafés in cities to file his stories," he said. "But most of the time we were in the countryside. In the devastated villages, they had no electricity, not even a generator."

In the wallet, she found only an expired phone card. The rest of the contents, she figured, had been cleaned out by Romeo the junkie. Dumped in the garbage. Gone.

She stroked the wallet, then slid her hand inside again. Empty. Nothing else. What had she expected to find . . . the murderer's name?

She put the wallet back inside the sack. She checked the bag itself, but found nothing else.

She pulled out the wallet again, searched each compartment, felt each seam and then felt a loose one behind the billfold compartment. She pried the fabric back and found a scrap of paper. With her fingernails, she pulled it out. A scrap torn from the lining of a La Perruche brown sugar-cube box. On one side of it were yellow and green parrots. She turned it over and in the street-light saw writing in unfamiliar script with dots over the letters. Her heart skipped. She held it up to Langois.

"Recognize this language?"

Langois stared, then pointed to one of the words. "*Kadeski,* that's Turkish for street. But the rest I don't understand."

A scrap of paper in Turkish in Yves's wallet?

"What do you think it means, Langois?"

"I don't know." He drummed his hands on the bridge's metal railings.

Battling tears, she said, "What haven't you told me?"

"When I came out of the bathroom in the loft," he said, "I overheard Yves talking about some network."

"Why didn't you tell me this before?" She thought of "the insidious network" Yves had circled in the newspaper.

"A vague mention of a network? It could mean anything. You know that. Besides, Aimée . . ." he said, drawing his words out, ". . . Yves wouldn't want you to get involved."

"Involved? A little late for that now."

"That came out wrong, sorry," he said. "I mean he cared for you; the last thing he'd want would be for you to be in danger."

First René, now Langois!

"It's a guy thing, right? Women can't handle this."

Langois shook his head. "You don't need to prove you're tough to me, Aimée."

For a moment, she wondered if she was too hard on him.

"He worked on exposés: political corruption, scandal, government ties with industry. You know that, he was an investigative journalist. But without his contact, he said he didn't know who to avoid."

"I find that hard to believe."

"From the way Yves acted, it was as if . . ." Langois paused.

She wanted to wrench the words from his mouth. "Go on."

"He needed another piece, proof . . . but I'm guessing. The AFP meeting earlier tonight was to tell if the ducks lined up, that's what he said."

She folded the shopping bag, putting it inside hers. And then it stared her in the face.

"But I think the ducks have lined up," she said, and looked at the paper in her fist.

She knew who would help her figure out how.

"Where can I drop you, Gerard?"

"Paul, remember Tintin's dog Snowy . . ." Nadira paused on page 18 of *Tintin and the Sceptre d'Otakar.* Paul's little sleepy breaths answered her. He was asleep at last! His blond curls were half under the duvet; his arm clutched his *doudou,* a stuffed bear with a missing eye.

She stifled a yawn and switched off the lamp. The blue room was painted with murals of Babar. It was a huge room for one child. In the Tehran orphanage, thirty of them had slept on the floor in a room half this size.

On the landing, a seam of light came from under Madame Delbard's bedroom door.

"Nadira?"

Caught, Nadira turned and smiled. Madame Delbard stood there, a robe over her cream peignoir, emitting the perfumed odor of La Prairie night cream. Madame spent more on face cream than she paid Nadira in six months. Yet it didn't diminish Madame's apparent age or the effects of butter and cream. Like all Western women, a soft, wasted life, Nadira thought, without prayer or purpose.

"*Oui,* Madame," she said. "Paul just fell asleep."

"You're a jewel, Nadira," she said.

Monsieur Delbard, she figured, hadn't returned and Madame was waiting up for him. Like she did every night. Nadira's eye fell on the empty open pill bottles on the dresser. And for a moment Nadira pitied this privileged woman with a straying husband.

Inside Madame's high-ceilinged peach-walled room, the late news flickered on the *télé.*

"Would you mind dropping my dress off at the dry cleaners tomorrow?" Madame said, a slight slur to her words.

"Oui, Madame." Nadira gave her a tight smile. On the *télé,* in the background, a uniformed CRS riot squad patrolled a Metro station.

Madame handed Nadira a blue dress on a hanger. *"Attendez s'il vous plait,* since you're going, my black suit's got a spot, too." Madame turned toward her armoire.

"In other news," the announcer said, "this afternoon Jalenka Malat, the first Kurdish member of Turkish parliament, visited a suburban infant *créche* serving Kurd asylum seekers."

The muscles of Nadira's neck tightened. Her target.

She saw a reddish-brown-haired short woman leaning over a crib. "Madame Malat, a Sorbonne graduate," the announcer continued, "thanked the French government for the generous subsidies making this possible. . . ."

"Don't forget Paul's playdate tomorrow, Nadira," Madame said, handing her another hanger.

"Pardon, Madame?"

"It's on the calendar," she said, slightly irritated.

Nadira summoned another smile. "But you've forgotten, Madame. Wednesday's my day off."

"*Desolée,* Nadira, I had to change it," Madame Delbard said, unruffled. "Didn't you notice? I wrote it in yesterday."

Madame couldn't change things when she pleased. Nadira's mission depended on Wednesday being her free day. She clutched the hangers. "Madame, I'm sorry but I made a doctor's appointment."

For once Madame could ferry her son to a playdate herself.

"But you must reschedule it, Nadira," she said, yawning. "Monsieur and I have an afternoon reception in Neuilly, followed by dinner."

Nadira bit back her frustration. "Madame, my appointment —"

"Your days off are subject to change,

Nadira. It's in your contract. Sleep well."
Madame shut her door.

The cook could take Paul . . . then Nadira remembered, Wednesday was her day off too. She'd ask Carla from the playgroup, she'd done the same favor for her. But she recalled Carla saying they were leaving *en vacances.* Stymied, Nadira climbed the stairs to her small attic chamber.

She washed her feet in the small basin in her room, covered her head, and pulled out her prayer mat. Then she prayed to over-come her shortcomings, her apprehensive-ness after seeing this woman on the *télé.* And then her mind cleared and the way unfolded to her. She'd take Paul. She'd use the stroller to hide the rifle. A perfect cover.

Tuesday Night
Aimée shifted into neutral and scanned the sloping street of neo-Classical white stone façades which gave little clue to the elegant townhouses and courtyards behind them. In this upscale slice of the quartier, few saw what lay behind the arched wooden doors. "Nice quartier, Gerard. Which way?"

"Make a right, then pull into Number 58."

She pulled into the courtyard of a Direc-toire style 18th-century *hôtel particulier.* The entryway was wide enough for a coach and horses. The Citroën made it with centimeters to spare.

"You didn't tell me you're a rich kid."

"I wish," Langois said. "Just a good friend of the owner's son. His family gives tours and capitalized on the fact that Napoleon's legation secretary lived here. Aristos have a lot of upkeep, you know. There's a loose connection to Balzac and a printing press in the backyard. He was hopeless with money, but at least his mentor, Madame de Berny, turned it into a prosperous venture."

Langois's hand paused on the door handle.

"I believe Berto," Langois said. "I doubt that he'd make that Turkish man up."

She agreed. "But the hard part is how do I find him?"

It would be like looking for one pebble on the quai. She didn't know where to turn. And then she grew aware of a stricken look on Langois's face.

"What's the matter?"

"I shouldn't do this." He reached in his bag and extracted a coffee-stained file folder. "If you breathe a word, I'll get in trouble."

She leaned forward, the steering wheel pressing against her ribs. "In trouble over what?"

"It's Yves's draft of his article on the Kurds," he said. "We were supposed to work on it tonight. I needed his text for the accompanying photos."

Her hand trembled. Small brown demitasse cup rings patterned the blue cover. Yves's coffee rings.

"But why didn't you tell me this before, Gerard?"

"By law, it belongs to Agence France-Presse. You know, intellectual property rights; they drill all that into us before we sign a contract."

"No problem. May I read it?" She wanted to grab it out of his hands.

"It's my only copy," he said. "Can I trust you to return it tomorrow?"

For a type who followed the rules, Langois was taking a big chance on her.

"Of course." She reached out and he handed her the much-thumbed file folder. "I appreciate your trust in me. I won't let you down, Gerard."

She gave him her number and wrote down his. "Call me if you think of anything."

"Read Yves's draft. It should give you the background. Like I said, he got tight with iKK radicals, the ones labeled by the Turkish military and everyone else as terrorists. But one night Yves argued that they were just what we'd term 'activists' here, protesting against a repressive regime."

She nodded. Now she had something to go on. She'd have to study it later. As she drove out of the courtyard, Langois waved and closed the massive dark-green doors.

She gunned up the deserted rue d'Hauteville, tired and needing more Doliprane. Yet she couldn't rest until she checked out that paper from Yves's wallet. She knew only one person to ask: a passing acquaintance, but she had to try.

She turned back on rue de Paradis, made a left, then parked. By the time she pressed the concierge's buzzer, chills racked her. She prayed he'd be up. She waited. In the dark street, a cat meowed from a doorway.

She heard the smaller door that was cut into the massive green entry creak open.

"Oui?" The Turkish concierge, Mehmet, to whom she'd spoken last night as he was sweeping the Microimages courtyard, stood there, worry beads clicking in his hand.

"Pardon, Monsieur, I consult with Michel at Microimages. You remember me?"

He blinked sleep-blurred eyes. "There's a problem? Michel said nothing."

"No problem. May I ask a favor?" She held up the sugar wrapper.

"I need my glasses . . . come inside."

She edged over the lip of the door frame into the dark portico and followed him inside the concierge's lodge.

On the wall, a framed black-and-white photo of Mustafa Kemal Atatürk stood above a tattered, much-fingered map of the quartier and a calendar with a nearby butcher's address.

"Forgive me; it's late, but. . . ."

"Sit down, Mademoiselle," he said, shuffling over to a single burner by the lace-curtained window overlooking the courtyard. The walls of brown wood patinaed by the years and the '50s floral wallpaper had seen better days. From the adjoining small room, she heard what sounded like a Turkish video.

"Café?"

"Non, merci," she said.

"But it's ready. No trouble, a custom for greeting guests, please." He set down a small cup of steaming thick Turkish coffee, spoon on the side. He gestured, opening his arms wide. "My home, it's your home . . . *chez vous.*"

"Very kind of you. I'm hoping you can help me. I didn't know who else to ask."

"Parfait." He smiled and several gold teeth showed. "I know many things. Things I don't know, I find out. I'm a good concierge.

Ask Michel, he trust me."

She nodded not sure of what he meant, and sipped the sweet coffee, which was so strong she thought she might grow the proverbial chest hairs. Grounds caught in her teeth. If she drank any more, she'd stay awake half the night. Dimpled lemons and oozing amber dates sat in a bowl on the small table.

"Fifteen years in the quartier, *oui,* you come to right person. First I worked in the sewing factory, then my own sewing-machine business."

"This paper, Monsieur —"

"Now I'm a concierge." He beamed, gesturing toward a well-used Pfaff sewing machine in the corner. He leaned forward, as if to speak in confidence. "But I contract to set zippers for a couture house. A sideline."

The coffee made him voluble; she had to work to get a word in edgewise.

She smiled. "Could you translate this for me?"

The smile still on his face, he moved his hands around the table, located his glasses, and put them on. "Let me see. Parrots?"

"The other side."

He stared at the sugar wrapper, his smile

fading. "Mademoiselle, where you find this?"

If he knew the quartier, as he boasted, he would have heard. A chance he'd know the little Turk. . . .

"Why?"

"Important you tell me, Mademoiselle." He pushed his glasses up on his wavy black hair. "Not only you in danger."

She clutched the glass. "What do you mean?"

He crumpled up the scrap, took a kitchen match, and was about to light it.

"*Non.* Tell me —"

"You're a nice lady. I take your work to Michel." He lit the match. "This not your business."

"Wait." She grabbed his hand, blew out the match. "It's the only evidence. You can't burn it. Please, you have to explain."

"Bad people. Kurds."

"The Kurds may be bad . . . but. . . ."

"I live here a long time; I'm not your usual narrow-minded Turk. I know good Kurds."

What in the world did he mean? She felt stupid, handicapped by language and a culture she didn't understand.

"Please. . . ."

He smoothed the paper out. Readjusted his glasses. "One time I read this. Then destroy." He pointed a grease-rimmed fingernail at the letters. "Not in Kurdish language, the government ban Kurdish in schools and on the *télé*. This says 'Institut Kurd, 9 rue Lafayette, Jelenka Malat, Wednesday 4:00 p.m."

He stopped.

"That's nearby. Who's she?"

"Woman elected to Turkish parliament. A Kurd, the first."

"What else does it say?"

His finger picked up his worry beads and he stared at her. "Give you more danger."

"Me?"

She wasn't in danger. Not yet. Then she remembered the second message from Yves's phone. The one without words.

"It say *hedef suíkast*."

"What does that mean?"

"Target assassinate."

Her shoulders tensed. "You mean this Jalenka's a target . . . of who?"

He leaned forward, whispered. "Kurds always targets. Even in Paris."

"Targets of who?"

He looked away.

And Yves had had this in his wallet. "So she's in danger of assassination?"

He rubbed his eyes. "You, too."

If they had killed Yves . . . Aimée willed

her fear down. "You remember the man who met me here last night?" she said, gesturing to the courtyard.

"Your boyfriend?"

She nodded. "I found this in his wallet."

His eyes widened. "So he know Turkish? But he didn't talk to me."

"They found him at dawn on rue de Paradis, his throat slit."

"Mademoiselle, I'm very sorry," he said, his eyes narrowing in understanding. "Better you forget this."

But she couldn't. He knew something, she could see it in his red-rimmed eyes. The silence was broken by a scratch of nails on the wooden door. He stood, opened the door, and a gray tabby, topaz eyes glittering, entered. The cat padded by her on his way toward the stove, his fur rubbing her bare legs.

"You saw, didn't you?"

"I saw nothing." He clutched his worry beads.

"But you heard about the murder. You know everything that happens in the quartier you said."

He fingered his worry beads, clicking them faster now. "I say that?"

"What time do you let your cat out in the morning?"

He blinked, caught unaware. "When the newspaper truck comes."

"Seven o'clock or so?"

He nodded, glad to change the subject. "Seven fifteen. I take the newspapers, let the cat on the street, then sort them into the mailboxes."

"Then you remember a little man running out of Cité Paradis this morning. A Turk who works at Gare de l'Est or Gare du Nord."

The man's eyes widened in terror. "I never say that."

"He must have passed right by here . . . by the foyer door." She took a chance. "Did he ask to hide here until the *flics* left?"

The man shook his head, his lips quivering.

"Of course, you heard the sirens, saw the patrol cars," she continued. "A fellow Turk and he asked for help. You saw he'd been crying, was in some kind of trouble. Why not help? You felt sorry for him and you hid him here."

"I didn't hide him," he said, his voice raised. "I lose my job."

"So you told him to run the other way. You know the passages between the buildings like the palm of your hand. You told

188

him to take a shortcut to the other street
—"

"You want me lose my job? My family go
hungry . . . sit in jail cell in Istanbul?"

So that was it? He was afraid, and it wasn't
of the *flics.*

"It's to do with the Turkish Member of
Parliament. And you're witholding information. Information about an assassination attempt."

"They take my *carte de séjour,* deport me."

Perspiration dampened her brow. "You
want this on your conscience . . . an assassination you could stop?" She rooted in her
purse, pulled out the amulet, and put it in
his palm.

Recognition shone in his eyes. "Where you
get this?"

"A Sufi gave it to Yves, for me. A betrothal
symbol . . . But . . ." She shrugged, blinked
away the tears in the corners of her eyes.
"Yves was an investigative reporter." She
took a guess. "This man was his contact."

"You don't understand."

"Maybe I don't." She took the amulet
back, pulled out her cell phone. "Then you
can explain to the *flics.* Right now."

He clicked the worry beads faster, his
mouth pursed.

"Or I will," she said. "Up to you. But if

189

you tell me, we can keep it between our-
selves."

He swallowed hard. He scanned the room,
then stood and went to the door. He looked
outside, then returned and sat.

"You promise?"

"You have my word."

"The newspaper truck," he said, so softly
she almost didn't hear it.

"You mean he hopped on the truck and
got away?"

"The truck driver's my friend." He stood,
setting her cup in the small sink. "I don't
know any more." Arab hospitality forbade
him to ask a guest to leave, but she knew he
wanted her to.

She rose, too, and pushed in her chair.
"But you can find out, you said so yourself.
Things you don't know in the quartier, you
can find out. Michel trusts you. Please, find
the little man." She pulled out her card.
"Tell him to call me. I'll be waiting."

Aimée's heels, clicking on the cobblestones,
echoed off the buildings as she walked back
to the car. The strains of a cello drifted on
the night air. She recognized a sonata by
Haydn. And then a bulbous shadow loomed
on the wall ahead. It was disembodied, as
though it was floating. The hairs on her neck

rose. She clutched the car keys in her hand, the tips pointing out between her fingers. The cello notes soared as footsteps beat a staccato rhythm ahead.

She'd been stupid to shrug off the concierge's insistence that she was in danger. The cello's notes drifted and lingered. She'd almost made it to René's Citroën when someone rounded the corner. She turned and thrust her fist out.

But it was an old woman, clutching a bunch of red balloons, a trace of wine on her breath. Rouged cheeks, rhinestone earrings, and diamonté paste brooch on her off-the-shoulder '50s–era turquoise cocktail dress. "It's my birthday, Mademoiselle," she said, giving Aimée a cockeyed, semi-lucid glance.

"Felicitations," Aimée said with a pang of sadness as she noted the old woman's scuffed house slippers.

"Join me," the woman said, a glint in her eye. She held out a bottle, handing it to Aimée. "Not a Pouilly Foussé, but a good year."

"A bit late for me, Madame."

"Think you're too good to celebrate with me? You with your chic outfit and firm skin?" She tottered toward the car, her tone turning belligerent. "Me, too, I was young once. Had them all on a string, one would take me to dinner, another to a *boîte de nuit.* Better make the most of it." She leaned forward, tottering. "I'll tell you a secret, there's only one way we leave the planet. Alone. And you, chic one, are alone, *hein!*"

She felt pity for this woman in her cocktail dress and worn house slippers. "May I help you home, Madame?"

The woman gave a short laugh. "No one gets out of here alive, why should I?" She handed Aimée the string of one of the balloons. Before Aimée could grab it, the balloon floated up, caught on an air current, and bobbed over the rooftops. Transfixed, Aimée watched it. And then it disappeared. Here one moment, gone the next. Gone. Like Yves. Leaving behind questions but no answers. The old woman's footsteps faded into the darkness, leaving Aimée more alone than ever.

In her bedroom, Aimée searched her drawer and found the cords to several rechargers. The third one fit Yves's phone and she plugged it in. She lay down on the duvet, too tired to undress. René's caution to change her cell phone number was uppermost in her mind; yet if the Brigade had cloned it, as she suspected, she doubted if it was worth the effort.

Her open windows let in a breeze and night sounds: lapping waves hitting the stone bank bordering the river in the wake of a barge, the song of a lone nightingale in the distance.

She set Yves's photo and the amulet on the duvet. She was bone-tired; her body craved sleep. But sleep eluded her.

She was alone, like the old woman, but she had no balloons.

She wondered for the millionth time why Yves had kept his secrets from her and why he had ended up in the morgue. He had been so full of promise, with his whole life before him. A life that could have been spent with her.

Together. A baby. . . .

Or maybe not.

Who knew if it would have worked out, but at least they could have tried. Her shoulders heaved thinking of his warm legs wrapped around hers, the way his tongue tickled her ears. She buried her head in the pillow.

But she couldn't wallow in grief. It wouldn't help Yves. Nothing could.

With shaking hands, she opened the file Langois had given her. Inside, she found several pages with red pencil marks and crossed-out words. The title read: Kurds Little Davids Hurling Stones Against Goliath-like Turkish Military, bylined Mas, Anatolia, Turkey by Yves Robert:

The Kurdish freedom fighter pointed to Mas on the map, the page whipping in the mountaintop winds. "My village, gone," he said. Mas, one of 4,500 Kurdish villages, now just scattered stones or submerged by the floodwaters of the Anatolian dam, courtesy of the Turkish military. Few Kurds are left to tell, only an outlaw band of weary, hungry freedom fighters in the Anatolian mountains. Half the time they move, hiding deeper in the valleys, scaling ravines to avoid the scouts of Colonel Ehret, leader of the Turkish forces in charge of "resettling Kurds." They are the few who haven't managed to flee Turkey for Iraq. "We're always on the move," the leader says. The Kurds are a tribal mix of Sunni Muslims and adherents of the banned Alevi sect who trace their beliefs to the ancient Zoroastrians and Sufis. These wandering tribes from Turkey, Kurdistan, Iraq, and even Syria have been seeking a homeland since the twelfth century. They thrived during the Ottoman rule of Turkey. The Treaty of Sèvres proposed by Allied powers after WWI was to provide an autonomous Kurdish region in Turkey. Then Atatürk gained power and united the dispar-

ate sects and Muslim groups, proclaiming Turkey a secular republic. There were to be no Kurds, no Alevis or Sunnis, anymore; all were Turks. Like France, in Monsieur Chirac's words: "We are not Algerian, Tongolaise, or Libanais, we are united as French." "Turkey will never join the EU," insists the freedom fighter, "as long as Kurds can stand up to the military and tell the world what's happened here." Yet world opinion has hedged its support for the Kurds and the radical iKK party after evidence surfaced of their brutal killings of fellow Kurds suspected of informing to the Turkish military. . . .

Yves's article continued chronicling the destruction and struggles of the tribal Kurds. Yves balanced the piece by citing the Kurds' often-violent retaliation. His draft ended with the fact that Ankara might finally be forced to deal with the Kurdish movement since a woman, a Kurd, had been elected to parliament. A small step, but a huge one for the previously un-represented Kurds.

This woman was a target. From what she'd found in Yves's wallet, if Mehmet the concierge had translated it right, she was going to be assassinated.

Right now Aimée was just guessing. Yet

her conscience wouldn't let her ignore her guess.

She owed it to Yves.

Bordereau, a contact in the DST — *Direction de la Surveillance du Territoire* — the elite intelligence unit, manned the night desk. She hated dealing with the DST; they traced calls in seconds. But reluctantly, she punched in his number.

"Unit 22," answered a voice on the first ring. Clipped and businesslike.

"Bordereau, please."

"Unavailable."

She hesitated. He was the only one she trusted.

"You have a message?"

"For Bordereau only."

"I'll make sure he gets it."

Right now she had no choice.

"Tell Bordereau, Aimée's got him a present."

Less than thirty seconds had passed. She hung up. Bordereau knew how to reach her. Her cell phone rang two minutes later. He usually called back sooner.

"Allô?"

"You've got a present for me, Aimée?" Bordereau asked, a wavering echo-like quality to his voice.

"A little one."

196

"I always like your presents." She heard a slight delay. "But we're away for diving exercises so I can't receive this one in person."

A champion swimmer, no doubt he was performing some amphibious exercise somewhere in the Indian Ocean or Celebes Islands and was using a satellite phone.

"You're calling on Telsat?"

"You string the beads, Aimée." She heard a sharp intake of breath. "Damn sharp coral. Give me a verbal."

"Jalenka Malat, the first woman Kurd in the Turkish parliament."

Silence except for a wavering static relay click.

"That's it?"

"It's significant, Bordereau."

"Not if I don't know the context. Give me details."

As she did so, she realized how far-fetched it sounded. What else did she have beside the sugar wrapper? But she related Mehmet's translation and Yves's article.

"And from *that,* you surmise an assassination attempt?" Bordereau said.

"Yves is . . . was an investigative journalist writing exposés of the Turkish military regime's repression of the Kurds. A Turkish member of parliament may be a target on

French soil. I'd think that would be more than embarrassing to the Ministry of Foreign Affairs."

"Not my arena now," he said.

"You've been kicked upstairs?

"Let's just say I'm operational in another way."

She drew a breath. Her one trusted contact in the DST was out of day-to-day operations.

"But you'll pass this on?"

"It doesn't even amount to a rumor, Aimée. Every branch's stretched tight now with three quarters of our forces patrolling the Metro. You know they're concentrating on the GIA . . . especially after Marseilles."

She'd seen the front-page headlines of *Le Monde.* AIR FRANCE FLIGHT 322 SHOT DOWN OUTSIDE MARSEILLES.

But Yves might have died for this information. She couldn't let go. "At least pass the info down the pipe to Rouffillac in the Brigade. He's not my biggest fan."

Bordereau owed her big-time for information she'd given him on a bomb plot in Montmartre. There was a pause filled with mounting static.

"No promises, but I'll try —"

"Sharks hungry this time of year, Bordereau?" The rest of her words were cut off.

The Doliprane took effect, her lids lowered, but her thoughts whirled. Like nagging bits of grit in the corner of her mind . . . A phrase, "Couldn't penetrate the world behind the veil" came from somewhere, but she couldn't place it. Yet she'd glimpsed the flash of red and whiff of perfume beneath the chador worn by the little girl's sister, a modernity that surprised her. Did these women dress fashionably at home but cover themselves out on the street according to custom . . . or had she worn a chador to hide an outfit for a later date? She wished Miles Davis were here, but tonight he slept off the effects of his minor surgery at the vet's. His least favorite visit. She couldn't sleep.

She stood up, shimmied out of her dress, and belted her father's old flannel bathrobe around herself. In the dark kitchen, crisscrossed by rays of light from the streetlamps on the quai below, she squeezed a lemon and poured the juice and pulp into a glass of water. Mid-sip, it hit her where she'd seen women behind the veil. The Cahiers de Cinema Club last week, of course. At the screening of the classic 1960s film *Battle of Algiers*. Late from work, she'd missed the beginning, caught the last half. Now she remembered. The scene of apprehensive

Algerian women applying makeup and donning short skirts, passing the Casbah checkpoint and flirting with occupying French soldiers while bombs were hidden in their breadbaskets. The youngest one entered a café in the European quartier, slipping her basket under the stool. On her way back, she put on her chador and re-entered the Casbah, joining the other women. Anonymous.

She ran back to her room, scrambled on her desk for the film brochure, found it. Under a brief synopsis of the film, she read the accompanying notes excerpted from a Muslim woman's short story.

"Why do we conceal? They never understand . . . we stay behind the veil, the wall, that is our way. A secret, a private truth is no longer private if it goes past these borders. A dropped word, our ancestors knew, becomes a newspaper headline, broadcast to one and all, for if one person hears it, down the road, a trickle here, there, it's public knowledge. Like the growing mint by the fountain in the courtyard compound, it flourishes protected from the wind. Words do not trail on the hem of a chador in the dust of the market street."

Poetic, haunting, and secretive, this glimpse behind the veil. How could she penetrate this world?

She lay down, set her alarm, worried that she'd missed something important staring her in the face. The next thing she knew, her cell phone rang. She must have closed her eyes. The red digital clock beside her bedside said 4:57.

Her mind cleared and she grabbed her cell phone. But the ringing came from Yves's phone, which was re-charging on her secretaire. Startled, she reached over and picked it up.

"Allô?"

Silence.

"Who's this?"

"I'm Yves's friend," Aimée said, trying to gain trust, to get someone to speak. "You can talk."

A passing barge cast blue oblongs of light over the carved woodwork ceiling. She waited, fingering the phone cord. The caller must have something to say, something vital, important.

"Please, it's safe; talk to me."

She'd given Mehmet her number; why hadn't he called her on her own phone?

"Allô?"

The phone clicked off.

And the realization dawned as she shivered with fear. Someone had heard her voice and now knew she had Yves's phone. Her hand tightened on the phone in dread, wondering if it had been his killer.

Wednesday Morning

Vatel pulled the baseball cap low over his eyes. A rose-violet hue spread in the sun-deepening sky. The narrow street lay quiet and expectant, as if the sleeping populace held its breath.

Vatel's feet crunched on the pavement. His eyes caught the beige grains, the fine Saharan sand borne by the African scirocco dusting the cars and street. He'd only seen it happen here once before. An omen. But of what, he didn't know.

At rue du Faubourg Saint-Denis, he checked his watch, waiting across the street from No. 83. Inside, he knew the three-deep courtyard building held a small mosque. The dark green doors parted, revealing men bent in prostration on prayer mats, overflowing the cobbled space and narrow foyer, under mailboxes with names in Chinese, Tamil, and Turkish.

He knew the prayers. In his village, the Alevis had been forced to worship at the mosque. Otherwise the Turkish mayor would withold the Kurdish schoolteacher's salary. Mehmet appeared: grizzled black hair, suit jacket over a sweater-vest in the heat. In a sea of Turkish men scurrying off to work, Vatel caught Mehmet's gaze. Mehmet shot him a look and nodded. But instead of nodding back, Vatel lifted his chin slightly and kept on walking.

Vatel passed the crowded café, the preserve of smoking men drinking tiny cups of coffee. No women. Like back home. He paused in the doorway of a small shop crammed with telephone cabinets for overseas calls, to make sure Mehmet followed. Then he moved at a fast clip through Passage Prado, rundown art-deco steel-and-glass ceiling overhead, lined with small clothing shops.

Vatel pushed down his fear of recognition and kept several feet ahead. Just before the looming arch of Porte Saint-Martin, he turned into a narrow street and looked back. No Mehmet.

He panicked. And then the black grizzled hair came into view.

"*Ssss,*" hissed Vatel. He'd reached the Second-Empire Theatre de la Renaissance, named by Victor Hugo for then-popular opera-comique performances. He knew the stagehand kept the side stage door open in the morning for deliveries. He stepped into the doorway and beckoned to Mehmet.

Mehmet joined him inside the narrow musty-carpeted corridor stacked with chairs. Vatel pointed to a room with a sign, "Wardrobe." Inside, on wheeled racks covered by clear plastic, hung costumes, period pieces by the look of them.

"How did you find this place?" Mehmet asked, looking around.

"More important, Mehmet," Vatel said, "how can I find the Yellow Crescent before they find me?"

"You?" Mehmet's protuberant eyes popped.

"The *mec* who was slit on rue de Paradis? He had their signature. . . ."

"Signature? He wasn't a Turk, or even a Kurd!"

Vatel froze. He remembered the dark hair, dark complexion . . . and the knife curl of flesh slashed under the ear just like on the bodies in his village. The Yellow Crescent's signature to send a message to the Kurdish Rebels.

"The *mec* was a French journalist." Mehmet clicked his worry beads, shaking his head.

No wonder the Brigade was investigating.

Vatel cast a nervous look at the costumes.

"Why so curious?"

Vatel heard suspicion in Mehmet's voice.

"I work across the street, remember? The Brigade's been asking questions."

"So has the journalist's big-eyed girl-friend."

More complications.

Cold filled his insides. Mehmet kept his ear to the ground in the quartier. This grew more complicated, more twisted all the time. Had he figured wrong?

Even for the Yellow Crescent, this move struck him as bold. Arrogant. Though he knew the authorities, much less this woman, couldn't begin to penetrate their web.

"Eyes watch everywhere," Mehmet said. "But this feels wrong for the Yellow Crescent."

The *flics* avoided internal rivalries in the closed Turkish community; but with a murdered journalist. . . . No wonder this Florand wanted him to inform.

"What's the word on the street?"

"The dead junkie, you know the types from the Canal? He got nabbed with the journalist's wallet."

Probably one of the two-way hustlers he'd seen in the doorway on rue de Paradis.

"So far, they put it down to robbery."

Vatel doubted it.

"It's more," Vatel said. "You know that."

Mehmet clicked his worry beads faster. "I

know nothing."

"Yet last week in the café, you insisted that the Yellow Crescent had posted that article in the laundromat."

Mehmet shook his head. "Yellow Crescent, the Turkish military . . . ? They'd never dare kill a journalist. You must talk to the wise one."

"He's not back."

Mehmet nodded. "He returns tonight or tomorrow."

Vatel marshaled his thoughts, trying to figure out what was bothering him.

"Count me out," Mehmet said. "I know nothing. I can't get involved."

But Vatel had to give some morsel to Florand. Mehmet had been a concierge in the quartier for years; he knew everyone, and everyone knew him.

"What did you leave out, Mehmet?" Vatel advanced closer, hemmed in by costumes. The walls were lined with waistcoats on hangers and knee-high boots lined up like soldiers.

"Finding a scrap of paper in the wallet . . . who knows what it really means, eh?" Mehmet averted his eyes, shrugged. "It's just a sugar wrapper."

"I'm waiting."

"For what? I told you. . . ."

Vatel visualized rue de Paradis: the breaking dawn, the ceramic tiled doorway, the hustlers down the street, the black chador, the street cleaner dropping his broom, and the figure. . . .

"Who else saw, Mehmet?"

"The blubbering mouse from Istanbul." Mehmet sighed. "He cleans the trains at Gare du Nord."

"His name?"

Mehmet shrugged. "I told you, *fare*."

"Mouse?"

The sound of footsteps and whistling came from the hall. An old Georges Brassens tune. Mehmet leaned closer, lowered his voice, and lapsed into Turkish. "*Ufak bir fare gibi,* little like a mouse."

"There's more, I can tell."

"Jalenka Malat's the target," Mehmet said, looking at his feet. "Tonight."

Wednesday Morning

At her window overlooking the Seine, Aimée sipped an espresso and checked e-mail. One from Michel requesting her to check in at Microimages. The next from Laure: *No dice with the homicide report.*

Too bad. She had learned nothing about Yves's murder. But knowing Bordereau, he'd pass on the information about the possible "assassination" even if the only evidence was a sugar wrapper written on in Turkish.

She wished she understood. At least the fever and chills had gone. She tried to repress her unease at the early-morning call on Yves's phone, knew she had to concentrate on things at hand. She looked at the clock.

Late.

She was late to pick up Miles Davis at the vet. She donned a black raw silk spaghetti-strapped agnes b. dress from the seconds bin at Porte de Vanves flea market, slipped into heels, and grabbed the dog carrier.

The Metro journey to the clinic involved crossing to the Left Bank and changing three times. But in her book, Dr. Rouzeyrol rated as a surgical genius after he'd stitched Miles Davis's paw back on following a vicious pit bull attack. And Miles Davis adored him.

"Came out of it like a champ!" said Dr. Rouzeyrol, a smiling rosy-cheeked well-built man in his thirties.

Miles Davis, hair clipped short, sporting a new tartan collar, scampered into her waiting arms.

"Shots up to date, microchipped, and with

pearl-white teeth; you can take him any-where."

"Hear that? I can take you to Fouquet's now."

Miles Davis responded by licking her ear.

"Speaking of Fouquet's, they have a *sud-ouest* prix-fixe menu, Aimée," he said. "We had a veterinary dinner there the other night. A superb seared *magret au canard* crusted with lavender and cracked pepper."

Miles Davis's ears shot to attention.

"I'd love to meet you and Miles Davis there," he said. "Some evening this week?"

She liked him and wished that sparks flew. Martine would insist she go; he had a booming practice, Miles Davis loved him and he didn't hurt the eyes. But after Yves, the thought of dinner with another man felt wrong.

She shrugged. "Dr. Rouzeyrol —"

"Antoine," he said, moving closer. "We've been saying we'd do this for ages. Tomor-row?"

"I'd love to, but with work and this cold. . . ." She saw the disappointment in his blue eyes, his hands clenching in the pockets of his white coat.

"Dr. Rouzeyrol," said his middle-aged receptionist, appraising Aimée's outfit. "A poodle in room three and Madame de

Songe's Siamese in room five."

"Another time." He squeezed Aimée's arm and disappeared into a consulting room.

She set Miles Davis down, leashed him, and pulled her checkbook from her bag. A crumpled paper fell on the tiled floor. An old fax receipt. And her mind went back to the fax from the State Department.

Outside, on Avenue Lowendahl, a light breeze dispelled the wavering heat. Instead of heading to Cambronne Metro station, she walked toward Place de Fontanoy. UNESCO headquarters lay a block away.

A fleeting chance that she'd find some link to her mother.

The hundreds of world flags surrounding UNESCO's headquarters waved in the light wind, their ropes pinging against the metal struts. The building, a swooping white-roofed '60s design of concrete and white blocks, could use a steam-cleaning, she thought. She crossed the yard of white flagstone to the entrance. Her mother had walked across these stones years ago every day for her job. Aimée wished for some feeling of connection. But all she felt were the ripples of hot air as men in three-piece suits, engaged in conversation, passed by.

Miles Davis was in his tartan carry bag slung over her shoulder. Inside, she paused at the reception desk and looked around. Groups of people gathered, others entered the double walnut doors to large meeting rooms. A conference sign read: UNESCO Bridging the World.

What could she hope to accomplish here? It had all happened more than twenty years ago.

"May I direct you to a conference room?" A woman wearing a beige suit with red-framed glasses smiled at her. "These large events get confusing, and we've had some room changes."

Aimée frowned. "I don't know if you can help." She hesitated. The smart thing would be to excuse herself, turn around and leave. "My mother worked here in 1968." She couldn't believe she'd said . . . her mother. But it had slid out without a stammer or a missed beat. "I wondered. . . ."

"Ah, you want to know about Roberta Tash's retirement party." The woman nodded. "You're the third one today. We're getting so many queries from past employees, project members and their families. Such a great outpouring, a testament to Roberta's more than twenty-five years of service."

The woman patted Miles Davis's head, took Aimée's elbow, and edged her toward a reception area. "The party's at Hotel le

211

Bristol. More invitations are being printed up, but here . . . take this."

Aimée stared at the embossed card in her hand.

"Don't forget to call that number and RSVP."

"RSVP?"

"Everyone's invited who's worked here during the past thirty years. Roberta's touched every part of our work at UNESCO, and it's our way of celebrating her accomplishments. Of course your mother . . . what did you say her name is?"

"Sydney . . . Sydney Leduc."

The woman gave a brief shake of her head. "Before my time, but we're a big family here. I'm sure you've heard this from your mother, but it's like we say, 'No one really leaves.' " The woman grinned. "We've got people flying in from Africa, the Middle East, you name it, Roberta's influenced generations of us at UNESCO."

Aimée cleared her throat.

"What's your name?"

"Aimée, but. . . ."

"I'll just write your name down and I'll tell Roberta later."

"Pardon?"

"Well, Roberta likes to prepare for her guests. A stickler for detail. Will you be attending with your mother?"

Struck dumb one of the few times in her life, Aimée just blinked. A group of women in saris crowded the reception. Distracted, the woman smiled again.

"Wonderful. Here, I'll RSVP for you, the caterers need to know today . . . Roberta will be delighted."

Aimée sat on the bus, Miles Davis on her lap, reading the thick cream-colored engraved invitation. "UNESCO requests your presence to celebrate Roberta Tash's retirement from our 'family.' No gifts, please, your presence is enough, donations accepted in Roberta's name to Save the Children, Roberta's pet project."

Roberta must have known her mother, maybe worked with her. Again she felt a fleeting hope that her mother would appear at the party. Impossible. A woman on the world security watch list wouldn't risk that. Even if she was alive. But perhaps Aimée could get this Roberta's attention for five minutes and pick her brain.

At her local café-tabac on Ile St. Louis, she picked up a copy of *Le Monde.* Then around the corner from her apartment, she stopped at the butchers'. Jules, in a blood-stained white apron, greeted her with a

213

knowing smile.

"A visit to the vet, eh?" Jules said. "The usual?"

She nodded.

Jules wrapped a kilo of horsemeat in waxed white paper, threw in some bones for Miles Davis. "Just in time, Aimée. I'm closing for *vacances.*"

"St. Malo?"

"Where else?"

Every year, Jules and his family decamped to his mother's at the seaside.

"And you?"

"Work. No rest for the wicked."

"Everyone needs a break." Jules winked. "Even sinners."

She set the franc notes on the counter. Her gaze fell on the row of sharpened knives in holders on his wall. Bone-handled, individually crafted by Laguiole, the premium knife maker.

Jules noticed her gaze. "Perfect for lamb. Slices the cartilage with a clean line."

She winced. But couldn't help wondering what kind of knife had been used to slit Yves's throat.

"Jules, would you need a special knife, say one that curved, to carve a curl in flesh?"

"Been reading Agatha Christie, eh?"

He applied a goat-horn-handled knife

from the marble-topped cutting board to a glistening slab of white fat suet and flicked his wrist. "Like this?"

A curl like a c resulted.

Her hand trembled. Any sharp blade could have made the swirl under Yves's neck. But from the way Jules carved, she learned an important thing: There was no way someone could have *faced* Yves and done it. They would have had to come on him from behind.

A coward. And afraid of recognition.

The bells jingled on the butcher-shop door as she shut it. She rounded the corner to quai d'Anjou, pressed the digicode to her building, followed a scampering Miles Davis up the worn grooved steps of the marble staircase to her apartment. And faced a pile of mail, bills and more bills at her door.

Inside the kitchen, she unwrapped the butcher's package.

Miles Davis's paws clicked over the wood floor as he made a beeline for his bowl.

Her mind couldn't rest. Did the Brigade have more suspects? Or did they still link the murder to Romeo? Morbier, her godfather, a Commissaire, worked at the Brigade part-time but she hesitated to call him. She doubted he'd do her yet another favor; but with no other leads in Yves's murder. . . .

She crooked the phone between her neck and shoulder and punched in his number.

Miles Davis hunched over, eating from his chipped Limoges bowl.

"Paulet," answered a clipped voice.

"Commissaire Morbier, please."

"En vacances."

Morbier hadn't taken a vacation in six years. *Incroyable!* The city under terrorist attacks, and this is the year Morbier decides to take his vacation! By now, Yves's homicide report would have been filed at the Brigade, his dossier swelled with investigative notes, interviews, lists of possible suspects.

"Who's calling?" Paulet said.

Desperate, she realized she had to somehow enlist this Paulet's help.

"Leduc," she rooted in her bag, read off her father's old police identification number. "I'm en route to question a homicide suspect. The name's. . . ." She thumbed her checkbook. "*Merde!* Found it, it's in the last page of paperwork they gave me. Renaud Vorner, aka Romeo Void. I need to finish this before my vacation. Commissaire Morbier's an old friend, my mentor from Brigade Criminelle. Save me some time, eh?" She spoke fast before she lost courage. "Vorner's the suspect in a homicide on rue de Paradis. Don't even have the Brigade case number, can you believe it?"

Miles Davis, now sated, and exhausted from his overnight stay at the vets, lay on the floor. His nose twitched in the sun.

"Rouffillac heads this investigation. . . ."

"That's just it; I can't reach him."

Pause. "What division did you say you're with?"

She thought fast. "Vigie Gare de Nord. It's a crossover crime."

She heard what sounded like metal file cabinets shut.

Pause. "Your name again?"

"Leduc."

"Renaud Vorner, aka Romeo Void?"

"That's right."

"You'll find him in the morgue. Lacerations on his upper body . . . the report indicates he's . . . was the main suspect in homicide Case 319."

She wrote the case number down.

"Any others? Just don't want to call you back if the Brigade's got other irons in the fire, you know, and they're in process of clearing him."

"That's the only suspect report in the dossier."

No other suspects.

"Merci." She hung up. And faced a blank

217

wall. She racked her brain. She sat and re-read Yves's article. She found what she had missed earlier, several paragraphs down. 'The iKK Kurdish workers party.' Time to question these radicals using terrorist tactics. She'd seen the posters for their protests. In the phone book she found them listed on rue d'Enghien. And now she had a plan.

"You're too late," said a woman, locking the door.

Aimée paused on the landing outside the iKK party office. Plaster had fallen from the walls, and the wood floor hadn't seen a broom in days. On her right were iKK post-ers, taped to the wall like those plastered on rue de Paradis. Horrific! There was a blurred, much-copied photograph of a heap of bodies wearing Kurdish *pejersh* and grin-ning Turkish soldiers pointing guns. If Turks hated a group more than the Armenians, it was the Kurds. They'd taken care of the Armenians in massacres before World War I. In the corner of the posters was the iKK symbol, a red circle — the red taken from the blood of the Paris Commune — a star, and a crescent.

"The office is closed," said the woman, putting the key in her pocket.

"But it says 10:00–18:00," Aimée said, pointing to the sign.

The woman, in a blue smock and clogs, shook her head. Not what Aimée would have expected a member of the so-called "terrorist radical Kurd worker party" to look like.

"My nephew runs the office, but he rushed off unexpectedly. The Tribunal," she said as if Aimée would understand.

Aimée didn't.

"The lawyer called him to be a witness at court. I promised to lock up for him."

"Aaah," she said. "But you're a member, can you help me, Madame?"

The woman shook her head. "Not me." A bottle of Persil liquid soap and a brush stuck out of her smock pocket.

Aimée caught a flash of fear in the woman's dark eyes.

"I work nearby. Excuse me. I must go."

"When will the office open?"

"Come back tomorrow."

A wasted trip.

"But I came all this way." Aimée sighed, hoping the woman would relent.

The woman, anxious to leave, started down the steps. By the look of the exterior, Aimée figured the office operated on a shoe-string.

Aimée picked the first thing that struck her. Money. "My appointment concerns our donation to the iKK party's legal defense fund. It would help so much if you could direct me to the person who accepts donations."

The woman stopped and looked back up at Aimée.

A look Aimée couldn't fathom.

She thought quickly. "I represent a human rights organization concerned over the atrocities in Anatolia. Our donation's confidential," she said, lowering her voice. "A large sum, our name not associated with . . . well, we ask for discretion."

The woman hesitated, her foot on the bottom step, unsure. Her watch alarm beeped. "I'd like to help, but I'm due back at work."

Aimée noticed her calloused work-reddened hands. Wariness battling something else, from her expression. For a moment, Aimée thought the woman would talk. But she continued down the wooden steps, her clogs echoing.

No luck. The woman was scared. Undeterred, Aimée knew that even if the office was a front, someone paid the rent.

Downstairs, she knocked on the lace-curtained concierge's door. A young woman holding a baby on her hip answered.

220

"*Oui?*"

"*Bonjour,* I'm looking for the landlord."

"No vacancies, *desolée.*"

"I'm dropping off the rent check."

"You're early. But I'll take it. Which unit?"

"Third floor, the iKK party office."

The baby whimpered, applesauce on her mouth.

"Already paid through September."

Curiouser and curiouser, Aimée thought.

"That's impossible."

The young concierge rocked the child on her hip.

"There's a mistake," Aimée said.

"Mistake? I just told you it's paid. The landlord collects the checks from me."

"I'll get in trouble if I don't pay you this rent."

The baby's whimper escalated. "She's hungry, if you'll excuse me."

"Look, I'm not going until I pay —"

"You want to pay the rent twice?" The young concierge reached for some papers by the door. "Up to you. But I don't want the landlord on my back saying I didn't tell you. This gentleman paid."

"Maybe I should confirm it with him before I pay."

"Good idea. Take it up with him." The young concierge thrust an empty, torn envelope with the return address Tamin Ansary, Ansary Ltd, 2 Boulevard de Strasbourg at Aimée and shut the door.

At last, Aimée thought, with relief.

Aimée approached the Porte Saint-Martin arch, scanning the building numbers for Ansary's office. Pigeons fed on crumbs in the arch's shadow, a smaller sandstone version of the arc de Triomphe. Then a horn blared and the pigeons fluttered away.

Bands of heat wavered and her dress stuck damply to her thighs. She wanted Ansary to illuminate the iKK party's background and Yves's connections to them, if any. If only she got Ansary to talk. Since they were described in the press as "Kurd terrorists," iKK party members had more than one reason to keep quiet. If the Kurds had engineered Yves's murder, no Kurd would talk. Yet right now, with nothing else to go on, he was her only shot. She stifled her unease and kept looking for the right address. Then she felt her cell phone vibrating in her pocket.

"Oui?"

"Aimée," Langois said in a whisper. "I couldn't sleep last night, I can't focus. Something Yves said kept going through my head."

"What was it?"

She heard voices in the background.

"Can we meet?" he said. "I can't talk now. And I need the draft of Yves's article back."

"Meet me at noon at the Eurostar exit in Gare du Nord," she said.

"Yves helped me more than I can say. I owe him a lot." Langois's voice was choked with grief. "Noon. Gare du Nord."

He hung up before she could ask him if he'd spoken with Rouffillac.

She hesitated in front of the building. Langois had information; she could walk away. She didn't relish questioning a supposed Kurd radical. Yet, like her father always said, leave a stone unturned and you'll trip over it later. Determined, after coming this far, she pressed the buzzer of Ansary Ltd. No answer. Several theatrical agents' offices were listed. She put her hand out to press another buzzer.

The glass door flew open and two men rushed out. She ducked inside, hoping in their haste they hadn't seen her. Old wooden stairs led to a series of offices. A sign with an arrow pointed across a wooden landing to another series of stairs. It's like a musty labyrinth, she thought. She mounted the creaking stairs and found herself at a dark wood-framed door with a frosted glass upper panel. The letters on the panel said ANSARY LTD. The door stood ajar, but she knocked.

"Monsieur Ansary?" she called.

No answer. She peeked inside to see a dark nineteenth-century wood-paneled waiting room. Probably still had gas fixtures instead of electricity. Not the way she imagined the office of the financial mastermind of the radical iKK workers party would look. And it was empty.

She turned to leave and heard voices from the hall. She walked on. A small sign read MUSÉE DE L'EVENTAIL, OPEN BY APPOINTMENT AND FROM 14:00–18:00, MON–WED, EXCEPT HOLIDAYS AND IN AUGUST.

Talk about hard to find and exclusive hours. But here it was August and the tiny third floor fan museum door stood open.

"They robbed the museum, Monsieur Ansary!" a woman's raised voice met her as she walked inside. Aimée picked up a brochure. The fan museum also doubled as an atelier for the last fan maker in Paris.

"The till's empty."

Aimée peered around the hall door to see a woman, her white floss hair arranged in a chignon, fluttering her hands. The woman lifted a small green and white factures' books of receipts. "The proof's in these receipts. I know how much the hoodlums took."

"*Tiens*, Madame Lange," a man said, concerned. "You're safe, that's the most important thing. With your blood pressure, *alors,* please sit down until the owner comes."

"No, we must check to see if they've taken anything else."

If the men she'd passed had robbed this museum, she'd be of no help; she'd never seen their faces. Better to keep that to herself, Aimée reflected. The floor creaked under her feet, and the woman looked up, fearful. Noting the brochure in Aimée's hand, her expression turned to annoyance.

"Mademoiselle, the museum's closed," she said.

"*Excusez-moi,* but I'm looking for Monsieur Ansary."

The man turned. Thick black hair, big-boned, wide-shouldered. Surprise was painted on his full face. He wore a tan suit, Hugo Boss by the look of it, and an open-collared white shirt. "Am I expecting you, Mademoiselle?"

"If you'll give me a moment? The iKK worker's party. . . ."

"I don't understand," he interrupted.

"Madame's upset; I'm busy." He took the old woman's arm.

"But go ahead, Monsieur Ansary," Madame Lange began.

"*Non,* Madame,"

"I can wait, Monsieur," Aimée said. "It's important."

His mouth narrowed. "Over there."

She nodded and brushed by a wooden-wheeled machine labeled *tabletier* for mounting the finished fan. Above her, wall photos illustrated ancient fan-making techniques. Judging by the contemporary photos, the same intricate process was used today.

"Now, Madame," Ansary said, guiding the old woman. "Walk me through so I can make sure you're safe."

Aimée peered around the small room under its coffered ceiling. Her gaze took in a display of seventeenth-century fans composed of swan skin, gauze-like silk, and lace. Some were painted, others needlepointed, gold-leafed or studded with pearl nacre. And their holders were equally embellished. Exquisite, of another age, a time when women powdered and dressed up in this district full of theaters.

Madame Lange strode over the creaking floorboards, waving him off.

"You're too kind, Monsieur Ansary," she said. "I'm fine, *merci.*"

"Who are you?"

Ansary stood glaring at Aimée in front of his closed office door, blocking her way out. The kind streak she'd seen in him had evaporated.

Not a smart move, to have entered his office first and let herself be cornered. A quick scan of the office revealed a solid walnut desk, heavy wood straight-backed chairs from the nineteenth century, an old oil landscape painting on the wall. And nothing to defend herself with.

"Florence Raymonde, a journalist," she said, with more confidence than she felt. She handed him a card from the collection in her bag.

"How did you get my name?"

"I'm with Reporters Without Borders. We believe Yves Robert, the investigative journalist murdered in the rue de Paradis, had contacted the iKK. Can you corroborate . . . ?"

"I asked who sent you here." He reached for the cell phone in his pocket and punched in a number on his speed dial.

"There are allegations that the iKK party

227

was involved in this murder. Any comment?"

"You're asking me? There's a mistake, I'm a restaurateur." He gestured to the photos of Andiamo, an Italian restaurant on one of the *grands boulevards.*

"That's not what Yves's notes said. I'm now finishing what he started."

Ansary paused a nanosecond. "You don't seem to understand, Mademoiselle Raymonde; this has nothing to do with me. Now if you'll tell me how you got this idea. . . ."

He said something she couldn't catch and snapped the phone shut. Great . . . calling for backup? Uneasy now, she wanted to get some answers, then get the hell out.

"Monsieur Ansary," she said, improvising as she went along. "These police allegations are confusing since Yves Robert wrote favorable articles supporting the Kurds' struggle in Turkey. Yet he was critical of the Kurds' methods. Can you comment on that?"

"Once again, I'm a restaurant owner —"

"*Mais non,* Monsieur, you're a very successful businessman who helps your fellow Kurds. You're paying the party's office rent. No law against that."

A muscle in his jaw twitched. "You've been following me."

"*Non,* it's called investigation," she said. "Reporters Without Borders's mission is to shed light on the cases of journalists who've been tortured, kidnapped, or silenced. Yves was murdered while investigating the iKK, so we're now investigating."

He stared at her.

"This won't go away, Monsieur Ansary," she said. "*Le Figaro*'s interested in your comments, in exploring the Kurds' position; but if you don't want to talk to me. . . ."

His shoulders sagged. "You put me in a difficult position. I'm a businessman. And a Kurd patriot. I don't speak for the iKK. I support the cause. But I do it the only way I can. Financially."

At least he'd admitted it. "Yet don't you want to clear up these allegations against the iKK party? You did speak with Yves?"

Silence.

"Did the iKK take offense at his articles criticizing their methods?

"Everyone criticizes the iKK's methods, Mademoiselle," Ansary said and sighed. "He's not the first, nor the last. You think the party would murder a journalist sympathetic to the Kurds' plight even though he disapproved of 'certain' methods?" Ansary didn't wait for an answer. "Every time an article accuses us of brutality, why, fifty young men line up to join the party, wanting to further the cause. We disabuse them of violent ideas right away. But it helps us more than it hurts us. Ironic, eh?"

"What about the death threat to Jalenka Malat?" she said, taking a chance. "Any truth to the rumor that the local iKK party disagrees with her stance? She has said publicly that she, too, opposes the iKK's methods to obtain an autonomous Kurdistan within Turkey's borders."

"Does it make sense that we'd want her dead?" His thick eyebrows raised in his forehead. "I ask you. The first Kurd elected to Parliament? Why would the party threaten her? You've got it wrong. Jalenka lives with death threats. She's made Kurdish women restive. They now meet at community washbasins and talk about their rights . . . at last." He paused as he considered an afterthought. "Regarding the journalist, you're looking in the wrong place."

"What do you mean?"

"The Turkish military."

Of course, he'd blame the Turks.

"What's their motive, Monsieur Ansary?"

"Let's say they disapprove of Kurd sympathizers."

"That's no reason to kill him."

"Then, Mademoiselle, I don't know."

230

Footsteps sounded on the landing.

The phone call he'd made . . . his backup. Forget his speech about Kurds. Her shoulders tensed and she stepped back. Looked again for something with which to defend herself.

Ansary opened the door to reveal a *flic* in a blue uniform standing, notebook in hand. "Monsieur Ansary, a few questions in the museum, if you don't mind."

"Of course, Officer. I'll join you."

And the successful businessman reappeared.

On her way out, she noticed the bowl of tamarinds, labeled "monkey fruit" in the Asian markets. Pod-like and the color of shoe leather. Soft but once crackled open, revealing a hard stone pit. Like Ansary.

Out on the scorching pavement, she shouldered her bag. She felt sure that Ansary had spoken with Yves. And for the rest, she counted on Langois to supply answers.

She parked at Hôpital Lariboisière, the old cholera hospital abutting the Gare du Nord rail lines. Its courtyard held cars now, not the wagons that had once brought the infected and carried away the corpses. In the distance, gray poles and wires supported gray canopies of glass, draped umbrella-like over the nineteenth-century rail station. Gray and more gray. Several carved heads of statues poked over the glass roof, somber and vacant-eyed guardians.

Léon-Paul Fargue's ode to his neighborhood came to her: "A bustling and noisy circus where iron mingles with men, trains with taxis, cattle with soldiers: a country rather than an arrondissement made up of canals, factories . . . a neighborhood of poets and locomotives."

Locomotives, all right, but the poets she didn't see.

On her right lay the rambling headquarters of the French National Railroads, an old-fashioned monument to bureaucracy.

She glanced at her Tintin watch and ran. Inside the Gare du Nord, crowded at noontime and all the time, the crackling loudspeaker and the old metal clock brought back memories of school field trips and harried teachers.

One could set one's clock by the Gare du Nord's arriving morning commuters, her father said once after a stakeout. Five to six a.m., the African workers with their lunch pails from the suburbs; seven to eight a.m., local secretaries and receptionists reading *Femme Actuelle;* nine to ten a.m., the executives carrying briefcases arriving from the rapid RER lines.

However, now as she made her way under the cavernous slanting glass roof, it was among knots of people in summer attire, vacationers with suitcases crowding toward the platforms. Numbers and letters whirred, clicking into place on the black electronic schedule board indicating gates for arrivals and departures.

At the Eurostar gate exit, a surge of scurrying people erupted, pulling wheeled bags. To the right, submerged in the crowd, she made out the train cleaners in blue coats waiting with their carts. Here. This had to be the place.

She saw two men, but neither was small nor moustached. The clock read 12:10 as she scanned the faces for Langois. A trio of uniformed *flics* on floor patrol approached through the sea of travelers. Their pace was unhurried.

Had the Turkish worker been scared off by the *flics?* She still saw no sign of Langois. She pulled out her cell phone to call him when a scream carried above the bustle, loud and piercing. Then there were shouts as people parted and another surge of passengers hurried from the platform trying to elbow their way through the knot of congestion.

Worried, Aimée pushed through, registering the shocked faces in the crowd. An old woman in a wheelchair, travel bag on her lap, screamed and pointed to a figure slumped against a baggage cart. Jostling bystanders blocked her view until the *flics* shoved them aside.

Blood pooled on the station floor. One of the *flics* kneeled down. And then she saw the camera bag labeled Hôtel Marriot-Sarajevo, and her stomach wrenched. The *flic* turned the man's head.

Aimée stared at the expression of surprise on Langois's blanched face. She stepped back in horror. More *flics* arrived, shoving aside the bewildered crowd. One of them felt for a pulse, and shook his head. It was too late.

Frantic, she looked around. Behind her, people sat at tables in the restaurant to the rear of the information booth, trains like long dark snakes stretched down the tracks, a constant rush of travelers brushed her shoulders. And always there was the booming loudspeaker: "Gate change for the 12:18 departing for Troyes."

The killer could be anyone, he could be anywhere now. Melting into the crowd after picking a perfect place to murder Langois, in plain sight, midday, and in the midst of

234

thousands of people. All of them intent on catching a train, carrying their luggage, and on their own agendas. A quick thrust of the knife from behind, covering the movement with a jacket over the arm, and then moving on, keeping pace with the other passengers. Not looking back, disappearing into the Metro, or leaving by the front exit.

But she didn't think so. Not just yet. The killer was still here, watching; she felt it. Scrutinizing her moves from behind a newspaper, or while drinking coffee at the buffet, or checking a train schedule. Even in this station jammed with people, the killer was waiting for her.

Had they been followed from the canal last night . . . the phone call . . . ? Now she'd never know what Langois meant to tell her. But she couldn't think about that now. Not yet. She had to get away.

She joined the rush of perspiring travelers, not sure of where to go. But she knew she had to keep moving, stay with the crowd, not too close to anyone. The Metro? No . . . too exposed waiting on a platform for the train. Go out an exit? But then, that's what the killer would expect. . . . She had to disappear here.

The tunnel. She had to find the tunnel Yves and Langois used to get to Gare de l'Est. And then Yves's phone rang.

Her hands trembled as she pushed the answer key.

"I know you're here," she said.

The station loudspeaker echoed over the line. A conversation trailed, the cry of a child. She searched the crowd. No women in chadors. Only women in halters, pastel tank tops, straw hats — vacationers.

The child's cry sounded louder now. Of course the killer was calling from a pay phone . . . and she'd slipped from his view.

"Who are you?" she asked.

Then Yves's phone went dead. Out of battery.

She saw the sign for pay phones. A woman cradling a crying toddler spoke into one, and from the other a receiver dangled. Her spine tingled. Keep moving, she had to keep moving.

Signs pointed to the Metro a level below. Several construction workers paused at a metal service door, opened it, and went inside. Before the door could close, she caught the handle and slipped after them. A lighted stairwell with the smell of concrete and whiff of burning rubber met her. She waited until she heard their footsteps disappear, then followed the stairs down.

She saw signs outlining the platforms

above. Diagrams with intricate details of rail lines and freight hubs; placards with the locations of electrical substations. She had had no idea that a small city existed down here.

A loud metallic clang sounded as the door above shut. More workers? Or had the killer followed her? No time to find out, and no reason to wait here like a sitting duck; she had to escape. She saw staff lockers and a sign labeled laundry/changing area. Inside the changing area, she heard voices and then she saw a pile of freshly laundered blue jumpsuits in front of her. Not ironed, but who needed to make a fashion statement right now? She stepped into one. Huge. She rolled up the pant cuffs and sleeves, and zipped it up. For now it would do. Back in the changing area, she saw white hard hats on the wall and took one.

She stepped into the tunnel and headed in the direction she figured was east. This narrow curving gray stucco tunnel lined with electrical cables had Gare de l'Est written on a sign with an arrow.

A construction worker approached. She felt out of place with her second-hand Kelly bag over her shoulder. But he merely nodded as he passed her. She nodded back and kept going.

Lights and the thud of drilling came from ahead. A room built into the tunnel labeled *bureau* held a copy machine, several desks with phones, and clipboards hanging on nails from the wall. Lunchtime . . . everyone was out for lunch. She had to take advantage. Right now, wearing the jumpsuit and hard hat, she fit in. And, hopefully, if the killer had followed her, she'd be able to avoid discovery. She ducked inside. The clipboards held employee assignment sheets: laundry, train maintenance, food service. Headed by numbers and times, they read like code. She might find this Turkish worker if she could figure it out. But where to begin?

Langois had mentioned Yves joking with the maintenance workers. She scanned the names on the train maintenance sheet for a Turkish name. There were at least five. That got her nowhere. She racked her brain. The information was here; she just didn't know how to find it. How long could she stand here before an employee came back from lunch? If the Turkish man she sought worked here, he had to be assigned a shift; but which one? How could she tell? She took the clipboard, flipped through the sheets, and found the ones dated Monday, the night Yves had met Langois at the Eurostar. She looked for the shift that covered 6:30 p.m., when Langois had arrived and Yves had insisted they wait for his contact. There was no time to study each name, so she went to the copier and pressed POWER. The machine grumbled as it warmed up. Voices came from the outside tunnel. She kept her back turned. The green copier light came on.

"Where's Basquiet?" a man's voice asked.

Though she was startled, Aimée controlled her panic and pressed COPY.

"Didn't he leave the report for me?" the man asked.

"Look on the desk," she said.

Papers rustled behind her. The red light of the copier flashed: misfeed. The copier was jammed.

"*Alors,* not *this!* I want today's unloading dock assignment." The man's voice rose in frustration. "Check the dock assignment log for me."

"Can't right now. . . ."

"You're closer to it than me."

She looked up to see a row of fat black binders, grease-stained and heavy. She picked the one labeled "dock assignments," turned around, and handed it to him.

A sallow man eyed her, his shirtsleeves

239

rolled up and tie askew. "That's not your job." She looked down at "Food Service" embroidered on her jumpsuit.

"Damn thing's jammed. Now I have to bring the originals."

"No one removes those papers from this location." His eyes narrowed in suspicion.

She thought fast. "A man's been knifed on Platform One. The *flics* demanded assignment sheets; they want to question the whole staff. The station's gone to lockdown."

Or it should if they could manage to corral thousands of passengers. She imagined the chaos upstairs while the killer slipped away.

"I didn't hear about this."

"You wouldn't down here, would you?"

She put the clipboard under her arm. "Or would *you* like to bring them to the Commissaire? Be my guest."

Before he could answer, she edged past him and out of the room. She kept her head down, clutched the clipboard to her chest, turned into another tunnel, an older one with age-darkened stucco, and passed a group of men working with blowtorches.

She took the train cleaning clipboard, flipped to Monday night, and scanned the list. The shift ran from noon to eight p.m.

"Where's the train cleaning section?"

"Where it always lives." A man pushed his welding visor up to reveal a sweaty face.

"And that would be?"

He leered. "Don't have many lookers like you down here."

The fumes of burnt oil and solder that filled the dark bowels underneath the station, with trains thundering overhead, wouldn't make it a sought-after workplace. For women or anyone.

"I'm food service." She gave a small smile. "New."

"What time do you get off?"

Never, she wanted to say

"But I'm late, can't you help me, I have to deliver this to train. . . ."

"Second tunnel on the left." He caught her sleeve, held it. She gritted her teeth and managed another small smile. "The buffet, say in an hour?"

He winked. "If my heart will take the wait." And let her go.

She followed the curving tunnel and saw metal carts filled with cleaning supplies.

A salt-and-pepper-haired man stood loading boxes onto the carts.

"Monsieur, I need to speak with these members of the crew . . ." she scanned Monday's sign-in and found three Turkish names ". . . Tariq, Faroum, and Ketzal."

He opened a door to what appeared to be a dumbwaiter and shoved a cart inside. "Up on 11."

"Which way, monsieur?"

"Take the shortcut. They do." He pointed to a narrow tunnel and stairs. He looked at her and grinned. "Like the Huns did." On the flaking wall she saw faded painted words: ACHTUNG, RAUCHEN VERBOTEN.

"A sign in German?"

"There's a whole Wehrmacht command room in these tunnels, still intact."

"Even now?"

"They didn't have time to empty it. Our SNCF Resistance loved to garrotte a few, then escape out on the platforms." He grinned again. "Those stairs are still the quickest way up."

"Merci." She ran ahead, began climbing the dark stairs and then she hit her head. A sheet of metal blocked her way. Had the man played a joke on her? Would she have to go back? Her fingers felt across the smooth surface, then hit a metal ring. She tugged it. The metal door moved aside, operated by a spring mechanism.

She emerged and found herself on a platform. This time there were no passengers about. A cleaning crew made trips in and out of the standing cars. "LILLE" read the sign in a slot on the siding. The train blocked her view of the station, but she saw no evidence of *flics*.

Yet.

"Where's Tariq?" she asked one of the blue-coated women, a bandanna around her head.

"Out sick today," she said.

With her luck, he was the one she wanted and he'd reported in sick because he was afraid to come to work. Running scared. She glanced at the two other names. "What about Faroum and Ketzal?"

"Inside, servicing first class." She paid Aimée no more attention after she'd hefted a plastic container of disinfectant. The container gave off that cloying sweet odor particular to train lavatories.

Aimée climbed the first class car's steps and walked down the aisle. A heavy-set dark bearded man swept the floor.

"Faroum?"

"*Fare,* we call him. Mouse." He shook his head. "What's the matter?"

"He's got a phone call," she said making it up as she went along, using the clipboard to cover the food service logo on her jump-suit. "The boss said it's important."

He jerked his thumb toward the next car.

She prayed Faroum was the one she was seeking.

She kept walking through first class until she reached the last car before the engine. She saw no one. About to leave, she called out "Faroum?"

A hand popped up from under the seats with a rag in it, and then a head with a moustache. "Cabin's half done," he said with a heavy Turkish accent. And then he stood, and she saw his blue jacket embroidered with the words Gare du Nord. He reached her shoulder. Almost.

The little one with a moustache, afraid to use a cell phone. Yves's contact. She'd bet money on it.

Her hands shook as she set the clipboard on a leather first class seat. She told herself to proceed with caution, not to scare him off. "Can you take your break?"

"I just started my shift." He spoke slowly, as if he had to think of the right French words.

"We need to talk, Faroum. I'm Yves's friend. Didn't you call his cell phone last night?"

He looked blank, then shook his head. Superb, she'd done it again. Barked up the wrong tree. While the killer. . . . Calm down, she mustn't give up so soon. She had to get through to him, he might know who Yves's contact was. She reached into her bag.

"I'm looking for this man's friend; he works here, like you." She lifted up Yves's photo.

Faroum dropped his cleaning rag. He spun around. Quickly. But she was quicker and locked her arm around his shoulder. She wished she'd gone to the dojo with René and picked up a few jujitsu moves. He struggled as she pulled him down to the seat. She had to keep him still and make him talk. But now he seemed too scared to move.

"You knew Yves, didn't you? It's okay, I'm a friend."

"Non, non." And then he lapsed into Turkish, his eyes pleading.

"Yves." She pointed to the photo of Yves wearing Kurdish clothing.

He shook his head. He was stubborn.

She ran her free hand across her throat. "You were meeting him . . . a rendezvous, right? But the killer got there first."

He kept shaking his head.

"Another man, his photographer, was just murdered," she said, trying to keep her voice level. "On the platform by the Eurostar, where you were supposed to meet him."

His body trembled.

"Tas." And then he mumbled something in Turkish.

"Tas?"

He pointed to Yves's photo. "Tas."

Now the centime dropped.

"You called him Tas?"

His lip quivered. "Turkish name. Good man."

"Will you talk to me? Please? Don't run away."

He shook his head. "Must finish my work," he said nervously. "Late."

"Okay, I'll help you, then we'll talk." She grabbed a rag from a bucket. "Did you see Yv— Tas killed?"

He shook his head. "I found him. Then I ran."

"Did you see a woman in a chador?"

"No one."

"But the two men who ran into you in Cité Paradis said you were crying."

"Coward. I'm a coward. I wanted to go back see what I could do, but . . . it's no use."

"You helped Tas by feeding him information, right?"

"Tas knew the valley of my ancestors; he loved my country. He spoke good Turkish, wrote good things about my people. Kurd-

246

ish, you know." He sprayed a window, then rubbed it clean in circular motions.

"You're Kurdish?"

He nodded. "No one tells the truth about my people."

"Jalenka Malat's in danger, isn't she?"

His hand stopped. "You in danger, now, too."

"What does she have to do with Tas's murder?"

"They have contacts here, I tell Tas."

"Who?"

"The Turks."

Ansary had said the same thing.

"The Turks? You mean a hit squad?"

"Hit squad? I don't understand."

"Hired killers."

"At the mosque, I hear things. That's all I know."

Pause. Talk . . . why wouldn't he talk? But she forced herself to take a breath, to curb her impatience. "Please, go on."

He lowered his voice. "The Imam died two weeks ago. Such a good man. A Sunni, a liberal cleric who wanted to open Islam, to make discussions with the Shi'a mullahs and all sects."

"Meaning?"

"Shi'a fundamentalists have taken over."

She tried to figure out what lay behind his

words. The rash of Metro bombings, the attack on the Marseilles airliner, the *Le Monde* article in which the government attributed terrorist attacks to several groups like the iKK Kurds or the radical Algerian GIA.

"A shield, was Tas's word. Someone's using the network."

A shield, deflecting attention from their real purpose . . . she remembered Langois repeating Yves's words . . . an insidious network.

"But Jalenka Malat's a target. I found this in Tas's wallet." She showed him the scrap of paper.

He nodded. "I left it for Tas in the letter box."

"Letter box?"

"Tas teach me. In letter box where he stayed."

She tried to make sense of it.

"So because you missed meeting him on the platform and wanted him to meet you later, you threw pebbles at the window?"

He nodded, hefting the bucket. "But now I heard that Jalenka's meeting a local Kurdish woman's group before her talk. Early."

Alarm bells rang. "At the Kurdish center?"

"Faroum!" The stocky man beckoned from train coupling. "Next train's here."

Aimée looked at her watch. "An assassination attempt?"

"Tas wondered too."

She thrust her number and a phone card at him. "Don't be afraid to call my cell phone number. The line's secure, use this phone card if you hear anything. Anything at all."

"But it's too late."

She stepped down to the train platform. "Not if I have anything to do with it."

Wednesday Noon

Nadira smiled at Monsieur Delbard as she climbed into the back seat of the air-conditioned chauffeur-driven car. "We're feeding the ducks in Canal Saint-Martin. You're so kind to give us a ride."

"It's on my way, Nadira," he said.

She could never lay it on too thick for Monsieur Delbard. He was trim, if pallid. In his fifties, he wore a blue shirt and linen trousers, and his blue blazer hung from the window hook. "Paul loves the interesting places you take him."

Juice from an orange segment dripped from the corner of Paul's mouth. "We saved our old baguettes, Papa. Nadira says it's better for the ducks. And 'Waste not, want not.' "

"She's right, Paul." Monsieur Delbard

flashed a huge smile at her and brushed back the hair from his graying temples.

"We'll picnic, watch the barges go through the nine locks. Do you remember how many swing bridges we'll see, Paul?"

He held up two fingers.

"So educational, too."

"I'm applying to the Sorbonne teaching program next year," she said.

She cast her eyes down as she'd seen cook do when suggesting she'd like to attend a pastry course. Impressed by the chef, who'd attained two Michelin stars, the frugal Delbards agreed. The cook holed up with her boyfriend at the hotel during the course and came back radiant. "Watch how I play it, Nadira. Learn." And Nadira did.

"That's my dream, Monsieur Delbard, to teach at a school for children with special needs."

"Admirable. You'll be wonderful."

The Canal Saint-Martin wound alongside on the left framed by chestnut and plane trees. Two men sat with fishing poles watching the lock fill with water. Paul shouted with glee: "Look, Papa!"

The chauffeur parked the car and opened the trunk. He reached for the stroller, but Nadira stopped him. "*Merci,* but it's tricky. Let me do it."

She lifted it out, careful to compensate for the added weight of the rifle, and strapped Paul in.

"Have a wonderful evening, Monsieur," she said.

He pressed a wad of francs into her palm, folded his hand over hers, and held it a moment longer than necessary. It was only a matter of time, she knew, until he hit on her as he hit on all the female staff. "Take a taxi back, Nadira, it's so hot. My treat."

She disengaged her hand. In her culture, no man touched a woman unless they were married. She felt defiled, but the mullah had given her dispensation to cover such situations. Her mission, he said, overrode the usual precepts.

She and Paul waved good-bye until the Renault disappeared along the quai.

Paul ate a sandwich, then fed the ducks, marveling at the lock man's patient explanation of how the canal system worked. "It's our route to the north and the Belgian waterways, *petit,* four and a half kilometers long." He detailed a several-hour journey stretching from Bassin de Villette part of the way underground to the Seine.

"Nadira, I want to ride the *peniche;* you promised me a treat!"

"And you will get your treat, Paul." She

251

smiled at the perspiring older man and pressed ten francs in his hand. Now he'd remember them. "But today it's too late. We'll plan it and ask your Papa to join us. You'd like that, wouldn't you?"

Monsieur Delbard, busy at the office and with his new mistress, rarely at home even on the weekends, would weasel out of it.

Paul blinked. A bright little boy raised by nannies, he'd grown accustomed to the absence of his parents. "Papa would come?"

Even in this affluent family, she saw how he was neglected. Yet he'd be spared the half-bombed-out concrete blocks of her orphanage; would never hear the bleating cries of malnourished infants or shiver, sleeping on the cold stone floor in winter, enduring the constant ache of a hungry belly. All the fault of the Western Imperialists.

She had been chosen; she must concentrate on her mission, ignore the twinge of unease at her target: a Muslim woman.

Paul tugged her arm. "Let's ask him right now. Call Papa."

"And miss your surprise?"

Paul's eyes lit up.

She kicked off the stroller brake and pushed Paul over the cobblestones. Perfect timing. Fifteen minutes later, they passed the fun fair on Place Franz Liszt, a small carousel with red and blue cars, a dart balloon booth and a *barbes de papa* stand.

She paused, wiped her perspiring forehead, and shook the Orangina before she handed it to Paul. The half of a sleeping pill she'd put inside had dissolved. "Here you go. Now if you're a good boy and listen to Nadira, we'll come back."

"But I want to ride now . . . you promised me a treat!" His blond hair lay matted on his flushed forehead; his lips were swollen in a pout. "Now!" His little voice raised in a whine. "I'm hot."

"Drink this; you'll cool down."

"Non." He unbuckled the stroller strap and scrambled out before Nadira could catch him. He kicked at her, and his whine escalated into a scream. "You promised!" Doting grandparents under the shade of the trees turned their heads. Her careful plan was deteriorating by the second. Paul was making a scene and her few minutes of leeway were evaporating.

She got down on her knees. "Paul, drink this. Then we'll come back. I promise."

He burst into tears and lay on the pavement, kicking. She had to salvage this. She hated Madame Delbard for forcing her to bring Paul. A spoiled, selfish Western woman whose husband cheated on her with regularity and whose child she regarded as a trinket.

"*Bon.* Drink this and you may have one ride," she said, her voice stern.

Paul sat up, surprised at her tone. Nadira never spoke like that. He wiped his eyes.

"Do you understand, Paul?"

He nodded.

At the ride's end, his eyes were glazed and she had to lift him out of the car. One of the watching grandmothers clucked knowingly. "The heat gets to the little ones." Nadira just smiled.

Her timing was off now, she had to hurry. She'd change her plan, switch to the alternate, and, if necessary, improvise. She'd been trained to improvise, and with Paul now asleep in the stroller, she'd manage.

On rue Lafayette, she entered a narrow seam in between 19th-century Haussmann-designed buildings which led to the triangular space fronting the Institut Kurd. A group of women in Kurdish baggy pants, tunics, and scarves mingled with those in Western dress, filing up the outside stairs to the Institut. Nadira joined them and, declining the offered assistance of several of the woman, lifted the stroller into the foyer. Instead of joining the crowd heading to the theater, she veered into the exhibition room lined by cases of books and Kurdish tapes, off which there was a small office. Leyla stood at her desk, gathering papers.

"Bonjour," Nadira said, smiling.

Leyla returned her smile. "Welcome. I noticed your name on our guest list. I'm so glad you made it for this earlier talk. More intimate . . . but excuse me, I have to hurry. I'm introducing her. . . ."

"The boy I babysit's exhausted," she said. "It's so crowded in there. All the chairs are taken, so I can't hold him. Someone told me they don't allow strollers. May I ask a favor?" She didn't give Leyla time to answer. "Can he stay here?"

"Well, we've never done that," Leyla said, raising her eyebrows. "It's such a small space. . . ."

"I'll check on him often; if he wakes up, we'll leave," she said. "I'm thrilled to hear even a bit of her talk. Please, otherwise I'll have to miss it."

Leyla hesitated, torn between saying no and her hurry to leave.

"Please, I promise he won't touch anything or be a bother."

Leyla smiled and shrugged. "I wouldn't want you to miss this. Just keep an eye on him."

"I so appreciate it, Madame," Nadira said. "Go ahead, I'll make him more comfortable."

Leyla left, and Nadira closed the office door. She pulled the plastic bags from under the stroller. From one she took the chador, draped the black folds over her tank top and jeans, and, using it as cover, with her back to the door, took the Lego backpack with the rifle pieces and gripped it to her body under her left arm.

Paul's measured breaths reassured her. She left.

Instead of entering the crowded room and giving her reservation ticket, she asked the pink-scarved ticket taker for the restroom. She was directed behind a screen to a row of doors. She thanked her and waited until her view was blocked, then took the stairs. Avoiding the library and those working there, she turned right into a narrow hallway and followed it as it curved around to the left until she found the restroom. In it was the stall with a toilet and a long rectangular window.

She unfurled her chador, set the rifle pieces on the tiled floor, and climbed onto the toilet seat. She applied WD40 to the window, which had taken her several tries to open last time. Now it opened on her first try.

Not even twenty yards away, across a small oblong courtyard in which a lone tree stood, lay the theatre. The windows were wide open. Through the farthest window, she saw a wooden podium with a microphone on it. On a cloth backdrop were the words KURDISH WOMAN'S LEAGUE WELCOMES JALENKA MALAT MP in bright green and red script.

Sunlight reflected off the windows. Inside, veiled heads leaned toward each other in conversation. Laughter and words in Kurdish and Turkish drifted out the window. Veiled women talking together, comfortable and familiar. Like home.

She ground her teeth, gripped by doubt . . . she, a Muslim, was about to shoot another Muslim woman. The mullah's words came back to her: "We trust in Allah to show the way; never question his teachings. We are his servants, we are his instruments." But weren't mullahs human, people who could make mistakes? she'd asked Ruhal once. And he'd answered "But if innocents are killed, they will go to heaven. The mullah will have the price of their life on his head. And he will pay. Not you; you are the instrument."

She stepped down from the toilet, assembled the stock, barrel, forearm, scope, mount, and silencer. Not an easy job with her hands shaking. She re-checked the bullet chamber. Full.

She glanced at her watch, her upper lip beaded with perspiration in the heat. Her body was baking in the chador. Three minutes, according to the schedule. She again stood on the toilet, set the rifle end on the wooden windowsill, crouched, and looked through the crosshairs of the sight. "Allah is all-powerful, we are but the instruments of his will," she murmured.

She aimed, adjusting the magnification, aiming a little above the podium as she remembered from the *télé* that Jalenka was short. With the sun overhead, she kept the rifle tip just inside the window frame to avoid having it glint in the sun, giving away her location. Still, in the resulting chaos and horror, with people rushing to give Jalenka aid, she doubted anyone would look up before she could disappear.

Then she heard excited voices rising and saw the flash of colored scarves inside the windows. Two minutes. Two more minutes.

Wednesday Afternoon

Aimée screeched to a halt at a curb on rue Lafayette. She was in a red zone, but it was the only spot she could find. Never mind, she'd pay René's parking ticket later. She ran across the busy street, just avoiding a bus, and entered the walkway leading to the Institut Kurd, crossed the small courtyard, and climbed the stairs. A crush of women stood at the doorway of a large meeting area. A mixed group of earnest intello journalists in black, Kurdish women in *pejershe,* the native costume, human-rights activists wearing red armbands, and a celebrity or two whose faces she recognized. Jalenka Malat was quite an attraction.

And not a *flic* or any security in sight.

Merde! Bordereau only knew about the evening event, not this one that she'd just discovered. In the corner, she pulled out her cell phone and punched in Rouffillac's number. Only his voice mail answered. Great, he screened his calls.

"Rouffillac, it's urgent . . . pick up!"

Her knuckles whitened around the cell phone. He didn't pick up. She waited for the beep.

"No. 9, rue Lafayette, an attempt on Jalenka —"

And the message cut off. Full.

Meanwhile, the crush had dwindled and the doors were closing.

All she could see were the backs of women's veiled heads. Her fingers trembled as she punched in the DST number. A recorded message asked her to hold and her call would be answered in the order it had been received.

"Your name, please," said a young woman wearing a pink scarf, holding a clipboard.

"How much?"

"No tickets. It's a reservation-only event, I'm sorry," said the young woman. "And no cell phones permitted."

No *flics* in sight, the DST keeping her on hold, a crowded room . . . How could she pick out an assassin?

"Again, I'm sorry, Mademoiselle." The young woman put her clipboard under her arm and reached for the door. She wore an armband bearing the slogan "Muslim Kurds for Peace."

Aimée opened her wallet and flashed her father's old police ID with her name on it. "Emergency. We need to talk."

The young woman stared, wide-eyed. "Something's wrong?"

Aimée motioned the young woman outside. "What's your name?"

"Iqbal."

"Iqbal, I need your help. Is there any security here?"

The young woman shook her head. "I

260

don't know, Jalenka just confirmed this, we weren't sure —"

"Her bodyguards?"

"Jalenka? Never uses them." She thought. "At least I don't think so."

"Has she arrived yet?"

"She's backstage. When everyone's seated —"

"DST, how can I route your call?" came over the line.

Aimée put her hand up to silence Iqbal. "Terrorist division."

A series of clicks. Aimée waited.

"Oui?"

"There's going to be an assassination attempt during Jalenka Malat's talk at No. 9, rue Lafayette. Now."

"How do you know this, Mademoiselle?

She hung up.

Iqbal's mouth had dropped open.

"No time to explain," Aimée said. "I want you to gather the other ticket takers and available staff and line the stage facing out so you can watch the crowd."

Iqbal stepped back in horror. "But I don't believe anyone would want to —"

"I don't know when security will come," Aimée interrupted. Or the Brigade. Or if any of them would appear in time. "This threat's real. Her life's in danger. Do you

261

understand, Iqbal? Answer me."

Iqbal nodded. *"Oui."*

A child's cry came from somewhere in the other room, but Aimée ignored it.

"Do it in a quiet way; we don't want to alarm a room full of women if we don't have to. Yet."

"But what do we look for?"

"Watch for women wearing chadors," Aimée said. "I'll be walking around the room. Point out anyone acting oddly. And stay with Jalenka. Don't let anyone get too close."

A serious look appeared in Iqbal's eyes. "Her work's important for women, for Kurds. I will help her."

"Good." Aimée paused. "Now tell me what you're going to do."

"Get the staff and have all of us stand around the base of the platform facing out, watch the crowd, point out. . . ."

"Now go."

Of all the times to have left her Beretta at the office, Aimée thought, following Iqbal into the close hot air of a room full of too many women. And why the hell hadn't anyone thought to provide security?

Inside the small theatre, there were more than two hundred women. They filled every chair and stood, lining the walls. A video camera on a tripod was operated by a woman in Kurdish dress. Not a single man was present. Aimée's eyes rested on the many open windows. One was right alongside the podium.

She scanned the walls for a fire alarm. Not a one. She hoped there was one backstage. Iqbal had gathered several women and was making her way through the crowd, stopping to speak to others who stood and joined her.

Good. Their presence might offer a deterrent. Or, the awful thought came, they'd be picked off like flies. Aimée shoved that aside. It wouldn't come to that if she could help it. Or if the DST got here in time.

A woman in Kurdish dress stepped onto the stage. "I'm Leyla, Resource Director of the Institut Kurd, and it's my great honor to welcome our guest, Jalenka Malat. Tomorrow she's flying back to Ankara to put the Kurdish settlement proposal on the Turkish parliament's agenda. A historic proposal that includes the teaching of the Kurd language in schools and reparations for forcible resettlement and for Kurd lands appropriated by the government."

Deafening applause drowned out the rest.

Leyla smiled and held up her hand. "Please, I know you want to hear her, but remember Jalenka has graciously carved time out of her packed schedule to address your League which she deems of vital importance. Right after this, she's addressing the media and our Institute members here on the topic of "To veil or not to veil: Muslim women's role in modern society," so I'd appreciate your keeping your questions brief."

Aimée worked her way toward the windows. Think, think like an assassin, she told herself. How would one kill Jalenka . . . a quick thrust of a knife, the way Langois had been taken out, but that meant close contact with Jalenka and a quick exit during the confusion. It would depend on whether Jalenka walked among the crowd, but that would be after her talk if she had time to do so. Or would the attack come later, when she addressed the media during the reception?

What could happen right now? Iqbal and the women had lined up, a few arm's-lengths apart, and stood below the stage. They now wore red and green armbands with the emblem of the Kurdish Women's League, like an honor guard. No one questioned their presence; they took it for granted.

And then Jalenka, a small woman with

reddish brown hair and sparkling eyes, wearing a black suit, appeared on the stage in a burst of energy.

"Thank you for coming," Jalenka said in flawless French. "I'm humbled by your support. As many of you know, my husband Demir, a former member of parliament, has been in prison for five years. It's through his urging that I campaigned and won the votes of his former constituency so I can carry on the work he started and further our goals for Kurds."

Another round of deafening applause, and the audience stood.

Jalenka's expression turned serious. "The eyes of the world will be on the Turkish Parliament when it considers this proposal. Turkey's bid to join the EU will be turned down unless it can demonstrate respect for the Kurds' human rights."

No wonder Jalenka was a threat.

A fine sheen of perspiration beaded Aimée's forehead. She caught Iqbal's gaze. Her raised finger indicated several women in chadors. Old women with wrinkled faces, their chadors half open in the heat.

More applause, and Jalenka raised her hand. "Since the 1920 Treaty of Sèvres, forged in this country to establish a Kurdish territory for our people, France has been our friend and supporter. We all know the military dictatorship ignored this. But, with my French friends' indulgence, I will now speak in Kurdish, a language forbidden in my country."

Aimée edged along the windows. From outside came the scent of a late-flowering plane tree. She saw the copper wings of a hovering dragonfly and heard the sound of splashing water. An old man leaned out of a window opposite, watering red geraniums. A peaceful torpid afternoon.

She had to keep alert. Langois had been murdered amid thousands of people in a busy station before he could tell her . . . but now she'd never know. What she did know was that Yves had been murdered for this.

All the windows across the courtyard facing the Institut Kurd were closed, except one a floor up. But there was no movement there, just darkness.

Wednesday

Nadira squinted, eyeing the telescopic sight. A spiky-haired woman's head bobbed in her crosshairs, blocking the podium. Where had she come from?

Nadira glanced at her watch. One minute. Barely enough time to realign. She shifted the rifle on the ledge, re-adjusted the mount and the sights.

Eight centimeters would do it. If only the bile didn't threaten to rise up in her stomach. She steeled herself to concentrate, block everything from her mind but her target. She would do this; she'd been trained almost her whole life for this mission. The viewfinder appeared, the familiar markings, and the red center dot aligned on the target. A centimeter more to the right.

The charm on her neck caught. The tiny blue horse. And that warm afternoon — like this one — came back to her. A breeze fluttering the hospital's window curtains. The nurse's kind eyes as she pressed the charm into her palm, mumbling about lost childhood. . . .

Then the woman moved. Thirty seconds, no time to realign her sights. Nothing for it, Nadira realized, but to take her out with the first shot.

Wednesday

Aimée cocked her head, about to turn toward the podium. She barely caught a glint. The briefest flicker at the window. She stared. She saw the unmistakable sight of a long-barrel rifle. Then it was gone.

Her adrenalin kicked in. She sprang into

action, running the few feet toward the stage.

"Get down, Jalenka!" she yelled.

Jalenka paused, looked surprised, and glanced to her left. Aimée heaved herself up to the stage and tackled Jalenka, pulling her down behind the podium.

Short cracking noises. The podium splintered above them. Puffs of wood powder and metal. The wavering microphone screeched with static. Screams erupted in the audience. Aimée felt Iqbal crawling and hurling herself over Jalenka's shoulders. More short bursts of noise. Rifle shots shredded the podium. Wailing and more screams.

"Get her backstage, Iqbal. Now. Sound the fire alarm."

But Iqbal didn't move. A fine blood spatter covered her pink scarf; her unblinking gaze was fixed on the ceiling. Aimée gasped. And then someone was crawling, pulling Iqbal's lifeless form off Jalenka. The rifle fire had ceased. Someone on a cell phone was calling SAMU, an ambulance.

The assassin would escape if she didn't hurry. Aimée got to her feet and ran down the aisle of terror-stricken women huddling on the floor. "Stay down," she called.

She had to reach the assassin before the

panicked women fled, choking the exit. Out in the foyer, she took the stairs two at a time, keeping in mind the location of the small window. She found a warren of little rooms and a library connected by a narrow dark hallway and kept going, winding to the left. She passed several doors, then tried the one with WC written on it. The rectangular window was open; there were smudged footprints on the closed toilet seat. Nothing else. Then she saw a backpack, a child's, behind the toilet and grabbed it. Rooting inside, she found a cardboard box of bullets and a bottle of Orangina.

Her spine tingled. The assassin had used a child as a front . . . and then she remembered the child's cries from the foyer that she'd put out of her mind. She ran down the stairs.

"Did you see a woman in a chador just now?" she asked one of the women spilling into the hall. The woman shook her head. Leyla, the director, rushed to her office and Aimée followed.

"They're gone," Leyla said.

"Who?"

"The little boy was asleep in the stroller and his nanny —"

"Did the woman have a bag, several bags . . . this one?"

Aimée held up the Lego backpack.

Leyla nodded, her face anguished. "A young nanny, so sweet, in jeans and tank top. I wanted her to wait. With all the chaos, I was going to help her after I —"

"Did she wear a chador?" Aimée interrupted.

Leyla shook her head.

A false lead again. Her hopes dashed.

"But I saw a chador trailing from her bag . . . what does it mean?"

Aimée ran through the throng of women, into the courtyard, and out into the street. She saw a taxi pulling away, a little boy's blond head and a woman's dark one just visible in the back window. Then it was swallowed in traffic. In the distance, sirens hee-hawed. The *flics,* after the fact. She pulled out René's car keys, threaded her way past a bus, and unlocked his car door.

She ground into first gear and took off. At least she'd seen the taxi's direction. The afternoon heat hovered in a mist on sloping rue Lafayette. Then she saw the taxi, a blue Parisien, like so many others, waiting ten cars or so ahead at the intersection.

Several cars made right turns. She advanced and zipped across the intersection on a yellow light. An ambulance tore past with its siren blaring, and her mind went to

Iqbal's blood-spattered pink scarf. She couldn't help feeling that it was her fault, such a waste. She'd prevented Jalenka's assassination, but at a cost. And Yves . . . she couldn't push away the image of the slit in his throat. Sickened, she wanted to mow the cars down and catch that taxi.

Langois's words in the Gare du Nord spun in her head. "The way Yves kept staring." She'd taken that to mean his informant was a worker and located Faroum, but what if Langois mentioned it because it had struck another chord . . . Had he been looking at a woman in a chador?

More questions loomed. How had this assassin known of their Gare du Nord meeting? How did she keep one step ahead every time? So far, each theory she'd come up with had failed to work. She went back to Yves's words . . . "an insidious network" . . . What if this assassination attempt was only the first act? She had to catch the assassin and find out.

The taxi crossed Place Franz Liszt and turned into the ninth arrondissement, down a clogged narrow street of elegant art nouveau buildings now connected to street-level copy shops and dry cleaners. The taxi stopped, stuck in traffic. She hoped the woman wouldn't jump out and take off on

271

foot. Horns sounded and traffic moved once more. She grabbed a pen and on her palm wrote down the first three numbers from the ID number on the taxi's side. It sped off before she could make out the rest. She kept three cars behind it, skirting the *rond-point,* drove down rue Rodie and through a soot-stained alley into a maze of winding thread-like streets and small squares. She glanced at her fuel tank: just above empty.

Now the taxi headed across rue des Martyrs, passing a fish store, a *boulangerie,* and a café jammed with afternoon patrons. A nanny with her charge, returning to a posh *quartier.*

Her cell phone rang.

"Aimée?" René's voice sounding peeved. "I'm at Gare du Nord."

Merde, did she forget to pick him up?

"I've come back early to talk to the real estate agent."

She set her phone on the leather-upholstered seat, put it on loudspeaker. "Sorry, René, but I'm tied up right now."

"Tied up? Knowing you, you're off on some wild-goose chase."

"I'm tailing the assassin who just tried to kill Jalenka Malat."

"Assassin?" She heard his intake of breath over the phone. "No wonder the *flics* are

272

questioning everyone. But how . . . ?"

"And who may have stabbed Yves's photographer."

"What's that got to do with you?"

"You've missed a lot, René. I found Jalenka's name on a bit of paper hidden in Yves's wallet."

"And that means?"

"The assassin killed Yves because he knew of the plot. Jalenka just missed being killed at the Institut Kurd a minute ago. But a young Kurdish woman on the podium wasn't as lucky."

"You mean you saw the assassin?"

"A little more than that. She's a couple of taxis ahead of me now, using a child —"

"Where are you?"

Aimée kept one eye on the taxi, the other on the street signs. "Headed uphill on rue Notre Dame de Lorette."

"Rue Notre Dame de Lorette, quick," Aimée heard René shouting at a taxi driver.

"I'm jumping in a taxi. Keep talking, stay on the line, and don't do anything foolish."

Her? What about him?

"But what can you do —"

"I'm a black belt, remember?" he said. "We can sandwich her."

"She's got a high-powered rifle," Aimée said. "She might take the child hostage."

Or arm herself with explosives, return, and walk into the reception.

"So you have a plan?"

"Playing it by the hem of my skirt, René."

"As usual," René said. "Whatever you do, don't stop the car when she gets out, keep going."

"The taxi's heading into Place Saint Georges."

And then the bus ahead of her stalled. Horns honked and drivers stuck their heads out the windows shouting. Fuming, she punched the steering wheel. Nowhere to go, no way to turn. Stuck.

She left the phone, jumped out of the car and ran, weaving her way among the stopped cars surrounded by the black billows of bus exhaust. When she reached the corner, the taxi had disappeared.

Back on the crowded street, traffic moved and a chorus of horns greeted her. Irate drivers yelled, shaking their fists, as they were jammed behind the Citroën. She turned on the ignition, ground into first. The car shot ahead, sputtered, then died. The red fuel arrow was on empty. Stupid, how stupid. She'd lost the assassin and blocked the street. Now there was a lynch mob of drivers behind her.

She set the gear in neutral and opened the door. One hand guiding the steering wheel, she began to push. Nothing. Vintage Citroëns weigh a ton. Sweat broke out under her arms and she heaved again, hearing more shouts behind her.

The car rolled. And stopped, like a stubborn shiny black beetle, refusing to budge. Right by Garvani's pigeon-spattered bust mounted on a pedestal. Elegant, well-maintained *hôtel particuliers* surrounded small, circular, tree-lined Place Saint Georges. Two Metro entrances on opposite sides were hidden discreetly by the trees. The Theatre Saint-Georges with its neon billboard angled away unobtrusively on the sloping street toward the church.

She turned around. "How about helping me if you want to move?"

Horns honked but no one got out of their car. The waiter from the one outdoor café on Place Saint Georges, in his long white apron, set down his serving tray and shook his fist at the cars. A faint breeze stirred the diesel fumes and plane-tree leaves.

He enlisted another waiter and, shirtsleeves rolled up, heaving and grunting, they helped her roll the Citroën off to the side.

"Merci."

"Our pleasure, Mademoiselle, it happens all the time," he said, his brow glistening with sweat. "Such a classic. Self-leveling hydro-pneumatic suspension makes the drive smooth, and it's wonderful rounding corners." He gazed with appeciative eyes at the Citroën. "Own a 1972 myself. You belong to the club?"

"Club?" she said, perspiration clinging to her shoulder blades. "It's my partner's car."

He pointed to papers in the side front-door pocket. *"Permettez?"*

Unsure of what he meant, she nodded, eager to get going.

"Aaah, of course," he said, displaying car club certificates. "Monsieur Friant, I know him from the rally."

"My bill, *s'il vous plait?"* said a man sitting at the nearest marble-topped round table.

"Excusez-moi."

She opened the car trunk, found the metal liter gas can, and shook it. Heard a swishing sound. Thank God, René kept spare gas in the trunk despite its illegality. She poured the gas into the fuel tank. An audience of smoking and drinking patrons from the café terasse watched her, glad of the entertainment in the doldrums of a summer afternoon. Frustrated, she angled the can higher so it poured faster. The pungent gasoline fumes joined the band of wavering humid heat.

A glass shattered in the café, someone said *"Merde!"* and all eyes turned. But she had the feeling someone was studying her. Watching her. Cold fear gripped her, as she thought of the assassin who had disappeared up the street. The assassin would have seen Aimée in her sights, could have noted her following in the Citroën. Instead of being the hunter . . . was she now the hunted?

She scanned the patrons who had returned to their drinks and conversations. The feeling had gone. Her imagination? Just nervousness? She capped the fuel can, put it back, closed the trunk, and walked past the townhouse of La Paiva, the celebrated courtesan who later became a marquise. The entranceway of the building, now converted to apartments, lay deserted except for a gardener spraying water from a hose at a green clipped hedge.

Puzzled, she walked back to the car.

"Where are you, Aimée?" René was saying over the phone in the front seat.

"In front of a café," she said. "I lost her. But I met your car-club friend. See you at the office later."

She picked up her phone. Punched in

the number. Now the DST couldn't ignore her.

She filled the fuel tank at nearby Pigalle, then headed back to the tenth arrondissement to a Turkish restaurant off rue du Faubourg du Temple, Bordereau's colleague's meeting place of choice.

A henna-haired older woman guided her to an empty back table and handed her an oversize menu. Murals of the Bosporus and Topkapi Palace lined the walls. She heard voices raised in the kitchen, then taped Turkish music with the twang of a *saz,* a mandolin-like instrument, filling the otherwise empty restaurant.

A man slid into the chair opposite her. He wore a green jogging suit. Muscular, midthirties, and not an ounce of fat on him. Brown-eyed, hair to match. Anonymous. He'd pass for another jogger on the Canal Saint-Martin.

"The *pide*'s excellent," he said. "So's the *esme,* their specialty."

"Coffee's fine."

He snapped his fingers, glanced at the woman, and settled back in his chair.

"Bordereau apologizes, but you can give me your little presents, now."

"Your name?"

"Call me Sacault."

She hated dealing with the elite terrorist squad, had only forged a connection with Bordereau because she trusted him. This wouldn't have happened if they'd listened to her. Now they would.

The woman set two Turkish coffees in small cups on the table and left. Two men walked into the restaurant. "We're closed," she said and ushered them out.

"I lost her taxi near Place Saint Georges."

"At what time?"

"Say thirty minutes ago." She slipped him the paper with the partially written taxi ID number.

"Pardonnez-moi." He reached for a cell phone in his jacket pocket, stood, and disappeared into the kitchen. The singer's voice rose like a lament accompanied by a shaking tambourine and thump of drums.

A minute later, he sat down again and gave her his total attention. "Please continue."

"The bus stalled, then I ran out of gas in Place Saint Georges, but I felt somehow she was watching me. She may have recognized me from the Institut Kurd. She murdered Yves Robert, the AFP investigative journalist. He knew of her plan."

His expression remained blank.

"I told all this to Bordereau," she said, trying to keep her frustration under wraps.

"How do you connect the two?"

She recounted what happened so far. Romeo, the dead junkie; the chador; the sugar wrapper; Langois's knifing in Gare du Nord. But she left out Faroum. And then she reached into her bag and set the Lego backpack on the table.

"She forgot this in the WC. She's operating undercover, disguised as a nanny."

He nodded. "That confirms our report. We've obtained her description and appreciate your information. Certain details corroborate our field reports." He took the backpack, didn't look inside, and pushed back his chair, which scraped on the tile floor.

She stared in surprise. "That's it? Can't you tell me anything?"

"It's forbidden to compromise an ongoing investigation."

"Compromise? I just prevented an assassination," she said. "By myself. None of you were there!"

"I can't reveal sensitive information; neither could Bordereau."

But he had let a few things slip.

"Answer me this: You're not linking it to the Algerian GIA and the Metro bombings, are you?"

"You'll see it in tonight's papers," Sacault said. "We identified a fingerprint on a bomb fragment belonging to a member of the rue du Faubourg Saint-Denis mosque."

She didn't see the connection.

"A fingerprint from who?"

"That I can't say."

"But why would the assassin target a Kurdish MP? She's a Muslim."

He paused, weighing his words. So far he'd said very little. "That's the link. It's clear."

She paused. As clear to her as the black silt layering the bottom of her cup.

"Meaning?"

"Think Iranian Shi'as against Turkish Sunnis, hardliners versus the more liberal clerics."

That echoed what Faroum had said. But it confused her even more.

"How does that make sense?" She leaned across the table. "Yves investigated Turkish repression of the Kurds. Have you investigated the iKK Worker's Party or the Turkish military?"

"Again, we appreciate your information." He set ten francs on the table. "And we'll handle it from here. Any interference from you could compromise our undercover field agents. Do you understand?"

In other words, leave it alone.

"But this assassin . . . murdered Yves." And she'd lost her!

"No one's attributed his murder to this suspect."

"What?" She handed him the sugar wrapper, translated it for him.

He paused, took it. "Mademoiselle Leduc, we've mounted sensitive operations. National security's at risk. All forces have gone on highest alert."

Yet they hadn't prevented the attempt to assassinate Jalenka, or Iqbal's death.

He stood. "Do you need further clarification, Mademoiselle?"

She shook her head.

He paused on the way to the door. Turned and scrutinized her. "You don't know what you're dealing with, believe me." And for a moment he sounded almost human.

"And you do?"

"We'll take care of that parking ticket you've just been given," he said. "Don't worry."

She wanted to kick him, but he'd gone.

Outside, on René's windshield, there was a ticket. She took it and tore it into little pieces, letting them flutter, confetti-like, into the sewer.

"Abort your cover," the voice said in Farsi.

Nadira clutched the cell phone to her ear. Paul slept in the stroller next to her in the rear of the Place Saint Georges café. A sirop de menthe sat on the table.

"Were you seen?"

Shame filled her. "Yes." And she'd left behind Paul's Lego backpack. It was only a matter of time.

"Then you know what to do." The phone clicked off.

Her mission, her jihad, ruined. A failure, and the mullah was disappointed. She must redeem herself. Follow Allah's will. Terminate the woman.

She sipped the mint drink, willing her hands steady.

"Jacques?" she called to the waiter, who put in orders at the counter.

"Another one, Nadira?" Jacques smiled.

"Non, merci," she said. She came here often to pick up courier messages left hidden in the downstairs cleaning closet. "You must be so strong to have been able to push that car."

He shrugged, but she saw gratification that she'd noticed in his eyes.

"Such a beauty, a vintage DS Citroën, like mine," he said, ringing up payment on the cash register. The cash tray rolled out with a ping.

She flashed him her best smile. "There are not many experts on classic cars like you, eh? You must know the owner, I saw you helping her."

She'd jotted down the license plate number. But it would take time to trace it. Time she didn't have.

"Matter of fact, we're in the same Citroën club," he said, rubbing his hands on his apron, then scanning the counter for his drinks order.

Nadira had to grab his attention. "I'd love to get one like that . . ."

"But the woman driving it is his partner," Jacques interrupted. "No real owner would let a treasure like that run out of gas. Not good for the rings."

"Think he'd sell it?"

Jacques shrugged, then his eyes narrowed. "To you?"

She smiled again. "At least I can ask if he knows of another one. What's his name, Jacques?"

A few minutes later, she walked out of the café and past the Place Saint Georges Metro entrance, pushing the stroller. At No. 16 she pushed the digicode, and entered the Delbard's 19th-century apartment building for the last time. Paul slept through their ascent in the wire-cage elevator and all the way into the apartment. She'd debated what to do with him. But her orders hadn't involved him. So she urged another sleeping pill into his mouth, rubbed his gums so it would dissolve, and left him asleep in his bed.

Nadira changed into a long dress, assembled her assortment of ID's and cash cards, and slipped them, along with another cell phone, into a money belt under her dress. She pulled out the memory chip from her other cell phone and cut it up. She took the prayer rug from the slats under her bed and discarded it and her few belongings in a garbage bag. She surveyed the now-stripped room. No trace of her remained.

Down in the chandelier-lit foyer, she took the plastic bag from the stroller and fit the rifle pieces into a backpack. It took her half an hour to wipe down all the door handles in the huge high-ceilinged flat: kitchen, bedrooms, bathrooms, and front door.

She wouldn't miss Madame Delbard.

She shouldered the backpack, gripped the garbage bag, and descended the back stairs to the topiary tree-filled courtyard. Beyond the old carriage house, she turned. In the next building's courtyard, she dumped the bag into the green garbage containers. Just before she reached the tall doors, she pulled out the chador, draped it over her, then pressed the door release button and emerged onto crowded rue Monnier. Slants of light drifted through the plane trees lining the street. She melted into the crowd waiting at the bus stop. She kept her eyes lowered. Anonymous, just another Arab woman in the mixed group waiting for the Number 67.

The bus sped past the church of Notre Dame de Lorette, sun splashing its soot-stained façade. Nadira hit the number for information on her new cell phone.

"Listing, please," said the operator's voice.

"Monsieur René Friant," she said. "That's F-R-I-A-N-T."

Wednesday Evening
René sat, fork poised over the Indian take-out container on his office desk. "If the DST warned you off, Aimée, listen to them. And you still haven't changed your cell-phone number."

Aimée paced before the tall window. Shadows filled the corners of Leduc Detective's office. The printer hummed in the background, spewing reports.

"I got the call in Gare du Nord."

"What call?"

"She called me right in Gare du Nord after Langois's murder."

"I told you to change it."

"On Yves's phone."

"Slow down, Aimée."

"Langois had information," she said. "We arranged to meet. Now I feel it's my fault . . . !"

"Someone else killed him, not you," René said, "and took advantage of a crowded train station. Smart. Now start from the beginning so I can understand."

So she told him about Langois, the killer's call, escaping in the passage beneath the station, and discovering Yves's contact. "Faroum tried to meet Yves after he overheard rumors at the mosque."

"If that's true," René began, then paused. "It's as if the killer knows you, knows your movements."

She'd felt the same thing. It sent a shiver up her spine. "I warned the DST about the assassination," she said. "They ignored it, and now they've taken my info and shut me out."

"Listen to the news, Aimée," René said. "There was another bomb threat this afternoon. No wonder they didn't respond at once. They're maxed out dealing with the

Metro bombings," he said. "What better time to plan an assassination of a Turkish politician?"

"You're going somewhere with this, right, René?"

"If the killer —"

"You mean this female assassin with the child," she interrupted.

René continued without missing a beat. "If she took care of Yves and Langois, then, besides Faroum, you're the only loose piece." René lifted a pakora and took a bite. Curry smells filled the office. But she'd left hers untouched; she couldn't eat.

"The DST man mentioned a network. Iranian Shi'as and Turkish Sunnis."

René paused, his gaze faraway. "That's a whole other ball game. I don't know . . . just somehow this feels personal, Aimée."

Her cell phone rang. For a moment, her fingers froze, then she punched ANSWER.

"Mademoiselle Leduc, forgive me for not calling sooner," said Gerard Drieu. "I know I promised but there's been a murder of another member of our AFP staff."

Should she tell him she knew? Explain that she'd been about to meet Langois? Better if she listened and learned what he knew.

"I'm sorry."

"And worse news, it's the photographer

288

who worked with Yves."

"Meaning there's a connection?"

"We've heard his murder is being attributed to a network of militant right-wing Turks. The Yellow Crescent."

Surprised she pulled out a pen and paper and sat at her desk. "The Yellow Crescent?" She hadn't seen that name in Yves's article.

"Turkish militants. They send in contract killers from Turkey," Drieu said.

"To take care of threatening investigative reporters here?" She thought for a moment. "Sounds like a stretch."

"We found some of the background information Yves filed from Ankara." He paused, cleared his throat. "You told me you wanted to know."

More ominous and twisted all the time.

"Did this connect? Wait, you're saying Yves was working on an exposé of the Yellow Crescent?"

"You got it in one," Drieu said.

She tried to fit it together. But if Yves's investigation of the Yellow Crescent based on Faroum's information had gotten him killed, it still didn't explain Jalenka's name in his wallet. Unless militant Turkish Sunnis wanted to kill a prominent Kurd . . . could that make sense? Yet the Turks were Sunni, and Sacault spoke of Iranian Shi'as. How did religion play into this?

"Turkey's secular. Any connection with a Sunni jihad?"

"None I know of," Drieu said, then paused. "Turkey's determined to join the EU. Right now, an important Customs Union Agreement between Turkey and the EU is about to be signed. It's a huge step, preparatory to Turkey becoming a formal candidate for admission to the EU. Turkey stresses the secular nature of their republic, likening it to France. They're proud of their separation of religion and state, unlike the rest of the Middle East."

"But Yves knew about an assassination attempt on Jalenka Malat."

Could these be two separate events, were there two networks? Or was the assassin acting solo and Yves had somehow gotten in her way?

"You're well informed, Mademoiselle Leduc," he said. "Did Yves tell you that?"

"I found her name listed as a target in his wallet."

Drieu said, "Yves had a spiderweb of connections. He knew things the Yellow Crescent wanted kept quiet."

"So you're saying Yves's knowledge of the assassination was just incidental, and these militant Turkish hit men from the Yellow

Crescent flew in to silence him before he could publish his article and expose their organization?"

Drieu sighed. "They're probably sitting in a café in Ankara right now. And we've lost the expertise Yves would have brought to the Paris desk."

She still found it hard to swallow. "Why not hire a hit man here?"

"A Reuters correspondent in Vienna ended up the same way," he said. "He'd gotten too curious about the oil-field concessions in Dirhan and the Yellow Crescent's involvement." He sighed again. "The Turkish military send them in, the job is done, and they're on the next plane out."

"But how did your photographer threaten them?"

"Out in the field, Yves would have shared info with him, *non?*" Drieu's voice lowered. "I'm deeply sorry you didn't realize how dangerous Yves's work was."

After hearing about the chador on the riflewoman, she didn't buy the Yellow Crescent . . . unless they employed female assassins. Or wait. A man could use a chador as a disguise, too. Her hands clutched the phone. The security guard had seen the assassin in the chador. She needed to find him.

"We're having a little staff memorial at Le Vaudeville later," Drieu was saying. "Simple, just colleagues, but you're invited. And I'd like to apologize again for, well . . . jumping to a conclusion. It's better to say you're sorry in person."

It was kind of him to invite her.

"You'd make a good correspondent, Mademoiselle. Dogged, determined —"

"Like Yves," she interrupted.

He sighed. More deeply this time. "*Oui, like Yves.*"

"I'll attend the memorial, but, to tell you the truth, they sadden me."

"Me, too." Pause. "But I think I owe you at least a drink."

He'd softened, seeming less businesslike. Maybe she could get more out of him, some detail that he didn't realize he knew. "*D'accord,*" she agreed, and hung up.

She stared out the window at the shadows deepening on rue du Louvre. The penumbra of fading light softened the stone building edges, blurring their definition into a play of shadows. She reached inside her bag and fingered the worn Ottoman coins of the talisman. Yves's words came back to her: ". . . for vision, to see your way . . . prevent being blinded by obstacles and false paths."

She wished it would guide her.

She grabbed her scarf. "See you, René."

He frowned, putting down the take-out container. "Forgetting something?" He pointed to the bills on her desk. "We need the Microimages retainer, Aimée."

"Right. It's ready; I'll pick it up."

Doubt appeared on René's face. "You're sure? I realize you're shocked by Yves's murder . . . I'm sorry, but we've got a business to run."

"Don't worry, René," she said. "The retainer will cover those bills."

René grabbed his car keys. "Let me give you a lift."

Aimée picked up the signed Microimages consulting contract and retainer from the receptionist. On her way out of the courtyard, she stared at the spot where Yves had waited for her only two nights ago. She pictured his tanned face, his warm arms folding around her, could almost feel the tense energy in those arms.

She made her feet move, tried to repress the cascading memories of that night.

The loge of Mehmet, the Turkish concierge, was dark, the glass door padlocked. The man who boasted that he knew everyone in the quartier was gone. She headed to

René's car where he was parked down the street.

"Not bad, Aimée!" Holding the check, René whistled.

High praise from René.

"*Zut!* We've got to get to work monitoring his system tomorrow."

Always the worrier.

A child on rollerblades skated over the cobblestones. His father ran to catch up with him.

"Aimée, the real estate agent called," René said. "He can meet us right now."

She looked at him as he perspired in his linen suit and had a vision of the future. A gutted floor littered by plaster, electrical wires hanging, plumbers shaking their heads. A money pit. For once, she seemed to be the practical one. Or was she running from commitment? After losing Yves, nothing felt permanent.

"Have you decided to do this, René? Do you think you can pull it off?"

"It's an incredible opportunity. To buy in the center of Paris, put down roots and have ample space."

"But we could expand our office," she said. "The place next door still looks vacant."

He pulled out a pocket calculator, hit

some keys. "With the low interest rates, we'd pay less to own than to rent."

"I don't know if I can swing it," she said.

Or wanted to. She hesitated admitting to René that she liked rue du Louvre, liked working at her grandfather's old worn desk, even liked the temperamental elevator from the previous century.

"Let me factor in the upgrades, make an offer, and see if the seller bites."

So his mother and the comte had come through, she thought. Would this signal a parting of their ways? She suppressed that thought. Right now, she couldn't think of the future or worry about René if he was determined to go ahead.

"Why not come with me and take another look?" René itched to leave.

"Not tonight." She had other things to do. Things he wouldn't approve of.

"Do you feel all right?" René stared at her. "Grief comes in stages. You go through shock, denial, then comes anger. . . ."

"So it's nice and tidy, in that order?"

She got out and slammed the car door, her hands shaking. Then shame filled her for shouting at René.

"I'm sorry, René," she said. "I know you want to help."

He shrugged. "I'm your friend."

"My best friend," she said.

She had no time to deal with grief. Yves's killer, the assassin, was on the loose. "But right now, I've got things to do."

She hitched her bag onto her shoulder and took off down the rue de Paradis. She didn't look back. After a few minutes, she heard his car start and then drive away.

Aimée noticed the iKK — the Kurdish Workers Party — *affiches,* not even proper posters, like those she'd seen outside their office. Here they were taped on the exposed drainpipes running down the buildings, slapped on pebbledash walls in a crumbling passage between buildings. That much-copied photograph of piled Kurd bodies was chilling. It sickened her.

And she thought about the iKK members, seeking revenge. Or, for that matter, militant Turks, this Yellow Crescent, taking action to silence Kurds here, like Jalenka. She remembered René's comment . . . what better time to assassinate someone than when the authorities were preoccupied by incessant Metro bombings. Were these groups still condemned to play out the thousands of years of hostility?

She stopped at her goal on the rue de Paradis, the porcelain factory showroom, intent on questioning the guard, Vatel.

Inside the glass doors there was a lighted hallway. A guard sat at a distant desk. She waved and got his attention.

Disappointed, she recognized Nohant as he took his time lumbering down the hallway.

"The building's closed," he shouted through the glass door.

"I'm looking for Vatel; he working tonight?"

Nohant shook his head. "He's reassigned."

Merde! With her luck, in some suburb.

"Where?"

Nohant stood, hands on his hips. "What's it to you?"

"Don't you have a phone number?" She hated shouting like this.

He shook his head. "Time for my rounds."

"Please, I need to speak with him," she said. "Help me out, Nohant," she pleaded.

He hesitated. He pulled some cards from his pocket, rifled through them, and held one up to the glass. His Sarko Security card with logo, main office address, and a penciled-in address on Cour des Petites Ecuries. She grabbed a pen and copied it on her palm.

"Tell him thanks for the overtime, he'll understand," said Nohant, or at least that's what she thought he said.

Vatel stood in the locker room unzipping his jumpsuit as he watched the small *télé* on the table. "A news bulletin . . . reports indicate an attempt on the Turkish member of Parliament . . . linked to the series of Metro bombings . . . in this video obtained from the Institut Kurd. . . ."

His fingers froze.

A spiky-haired woman dived onstage and tackled Jalenka Malat. Shots rang out. Puffs of powdery dust erupted from the podium. Vatel recognized the impact thuds of bullets from a high-powered rifle.

The camera angle wavered. Then there were loud screams. Women were scrambling under the chairs. Then the scene erupted in confusion.

"According to our correspondent, Jalenka Malat survived. However, a staff member suffered a mortal wound."

Vatel's hands shook as he checked the cell phone Florand from the Brigade Criminelle had given him. Four messages.

Terror rippled his insides. Florand expected information. For all Vatel knew, he'd be waiting at his apartment with a one-way second-class ticket to Istanbul, demanding to know why he hadn't made contact.

And he'd known. But then he hadn't

expected that there was truth in Mehmet's rumor. Wrong, so wrong. A dead journalist, now the assassination attempt. He had to find some way to placate Florand. Only an idiot would blame the iKK. He'd find out about the Yellow Crescent. Only one person would know. He slammed his locker shut and ran out the door.

Wednesday Evening

Aimée called the number Nohant had displayed as she walked toward the Cour des Petites Ecuries.

"Sarko Security," answered a male voice.

"Monsieur Vatel, please," she said.

"He's off shift," a man said, young by the tone. "Can I help you?"

Missed him again!

"Who's this?"

She thought fast. "His girlfriend — well, ex-girlfriend. We're still speaking, but . . . I have to reach him!"

"I'd have to ask the boss."

"Do you have to go to all that trouble?"

"Monsieur Belfont at the main office should okay this first."

"But, I really need to speak with him," she interrupted. "Would you know — ?"

A loud buzzer in the background drowned out her words.

"Sorry, I'm resetting the alarm."

"Look, he kicked me out, I'm desperate, I need my things. Please!"

Pause.

"He just went out the back door."

"Merci."

Aimée hurried to the Cour des Petites Ecuries, a T-shaped passage which had held the former royal stables. The last rays of the sun shone, then sputtered into a fading twist of light swallowed by the shadowed corners.

Vatel had seen more than he'd disclosed . . . she'd bet money on it. If he remembered the chador-clad assassin, he'd know more. She might be able to discover a way to find her.

She passed Brasserie Flo, open windows revealing the dark mahogany art nouveau interior. Number 54, an old fur warehouse had arching iron struts and floor-height half-oval windows, towering over a turn in the passage. It housed architecture firms, designers, and *pret à porter* clothing manufacturers, more upscale than the off-the-rack wholesalers a few blocks away in the Sentier.

A man wearing a jumpsuit labeled Sarko Security rushed out of a door. Dark-haired, mid-twenties, with a thermos hanging from a strap around his shoulder. She recognized

Vatel, the Kurd Nohant had described. More muscular and trim than Nohant, an ex-Legionnaire by his stance, he could pass for European with his light green eyes. Men joined the Legion to erase their past and obtain new identities. What secrets did he hide?

"Monsieur Vatel?"

Startled, he looked her up and down. Something like recognition showed in his eyes.

"Do I know you?"

There was a roll to his syllables, a slight accent. Coolness emanated from the stone passage corners, an evening respite from the heat. Conversations drifted from the open windows above them.

"I'm Aimée Leduc," she said, showing her PI license. "Nohant, your co-worker, told me you worked here. By the way, he says thanks for the overtime. I'm here because I'd like to talk with you."

"Why?" He stepped back.

"You reported an attack that took place early Tuesday morning on rue de Paradis."

He stood in the half shadow. She couldn't make out his expression.

"You described the woman as tall, wearing a chador. What else do you remember?"

He shook his head. "Excuse me, but I'm late."

"If you could just —"

"I told the Brigade all I knew," he interrupted. "Why is it so important to you?"

He'd bolt in a minute if she didn't persuade him to talk.

"A man's body was found on rue de Paradis," she said, keeping her voice calm. "Yves Robert, an investigative journalist who'd covered the Kurds and written an exposé of the Yellow Crescent."

Vatel backed away. She'd touched a nerve.

"He knew of the plot to assassinate Jalenka Malat."

"None of this involves me," Vatel said. "I don't know why —"

"But it involves me. He . . . we'd gotten engaged," Aimée said. "I prevented Jalenka's assassination. . . ."

"You're the one!" he said, his voice just above a whisper.

So he'd heard.

"A woman in a chador killed Yves to silence him. His boss feels the Yellow Crescent's responsible. But I don't buy that. I think the same woman tried to assassinate Jalenka, failed, and got away. You're the only one who saw her. Will you talk to me now?"

He pulled his collar up, watched her as if

deciding. "*Non,* but I know someone you should speak to."

"Who's that?"

"Someone who knows." He glanced at the sports watch on his wrist. "You ready?"

"Oui."

"But I need to blindfold you when we get there."

"What?"

"There's a fatwa on him. He's in hiding." She tried to control her fear.

"Fatwa . . . you mean a contract?"

He nodded.

"But why, who — ?"

"You agree or not?" he interrupted.

What did she have to lose?

A cold draft swirled around Aimée's legs. She'd followed Vatel through several passages, keeping off the main boulevards. The last street they'd crossed had been rue du Faubourg Saint-Martin where the Mairie was located, a nineteenth-century spired confection more like a château than a city hall. A large remodeled warehouse fronted the street with a plaque on it: "Here Jews worked for the Occupiers. . . ." Before she could decipher the rest, Vatel gestured her forward.

"Close your eyes."

She complied and felt her arm clutched, heard a door buzz open, and then was escorted inside, a cloth tied around her eyes. In the darkness, for a moment, her bout with blindness came back to her . . . that helplessness, only able to rely on her senses. Stop it . . . she wasn't blind, could rip this cloth off any time. And she fully intended to, once she'd met whoever they'd come to see.

"He's supposed to have returned this afternoon," Vatel said.

"Who?"

"It's better you don't know," Vatel said. "But if anyone understands the Yellow Crescent, he does."

She stifled her unease. Better not to think she might be about to interview a wanted criminal while wearing a blindfold.

"You want to talk to him, too, don't you, Vatel?"

Vatel stopped suddenly, and she plowed into his shoulder. "Sorry."

"Keep quiet."

She shut up. Felt uneven cobbles under her feet, heard the creak of a door.

"There's a step down," he said.

Then they were inside a damp, mildew-smelling tunnel echoing with their footsteps. The creaking of a door. Now, fresh cool evening air brushed her arms and she heard the clink of cutlery, the hiss and spatter of frying food. A scent of cardamom and mint. More uneven cobblestones. Vatel halted. A faint buzz, then a door opened and a cold rush of rotten-smelling wood. A cavern? And then she felt a cloth being draped over her shoulders, brushing her ankles, fabric being stretched over her head, around her face.

"What's going on?" Stupid, trusting him. Had she let herself be kidnaped?

"You need to wear it, please . . . shh! Hold this."

She felt clumped fabric being placed in her hand. "Don't trip. We're going up stairs."

Even with her hand clutching the railing, she tripped several times mounting the steep winding staircase while swathed in the hot cloth.

She heard Vatel's knuckles knocking lightly. Then again. Quiet, except for the creaking of floorboards somewhere, the muted sounds of a violin on the radio, and a child's cry from somewhere below.

"Roj baş."

And then Vatel's arms ushered her forward. She knocked into what felt like a doorway, heard what sounded like windows cranking closed.

"Sit down here." She felt for a chair, with no success. She gathered the material and sat on the floor, cross-legged. A conversation ensued in a guttural language; Arabic, Turkish, she had no clue.

And then she smelled the acrid aroma of coffee and tobacco.

She felt the cloth over her eyes being untied, rubbed her eyes, and opened them. A black chador covered her; a veil covered her head and half her face. She sat on a red Kilim rug in a white-walled room, the only decoration a large black-and-white photo of a snow-capped mountain. A plugged-in high-end laptop stood on a table beside a French–Turkish dictionary and an open notebook. She turned to see a smiling bearded man, hook-nosed, with sharp brown eyes. He nodded. A hookah bubbled at his side. "Excuse the cloak and dagger, Mademoiselle. I apologize. But may I make one more imposition?"

Fluent non-accented French. Polite, almost academic.

She nodded, noticing another bearded man in the corner, sitting cross-legged, his eyes averted.

"May I see your ID? I'm not paranoid, I assure you," he said. "It's necessary."

306

She reached for her bag under the chador, found her *carte d'identité* and PI license. This slight exertion in the hot engulfing robe and stifling room made her light-headed.

"Merci," he said.

She reached to pull the veil from her head.

"Please, keep your hair covered," the man said, "if you don't mind. Some of us here follow the Koran in its strict interpretation."

"Of course," she said, feeling awkard. She didn't know the customs or etiquette. She'd probably violated a few Muslim precepts already.

Vatel placed a demitasse of steaming coffee on the floor by her, careful not to touch her hand. Then he sat across from her. She sipped it, the grounds sticking in her teeth. This man's face . . . something about his face seemed familiar. But she couldn't place it.

"What do I call you?"

"Kat. I hear you have questions," he said, then inhaled deeply from the hookah.

"And suspicions. Vatel said you have answers."

He shrugged and shot a glance at Vatel, who leaned forward staring intently at Kat.

"Experience has taught me a few things," Kat said. "In Istanbul, I lived under what amounted to house arrest, though the government called it 'security surveillance for my safety.' Here I hide in plain sight, Mademoiselle, do my work, blend in with others in the quartier, even visit cafés. Impossible for me in Istanbul. But more pertinent to you, I think . . ." he paused and tugged his beard, ". . . the Yellow Crescent hasn't made an attempt on my life in more than a year."

He'd got right to it.

"Meaning?"

"Vatel saw similarities between my situation and that of the murdered journalist," he said. "Let's say he has intimate knowledge of the Yellow Crescent's methods. However," he said, "I disagree with his conclusion. Their leader is Colonel Ehret. His secret military funding for hit teams has dried up. The Yellow Crescent operates by instilling fear; it does its dirty work in Turkey, not here. And professional killers leave no calling card or signature."

"Signature . . . I don't understand."

"A distinctive curling slit under the ear of their victims."

Yves's lifeless face, his slumped head, the knife curl and makeup behind his ear, flashed in front of her.

"Then how do you explain a Reuters correspondent in Vienna —"

"But that occurred more than a year ago."

"You're implying Yves's murder was deliberately made to look like Yellow Crescent's work?"

He took another drag from the hookah.

"By their enemies in the iKK Kurd party?" she asked.

"I don't think they'd kill a journalist who told their story, albeit from his own perspective." He shook his head. "He disagreed with the iKK's tactics, but it would do the party more harm than good to silence him. No one else had the courage to write an exposé of the Yellow Crescent."

That theory put her back to square one. Without a reason for Yves's or Langois's murder. Nowhere.

"Turkey's applying to the EU; everyone's on their best behavior." He gave a short laugh. "At least on the surface. This is not the time to dispatch contract killers to France. And your government desires the fat contracts —"

"What contracts?" she interrupted.

"For a start, dam construction and hydroelectric power plants to be built in the reclaimed Kurdish area."

"Jalenka mentioned Kurdish resettlement."

He nodded. "They resettle Kurds wherever it suits their policy."

Doubts stirred in her mind; the implications were too complex to understand quickly.

She glanced his way, then turned to Vatel, who'd remained quiet and attentive to this "hero." That bothered her. Now she finally realized. "But it was you who found Yves's body, wasn't it Vatel?"

He didn't deny it. The water in the hookah bubbled. The close air and dense heat were stifling her.

"You witnessed the murder! You saw the assassin! Why didn't you tell the Brigade?"

Vatel shook his head. "All I saw was a chador. I heard a scream," he said. "She was tall, that's all I remember. Then when I found him —"

"You saw the slash under Yves's ear."

"True. It was just like a Yellow Crescent murder," Vatel said. "To send a message to Kurds in the quartier. . . ."

"But would they hide behind the veil to kill?" Kat shook his head. "It's not their style. Or the iKK's."

Then who was the person who'd killed Yves, and tried to kill Jalenka, working for?

She pushed the folds of the chador back. "Yves's contact heard rumors at the mosque. The DST are trying to connect the assassination attempt to the Metro bombings."

"But the Shi'as are claiming responsibility for Jalenka's assassination attempt," he said, a calm authority in his voice.

She stiffened. "The Shi'as? How do you know?"

"The rumors are running rampant in the mosque and cafés. An Islamic jihad's forming. But, Mademoiselle, this is different."

"Shi'a Iranians against Kurdish Sunnis?" That's what Sacault had intimated?

"Ask me if I'd be surprised," he said.

She couldn't stem her curiosity. "And the fatwa on you?"

"Made me more important than I am. But a man cannot be too careful in his choice of enemies, as Oscar Wilde pointed out." He gave a little smile. "I'm just a scribbler who has written things that they deem offensive."

Now she recognized him. Kat Ahmet, the famous Turkish novelist who'd spoken at a UN Human Rights Watch meeting in Switzerland last week about Turkish atrocities against the Kurds. Amazed, she looked around at the simple, bare apartment.

"They banned your books in Turkey."

"Past tense," he said. "Due to worldwide sales, the London publisher's partner in

Ankara is publishing an English–Turkish edition. Me?" He gave a little shrug. "Now it's too embarrassing to eliminate me."

He took a sip of coffee, indicated that she should do the same. "Please, or it will get cold."

A curious mixture, this novelist: traditional customs, surprising open worldview, and with a connection to underground Turkey, as well as a fatwa against him.

"But you're not a Kurd; you're Turkish," she said.

He smiled. "That surprises you, I see. But my wife is Kurdish. You saved Jalenka Malat, Mademoiselle. That's why Vatel brought you here, and for that I must help you."

Surprised, she realized he trusted her.

"Can you point me to whoever murdered Yves?"

"Look at the contracts the French stand to gain. An investigative journalist worth his salt, as you say, would know about them. Would report them. But where are those stories?"

Mystified, she set the bitter coffee down. "By that, you mean . . . ?"

"Let me tell you the story of the famous cats in Van, a Kurdish city. All the white cats had one blue and one amber eye.

Remarkable, everyone said. Unique." He paused to inhale from the bubbling hookah. "Word spread throughout Turkey about the beautiful Kurdish cats. Poems and stories were written. These cats became famous."

There was a point to this, she assumed.

"But the government panicked. They weren't simply cats, you see; they were *Kurdish* cats. A symbol of the Kurds. And then one day, the cats disappeared. All of them."

She waited, wondering what conclusion he expected her to draw.

"There was no mention in the newspapers. Later, rumors floated that a garbage man, paid off by the military like everyone else, had poisoned hundreds of them."

Was he implying that Yves was dirty? Her eyes flashed. "You're saying Yves took bribes not to report . . . ?"

"I've offended you. Forgive me," he said. His eyes narrowed. He leaned forward. "I'm saying *someone* might have."

"Yves wrote articles supporting the Kurds. He produced an exposé of the Yellow Crescent," she said angrily. "There's another possibility. Say he'd found out who was taking bribes and somehow it involved these contracts."

There was a knock on the door. Then

another. "Now if you'll excuse me," Kat said.

Vatel motioned to her. Awkwardly, she rose to her feet despite the chador folds wrapped around her legs. The bearded man in the corner had not uttered a word. The short audience had ended, but still she had more to ask.

"One last question, please," she said. "I'm ignorant of your culture, but you said the Yellow Crescent wouldn't hide behind a woman's veil."

"No man in our culture would," he said. "I hope Vatel's convinced of that by now. Oh, Jalenka sent word to thank you."

"But the assassin may try again. Jalenka's not safe. She needs protection, security."

"The incident caused your authorities profound embarrassment, I know. If anything happened on French soil, there would be repercussions. But Jalenka hates security and evades it to meet with people. That's what happened today. . . ." His words trailed off. "However, the student. . . ."

"Iqbal?" she said. Feelings of guilt shot through her. "I feel responsible."

Kat raised his hand. "*Inshallah.* You did what you had to do."

"How do you know?"

"Watch the *télé,* Mademoiselle," he said.

314

"They're showing the video from Institut Kurd. You're on the news."

She didn't own a *téle,* or want one. Now here she was on the news with an assassin on the loose. A chill invaded her bones.

"There's something you should read."

His book? she wondered. But Kat motioned to Vatel, who stood, opened the Turkish–French dictionary, then took an envelope from inside the cover and handed it to her.

She stuck it in her bag.

"For your sake, I'd stay out of sight and never mention our little visit."

Vatel opened the door to a wizened man with a gray tonsure of hair. Ignoring the heat, he wore a sweater vest and wool trousers. He handed Kat several evening newspapers and then beckoned to Aimée, reached up, and tied the blindfold around her eyes again.

"I'll escort you, Mademoiselle," he said. A definite Yiddish accent.

"The blindfold's unecessary."

"*Desolé,* but that's how all monsieur's visitors arrive and leave."

At least she'd gotten a good look at the steep staircase to prepare herself. She reached one hand out to the worn railing, gathered up the chador in her other, and descended in total blackness.

"You work for him, Monsieur?" she asked softly.

"I protect him," he said.

Again, the rotting smell of age and decay reaching the bottom of the stairs. She wished the chador weren't so hot and awkward to manage. The old man guided her by touching her arm. Cold air radiated from the stone; there were smooth worn pavers under her feet. The clink of a door unlocking and then the pungent smell of sandalwood incense and what sounded like muffled Hindi coming from somewhere in the hallway. She heard the creak of a door. His hand guided her into a musty-smelling space. "Wait here for a moment, Mademoiselle, until it's safe to leave."

The blindfold was untied. She found herself in a neat narrow envelope of a room. A double-ring burner and plug-in Bodum kettle stood on a counter by the window; a faded brocade couch hugged the wall. The many framed photos on the ochre walls caught her eye. Black-and-white snapshots from the forties. Men in caps, women in wooden-soled platform shoes and turbans enfolding their hair, teenage boys wearing work aprons in what looked like a furniture warehouse. In the middle of the photos was a dried corsage wrapped in cellophane, browned stiff petals, tricolor ribbon hanging from it with the faded gold letters FFI.

"Quite a collection," she said. Like a shrine, she thought, but she kept that to herself.

He followed her gaze.

"I like to remember them. No one else does."

She stepped closer and stared. Now she noticed the yellow stars on the men's lapels and the women's sweaters, the uniformed Wehrmacht soldier to the side.

Her throat caught. "They worked in the quartier?"

"At Lévitan, next door. And at Bassano and Austerlitz, the other labor camps on the Left Bank."

She'd never heard of these camps.

"Labor camps? I had no idea."

"Few do. Under *L'Opération Meuble,* the *Boches* took skilled workers from internment camps: jewelers to repair clocks, artisans to restore furniture and musical instruments, women couturiers to bleach and press linens — you name it — all looted from Jewish *deportés* apartments."

"But why?"

"Goering needed to fill his boxcars at Gare de l'Est, *hein?* After 1943 it was not just paintings. His bombed-out *Vaterland* needed goods, and these were here for the taking."

In essence, a goods depot for the Third Reich.

He shook his head. "Quiet as it's been kept, on the outskirts of Paris there's still a warehouse with hundreds of pianos. All of them still tagged for Dusseldorf."

"More than fifty years later?" she asked, shocked. "How's that possible?"

"No one wants to know, no one knows how to deal with descendants, property claims and the lawsuits it would raise!"

He shuffled to the small oval window and looked out.

"And you, Monsieur, were you one of them?"

"A Resistant, if you call a fourteen-year-old that." He smiled tightly. "My mother was the concierge here. What better location for sabotage?"

She swallowed hard. "You didn't wear a yellow star?"

"I took it off for my courier jobs," he said, his voice matter-of-fact. "But just before Liberation, the *Boches* deported the last workers to Bergen-Belsen. That's when we set explosives in the Wehrmacht's barracks at Republique. You can still see the bullet holes in the walls."

The old, sad stories of the Occupation. One never got away from them, she thought. For him, the place was redolent of memories.

"Yet you stay here, Monsieur, and help Kat. Why, may I ask?"

"Things never change, do they? He's in hiding."

"And you're saving him, like you tried to save them?"

The small wizened man edged the door open. "It's safe for you to leave now, Mademoiselle."

Aimée set the chador on a hook near an age-speckled beveled mirror.

"You won't visit again, eh, Mademoiselle?"

She shook her head.

Outside, on the limestone façade she saw a plaque about Camp Lévitan and knew she'd been in part of the warren of buildings behind it. Not that she'd ever be able to find this place again. Or want to.

She kept to the shadows and turned right into rue du Chateau d'Eau. The streetlight illuminated a building plaque. Jean Cazard and Pierre Chatenet, both eighteen years old and members of the Red Cross, shot by Germans, August 18, 1944. Just days before the Liberation. There were fresh lilacs in a vase fastened to the plaque. She shivered and hastened her steps. The past clung to these cobblestones and buildings as if it were just yesterday.

She walked and walked. Past the yawning, dark windows of vacant *hôtel particuliers* with chipped cornices, and bearded men clustered on the street, prayer beads clicking through their fingers. She considered the words of the novelist. A different network, the attempt to assassinate Jalenka a jihad, Shi'as against Sunnis . . . the more she learned, the more questions arose. Hoping to clear her mind, she kept walking and found herself on Place de la Bourse, opposite the stock exchange and the Agence France-Presse building, the purple awning of Brasserie Le Vaudeville on her right. Once a theater bar, it was now patronized by stockbrokers, journalists, and taxi drivers.

Maybe she'd intended to come here all along, to take a step and ascend the ladder of grief, following the steps René had pointed out she needed to tread. Anger only got her so far.

She'd pump Drieu for information about contracts France stood to gain in the Kurdish territories.

■ ■ ■ ■

"*Bonsoir.*" A smiling black-suited maître d' flicked his gaze over her. "You're joining someone, Mademoiselle?"

"Monsieur Gerard Drieu with Agence France-Presse."

"His table's this way." The headwaiter guided her under the art deco domed ceiling, past the etched glass and intricate ironwork decor. A pianist played an old Charles Aznavour song to the accompaniment of low murmured conversations and the clink of glasses. Small white candles flickered on the white linen tablecloths. At the table by the window, swirling a snifter of brandy, was the man whom Langois had referred to as the "attending" in the AFP newsroom cubicle. The balloon glass of amber liquid caught the light.

"Take a pew," he said.

She sat on the leather banquette, not knowing what to say. Her feet ached from walking, fatigue made her shoulders ache, and her skin still burned with the memory of the heavy, thick chador.

"Mademoiselle?" said a waiter who'd appeared without a sound at her elbow.

"I'll have the same, *merci.*"

"You missed the memorial. Drieu got a phone call, an emergency. He sends his apologies."

She glanced at the time. Too late to call him with the questions Kat had raised. But maybe this man might furnish some answers.

She shook his hand. "I'm Aimée."

"Georges." He raised his brandy snifter. His red-rimmed eyes behind tortoiseshell glasses, sunken cheeks, and gray hair gave him a vulnerable look. "You're the one Yves talked about."

"He did?" Pain rubbed her raw. She shouldn't have come. And she longed for the brandy to hurry up.

"A pitiful good-bye, eh?" He rotated the brandy snifter again, watching the amber liquid swirl in a vortex. "Half of the newsroom's off, the other half stopped in, then left. Not like the old days when there would have been a good send-off, but then, what is? My retirement's in two days. Officially, on Friday. I'll be lucky if anyone shows up."

Her brandy appeared on the table in front of her.

"Salut." He clinked her glass with his.

"When did you last talk with Yves?"

"Monday. As usual."

Surprised, she leaned forward. "You're

sure? Wasn't the staff meeting on Tuesday night?"

"Yves didn't show up."

"But what did he do on Monday?"

"I saw him in the office."

"At what time?"

He shrugged. "Just before I left."

"And that was?"

"Around ten."

Just before he'd met her in the Microimages courtyard. So he'd gone to AFP after Langois left, and before meeting her.

"Did Yves have anything with him?"

"I'm not sure," he said, then paused in thought. "A laptop."

"Neither Drieu nor Langois mentioned it."

"Eh, why would they?"

"I don't understand. According to Yves, he'd been transferred here."

"There's been a big shuffle. 'Reorganization,' that's the term for layoffs these days," he said. "They were kicking Yves upstairs. The award, for excellence in the field, you know? We're a news service, we provide in-depth coverage for dailies and the weeklies that don't have correspondents in the area. It's cheaper for everyone. And Yves was a star. He could work a bureau desk as well as report from the field. Only a few can do that . . . could. . . ."

Georges's mouth sagged. Small licks of candlelight reflected in his glasses. She still didn't follow, and he still hadn't answered her question.

"I pulled an early shift Monday." He shrugged. "Yves wasn't due until Tuesday. He surprised me. I don't know who else saw him."

She had to try another tack.

"Did you read the exposé Yves filed on the Yellow Crescent?"

"You're not drinking." He pointed to her brandy.

She took a sip. The liquid burned her throat, leaving a toasty aftertaste.

"You're chasing phantoms. He's gone."

She pushed away the horrible feeling that his words were true.

"But didn't you see the article?" she asked again.

Georges shook his head. "Like I said, he stopped in and then I went off shift. He sat down to file his story as I left."

"Then where's his laptop?"

"If he didn't take it with him, it's still there."

She clenched the glass stem tight.

"Where?"

"He used the night editor's office."

She leaned back, a plan forming in her mind. Then took a deep gulp.

"*Alors,* I've had too much of this," Georges said, pulling out his wallet. "And my bus line stops running in twenty minutes."

"And Gerard Langois?"

"A kid, full of promise. I met him for the first time on Tuesday night. . . ." Georges's words trailed off.

A sad, tired older man.

"As a favor, do you mind checking out the night editor's desk?" She pulled a card from her bag, pushed it over the white tablecloth into his hands. "See if you can get me a copy of his story. Or anything else he filed."

"Why?"

"It may have gotten him killed, Georges. That's why."

"You have to let this go. Let him go."

"What do you have to lose, Georges? You're retiring. Help me out. Dig around a bit."

She pressed her card into his hand. At least he didn't give it back.

"This should cover the tab." He set a fifty-franc bill on the table, shaking his head. "Digging around won't bring him back, Aimée." A wistful look appeared in his tired eyes. "No wonder you're all he talked about."

The waiter slid another cognac in front of her. "But I didn't order . . ."

"From the gentleman over there," said the waiter, lifting his eyebrows. "He'd like to join you."

A man standing at the bar raised his glass. Tousled long black hair, fashionable stubble on his chin, lean, in white linen shirt and trousers. A hunk, he could have stepped off the cover of the August *Vogue Homme.*

"Tell the gentleman . . ."

Drieu appeared and slid onto the leather banquette across from her.

". . . *Merci,* but I have company."

The man at the bar shrugged, then grinned.

"Lucky I didn't miss you," Drieu said. "We've had a crisis at work."

"What's happened?"

"Haven't you seen this?" Drieu set down a copy of *Le Figaro.* "Marseilles airliner suspect caught in Lyon. President Chirac deploys army."

"Monsieur Drieu —"

"Please, call me Gerard," he interrupted. "No corroboration for our stringer's story, big legal ramifications." He shook his head. "Shop talk. Sorry, I'll stop."

But he'd set her thinking. "How many sources are required for a news story?"

"To verify?"

The waiter appeared.

"Monsieur?"

"A Vichy water, *s'il vous plait.*"

Drieu turned his attention back to her. She noticed the graying at his temples. Older than she'd thought, early forties maybe. "A minimum of two," he said. "At least that's our requirement."

"So Yves would have needed two people to verify his exposé of the Yellow Crescent?"

"That doesn't sound like a question," he said with a tired smile. "But to anticipate your next question, at legal admin's insistence, all files concerning Yves were routed to the Brigade."

She blinked. For once, Rouffillac seemed to have been on the ball.

"His articles too?"

"That part, well, I know I said I'd look; but with the pressure I've been under at work, I haven't had time to check."

She had Yves's draft, which Langois had given her. She hesitated to give it back. Yves had written it, touched it, spilled his coffee on it, and she couldn't bear to part with it. Yet.

"Langois's parents called from the

morgue. . . . Terrible," Drieu said. "Their only son."

Aimée didn't know what to say.

With a deft movement, the waiter flicked the metal bottle cap off and set the moisture-beaded Vichy water on the table. He poured it into a tall glass and discreetly disappeared.

"You don't drink?"

"Not when I've got forest fires to put out." He took a sip, then met her eyes. "I feel guilty."

That he'd bought the idea that Yves had gone with a male hustler? That he hadn't accessed Yves's work? Or something else?

"How's that?"

"I pride myself on listening. Actively listening, helping journalists. One referred to me as a father figure, but with Yves. . . ." He let out a small sigh. "He followed his own path. But I should have tried harder."

"You mean in Ankara?"

"Yves worked in the field. He kept saying we needed to talk . . . but I didn't push it, and that time never came."

"But in that climate. . . ."

Drieu shook his head. "I was Admin chief for the Middle East bureau. Still, I should have been more on top of things." He sat back, his eyes somewhere else. "But last

328

month my wife had an accident." He spoke in halting phrases, ". . . run over . . . in front of the house."

She remembered Langois's words. Drieu's wife had walked out on him and then been hit by a truck.

"I'm so sorry," Aimée said.

"I sympathize with you," he said, sighing. "When it's sudden, the loss is almost worse."

He exuded a warmth she hadn't felt before. Yes, he was a person one could talk to. And feel that he listened. But the cognac was making a mist of her thoughts.

"Did Yves ever talk about an Iranian Shi'a agenda involving the assassination of a Kurdish member of Parliament?"

He shrugged. "You asked me this before. But then, I'm in admin. Yves's senior editor's in Brussels covering a conference. From what I've heard, the Brigade's in contact with him."

Score another one for Rouffillac.

But Drieu must know something. She tried again. "Or did you discuss French government contracts for projects in Turkey?"

"What do you mean?"

She didn't know what she meant; she was fishing.

"Articles he might have written concerning French contracts with the Turkish government that have not been picked up by the news wires."

Drieu ran his finger around the glass's edge. "I could put in a research department request. They have access to our complete database. It might take time. And that's if he filed such stories. But why do you ask?"

For a moment she felt guilty about pressing him. After all, his job dealt with the administration side. And he was doing her a big favor to even offer to make a request to the research department.

Aimée said, "A source suggested to me that there may have been payoffs to keep these stories from appearing in the press."

Drieu's brows knit. "You know what you're saying?"

"All I'm saying —" She paused, realizing she was asking a lot of Drieu, asking for information that even Georges had refused to give her.

"You want me to point a finger at a colleague or a senior staff member," Drieu said. "And on what basis?"

He'd thought about it, she could tell. He hadn't mentioned the Yellow Crescent threat again.

"If I had proof, I wouldn't ask you."

He sipped his Vichy water.

"Forgive me for insisting." He must think she was obsessed. "But if a French firm stood to gain by relocating the Kurds and offered a bribe to suppress this information . . . ?"

His cell phone beeped, but he ignored it. "I imagine there's a long line waiting for the Kurds to relocate: Germans, French, Swedes. You could point to any of them. There's strong international competition for lucrative contracts But . . ." he paused, "Yves threw himself into his work with a passion. I don't need to tell you, but it's just a feeling . . . hard to pinpoint, but I felt that, along the way, Yves became disenchanted."

"Disenchanted?"

"With the Kurds, not with their cause but with their tactics."

His cell phone kept beeping. He shrugged. "Excuse me. I have to answer this."

Yves's words came back to her: *Nothing prepares you for . . . the red dust, baking heat, and the refugees . . . the children are the worst.*

After a terse conversation, Drieu hung up.

"I'm sorry, now there's a firestorm raging at work . . . I've got to go."

He stood up and took her hand in his

warm one. She wished instead that it was Yves's comforting grip. But it never would be again.

Wednesday Night
"*Desolé,* Monsieur Friant," said Boutarel, the real estate agent. He flicked his cell phone closed, then wiped a handkerchief over his brow. His seersucker jacket hung over his arm; a binder was held in his hand. "The owners received a higher offer half an hour ago."

René's shoulders sagged. The nineteenth-century building, its lighted windows like eyes, was out of his reach. Like everything else.

"We can raise your offer and see if it will be considered," he said. "But there are no guarantees."

If only he'd trusted his instinct, convinced Aimée, made a higher offer even though he didn't have the necessary capital.

"Let's keep in touch." The real estate agent shook his hand and then his footsteps echoed on the cobbles.

Dejected, René headed to his car. A motorcycle whined past. Patrons left the cafés closing along the dimly lit boulevard; a waiter was stacking rattan café chairs when a young woman bumped into René.

"Pardonnez-moi," she said. Her blond shag-cut hair was at odds with an olive complexion. She wore a lime tank top and jeans. A backpack hung from her shoulders. She stood close, a head taller than him, and her arm brushed his. "I'm looking for the New Morning."

"The jazz club?" René asked.

"I love jazz." She smiled. A bright smile for that time of the evening.

"Just around the corner. Look." René pointed toward an unprepossessing metal door on rue des Petites Ecuries, the old haunt of Chet Baker and Miles Davis.

For a moment, he had the strangest feeling that she was trying to pick him up. It didn't happen often. Flattered, he was about to show her the way when a foyer light blinked on. Two laughing couples spilled from the apartment building, crowding the pavement near them. The couples engaged in multiple cheek-kissing and loud good-nights with promises to meet tomorrow, punctuated by gusts of pungent red wine. And then René realized she'd gone, turned the corner.

Disappointed for the second time that night, he reached into his linen jacket pocket for his keys. He clutched them, and then reached for the money clip in his inside jacket pocket. Gone.

She was good. He wanted to kick himself. A professional pickpocket.

He hurried to the corner, ignoring the sharp pain in his hip. The humid dampness exacerbated his hip dysplasia, the curse of dwarfism. A line coiled out the New Morning Club door. He heard the moan of a saxophone and thrum of a snare drum but saw no blond in line or on the street.

From past experience, he'd kept his *carte d'identité* and credit cards in a pouch inside his trousers. He took precautions even with his black belt. Late night invited thugs eager to pick on someone smaller than themselves.

Chalk it up to a pretty face and his distraction. Dumb. Weary, he pulled the Citroën in front of the ATM near his street to get cash. Only then did he realize that his business cards were gone, too.

Wednesday Night

Nadira climbed the narrow spiral staircase. A single naked bulb cast a harsh light over the warped landing illuminating the business card she held in her hand. It read, LEDUC DETECTIVE, 18 RUE DU LOUVRE. No wonder, she thought. The woman was a detective. And now a plan formed, almost by itself, in her head. Easy.

She rapped on the third door. "Mouna?"

She heard shuffling, then the door edged open. A dark-eyed smiling woman wearing a head scarf stood in the doorway. Light behind her revealed a yellow-walled room and a galley kitchen with a beaded curtain separating the rooms.

"I knew you'd do it, Nadira." She reached out and grasped Nadira's cold hands, pulling her inside. "You've left him this time, haven't you?" The question hovered in the rose-water-tinged air of the apartment. A photo of the bearded imam and gold verses from the Koran embroidered on maroon velvet were framed on the wall. Doors led to other rooms where Mouna's family slept.

"This time for good, Mouna," Nadira said. She gave a little sob and rubbed her eyes.

Mouna wanted to help. Needed to help. That formed the core of her being. She was determined to succor Nadira, to rescue her from an abusive boyfriend. A French boyfriend, an infidel. Mouna believed the tales Nadira had fed her after the Koran study meetings at the mosque.

"I have nowhere else to go, Mouna," she said.

Helpless. Mouna needed to see her helpless. Desperate.

"I left him. But with no job. . . ."

"Sit down, Nadira." Mouna gestured to the low cushions on the floor. Next to them lay a leather-bound Koran and a small turquoise-green Egyptian glass kohl bottle. "We'll help you."

"Does your brother Rachid still work at the hotel?"

"He's been promoted. Now he's at the front desk." Mouna squeezed Nadira's shoulders, a smile of pride on her round face. "He'll find you a position. They're always short-staffed, especially now."

Perfect.

"Nadira, think of this as your home. Haven't I told you before that you could always stay here?"

Nadira brushed away her tears, careful to set down her heavy pack holding the rifle parts before Mouna could take it. "You're so good-hearted, Mouna. I mean it this time. It's over."

"The Koran teaches us, Nadira. Allah's words tell us to aid those in need. My sister will sleep with me. You can have her place."

"*Merci,* Mouna."

"You're safe, Nadira. He won't find you here."

Nor will anyone else, Nadira thought.

Wednesday Midnight

Aimée leaned against the Napoleon-era headboard with its bee motif. Miles Davis was snoring beside her on the bed's folded-down duvet. Despite the algae-scented breeze rising from the moonlit Seine, the smooth cotton sheets, and a glass of chilled Volvic water, nothing alleviated her feeling of hollowness.

The effects of the brandy she'd consumed earlier that evening had worn off. She tried to clear her mind and concentrate on the night sounds: the rustling leaves of the plane trees lining the quai, the wavelets from a passing barge slapping on the stone bank. But clarity eluded her.

She stared at the amulet, the embroidered cloth with worn Ottoman coins, wondering what to do next.

Drieu said Yves had grown disenchanted with the Kurds. She suddenly remembered the envelope Kat had given her. She sat up and found it in her bag. Opening it, she saw a stapled Amnesty International report filled with pages of Kurdish refugee stories. Horrific testimonies of destroyed villages and inhabitants fleeing Turkish military forces. A photograph of a woman's dirt-stained, ravaged face as she sat in the medical tent. What Aimée read shook her. "My eyes saw only the past. The memories of the apricot tree, the branches heavy with fruit, an entire kilo in one cluster as my grandfather would say. I was sitting on the steps of the house my grandfather had built, holding the keys to a house that no longer existed, broken stones and dirt now all that was left. Why does the world not witness this genocide?"

She tried to understand why a Shi'a Muslim group would try to kill a Sunni Muslim woman who stood for Kurdish rights. And what reason might they have had for murdering Yves?

Both the Sunnis and Shi'as were Muslim, but they were divided. What made them different? She pulled her father's robe around her and went to the library, a high-ceilinged room she seldom used, lined by bookshelves filled with musty volumes and a complete set of Michelin guides from 1945 through 1990. The sagging chandelier emitted a dim light; all but two bulbs had burned out. Too bad she didn't have a ladder. She found the thick leather-bound book about world religions next to a much-thumbed copy of the Civil Code 1956.

She lugged it to her bed and lay back next to a sleeping Miles Davis. Islam comprised a fat chapter. After skimming several pages, she found the basic explanation. Islam was founded by Mohammed in the seventh century and evolved into two branches, Sunnis and Shi'as.

The Sunnis believed that the first four caliphs — Mohammed's successors — took his place and that the heirs of each of the four caliphs were legitimate religious leaders, while the Shi'as believed that only the heirs of the fourth caliph, Ali, were legitimate successors to Mohammed.

Was this at the root of their division? She read further. In theory, Sunnis believed that the leader — imam — should be selected on the basis of communal consensus as to a leader's individual merits, while the Shi'as believed that it was the line of imams descended from Ali who had the right to interpret religious, mystical, and legal knowledge to the broader community. The most learned among these teachers were known as ayatollahs and mullahs.

Were these differences so great that each side of the schism hated the other? But then was that so different from the sects of Judaism, of Christianity, or of Buddhism?

None of this told her what the current Shi'a and Sunni conflicts were about.

The phone rang once. Stopped. Then rang three times. Apprehensive, she let her voicemail answer. She heard René's voice being recorded.

"Aimée, if you're still up. . . ."

As if she could sleep. She picked up the phone.

"You're home?" René asked. "Everything okay?"

She stared at the amulet in the duvet folds. She wished it was. "*Oui,* René," she told him.

"The owner took another offer, Aimée," said René. She heard the disappointment in his voice.

She stifled her relief. "I'm sorry."

"No, you're not," he said.

She had rarely known him to be so disappointed.

"You're a typical Parisian, content to rent and pay the landlord's mortgage."

Typical? Anything but. A misfit, like René. An outsider. She had a mother she didn't know and had been raised by a father who'd done his best, between police stakeouts, to pick her up after school.

But she didn't want to argue. The selfish part of her felt glad he'd missed out. The other part was sorry it hadn't worked out for him.

"Other opportunities will arise, René," she said. "The right place and the right time will dovetail."

He snorted. "Fine for you to say, you own —"

"Correction, *inherited* my grandfather's apartment," she said. "Along with the seventeenth-century plumbing, archaic electrical fuses, a chandelier I can't reach to replace the bulbs, and holes in the wall that I can't afford to pay my contractor to close."

A siren wailed in the background. She sensed that something else underlay his anger.

"What's wrong, René?"

"If I tell you, you'll say it's a good thing the offer didn't work out, that the area's dicey. . . ."

"What happened?"

There was a brief silence. "A pickpocket. Professional," he finally said.

Her anger mounted. This wasn't the first time. She hated that thieves picked on René.

"How much?"

"Not important."

"Did he hurt you?"

"The disturbing part is that my business cards are gone," he said. "And it was a woman. But that's not why I called. Remember the Fontainebleu problems? I found the new receptionist who fell for the trick —"

"Why do I feel you're really calling about something else, René?"

He drew a breath. "To safeguard the account, I could set up a proxy server, register a domain by entering a fake credit card number and address. The usual."

"For Fontainebleu? That requires time and work."

Light years ahead of the hacker pack, he still amazed her. She heard him clicking the keys. Then a pause.

"Regarding Fontainebleu, simple works best," she said. "Just as you always say. Give her a lesson, security 101."

She heard him sigh. But the idea intrigued him. He loved to crack puzzles.

"You're magic at security, René."

"It's not just that. I'm worried about the security services tracking you."

"That's at the bottom on my list, René," she said. "I met the rue de Paradis security guard, Vatel, a Kurd —"

"Didn't the DST warn you off in no uncertain terms?" he interrupted. "Aimée, it sounds to me like you're forgetting the Microimages IT consulting contract. And that you should rest."

The gauze curtains shifted in the night breeze. Miles Davis stirred in his sleep. No use arguing with René at this time of night.

"Pas du tout," she said, feeling her forehead. No fever. The chills were gone. "To-

morrow I'll start at Microimages and check on their terminal connections and file sharing."

The most lucrative and boring aspect of their service.

"Let me try a dial-up trick and see what I can do," he said.

"Why?"

"You could work from home."

That's what this was about.

"You need to be careful, Aimée. That woman's a killer and she's still on the loose."

As if she needed René to remind her.

Thursday Morning

Aimée walked Miles Davis along the quai on Ile Saint-Louis below her apartment. The air was still thick with heat. Parched plane trees, dappled with sunlight filtering through their dense green leaves, reminded her of Renoir's riverside scenes of long-ago afternoons at the turn of the century, of riverside escapes from the heat outside Paris. But there was no escape for her, she had work to do.

In the apartment she switched on the wire-framed fan. It sputtered to life. Warm currents of air swirled through her high-ceilinged apartment, but at least Miles Davis would stay cooler.

She needed to stop at the office of Leduc Detective before heading to Microimages. Down in the courtyard, she unlocked her bike from the grille surrounding the ancient pear tree, set her bag in the wire-frame basket, wheeled the bike over the cobbles to the massive entry door, and rode down the quai.

Crossing the Pont Marie, she passed open-topped tour buses whose occupants, tourists, were fanning themselves in the heat. A silver ripple of water fanned from the police diver battling the Seine current, swimming ahead of a Zodiac river police launch. Couples sat, legs dangling from the stone bank, under the shade of the plane trees.

As she unlocked Leduc Detective's frosted-glass-paned door, she heard the phone ringing. She reached it on the sixth ring.

"Leduc Detective," she said, catching her breath.

"I know who slit your friend's throat on rue de Paradis," said a singsong mechanical voice. A computer-generated voice.

Aimée gripped the receiver. She wondered how he'd obtained her number. Then she remembered the *télé* coverage.

"So tell me," she said.

"Bring a thousand francs to 108, rue du Faubourg Saint Denis."

"Not so fast; how do I know — ?"

"The swirled cut under his ear," the strange voice interrupted. "Noon."

Then he hung up. Was this the break she was looking for? Or a setup? Only one way to find out.

In the back of the armoire, she located her father's old bulletproof vest, pulled a jean jacket over it, knotted a scarf, and called René.

"René, still have that Glock 19?"

"I'm in a meeting, Aimée, hold on," he said, lowering his voice. She heard the scrape of a chair and, a moment later, what sounded like the gurgle of a water cooler. "You mean the one you lent me?"

"Right. Have you gone target-shooting?"

"Every week," he said, suspicious. "Why?"

"I've got a lead to Yves's murderer. In two hours at 108 rue du Faubourg Saint Denis, but I'd feel safer with backup."

"Wait a minute, we're running a business. Aren't you working from home?"

She reached in her desk drawer, found the Beretta and tucked it beside the mascara in her bag.

"I'm en route to Microimages. If you can't come, that's fine."

345

"Wait. . . ." Pause. "But what should I do?" he asked.

She told him.

Inside Microimages' sandblasted stone reception area, Aimée waited on a zebra-print-covered chair under a Venetian glass chandelier. The receptionist, wearing a '60s orange floral print dress and clear Lucite sandals, looked up and smiled.

"Go in, Michel's expecting you."

Michel's cavernous office overlooked the courtyard. He nodded, a cell phone to one ear, a landline receiver cupped to the other. He wore a camouflage green tank top and three-quarter-length striped pants. "I'm closing a big deal," he whispered. He motioned her toward several computer terminals facing the window. "Go ahead."

Aimée got to work. She had to keep her mind on the Microimages consulting job, make her high-paying client her priority. She had to force herself to focus on the work at hand and not on the phone call made by someone using a computer-generated voice.

She performed a routine check on Michel's terminal connections. The systems ran smoothly. Michel sat hunched over the phones, taking part in a low murmur of conversation punctuated by a *zut* every so often. By the time she'd checked the server connections in the other offices, the clock read 11:30. Back in Michel's office, she slipped on the bulletproof vest, then shrugged into her jean jacket over it.

"Cool fashion statement, Aimée," Michel grinned. "Part of Lagerfeld's fall line? The urban guerrilla look, right?"

If only he knew. She smiled.

"But I'd need your tank top to complete it, Michel."

She walked to the courtyard and peered into the concierge loge. Again it was dark, no Mehmet in sight. She tried to ignore the pang in her heart as she passed the spot where Yves had waited for her. But it wouldn't go away.

She gripped her bike's handlebars, heading to the street.

Passing the Gare de l'Est, Aimée remembered her grandfather's visits to the World War I memorial inside on Veterans' Day, the bouquet of white chrysanthemums he'd leave every year. He'd fought in the Verdun trenches, but never spoke about it. Her father once said that her grandfather had shipped out from the platform at the Gare de l'Est on the troop train a young man, and returned to the same platform an old one.

Past the Gare de l'Est, at the Paribas cash machine, she withdrew five hundred francs. Before she got the rest, she'd see if the information was good. The intersecting boulevards and cobbled streets, buildings adorned by wrought iron balconies and blue-gray roof tiles, reminded her of Caillebotte's paintings of this quartier. His quartier.

A few minutes early, she walked her bike past a glassed-in Alsatian restaurant on rue du Faubourg Saint Denis. The street displayed few vestiges of its former glory, when it had been the ancient royal route to the tombs at Saint Denis. Now there were mostly rundown seventeenth-century townhouses broken up into cell phone shops, cafés, and small grocers at street level. She kept alert, noticing lunchtime workers exiting the scrollwork door of the townhouse opposite Number 108. It was exquisite, whole, and in the process of a facelift. Gray netting covered the partial scaffolding that started at the first floor.

Uneasy, she watched each passing face for a look or nod of recognition. None came. There was no sign of René, either. She drummed her chipped red nails on her bike's handlebars. Still a minute to go. She took out her lock, ready to chain the bike to an exposed drainpipe.

A few women carrying bag lunches headed for the park, once the site of the infamous Saint Lazare women's prison. Anxious, realizing she was standing there exposed and without backup, she wondered why the caller hadn't suggested an indoor café out of public view. Already she could hear René's words . . . a wild-goose chase. A sixth sense impelled her to cross the street.

As she took her first step into the gutter, a whizzing passed her ear, then she felt as if she'd been punched in the chest. She jerked from the shot's impact, gulped for air and saw the small black hole in her vest. The chrome metal of her bike handlebars cracked and split. Pinging sounds erupted all around her. The shots came from a high-powered rifle equipped with a silencer.

She dropped and rolled on the pavement as another shot peppered the limestone façade. Grit and a fine sand dust spit over her face as she reached for her Beretta. The window shattered behind her. A woman screamed. The grocer weighing lemons outside his shop tipped the scale and ducked. Lemons scattered, tumbling over the cobblestones.

Aimée saw the gray mesh of the second floor scaffolding quiver. *She* was there. In broad daylight. The assassin. And Aimee had walked into her trap right on a busy street.

She realized René was at her side now, firing his Glock at the scaffold.

"Aimée, you okay?"

A man yelled and ran into the restaurant.

The shots had ceased. Trembling, she nodded and pulled herself up, wincing at the pain in her chest. Several car alarms had gone off and a child wailed in the distance. She thrust down her fear.

"Either she fled over the scaffolding or you hit her," Aimée said, breathing hard. "I've got to get up there."

"But. . . ."

"I'll get her this time, René. Call for backup. Hurry!"

She took off across the street, barreled past two women cowering in the doorway, and ran inside. Breathless, her heart pumping, she ran up the wide period staircase.

Lemairé, *Parurier de création — Plumes — Fleurs,* read an old-fashioned sign on the only doors on the second floor, double doors. She pressed the buzzer, then pounded on the door until it opened.

"We're closed for lunch," said a man wiping his mouth with a napkin. He peered at her through reading glasses perched on the bridge of his nose. The strains of Vivaldi's *Four Seasons* came from inside.

"Security!" She edged past him, stumbling into the white-paneled, gilt-trimmed hall of what had been an apartment. High-ceilinged rooms branched out from the hall. In them were marble fireplaces and work tables laden with beaded fabric, silk flowers. Built-in drawers stood open from which spilled peacock feathers.

"What's the meaning of this?" He grabbed her arm. The Vivaldi was louder now.

"You have a sniper!"

He snorted. "We do haute couture."

Framed *Elle* magazine covers lined the walls. Articles on Chanel's fall look with winter-white feathers accompanied them.

"You're deranged," he said, digging his fingers into her arm. "There's no one here beside me." His eyes widened as he saw the Beretta in her hand. "I'm calling the *flics*."

"You do that."

She shook his hand off, broke away, and ran toward a closed door at the end of the hall, clutching the Beretta. She opened the door. Inside the darkened, vacant workroom, tables strewn with beaded and feathered silk, the window stood open. A lace

351

curtain fluttered. She crouched and crawled to the window. The mesh around the scaffolding made a pattern of small sun-filled rectangles. She saw no one.

Had she lost her again? In the dim light, Aimée's eyes focused. The gold-edged mirror over the marble fireplace reflected strewn ribbons of lace, reams of ecru silk, feathery ostrich plumes — and another door. She reached for its handle, turned it slowly and opened it.

Inside, she saw what had once been a walk-in linen closet of a size most Parisians would feel lucky to have for a bedroom. Shelves above her were stacked with cream-colored lace fabrics. On the floor there were spent shell casings. And then she noticed a ray of light coming from a door that was ajar. The hair rose on the back of her neck.

She prayed her hands wouldn't shake, aimed the Beretta and nudged the door open with the toe of her black pump. A blast of sunlight blinded her. As her eyes became accustomed to the light, a drop of several stories was revealed. An old metal staircase led down to a dank space between buildings. She edged onto the staircase and looked down. It was empty.

The woman had gotten away. Again. Aimée ran, heels clattering on the metal stairs, to reach the unevenly paved concrete space between the buildings. Green garbage bins stood in a line by a door leading to the courtyard.

Her cell phone vibrated in her pocket.

"Mademoiselle Leduc?" asked Rouffillac. "We're outside on rue du Faubourg Saint-Denis."

"Thank God, but you have to hurry!"

"We're handling the situation. The situation's under control."

There were confused raised voices in the background.

"She almost killed me, Rouffillac," she said. "She's getting away."

"We received an anonymous phone call concerning a shooting. But it seems the owner of a haute couture atelier wants to press charges . . . breaking and entering . . . calls you delusional."

"What? There are shell casings in a closet of the atelier, if you don't believe me. Meanwhile. . . ."

"Come downstairs. Leave your weapon —"

"Listen, Rouffillac, the assassin's escaping."

"You're disrupting a highly sensitive operation in progress," he said. "Consider this your second warning."

Merde! Rouffillac must have a SWAT team on the stairs if he'd given her a second warning.

"Mademoiselle, you're in defiance of my order. You can explain the rest from a cell at the Brigade."

She clicked off and turned the door knob. Locked!

Thursday Morning

Nadira tucked her maid's cap behind her ears with the same precision she brought to folding the crisp corners of sheets on the hotel beds. The high-ceilinged hotel suite smelled of citrus soaps and the fresh laundered towels stacked on her cart.

"Not bad for a new girl." The floor matron, a thin, nervous woman, ran her hand under the mattress. "You're experienced, I can tell."

Nadira nodded. Based on Mouna's brother's recommendation, the hotel had hired her this morning.

"A small miracle!" The matron smoothed the duvet, centered the flower vase by the bed and spoke non-stop at a rapid clip. "We're short five staff this afternoon. Get to it now; there are four more rooms on this floor."

Nadira wondered if the matron took amphetamines.

"Don't forget, we've got a late check-out. Room 312. Do not disturb our guest; please remember to work quietly."

Nadira nodded again. "The guest's name, please? There are two lists. I don't want to make a mistake."

"She's a VIP. That's all you need to know."

Nadira waited until the matron disappeared into the bathroom for a final check of her work and scanned the matron's master guest list. She saw the name she sought: Madame J. Malat, Room 312.

"Satisfactory," the matron said.

Nadira pushed the room supply cart into the hall, heavy with the kilos of Semtex and the detonator she'd loaded under the sheets on the bottom tray. A jumpsuited terrorist squad member with an Uzi hanging from his shoulder guarded the small wire-cage elevator and adjoining stairway. Another man patrolled the end of the carpeted hallway. As he passed, she inclined her head and he doffed his blue cap. There could be no better cover than hers, she realized, thankful for her training.

And a calm certainty filled her. A serenity she'd not felt before. Her doubts all disappeared. Her mind went back to her mother — the last time she'd seen her alive

— sipping tea, smiling at her little brother playing under the spreading lime tree in their garden, the birds chirping . . . and then it was all gone. Her family, her home, her street bombed to rubble in the firestorm.

She'd join her mother and brother now. This time she'd fulfill the jihad, accomplish her purpose, the only purpose she'd ever discovered for her life: dying in the performance of her duty would guarantee her entry into Paradise.

While the matron fussed with more instructions, Nadira scoured the bathtub in the next room, her thoughts floating on a sea of peace. She bided her time. With a flick of her wrist, she'd flip the DO NOT DISTURB sign. If the matron didn't leave, she'd have to take care of her. A minor consideration, now that she had Jalenka Malat's room key on the ring in her uniform pocket.

Thursday Afternoon

Panicked, Aimée tried the third courtyard door. It opened. Now she found herself by a WC with the photo of Marlene Dietrich hanging on one door, Jean Gabin, for men, on the other.

She kept going and punched in René's number.

"Don't say my name, René . . . Do you see a short wiry mec with an attitude on the street?"

"Affirmative. With lots of his friends. And very close."

"*Bon,* I think I'm in a café . . . look to the right of the building."

"You're in Café L'Escalier," René said.

She knew the café; its wall was part of the foundation of the infamous Saint Lazare prison, torn down in 1940.

"I'll meet you inside, Aimée."

"Just don't bring Rouffillac with you."

She pulled on dark glasses from her bag and entered L'Escalier. Its recent incarnation as a café didn't hide its former origins as a factory. An upper balcony ringed a deep well of dark red walls; the thick wedges of masonry and stone were the remains of the seventeenth-century prison which had itself originally been a convent, then a leper hospital and, subsequently, a prison for the condemned, notably the Marquis de Sade and the blind and deaf Abbesse of Montmartre guillotined for "conspiring" against the Republic. Folklore placed the Revolution's beginning on July 13 in the prison courtyard with angry crowds who carried on to storm the nearby Bastille the next day. At the turn of the twentieth century, it had housed women. Among the inmates, in addition to prostitutes, had been Mata Hari.

On a blackboard, the chalked *prix fixe* special was *turbot à l'anglaise.* The tables were filled with lunch patrons. René patted down the bulge in his pocket at the entrance and joined her at the counter.

Aimée asked the ponytailed man behind the counter, "Do you have a rear exit?" He wiped his hands on his apron, scanning the scene outside the window.

"Why?"

"Here's why," she said, palming a hundred francs into his moist hand.

"Bien sur!" He grinned. "The service door."

Thank God she'd gone to the ATM.

She nodded to René, and they followed him through the swinging doors into a narrow galley-style kitchen whose huge frying pans sputtered with shallots, butter, and browning filets of fish. The chef in a white hat ignored them, intent on raking the pan back and forth over the blue flame. Fragrant steam wafted up, but Aimée didn't envy him in this narrow sauna of a kitchen.

The ponytailed man unlocked the rear metal door. It opened onto a weed-choked walled courtyard, which displayed remnants of limestone arches and dislodged stones. Sun beat down on the hot cobbles. She saw a small chipped statue of the Virgin Mary nestled in a niche of the peeling back façade among snaking pipes. They'd emerged into a remnant of the medieval cloister of Saint Lazare. From force of habit, Aimée made a small gesture, the sign of the cross.

"A lot of us do that," he said, grinning. A gold tooth sparkled in his mouth. "The place gives a feeling. . . ." He shrugged. "The cook says he's heard chanting at night. Swears it's the nuns."

What about the ghosts of the condemned female prisoners, she thought, recalling Aristide Bruant's famous song in which a woman writes to her lover before her execution: *"Je me fait un sang qu'est d'un noir à Saint Lazare."* My blood is now black with that of Saint Lazare.

Enough of the woo woo; they had to get out of here.

"Your boyfriend after you?" he asked.

"Like a hornet," she said. She saw a rusted door in the wall.

The ponytailed man noticed her gaze and shook his head. "Locked. Go through the back courtyards, three of them, and then make a left."

René glanced at Aimée.

"You know this escape route pretty well, don't you?" René looked around uneasily.

"Did you show this to anyone else today . . . a woman?"

The man grinned. "Only last month, Johnny Hallyday dropped in for a drink. Even at his age, the fans won't leave him alone. He had to leave the same way."

He led them to green garbage containers clustered around another door, rolled one away, and opened that door.

Aimée peeled off another hundred-franc bill and stuck it in his apron pocket.

"Keep this between us, eh?"

He winked. *"Merci."*

She and René followed the dark cool passage between the buildings to another courtyard. Lines of laundry hung between buildings, conversations drifted from windows, open in the heat. Then the winding space led them past another sagging building, and they found themselves in a courtyard in which clay crucible forms and rusted hollow metal glass-blowing rods leaned, abandoned, against the walls.

"Now I know how an aging celebrity feels," René said, grimacing as he stepped over a pothole.

"Over there, René." Aimée pointed to a double door on the left labeled Cristallerie. They entered and stood in a narrow hallway. At the other end, half obscured by a drape of red velvet curtain, lay long tables set with china and crystal goblets. A well-dressed crowd was listening to a speech. An immense crystal chandelier dripped refracted pinpoints of light dominating the frescoed banquet room.

"We thank you, Cristallerie Baccarat stockholders. . . ." a man's amplified voice droned.

Stunned, Aimée realized they'd crashed Baccarat Crystal's stockholders' luncheon. And she was wearing a jean jacket. She looked around, saw no other exit.

"Let's go, keep to the walls."

"Second nature to you, Aimée, but not my thing."

"Got any other ideas, René?"

They were trapped, like geese in a pen.

"Act like you belong. Head to the cloak-room." She pulled his sleeve. "And keep moving."

Frock-coated waiters poured champagne into gleaming stemmed goblets. Aimée kept close to the ornate walls, dodged servers with platters, and kept her gaze straight ahead. A few ministerial types in pinstriped suits, blue shirts, and red ties looked up from their Limoges plates. The speaker, standing at the head of the first table, raised his goblet.

"A toast to our recent resounding success, to Baccarat's best-ever quarterly earnings report! And to you, our shareholders."

Nice profits, if they could afford to toast with champagne and sponsor a function for a hundred or so.

She padded over the plush Aubusson carpet to the cloakroom, which turned out to be a parlor furnished with Louis XIV chairs and what looked like Corot landscapes on the walls. "We're almost there, René."

She threw him a glance, then turned back. A massive mountain of a man in a black suit blocked her path.

"This way, please," he said.

"Excuse me?" she said.

"If you make a scene, I will be forced to escort you out with force."

Nothing for it but to comply. High level security, if the suit was anything to go by. Ex-legionnaire, by his physique.

In the vaulted foyer, the guard stood framed against floor-to-ceiling glass vitrines showcasing a collection of Baccarat crystal: acid-etched neo-classical vases, nineteenth-century fluted perfume flacons, branches of a chandelier with faceted pendant crystal drops catching the light.

She had to come up with a plan. And fast.

"You're a Sarko Security employee, *non?*" she asked.

The guard's lips were immobile in his expressionless face. But he didn't deny it. She went with her hunch.

"You should know better, Monsieur."

"Show me your ID," he said, eyeing René. "I've called for backup experienced with gatecrashers like you."

"Shhh," a server said, peeking around the corner.

The guard gestured them farther away, toward a section devoted to the 1878 Exhibition with sepia photos documenting candelabra commissioned for maharajahs and delivered on elephants, and chandeliers hung in glittering Constantinople palaces, as well as a display of engraved certificates from Tsar Nicholas II.

She flashed her PI license, thought quickly, remembered the card Nohant had showed her.

"This goes into my report. Monsieur Belfont in the rue de Saintonge office will be informed." She pulled a notebook out of her bag, flipped it open, made a checkmark in it with her eye pencil, the closest thing at hand.

He blinked.

"We entered through the rear courtyard,"

she said, assuming a businesslike tone. "That shows a major lapse in security. I've noted that there was no guard stationed there. We're an independent contractor hired by Sarko to investigate for lapses in security such as this." She tapped her heel. "Given the prevalence of Metro bombings, and with several members of the ministry in attendance, this security oversight's inexcusable."

"But we did a thorough sweep before the banquet," he said, his tone defensive now.

Good.

"Not enough, Monsieur, as we've found out." She whipped out her cell phone. "Monsieur Belfont and your superior will see this in our report. My colleague here specializes in counterterrorist tactics, and your failure's duly noted. He'll require you to attend a security seminar, *de rigueur* to prevent further incidents like this."

She nudged René, who closed his mouth and nodded. "*Exactemente,* Monsieur."

"*Mais . . .*" His voice wavered. "It's not only me; what about the other staff?"

She glanced at her phone. "Of course. Now if you'll excuse us?"

"Wait . . . you can't just go —"

But Aimée spoke into her phone, hoping he couldn't hear the dial tone. "Monsieur,

364

we've just discovered security flaws at the Cristallerie Baccarat function . . . *oui,* I'm *en route.*"

Perspiration shone on the guard's upper lip.

"Assemble all the guards for a meeting in fifteen minutes," she said. "Be discreet, of course. Meanwhile, post a man on the back door."

She strode out of the building, René behind her, praying they'd get past the pillars and around the corner before the guard reached his boss on the phone.

They emerged on rue de Paradis. She shuddered, realizing that they were standing not a block away from where Yves had been murdered. No time to dwell on that now. She threaded past cars on the narrow street, hailed a taxi, jumped inside and edged over, making room for René.

"Where to?" the taxi driver asked at the corner of rue d'Hauteville. She looked back; there were no police behind them. She'd already written off her bike, now riddled with bullets.

"Just keep driving," René said, his fingers tapping the window. "Better yet, my car's near Gare du Nord. Drop us there."

"Rouffillac didn't sound concerned about Jalenka, René," she said. "What do you think he meant when he said the situation's taken care of?"

René wiped his brow with his monogrammed handkerchief. "Why, he meant they would guard her hotel! He was sending the DST there. I overheard him."

"You mean they weren't there already?" she asked, alarmed.

"I don't know."

"Never mind. What hotel?"

"Abotel Windsor on rue Gabriel Laumain. What's the difference?"

"But that's two blocks away! Don't you see?"

"See what?"

"First she'd want to take care of me and then. . . ." Aimée tapped the driver's shoulder. "Rue Gabriel Laumain."

"I know the hotel, Mademoiselle," he said. "I drop clients there all the time."

"But the big question is this," she told him. "Do you know the service entrance?"

"And if I do?" he asked, swerving and making a U-turn. A horn blared and a driver shook his hand from a car window.

She held the hundred-franc note up to flutter in the breeze. In the rear-view mirror, she saw his thick eyebrows lower as he calculated the size of her purse.

"And if I got you into the laundry receiving station?"

"How would you do that?"

He shrugged. "Pays to have friends, doesn't it?"

She ended up forking over more for a two-block ride than she would have paid for a trip across the Seine and back. But they were mounting the hotel's narrow back stairs without interference five minutes later.

"Where are we going?" René asked. "We don't know her room number. It's crazy. The DST's got this under control, Aimée."

She halted on the third floor, where they were met by a reeking chemical smell. Her throat burned.

"What's that?" René said, catching his breath and coughing.

"It's not good." She pointed to the jump-suited DST man sprawled on the carpet by the elevator. "Open some windows, quick."

She covered her mouth, jimmied open the hall window, inhaled huge gulps of fresh air, then ran down the hall.

"Look, Aimée." His handkerchief over his face, René held up one of several plastic liter containers that were lying on the carpet. He choked as he read the label. "Contains trichloroethylene. Breathing in TCE fumes may cause headaches, dizziness, confusion . . . higher amounts . . . uncon-

sciousness, death . . ." the rest was lost in
his fit of coughing.

She stuck her head out the window and
gulped more air. ". . . downstairs," René
said, "getting help."

She turned to see René's head disappearing down the stairs.

Yet she couldn't retreat. She had to find
Jalenka. But where the hell was she?

She had to be on this floor . . . and then
Aimée noticed deep tracks furrowed in the
wet carpet. Tracks ending at the door to
Room 312. She tried the doorknob. Locked.

With no time to waste, every breath burning her lungs, she pulled out the Beretta
with the silencer. She steadied her shaking
hands, shot the lock, and shouldered the
door open.

Inside the salon of the hotel suite, she
walked into a brocaded chaise longue.
Beside it, a grouping of period chairs were
empty. She closed the door behind her and
took a deep breath. No fumes in here. Nor
noise, except for piped-in '80s dance music
from a built-in wall speaker. She kept going, tiptoeing into a smaller dim room with
drawn red *toile de jouy* print curtains. A
lamp illuminated an ormolu-trimmed desk,
a pair of black heels in an open shoe box,

and the large walnut-carved armoire on her right.

Ready to turn and leave as quietly as she'd come in, she heard a voice speaking in a rapid, guttural language. She advanced farther to see a young woman wearing a maid's uniform leaning over a figure in the bed. In the small room, the maid was half hidden by the open armoire door. She was speaking into a cell phone held in the crook between her neck and shoulder. But Aimée saw the narrow-gauge rifle lying on the chair.

The assassin. Yves's murderer.

Her gaze fell on the wires running over the floor to the armoire. Noticed the fold-down ironing board inside with a white blouse hanging from the armoire door. Underneath it, there was an open bag filled with brown-gray clay-like material; the wrappings bore Cyrillic letters. Good God, it was Russian Semtex. She trembled as she recognized the detonator, a loose wire on the carpet next to it and the coil of copper wire on top of a suitcase. The woman was assembling explosives.

Aimée raised the Beretta, aimed, and moved to the edge of the bed.

And then, as if possessed of another sense, the maid turned and stopped talking.

Almond-shaped hazel eyes stared at her, eyes that were flat and dead. Assassin's eyes, scrutinizing her.

Young. So young, Aimée thought, amazed.

She said something and let the phone drop. Below her on the bed, Jalenka Malat, in a skirt and slip, lay across the disheveled duvet, twisted sheets binding her legs and arms, her mouth covered with duct tape. Her brown eyes were wide open and full of fear.

"Let go of the wires," Aimée said, keeping her tone level with effort. They still had a chance; the wires weren't connected to the Semtex yet.

The young woman reached out for the rifle.

"Nadira . . . Nadira," Aimée heard a voice repeat over the phone.

And in that moment Aimée saw the wire running down the woman's arm. Aimée shoved the armoire door wide open. She never saw the kick that struck her arm from below. She heard a snap, then a raging fire tore through her shoulder. Her Beretta fell onto the suitcase. Aimée winced as she reached for the gun, biting her lip as pain shot through her shoulder. She felt another piercing pain as Nadira's fingers jabbed her neck.

"You can't stop me," Nadira said.

"Don't bet on it."

Aimée lunged, knocking Nadira into the armoire. Copper wire rained down on them. Her Beretta skidded away.

Aimée grabbed Nadira's shoulders, struggling to pin her down. But her left arm hung useless. She felt Nadira's body heave under her. She twisted like a snake. Nadira's fingernails raked her neck. The Semtex and the steam iron had fallen to the floor; the iron's controls had been knocked into the ON position. It hissed steam at Aimée's face. She saw Nadira reaching through the jet of steam with the wire for the detonator. Panic filled her. She had to stop the woman from connecting the wire or they'd blow up.

Nadira's knee jabbed her in her rib as she half twisted out from under Aimée. Then Nadira's fingertips were clawing at the Semtex just out of her reach. She was pushing the wire toward the detonator caps.

"No, you don't," Aimée panted. "Not like you killed Yves."

"Who?"

Yves's death meant so little to her that she didn't even remember his name.

Nadira, her face beet-red, strained to push the wire toward the detonator. Just a few more centimeters.

With her good hand, Aimée took the hot iron and swung sideways at Nadira's head with all her might. A dull thud, a sputter of hot steam, and then a sizzle. Nadira's body shuddered. Then another swing and Nadira's fingers loosened. She crumpled, limp, onto the carpet, open-mouthed.

Aimée struggled to her knees, straddling Nadira. Panting, using her right hand, she lifted the wires away from the detonator. Then she wrapped them around Nadira's wrists and tied Nadira's ankles together. She listened to the cell phone. Dead.

As she was about to climb onto the bed to untie Jalenka, loud footsteps sounded. She looked up. René, wearing a mask so he could breathe, stood with a *flic,* and a woman with a horrified expression on her face who was pointing at her.

"*Une catastrophe!* You've killed her!" she screamed.

Aimée, collapsed against the bed, felt Nadira's pulse. It was weak but beating. She shook her head.

Aimée sat barefoot on a laundry table holding a glass of *restoratif* from the matron's bottom desk drawer after undergoing fifteen minutes of perfunctory questioning. On the floor above, the bomb squad, poison control unit, and a plainclothes DST team combed the hotel suite. Jalenka Malat had been whisked off to the airport under high security, Nadira dispatched in a guarded ambulance. Aimée hadn't managed to have a chance to speak with her.

René applied ice to her shoulder as Aimée downed her second drink. The hotel matron answered investigators' questions next door in a tearful high-pitched voice, protesting her ignorance.

"We'll treat your shoulder dislocation at the hospital," the medic said, dabbing Aimée's scratches with antiseptic. "Shot at, too." He shook his head. "Nice bruising. Still it's good you wore the vest."

As if she needed him to tell her that. Her chest still throbbed.

"Rotate my shoulder counter-clockwise and it will pop back into the socket," she said.

The medic and René exchanged looks.

"It's happened before," she said.

"I'll get fired if it goes wrong." He shook his head, applying gauze to the fingernail scratches on her neck.

"And I'm in a lot of pain," she said, gritting her teeth.

He packed up his medic kit, snapped it

shut. "I'll bring the stretcher."

René looked at her. "You don't look too good, Aimée."

She didn't feel too good either.

"Nadira's cell phone should lead them to —"

"It's a throwaway." René wiped his perspiring brow. "The woman at the Institut Kurd confirmed Nadira's description, and finding the high-powered rifle helped. The DST's connecting Nadira's attempt to the Metro bombings," René said. "There was another attempt today. Semtex. . . ."

"What?"

"I overheard the chief talking," René said. "They found several carte d'identité's on Nadira; they know she's Iranian."

She recalled the little girl's words about the Tehran mosque, the timing of prayers.

"Iranian? It's political, but. . . ."

"And the rash of Metro bombings aren't?"

Still it didn't fit, they were jumping to conclusions, clutching at the most convenient terrorist explanation. "Nadira's a trained assassin."

"Right, a hit woman," René said. "She murdered Yves when he got wind of her mission to assassinate Jalenka." He looked at his feet. "I'm sorry I ever doubted you, Aimee."

But Aimée still had doubts. Maybe Nadira hadn't known Yves; maybe she hadn't killed him.

"I'm not sure, René."

"What do you mean? Jalenka's name was in Yves's wallet, her chador —"

And then it hit her. Aimee shook her head. "Nadira's short."

"What?"

"She didn't know who Yves was —"

"You believed her?"

"How could she have gotten here so quickly from rue du Faubourg Saint-Denis, changed, and tied Jalenka up? It feels wrong."

Exasperation shone in René's large green eyes. "The liquor's gotten to you."

No. For once, it had made her head clearer.

"It wasn't her."

"Your imagination's run amok."

She didn't think so.

"They spoke with a Monsieur Delbard who'd employed Nadira as his son's nanny," Aimée said. "He'd dropped his son and Nadira at Canal Saint-Martin to feed the ducks a few minutes after twelve. Nadira couldn't have killed Langois at noon in the Gare du Nord."

It wasn't over. She had to find the truth.

She took off the ice compress; her shoulder, swollen and bruised, throbbed.

René knew pain, living with hip dysplasia. She had to convince him.

"Will you help me? Just try to do what I tell you, and it will work."

"Let them take care of you at the hospital," he said.

"René, if you won't, I'll do it myself and you'll get to watch."

"You're serious, aren't you?"

"When I say three, rotate it counterclockwise."

He hesitated. "The last thing I want to do is to hurt you, Aimée."

And she saw the strangest look in his eyes. A fleeting look she couldn't decipher.

"I've hurt you already by not believing you."

"Can't you pretend it's a socket wrench and you're putting the lugnuts back on your tire, nice and quick?"

"A socket wrench?"

"As my best friend, you'll do this for me, right?"

He just stood there, linen sheets and feather pillows piled on the shelves behind him.

She steeled herself. She'd have to do it herself before the drink wore off. And then she felt René's sure hand. She took the deepest breath she could.

"One, two, and three." And he pulled and rotated her arm.

Pain flashed through her. And then her shoulder popped into place in its socket.

René reached for the *restoratif*. "I need a taste of that."

She eased her arm into the sleeve of her denim jacket and edged off the table, wincing.

"Let's get out of here," she said.

"But Rouffillac wants to talk with you."

"He's the last person I want to see right now."

But she was wrong.

Outside, a flurry of journalists stood near the ambulance. Aimée saw news crews, cameras trained on the hotel, and kept walking. "Mademoiselle, Monsieur . . . a few questions please."

She shielded her face with her hand until a figure blocked her way. "Mademoiselle, is it true the attempted assasination of Jalenka Malat is linked to the Metro bombing incident this afternoon?"

She looked up to find a camera in her face. "Excuse me."

"Any comments on the rumor that Islamic

terrorists are planning to strike the entire transportation system —"

"Let me pass, please." She didn't need her face on the *télé* again for the jihadists to see.

"She's the one," said a voice behind the camera.

"Can you confirm that you prevented Jalenka Malat's assassination and were attacked yourself?" She pushed her way around him. Several *flics* provided interference; then she broke away and strode down the street.

A few blocks away, near Gare du Nord, René took off in first gear, one hand on the hot steering wheel, the other wiping his brow with his monogrammed linen handkerchief.

She leaned back, fighting waves of dizziness. The medic's pain medication, the ache in her shoulder, the *restoratif,* and the heat had gotten to her.

"You're very pale, Aimée," René said.

Small shooting pains ran up her arm. She held her breath and they subsided, merging into a dull ache.

"Want to hear some good news?" René asked.

She sat up.

"The Fountainbleu account's back on track," he said. "And it should stay that way after my mini security seminar."

"Bravo, René." And, not for the first time, she wondered what she'd do without him. "What's the bad news?"

René sucked in his breath. "Morbier left you a message at the office."

"He's back?"

"And not too happy," René said.

No wonder. Probably angry at her subterfuge; she'd used his name to obtain suspect information from the Brigade's report on Yves's death without authorization. But right now, she needed to go home, rest her shoulder, and sleep.

"He's waiting for you." René's green eyes blinked. "At the Brigade Criminelle."

Little fingers of apprehension tugged at her.

She wanted to soak her shoulder in a hot tub. She could contact him later.

René honked at a bicyclist darting into his lane. "You can't fob him off, Aimée."

Why not, she almost said. "I'll call him later."

"His message indicated that if you hadn't shown up in two hours, he'd arrange for an escort to pick you up. His words."

All she needed right now: an irate Morbier.

"Drop me at 36, quai des Orfevres," she said. "I'll talk with him."

"You do that," René said. "I'll do some work back at the office." Something like relief shone in his eyes.

Aimée paused in mid-step at the pock-marked stone prefecture and flashed her ID at the police sentry box.

"Not so fast, Mademoiselle," said the *flic,* catching her elbow and speaking into a walkie-talkie. *"Attendez, s'il vous plait."*

Heightened security? Or did Morbier have a surprise for her? She stood, shifting her heels, wishing this meeting was over and she could go home.

The préfecture's façade caught the light under spun-cotton white clouds floating in a cerulean blue sky. Citrus scents from the flowering linden trees carried from across the Seine. On the Pont Saint-Michel, a kaleidoscope of bicyclists, cars, and pedestrians streamed to the Left Bank. Peaceful, picture-perfect, until a blue-and-white police car screeched to a halt on the cobblestones. The *flic* opened the back door.

"Your chariot awaits, Mademoiselle."

"But, I'm meeting with . . ."

"Commissaire Morbier's waiting."

Ten minutes later, the car halted three blocks away from the hotel she'd left less than half an hour ago. No matter what, she kept being drawn back to the tenth arrondissement.

The *flic,* guiding her by the elbow, escorted her to a resto on the corner of rue des Messageries. The maroon wooden façade, adorned by black wrought-iron grillework with finials of lances and pineapples in front of the windows, hadn't changed since the Revolution.

Inside, at the old-style elevated cashier's desk, a woman sat, a chocolate-colored Labrador stretched out by her feet.

"Bonjour," said Aimée.

She raised her thin black-penciled brows. "He's in the rear salon, Mademoiselle," she said, and waved an age-spotted hand in dismissal.

A white-haired man rushed past her with a plate of steaming skate. "This way," he said. "If you please."

Morbier, with a white napkin tucked in his collar, sat below a tarnished beveled mirror. From the foodstains on the napkin, she could read the menu. Pale skin around his basset-hound eyes highlighted the tan of his forehead and jowls. Sunglasses perched on his thick salt-and-pepper combed-back hair. He was relaxed, wearing a light blue suit, tanned . . . she'd never seen him like this.

"About time, Leduc!" Using his knife and fork, he deboned a fish, separating spine from flesh, with an expert flick of his wrist. Lining the walls on the faded flocked velvet wallpaper were yellowed prints of guillotinings. They didn't seem to cramp Morbier's appetite.

"So you wanted a command performance, Morbier?" She sat in the black-lacquered ladder-back chair, keeping her hands steady with effort as she poured some Vittel into a water glass. "To what do I owe the honor?"

"*Tiens,* you're a celebrity, Leduc," he said, spearing a morsel of succulent white fish. "Every time I see the *télé,* you're on it."

She looked down into her lap. "Since when do you go on vacation?"

As if he didn't have the right to take some time off. She wanted to bite back those petulant-little-girl words as soon as she said them.

"Use it or lose it, they said." He ignored her tone. "I found a great three-city package to Agadir, Marrakech, and Fez."

"Morocco?" She stared, open-mouthed. He'd never before left France.

Morbier set a photo on the white table-cloth. It showed him with his arm around Marc, his half-Moroccan grandson, on a sand-dusted street in front of a minaret.

"Marc's grown," she said.

"They do that," he said, with a sigh.

So that's why he'd gone. Marc's Moroccan grandparents had custody. They must have relented to let Morbier visit. "If the mountains won't go to Mohammed, then Mohammed must go to the minaret? That it?"

"Something like that," Morbier said. "Which reminds me." He groped in his jacket pocket and set another photo on the tablecloth. "Seems you had a close encounter with her."

Nadira's almond-eyed face stared back at her. Number 4351, read the tag hanging from her neck in the mug shot.

"Closer than I wanted." She rubbed her shoulder. "Who is she?"

"Shareen Fekret, aka Nadira Abouz. A sleeper in a jihadist network. Activated this week."

So that's what this was about.

"You're saying that you didn't know about her?"

"The DST didn't," Morbier said. "And you've stepped on some pretty big toes,

Leduc."

She didn't need him to tell her that. So far, he hadn't mentioned her using his name at the Brigade. With luck, he wouldn't find out.

"What else is new, Morbier?"

"*Voulez-vous desirez,* Mademoiselle?" a waiter asked.

She gestured to a lavender petal-decorated *crème brulée* on the dessert tray.

"So you're taking all the food groups, Leduc. Dairy, floral. . . ."

"Look, Morbier, if that's all. . . ." She folded the napkin, about to cancel her order and stand up.

"But I've got a babysitting job."

"Marc's come back with you?"

He set down his fish knife. "You, Leduc."

"Me?"

"For your own sake, and to guarantee that you stay out of trouble."

She shook her head. "You mean keep out of the DST's way."

"Like I said, for your own sake. Seems you stepped on the jihadists' toes too. They put a lot of effort into arranging Nadira's cover; they had great plans for her."

The skin prickled on the back of her neck.

"Maybe. But she didn't kill Yves."

His brown eyes flashed. "Since when do

384

you use my name to try and access a police report, eh?"

"Let me explain, Morbier," she said.

"Make it good, Leduc."

And then she told him.

Before she could finish, he handed her a newspaper article in Turkish.

"Going to translate, Morbier?"

"Sorry, wrong one."

Did everyone understand Turkish but her?

He pulled out a version in French. "Osman Edlick's a famous columnist in the most widely read paper in Turkey. And in the palm of the military. Last week he wrote this column about a 'hero.' A Yellow Crescent hit man shot in Iran."

He paused and forked a parsleyed, buttered slice of potato.

"Seems you've heard of the Yellow Crescent, Leduc?"

She nodded. His basset-hound eyes watched her.

"But this 'hero's' last job in Europe, taking care of those offensive to the Turkish military, was more than a year ago."

"So?" But that corroborated Kat's comments about the fatwa on him; how funds for hit teams had dried up.

"But, and the article mentions this, he was a Shi'a. Interpol confirms that known

Iranian jihadists appeared last week at his funeral," Morbier said. He took a last bite and set down his fork. "Other than that, the connection remains unclear."

"What do you mean?"

"Pick any term you like: fluid, many-headed Hydra monsters; independent sleeper terrorist cells; jihadists following their own agenda."

"Meaning random actions with no central command?"

He shrugged. "Or maybe a united mission to destroy the West has rallied disparate groups. That's the current idea."

"But the DST insist that it was the *Algerian* GIA that bombed the Metro and the Marseilles airliner and that Nadira worked for them."

He raised an arm. "Alphonse, *une crème brulée aussi, s'il vous plait.*

"That's for public consumption, Leduc. And I never said that."

The impact of his words hit home. She was terrified. It would be like trying to swat a swarm of killer bees who flew from different hives.

"Since when does a Commissaire like you have access to such information? Does it involve Groupe R?"

Silence except for the scrape of his spoon

on the porcelain *crème brulée* ramekin.

"The less you know, the better."

She didn't get his connection with the intelligence service. "The DST's run by the Interior Ministry. It's a different branch. . . ."

He had never been one to give out information, so it surprised her to see him sit back and grin. "Let's just say that during the Cold War, I proved helpful. You do remember the Cold War, Leduc?"

The Berlin Wall, espionage, Le Carré novels. The implication staggered her. A man who left half his lunch on his napkin, darned his own socks, a dyed-in-the-wool Socialist . . . a spy? Her godfather, who'd played Santa on Christmas mornings until she'd pulled his beard off.

His expression changed. "According to certain Interpol reports, Leduc, you're on the bad side of a powerful mullah."

Her spoon clattered onto the saucer beneath the *crème brulée.*

"Now I'll have time to show you all my vacation photos."

"I don't get it."

"My babysitting job? You." He frowned and signaled for the bill.

"But she . . . they didn't kill Yves," she said. "It doesn't make sense."

"Doesn't make sense by the old rules, but we're playing with new ones now. Ones no one understands."

"You're not babysitting me for my own protection; it's so I don't —"

"Compromise ongoing operations?" He smiled, signed the tab, and stood. "That's what the DST termed it. Shall we go?"

On the corner, bright sun shone on the wrought iron railings. Morbier raised his arm to hail the waiting police car.

"But Miles Davis. . . ."

"Your concierge loves him, doesn't she?" Morbier ushered her into the back seat. Hot air blew in from the open window. "Have her take him for a few days."

"But I've got a business to run; I can't leave René on his own."

"We've taken care of that," he said, motioning the driver down a narrow street crowded with bicycles, delivery trucks, and women wearing chadors.

Taking over her life, her work. No way.

Ten minutes later, the police car bumped over the curb and let them off under the elevated Metro at La Chapelle. Brakes screeched and orange sparks flew on the overhead Metro lines. From below the bridge to their right came the clack of trains on the dark tangle of rail lines radiating from the Gare du Nord.

"Where are we going?"

"To the theater, Leduc. Time for your ration of culture today."

They crossed the street and entered a wormholed wooden side door labeled ENTRÉE DES ARTISTES.

"*Bonjour,* Commissaire," said a blue-uniformed *flic.*

"How's the wife?"

"*Bien.* Another one on the way, Commissaire," he said with a big smile.

Morbier patted him on the back and signed in on a clipboard. He walked on ahead, but the *flic* stopped her. "*Excusez-moi,* Mademoiselle," he said, running a metal detector wand over her. A loud beeping erupted. *Merde!* She emptied her bag, and the Beretta landed on top of her Leclerc compact.

"Leduc, I assume that's licensed," Morbier said, wagging his finger.

"As if I'd carry . . . why, *you* gave —"

"Officer," Morbier interrupted, "we'll just hold on to that for her, won't we?"

Nice save, she thought. Still, it would take her a ton of Brigade Criminelle paperwork and months to get back the Beretta Morbier had given her.

She followed him. She noticed his worn

brown shoes, one sock blue, the other brown. He still got dressed in the dark.

The passageway: scuffed saffron walls lined with pipes and electrical wires led to a black wooden painted floor marked with scattered blue tape X's. Beyond it was an expanse of darkness, like falling off the edge of the world.

She looked up and stared at the faded gilt-edged balconies and soaring domed cupola of the Theatre Bouffes de Nord. This nineteenth-century decayed jewel had been abandoned for years, then was saved from destruction and semi-restored. With klieg lights nestled among scrolled pilasters, chipped friezes, and the rose red exposed stone arched stage, it was now home to ongoing plays and musical performances.

"The season over, Morbier?"

"Rehearsals start next week."

She heard the murmur of voices, the tramp of feet. Once backstage, they descended a black wrought-iron staircase to a lower level. Uniformed and plainclothes officers sat before a bank of computers. Duct-taped strands of wires and fiber-optic cables crisscrossed the floor. Several men were gathered over a large map of the tenth arrondissement on the wall. A single fan blew hot air and cigarette smoke around in the air. No one paid them any attention.

An efficient temporary DST nerve center, a makeshift headquarters for operations. Morbier continued past a lighting panel and opened a door, then backed out, seeing a uniformed man curled up asleep on a couch.

Further on, he looked into a door to a small dressing room. A beveled mirror, and worn velvet brocade chaise furnished it. A blue feather boa hung from a screen; there was not much else. Taped to the mirror, a note written in faded lipstick read: *Bonne Chance on your premiere, Zou-zou!*

Her office bag containing her tango outfit for the lesson she never managed to make sat on the chaise. No doubt courtesy of René, the traitor! In cahoots with Morbier, and he hadn't told her.

"How long do I stay, Morbier?"

"Tonight, maybe longer. It's for your own sake."

They had mounted an operation for tonight and guaranteed that she'd be out of the way. She was still not satisfied that Nadira was Yves's killer, but now she was stymied. She wanted to kick something.

And she had no laptop. How could she work?

Out in the hall, he jerked a thumb at a

room labeled MAQUILLAGE and parted voile curtains to reveal a long, lighted makeup mirror and a Formica counter with dried-out pancake sticks and powderpuffs.

"You might want to clean up first, Leduc," Morbier said. For the first time, she detected concern in his eyes. "Change your bandage."

"You can wash up down the hall. Don't get any ideas about leaving," he said. "Sacault wants to talk with you."

No wonder her interrogation at the hotel had been so brief. They'd questioned Nadira by now and obtained more information. She'd turn that to her advantage and find out what Nadira's connection, if any, was to Yves.

"Morbier, if they'd listened to me in the first place —"

"I'm not involved, Leduc." He raised his age-spotted hand.

"I think you're very much involved," she said. "They probably called you back from vacation for this."

And for a moment, his shoulders drooped and he looked like the old man he was.

"You're right. My first vacation in six years, my grandson's birthday, and here I am, sweating in Paris with you."

Guilt washed over her. Not for the first

time, she'd thrown a wrench into Morbier's life.

"I'm sorry."

He sighed. "Just be a good girl, Leduc. Try? It's not the Ritz, but still it's better than a holding cell at the préfecture, *non?*"

She nodded. No doubt he'd saved her from that by exercising his influence. The last she saw of him, he was shuffling down the hall.

She found the showers, removed her bandage, and turned on the hot water. She stood under the spray as long as she could, soaped up, and then turned on the cold. Icy water needles blasted her skin. She stepped out, alive and awake again. Her shoulder was numb. She re-applied antiseptic and a bandage. In her bag, she found black leggings, a denim miniskirt, and a black tank top.

In the makeup room, she outlined her eyes in kohl, applied foundation to cover her neck bruises, and dotted her cheeks with Chanel Red lipstick for color. She pulled out her cell phone and arranged for her concierge to walk and feed Miles Davis. Dour mannered, opinionated . . . still Miles Davis loved staying with her. Aimée figured it had to do with the treats she kept on her shelf.

That accomplished, she tried to take stock of her situation. Her hands trembled. Everything seemed to have spiraled out of control. Her life, and business, were threatened, Yves was gone. She tried to imagine the rest of her life spent undercover, hiding. But she couldn't. Wouldn't.

Inside the dressing room, she inhaled the lingering scent of *muguet* — lily of the valley — from the chaise. A memory of first nights, but for her evoking the scent her mother had worn twenty years ago. And it was as if her mother had left yesterday. That sweet pungent scent trailing in her wake, the carmine-red lipstick she bought at the corner *pharmacie*, the flaking charcoal drawing sticks always in her pockets. The charcoal sticks her mother used for life drawing at the Beaux Arts Academy. She recalled something unfinished: the reception to honor the woman retiring from UNESCO. Too late? She rifled in her bag, found the invitation. Hotel le Bristol tomorrow, an evening reception. Stop, she had to stop, she told herself. This led nowhere.

Pounding came from the door. Frantic, she looked for escape. No window.

"Leduc?" Morbier's voice. "Sacault's waiting."

And then she remembered where she was.

"Un moment."

She had to finish dressing. No scarf, and she'd left her jacket in René's car. She grabbed the blue feather boa, buckled her ankle-strap heels meant for the tango lessons, and opened the door to Morbier.

The burning orange tip of a cigarette was held between his thumb and forefinger. His eyes narrowed at her outfit, then he pinched his cigarette out between his fingers. In the hallway, a half-open window overlooked the maze of rail lines leading to the Gare du Nord. The monotonous *clic-clac, clic-clac* of rolling freight cars rumbled below.

Backstage, in a darkened sound booth, Sacault huddled over an open file resting on a console. Stubble shaded his chin. He wore a black tracksuit this time.

"We'll make this short," he said.

Still a man of few words.

"To your knowledge, had Yves Robert visited the mosque on rue du Faubourg Saint-Denis?"

She shrugged. "No clue."

Sacault consulted the file, flipped a page. "In your statement, you mentioned a taxi ride to a loft on Canal Saint-Martin Monday evening. Did you stop anywhere?"

"Just for champagne."

"So a wine shop . . . open that late in the

quartier?" Sacault looked up, studying her.

The wheels in her mind began to turn. "Yves went into Afro Coiffeur on rue du Chateau d'Eau and emerged with champagne in a paper bag."

"You're the curious type; didn't you ask him . . . ?"

In her mind's eye, she saw the women's hair being braided in the packed salon and heard the bubbling African dialect drifting onto the street. There had been clusters of young hip-hop types and African men in robes on the pavement.

"He said it paid to have connections."

Sacault shut the file. Nodded to Morbier. She noticed that the "incident" room was nearly vacant, except for a few men working on computer terminals. Something was up.

"That's it?"

"For now."

"And Nadira . . . ?"

"Nadira Abouz is under suicide watch at the Brigade. Her mission — her jihad, as she termed it — was and is the destruction of Jalenka Malat for the glory of Allah. She's refused to answer any other questions."

Aimée remembered Nadira's eyes, assassin's eyes. She stood. "Her youth. Anyone that age, that focused, was trained young. She's a single-minded terrorist, her goal, paradise, after she takes her target with her."

"Sit down."

Aimée couldn't get Nadira's chilling eyes out of her head.

"But she's telling the truth, don't you see?" Aimée pounded the table. "A *tall* figure wearing a chador murdered Yves."

"When I want your opinion, I'll ask for it."

"What aren't you telling me?"

He stood. "Give her a sedative," he said. And was gone.

"Talk about rubbing people the wrong way, Leduc," Morbier said with a sigh. "Let's see the medic."

Let them drug her into silence? No way. She envisaged a DST sweep of the quartier: the mosque, the coiffeur. Stupid, why had she opened her mouth? But she had an idea.

The medic, wearing a red armband, smiled. "A little on edge, eh? Try this."

She managed a smile. "Me, on edge?"

Shot at, bruised, sore, and almost blown up by Semtex, and still everyone wanted to keep her in the dark. Morbier, her jailer; René, a traitor.

"A little, I guess," she conceded.

The medic handed her a big white oval pill and a paper cup of water. She swallowed, careful to keep the pill in her palm, and drank the water. Morbier escorted her to the dressing room, looked at his watch.

"Sweet dreams, Leduc."

And he padded away.

Like hell. She waited ten minutes, opened the door, and crept upstairs. The backstage area held two men at one end of the bank of terminals. Nearest her, a pockmark-faced young *mec* sat at a screen, inputting data from file folders. *TARILLE,* read his name tag. Smoke spiraled upward from his cigarette; the blue screen light was reflected in his eyes.

She sat next to him. "Got another one?"

He gestured to the pack of unfiltered Gauloises.

She took one, flicked the plastic yellow lighter, and inhaled. She felt the jolt hit the back of her lungs. Her eyes flicked over the data on his screen, code 0IP for interrogation files, if she remembered right.

"Merde!" she said. Gave a big sigh. "Interrogation transcript not inputted yet, Tarille? I'm supposed to read it."

His thick eyebrows rose on his forehead. "No one told me."

She shrugged, crossed her legs. "Not your fault, eh? But if Sacault expects me to question Nadira further without the file, he's dreaming. I can't do it."

"Your clearance?"

"Good question. He didn't pass on my team's access? I'm not supposed to disclose it." She shrugged. "*Bon,* I'll ask him."

Tarille averted his eyes from her legs. "The unit's gone."

Of course it was. The important thing was to act like she knew what she was doing. And play it right, so she could read Nadira's file. Yellow light from a halogen lamp pooled on the pile of papers.

"Typical!" She leaned forward, stubbing out the cigarette.

"You're undercover squad, right?"

She put her finger over her mouth. "Shhh."

His eyes glittered. The wanna-be type who thought late-night, rain-soaked stakeouts in rat-infested alleys were atmospheric.

"I'm taking the course," he said, "thinking of applying for undercover next year."

"Perfect for someone smart like you," she grinned, then winked. Hoped she hadn't laid it on too thick. "Tactics, you know; most times we move in after the sweep." She stretched her arms. "*Bon,* I'll read the print version," she said, as if in afterthought.

"But. . . ."

"You're backed-up, I know," she said. "Don't worry, I'll read the full file later."

"I'm not supposed to —"

"Tarille, we need your access code here," said one of the men.

"Go ahead," Aimée said.

He hesitated.

"And I'll bum another cigarette if you don't mind while I read what's here."

"Help yourself," he said, ingrained manners kicking in.

She wished he'd hurry up. "This file on top?"

He shook his head. "This one." He slipped a file from underneath.

While he stood talking to the man, she hunted for the interrogation transcript. Found four pages, starting on page 27.

She gave a big yawn, slipping them first onto her lap and then up under her tank top. Then she closed the file folder and wedged it back into the pile next to the terminal. By the time Tarille returned, she'd left.

In the dressing room, she packed her bag, looped the feather boa tightly around her shoulders, and descended to the bowels of the theater, looking for the fire exit. She found it two floors down, a large red fire door.

After several tugs and pulls, unable to use her full strength because of her shoulder, it opened. Below, a rusted metal fire escape led to a narrow concrete walk bordering train tracks, beneath electric wires, next to the rushing Lille Express. She kicked the safety latch, and the fire escape lowered. She took a deep breath and felt her way down the rungs. And then hung by one arm, her shoulder aching and legs swinging half a meter above the concrete, before she summoned enough courage. And dropped.

She landed on her knees, heard a rip, and saw a big hole in her right legging. But nothing worse. She picked herself up and ran down the walkway along the stone embankment, past switching stations, banks of signal lights, and abandoned crumbling concrete station points. The tracks narrowed now as they entered the terminal, and she hopped on the end of platform 12. She looked behind her.

No one.

She dusted herself off and joined the crowd departing the train. At the nearest pay phone, she looked up Afro Coiffeur, stuck in a phone card, and dialed.

"Bonsoir," she said. "The owner please. Hurry."

"Speaking," said a woman with a thick African accent.

"I don't have time to explain. But a man,

Yves, my friend, picked up a bottle of champagne from you Monday night, *non?*"

"Who's this?" Her voice was suspicious.

"The *flics* are en route to question you," she said. "You should close. Leave. Right now."

"Question me? Again?" In the background there was laughter and the hum of a blow-dryer.

Aimée's ears perked up. "What do you mean, 'again'?"

"Asking questions," she said. "Look, an old friend of Monsieur Yves knows my brother works in a wine shop. I helped him out. He got a discount and gave me a little *baksheesh,* you know, for the trouble. That's all."

"Can you describe this person. A man?"

"C'est-ça," she said. "Witch-doctor hair."

Nonplused, Aimée took a guess. "Black, wiry, like an Afro?"

"Hair only you white people have. Yellow."

She'd think about that later. "You really should leave now."

"And lose business? Evening's my busiest time, every chair's filled."

Women came after work, the process took hours, they worked late into the night.

"Your choice," she said. "But take it from me, this time the security service has mounted a raid on the quartier. Full-scale."

Sirens moaned in the distance.

"Look out your window if you don't believe me."

The woman said something in an African language. The blow-dryer shut off.

"I see armored trucks stopping on rue du Château d'Eau —" she said.

"Get out. Now. Go out the back." And Aimée hung up.

She hurried to the station buffet. Inside, she found a space at the counter and ordered an espresso. She stuck her bag between her feet, on the mosaic floor littered with sugar-cube wrappers and cigarette butts. Right now, even if the DST discovered she'd gone, they had more on their minds than her.

Next to her demitasse on the zinc counter, she opened Nadira's interrogation transcript and read:

Q: You've been in the country two years; who's your contact?

A: No answer.

Q: Who runs your cell?

A: No answer.

Aimée sighed. Three pages of questions with no replies from Nadira. On the fourth page, branded with a round tan coffee-cup ring, it became more interesting.

Q: How many missions have you accomplished here?

A: I follow the jihad.

Q: So . . . how many?

A: *cough* . . . It's time for my prayers.

Q: After you answer questions, you can pray . . . do you understand?

A: Yes.

Q: You were found with Russian Semtex. How many Metros have you bombed?

A: Not my directive.

Q: What directives do you follow beside assassination?

A: Courier. I receive the call to transport arms and, Allah willing, I do it.

Q: You're a Shi'a Muslim linked to a radical mosque in Tehran. Explain your mission here.

A: I follow Allah's will. Praise be to Allah.

Q: How does assassinating a Kurdish Turkish Muslim follow Allah's will?

A: We don't always understand the mullah's directives, but it is revealed.

Q: Revealed? The Shi'a Iranians want to destabilize Turkey. You're a political pawn.

A: Allah's will . . . *pause* . . . the mullah found me, trained me to carry out the jihad. I am proud to be chosen. I was proud to have been chosen, but I have failed.

Q: Proud to have killed Yves Robert?

A: Who?

Q: The investigative reporter in the way of your jihad.

A: I don't know this man.

Q: But you eliminated him. It will go easier on you if you admit it.

A: Jalenka Malat was my target. Others will take my place.

Q: Answer the question.

A: I want to pray.

Break, interview ended.

A trained undercover hit woman fluent in French, a sharpshooter, with a perfect cover as a nanny. It made sense to keep her concealed, to activate her for assassinations of specific targets. Not to murder Yves. Killing him could complicate her mission. Nor to blow up a train station. No sophisticated training was needed to leave a backpack with explosives in the crowded Metro.

Nadira hadn't known Yves. What reason would she have to lie now?

The steamer hissed as the milk bubbled. She needed to learn everything Yves had been investigating. But Georges, the retiring night "attending" at AFP, refused to help her.

A slim chance existed that he'd reconsider. But there was no other way for her to discover the articles Yves had been working on.

The loudspeaker announced that the Eurostar was boarding. Passengers scurried past the glass-windowed buffet, numbers and letters changed on the electronic arrival/departure board, and she remembered Langois's pale face, the blood pooling by his camera case that bore a Marriot-Sarajevo sticker.

She knew in her bones that Yves's and Langois's killer was out there. Gunning for her. Morbier was trying to protect her. The DST had a killer, but the wrong one. No one could help her. She had to do this herself.

Thursday Night

As he stood in the shadows of rue de Paradis, Vatel fingered Mehmet's message in his pocket. Mehmet, who'd never taken a day off since he'd left Turkey, was *en vacances.* Or so the sign on the concierge's loge door read. Frightened and fleeing, more likely, Vatel thought. But Vatel recognized the small crescent etched in the windowsill dust, a signal indicating that a message was waiting behind the row of mailboxes. Mehmet owed him, and he'd delivered; now they were even. And now Vatel had information for Florand.

Vatel took a deep breath, the image of his village filling his mind. The whitewashed stone houses; the rows of apricot trees in his father's grove; the cries of goats carrying on in the wind; cypresses, waving like tall sentinels, bordering the dirt road. The snowcapped peak of Mount Ararat framed in the indigo sky . . . a wash of color seen nowhere else.

A siren blared, bringing Vatel back to this narrow, dark street. This dense street of people packed on top of each other in old buildings. No trees or greenery, except for the poor excuse for a garden near the old chapel around the corner.

Now the apricot trees only existed in his mind. His village lay in rubble and ruins. Yet he had a chance to save other ones.

Once an informer, the Kurd saying went, always an informer.

He keyed in Florand's number on his cell phone.

Florand answered on the first ring. "Where are you, Vatel?"

Startled, Vatel almost dropped the phone, then recovered. "I heard —"

"Not on the phone, Vatel. Your location?"

He glanced at the corner street sign. "At rue du Faubourg Poissonnière."

"I'm nearby."

"I noticed, it's hard not to, the way your people cordoned off the quartier."

The whine of sirens echoed and blue and red lights flashed on the street behind him.

"Wait for me in number 58. Back of the courtyard, in the construction area."

"And consider this more than fair payment, Florand."

But Florand had hung up. Vatel heard a movement in the shadows. He put his head down, kept to the shadows of the buildings, and started walking.

He had one more call to make.

Thursday Night

René nodded in time to the Mozart concerto on the radio. The halogen desk lamp was angled on his computer screen in the darkened office. One last scan of the Fountainbleu account statistics, and then he'd — the phone rang.

"Leduc Detective," he said. "René Friant speaking."

"Mademoiselle Leduc, please."

Who would call Aimée this late at the office, he wondered.

"She's not available. May I take a message?"

René heard sirens in the background.

"I'm her partner," René said. "Perhaps I can help you?"

Pause.

"The phone's not safe."

René sat up in his specially designed chair and hit SAVE on the computer screen. "Who's this?"

"She knows me. It's important."

René heard the slight rolling of syllables. A faint foreign lilt. The Kurd?

"You're the guard, Vatel?"

"And if I am?" Another pause. "I made a mistake. Forget it."

"Wait, don't hang up," René said. "Aimée told me about you. She's at the Brigade —"

"The Brigade Criminelle?" he interrupted.

"She's answering questions. Jalenka Malat's assassin's in custody."

"Then it's too late."

Warning bells went off in René's head. "What's too late? Tell me, and I'll pass it on."

"Not over the phone."

"What's so important?"

"But she's not safe. . . ." Vatel stopped.

"Aimée?"

Of course Aimée was safe. Hadn't René made a deal with Morbier, turned her over for "safekeeping," or so Morbier promised.

"We need to meet." René stood, grabbed

his keys, and reached for his linen jacket. "Tell me where."

"Can I trust you?"

René heard him panting, then footsteps. Was he running . . . running away from someone?

"More than anyone else right now, Vatel."

"An old townhouse . . . the sign says Hotel Titon."

The phone buzzed.

"Allô?"

Then clicked off.

Alarmed, René hit the callback button. No answer. He wanted to throw the phone across the room. Instead, he pulled his chair to the bookcase, climbed it, his hips protesting, and stretched for the guide to buildings and monuments, a thick-bound book of 464 pages. With laborious steps, he climbed back down, then thumbed open the book's index. Titon . . . he scanned the entries and found it listed near a neighboring *hôtel particulier* owned by the model for Boucher's *Odalisque,* Louis XV's mistress. After discovering that a one-time owner, a magistrate, had been guillotined in the Revolution, he found the address. He hurried, locking the office door to the last strains of the Mozart concerto.

■ ■ ■ ■

René parked two blocks away to avoid police roadblocks. The quartier resembled a battle zone. Cracks of thunder rumbled in the eastern sky. Above, he saw the slanted rooftops and chimneypots outlined by a dull glow.

Neo-Classical seventeenth-century townhouse façades of white stone and delicate Louis XV iron-railed balconies, sloped up rue du Faubourg Poissonnière. The Hôtel Titon could use a facelift, he thought, when he faced it. And by the evidence of the cement mixers and sand piles standing in the dim semicircular courtyard, it was getting one. The rays of moonlight didn't hide the exquisite neo-Classical busts and figures in the niches on the curved façade, nor the sculpted-stone garlands and wreaths and the vaulted, column-bracketed windows. Uneasy, he made his way over the vast cobblestone courtyard. Why meet here, René wondered. More important, where was Vatel?

Scraping sounds came from the tall rear doors. One door was open. He took a step and walked into a shovel that had been propped against the wall. The clanging noise

411

it made as it fell on the cobblestones would alert Vatel to his presence, René thought. And then he heard footsteps, running. With his luck, he'd scared him away.

René sprinted over the sand-dusted cobbles to the rear. Even with his short legs, he'd catch him. Had to. But inside the door, he found himself in a dim sawdust-filled room, a street lamp illuminating faded murals on the gilt-edged recessed ceiling. Through the open tall glass door leading to Cité Paradis, he saw a dark figure running in the shadowed alley. The figure turned the corner. Gone.

He'd never catch him running, but in the car he stood a chance. He turned and rushed past sacks of dry cement. He put out his hands to feel his way. His fingers caught on what felt like a zipper, the seam of a pocket, then a mound sprawled over what appeared to be a table saw. Just at René's height. Unmoving, inert.

René stood rooted to the sawdust-covered floor. He'd never felt a dead body before. He'd never attended a funeral; his relatives were long-lived; even the château staff hung on.

But now, he knew, he'd walked into one. Still warm but very still. With shaking hands, he fumbled in his jacket pocket, found a matchbox, and struck a match. The flame sputtered, illuminating a figure wearing a blue jumpsuit with Sarko Security embroidered on the pocket and a red rimmed, pinkish-gristle slash where the man's neck had once been attached to his head.

Blood pattered onto the sawdust with a steady drip. Death wasn't like René had imagined it. But he did recognize the distinctive curl in the slice near where the ear would have been that Aimée had described. He realized that it was too late to hear what Vatel had to say, now or ever.

Vatel's fists were still semi-clenched. The match burned René's fingers. He struck another. With his other hand, he unclenched Vatel's fingers. A torn bite-size shred of paper was stuck between his middle and ring finger. René smoothed it out and deciphered the half-word Pamlu . . . the rest had been torn off. It meant something. But he didn't know what. Or how it connected to Aimée's danger.

The knock of a diesel engine echoed from the courtyard. René moved away from the table saw, avoiding Vatel's half-severed head, and peered beyond the door. A blue diesel Peugeot stood bathed in the moonlight, the model favored by undercover security types,

Aimée had told him once. And judging by the broad-shouldered man who got out, he figured she was right.

His conscience, *non,* his duty as a law-abiding citizen demanded he share his information with the *mec.* Give a statement at the Commissariat while the murderer walked free. Playing by the rules: where did that get you, René thought, except maybe dead like Vatel. He stuck the paper into his pocket, slid out the back door and into the alley, following in the steps of the killer.

Thursday Night

At the zinc counter in the Gare du Nord buffet, Aimée punched in the Agence France-Presse number on her cell phone.

By the time she reached Georges Millac, she'd downed her espresso and ordered another.

"It's Aimée Leduc, Georges," she said. "Forgive me for bothering you."

"The big-eyed wonder," he said. "Knew I'd hear from you again."

Hope flared in her. "Did you find something?"

"And here I thought you liked my company or wanted another brandy!"

The thought of brandy curdled her stomach. "That, too, but —"

414

"You have a fax number?"

Excited, she realized he had something. Her office? But she couldn't go there. Too dangerous.

"Hold on." She rifled through her worn Vuitton wallet for the Internet café cards she used sometimes. Found the closest one.

"Café Panique, an Internet café. Put 'Attention Aimée.' Ready for the number?"

There was a silence.

"Georges?"

"Something's come up," he said, his voice lowered.

"Take down the fax number. 01 83 79 66 50."

Another pause.

"Georges, did you get that?"

"Oui."

"Fax it when you can," she said. "I'll wait in the café."

He hung up.

She threw some francs on the zinc counter, left her second espresso untouched, and grabbed her bag.

The CRS would patrol the Metro and reroute the bus lines. Better to take a taxi. She joined the line at the taxi rank, fanning herself in the heat. At her turn, she jumped in a taxi's back seat. "Bourse de Travail, *s'il vous plait.*"

The driver ground into gear, wound through lines of buses, and entered Boulevard Magenta. On the wide boulevard, dotted by globed street lamps and shadows cast by the trees, they passed the glass canopy of Marché Saint-Quentin, the covered market, now dark. To the right, she noted armored vehicles blocking the area of Château d'Eau and a burning car, the rioters' target of choice. The crackdown already heralded an ugly night. So far, there were no roadblocks or car checks on Boulevard Magenta. It was a straight shot to the café.

She slipped the taxi driver a twenty-franc tip for the short ride. It never hurt to earn rainy late-night taxi karma. She got out in front of the Bourse de Travail, a Corinthian-pillared palace of the workers' unions, more Italianate than utilitarian.

The Place de la Republique lights shone through the manicured trees, glinting on the red metal airplanes of a children's fun fair. The humidity felt so thick, she could taste it; the distinctive ozone smell signaled a storm. She crossed the pedestrian zebra's white stripes to Café Panique's outdoor tables under an awning, and continued inside the turn-of-the-century café with its red velvet curtains, gilt-scrolled alcoves, and blazing chandeliers. She walked to the rear, behind the leather banquettes, to the Internet access desk. A shaven-headed man, a gold hoop in one ear, looked up.

She handed him her punch card. "I'm expecting a fax."

He breathed out and shrugged.

"You, too? The lines were down. Let me check again."

She scanned the clientele: a young *bourgeois bohème* couple in stylish rumpled linen holding hands; a man in a suit with a loosened tie nursing an aperitif, who glanced up each time a woman entered the café; two old women in faded housedresses sipping fresh-squeezed *jus d'orange;* all escaping the heat of their apartments. A mix, like the quartier. And she imagined sitting with Yves at a neighborhood café, like this, his arms around her, nibbling her ear, whispering. . . .

"Mademoiselle?"

She blinked.

"Partial transmission." He handed her three curling Thermo-fax paper sheets. "We should have received more, but the lines go up and down."

Thanks to the DST disrupting land lines to receive satellite feed. Or the storm.

"No problem; I'll wait."

He punched three holes in her card.

She sat by the dark wood-framed window and ordered a *citron pressé* from a waiter with a serpent tattoo disappearing up his arm under his wrinkled white shirt. She set her cell phone down on the white napkin and poured the sugar water into the squeezed lemon juice, added more water, and sipped. Tart and sweet.

The cover page read: From Georges, AFP to Aimée. The next was a blurred series of lines, the bottom section wavering off the page. But, squinting at the first paragraph, she got the gist of it. "*Molry Chimie traitment d'eau industriel* and SAHE, *Sociéte Anonyme de Hydroelectricite,*" a press release read, "announced today August 15 a joint venture with the Turkish government to take over the construction of the Ilisu Dam and supply hydroelectric power in Southeast Turkey."

The next page came out more clearly. It was titled *Bulletin of the Kurdish Human Rights Project KHRP* and stated, "The Ilisu dam project in the predominantly Kurdish area of Turkish Southeastern Anatolia is located on the Tigris River. The largest hydroelectric power plant in Turkey, its construction has been troubled. It is estimated the dam will create a reserve with a maximum volume of 10.4 billion m^3 and a surface area of 313 km^2, creating a power capacity of 1,200 MW. The completion of this dam would cause flooding of the ancient archeological site of Hasankeyf, a site estimated to be more than 2,000 years old with cultural and historical significance to the Kurdish people. The KHRP believes the project is motivated by a desire to cleanse the region of Kurds as an ethnic group. Between 50 and 68 hamlets and villages will be flooded, an additional 57 villages will have their land partially flooded. Estimates run as high as 80,000 local inhabitants affected. Many villages have reportedly been evacuated at gunpoint by the Turkish military and in some cases houses have already been flooded or burned to the ground."

Below that, running off the page, were scribbled initials. YR. Yves Robert. Her finger traced the letters. First Kat, the novelist, intimating that French contracts were at stake in Turkey, and now this, from Georges. She needed to think. More than that, she needed to see. The answer had to be here. She rubbed the worn Ottoman coin amulet.

Bribery and kickbacks were endemic to such a project. But key was Yves's initialed copy of the Kurdish bulletin. Yves *knew*. If Molry *Chimie* and SAHE had greased palms and were allied with the Turkish military. . . .

She needed another piece of the puzzle.

She punched in Sarko Security's number. "Vatel still working?"

"Aah, you're the ex-girlfriend, right?" It was the voice of the guard from the other night. RadioEurope with 80's pop music played in the background.

"Right . . . hope I didn't miss him again."

"*Zut!* He didn't show up tonight."

An uneasy feeling stayed with her after she hung up. She stirred the *citron pressé.* Who else could she telephone? The only other Kurd she'd met didn't like her either.

She doubted that Ansary would be working at his office this late, but she tried it. No answer. Then she tried Andiamo, his Italian restaurant.

"*Buona sera,* Isabella speaking," a woman answered. "You'd like a reservation?"

A plush place, by the woman's manner.

"Monsieur Ansary please."

"The owner? A moment, please."

She thought a hand muffled the receiver as someone spoke. Then, "Monsieur Ansary's not here. If you tell me what it's regarding, I'll make sure he —"

"I must speak to him, now," she said. "Can I reach his cell phone?"

"We don't give that number out."

She tried to remember if he'd had photos

on his desk . . . children, a dog? *Non,* she couldn't recall even seeing a wedding band.

"Mademoiselle," the woman said, "we're full this evening. I've got patrons waiting. I'll write down your message."

"It's an emergency."

"What do you mean, 'emergency'?" Suspicion laced her voice.

"A fire in the building," Aimée said. "I saw the flames. I need to reach him."

True, she'd seen a burning car. Who knew? A riot could be in full swing.

"You mean Monsieur Ansary's apartment?"

A trick question?

"The office . . . what's with the questions? The firemen have their hatchets out, about to chop down his door. What's his cell phone number?"

"He told us never to —"

"Give it out? And let his office burn to a crisp?"

Silence except for the clink of cutlery and hum of conversation. "Fine, Isabella. I'm sure he'll thank you when . . ."

"06 21 94 33 65."

"Merci."

"One thing," she said. "Forget my name."

Ansary's phone rang five times, then his voice mail requested that she leave a message or, in an emergency, try 06 30 44 22 42.

She had already classified this as an emergency. She punched in the new number. Another message in Ansary's voice, in both French and, she figured, Kurdish, instructed her to leave her number. He was cautious and hard to reach. But then, if she were financing a reputed "terrorist" Kurd party, she might be also.

She tapped the long-handled spoon on the tall frosted glass. Glancing back at the desk, she saw the shaven-headed man signaling her.

With the phone crooked between her good shoulder and her ear, she picked up the next sheet.

"Another transmission," he said.

Thermo-Fax paper with a few waving lines and a blurred grayscale photograph displaying indistinguishable figures. No facial delineation, but she could tell they were men. One was stocky and broad-shouldered in a type of uniform, pinpricks of white from medals on one side of his chest, braid, epaulettes on his shoulders. A tall figure was partially cut off. There were words in Turkish with those funny little dots.

Her cell phone rang.

"Allô?"

"There's no fire. Why did you call me at work?" said Ansary, sounding irritated.

He'd know Nadira had been caught by now. Or did he?

"Do you have a comment concerning the Iranian assassin in custody?"

"What's there to say?"

"Do you question her involvement in Yves Robert's murder?"

Ansary sighed. "And what if I do? That's the last thing on my mind. Security forces have thrown a cordon around this part of the quartier. They raided the iKK party office and rounded up party members from the cafés. Write that in your article."

She stared at the fax. "Do the Ilisu dam or Hasankeyf mean anything to you?"

Pause. "Hasankeyf?"

"The archeological village —"

"I know. I come from the hamlet five kilometers away. My family. . . ." His voice broke. "Gone. The military blamed it on water-level testing necessary to attract French company contracts. But they wanted the Kurds out. And efficient as always, the military —"

"Can you help me, Ansary? I have a photo but can't understand the Turkish words. One of them looks like Ehret."

He drew a breath heavily.

Stumbling over the pronunciation, she read, *"Albay Ehret ve meshru Turk-Fransiz aile evladi dedi telafuz ederken Umut. . . ."*

"Colonel Ehret and the scion of the prominent Turkish–French family Umut. . . ." he said, translating.

"Ehret's the colonel . . . ?"

"In charge of Anatolian military operations. He commanded the Yellow Crescent five years ago. They flooded my village."

"You have proof of this?

"It took me years to find it. I gave the documents to Yves Robert," said Ansary, his voice now distant. "And what good did it do? None."

Her knuckles grasping the phone whitened.

"And this other man mentioned in the article?"

"One of the elite?" he said. "I don't know."

"His picture runs off the page," she said. "But he's tall."

Her words hung in the air.

"Look, I'm working. I have to go."

She missed it and it was right here. "Please, let me read it to you again."

He said something, but as he spoke a buzzer sounded in the background.

"What?"

"Umut."

"Is it a name or a place?"

"Both. I have to go."

"Wait, please, one more question. What does *Roj baş* mean?"

Vatel had used these words as he entered Kat's apartment.

"*Roj baş?* Kurdish . . . a greeting."

"Like *Salaam Aliekoum,* would you say?"

The greeting used by Arabs and Turks, the response *Aliekoum Salaam,* with the hand over the heart.

"It's the Kurdish equivalent."

He hung up.

Yves had said *"Salaam Aliekoum"* on the interrupted cell phone message. It seemed unlikely then that he'd met a Kurd who'd knifed him from behind.

Shadows draped the ornate iron balconies of the six-story white stone buildings across the street. A late-night bus, half empty, trundled by. The bark of a dog came from the open window.

She debated calling Georges to ask him about the whereabouts of Ansary's documents. She'd have to use tact, a quality René often said she lacked. But Georges didn't answer the phone.

She handed her card to the desk man.

"We close in twenty minutes."

She had to hurry. She picked a terminal,

logged on, and started her search. One entry for Colonel Ehret listed his military service. She cross-referenced the entries with "Ilisu Dam."

Nothing.

Then she searched newsgroups for prominent Turkish-French families. Fifteen or so came up on various philanthropic news group sites. She had to winnow it down . . . to what . . . tall men?

The café lights dimmed. *Merde* . . . was the power going out? She looked up to see a young man, bloodstains on his tank top, entering the café. At the counter, he ordered a Pernod.

"I've never seen anything like it," he said, shaking his head. "The Citroën DS shot through rue de Paradis like a flying saucer."

The barman nodded. "Those DS road-handle like gazelles, that's why they call her the 'goddess.' My uncle drove one."

"Then it crashed into the statue." He took a gulp of the Pernod. "And a dwarf spilled out!"

Aimée froze. René! She forced herself to stand and approach the counter. The blood staining the man's top made her stomach lurch. She had visions of René's mangled body encased in twisted steel, remembered his attempt to protect her, their argument over real estate, her last angry words. . . .

"He . . . he's dead?"

She'd take it all back, take every word back, rob a bank to pay for . . .

"Eh?" The man grimaced. "I ran to help him and I cut myself. See!"

"Please . . . tell me the truth. . . ."

He blinked at her.

"The dwarf dusted off his jacket, not a scratch on him or the DS, just a fender gone." He shrugged. "Damnedest thing!"

The bartender nodded. "The hydraulic suspension in de Gaulle's DS saved him, too. The OAS ambushed him with machine guns, but the old bull drove away, cursing them. They're built like tanks, those 'goddesses,' " the barman said. "Of course, they guzzle gas like there's no tomorrow."

Aimée grabbed at the zinc counter ledge as she tottered, then fell.

Her cell phone rang.

"Allô?" she managed to say, as she sat up.

"You all right, Aimée?" said René, sounding sheepish. "If you're angry at me for telling Morbier, I understand, but it's better that you're safe . . ."

"Me?"

"Listen —"

"You emerge from the jaws of death and — !"

"An exaggeration. The car needs a little work."

Poor René, his beloved car injured.

"Forget any ideas about leaving the DST," he said. "The quartier's in lockdown."

"I can see." She pulled herself up. "What do you mean?"

"I'm in the café Panique near the Place de la Republique," she said. "Trying to decipher a fax."

"But you were supposed to — !"

"Hold on, René." She walked back to the computer terminal and scanned the screen.

"Listen, Aimée, Vatel said you were in danger. But when I went to meet him, I found him —"

Her fingers halted on the keyboard. "You saw Vatel? Did he tell you anything?"

"He couldn't. His throat was slashed. Like Yves's."

She gasped, envisioning again that swirl, that mark.

"Does 'Pamlu' mean anything to you?" René asked.

"Should it?"

"The paper was torn off, but I found it gripped between Vatel's fingers. He wanted to tell you something. Get out of there, Aimée."

"I will."

She hung up before he could protest further. She searched the newsgroups for the names Umut and Pamlu. At the bottom of the page, a genealogy newsgroup for the Pamluk family, caught her eye. An Umut Pamluk was listed as an Ankara correspondent, now the Agence France-Presse administrator.

She stiffened.

"Mademoiselle, we're closing in two minutes."

She kept reading. Umut Pamluk, an accomplished stage actor in his twenties, had changed careers. He wrote under the pen name of Gerard Drieu, using his father's last name. He published a well-received history of the Turkish military. His father was a SAHE manager; he'd had a Turkish mother, a Pamluk; he'd married a French wife. There had been an acrimonious separation after her supposedly blatant affairs with foreign correspondents splashed over the Ankara society column. An obituary noted his wife's recent death.

Aimée froze; then she began to berate herself. Not only had she believed Drieu, she'd been blind. Nor had Yves seen, until it was too late. But Drieu wouldn't get away with it.

She hit PRINT. The café lights dimmed.

Outside on the terrace, the waiter was stacking the rattan chairs. Her hands trembling, she grabbed her bag and picked up the printouts.

The waiter saw her out the door and locked it. There was no one on the street except an old man walking his dog. She hurried up the first road to her left, her mind turning over the changes in Georges's voice, the partial fax. What if Drieu had been there . . . listening? What if he'd figured out where she was?

She headed to rue des Vinaigriers, the old street of the vinegar merchants. And to the only person she knew in the quartier. She called Drieu and left him a message to meet her there as soon as possible.

She answered René's call on the first ring. "It's Gerard Drieu," she told him. "He killed Yves."

"You mean the admin at Agence France-Presse? But that doesn't make sense."

A taxi whizzed by, horn blaring. "It makes a lot of sense."

"Wait a minute, where are you?"

"Heading to rue des Vinaigriers," she said. "You know the place."

"But —"

"Drieu's half-Turkish, his French father worked for SAHE. The company that snagged the Ilisu Dam project. Yves found out. It all makes sense now."

She knew what she had to do. She heard footsteps, and broke into a run.

Thursday Night

René limped from the all-night garage at a half-run. Rue des Vinaigriers. That meant only one place.

How could she have escaped the DST and safety, the protection guaranteed by Morbier? But never mind how: *Why?* Bullheaded and stubborn as always. Wrong or right, she was loose on the street, in danger. Never mind the why.

His hip ached, the Glock sat in his desk drawer . . . what use could he be? And Morbier? He'd bring the wrath of the security service to bear on Aimée. When he found her.

One more block to go. René wiped his forehead as he crossed Boulevard Magenta.

"Monsieur, not a nice time for a walk. Your papers, please."

A jumpsuited figure stepped in front of him.

"Excuse me, you don't understand —"

"Wasn't your vehicle involved in a collision?"

"Yes, but —"

"It seems you left the garage without making a full report to the officer. Now, if you'll come this way."

He gestured René to a gray van.

Thursday Night

Aimée panted, catching her breath in a doorway on rue des Vinaigriers. Streetlights punctuated the shadowed, stone buildings with their mansard roofs and tall shutters. She caught the tang of leather emanating from inside. Behind these entry doors were leather workshops full of pelts and hides. Even the stairways reeked with the odor of leather.

Drops of warm rain fell on her face. Leaves rustled. She passed a ground-floor establishment with a black façade over which gray metal shutters had been rolled down. Above them were gold letters in scroll reading S. Poursin, established 1890. She edged into the shadows of the massive black doors, and buzzed. The doors swung open. And she went inside, leaving one door ajar.

"Albert?" she asked.

Tall glass showcases displayed every kind of buckle known to man. Brass, copper, metal. And then some she couldn't identify.

"Mademoiselle Aimée, long time no see." Albert, in his grease-stained blue work coat,

432

pockets overflowing as usual, peered over his reading glasses.

"The usual, a new client, I take it?"

The thump and clack of machines came from the factory in the rear. A huge peaked glass ceiling extended over a workspace filled with machines that reached to the next street.

"You might say that, Albert. May I use the back office?"

"You know where it is." He scratched his grizzled gray hair. "I'm running the sanders, can't stop and chat."

"I appreciate this, Albert," she said. *"Merci."*

"Your father was a good man. I owed him," he said.

He left the rest unsaid.

Pangs of guilt assailed her for using Albert's workshop to lure Drieu, but it was the only place she could think of. She glanced around, then scanned the printout and faxes.

Taking bribes from SAHE, working with Ehret . . . Yves must have found out. She'd still have to locate the proof that Ansary had furnished Yves, but maybe she could get Drieu to admit it. If he bit.

She heard a distant click and scrape as the garage door opened.

He just had. And sooner than she expected. There was no time to prepare. In the grimy glass-windowed office, she searched her bag. She'd left her microcassette recorder back at the office.

Footsteps. She looked around the office. An old Olivetti typewriter, brown ledgers, an inkwell. Albert's business practices hadn't advanced to the 1990's. But he had an old beige plastic answering machine. It would do. Had to.

"I just got your message," Drieu said, a bewildered look in his eyes, his blond hair damp and tousled as if he'd been running. "Why are we meeting in a buckle factory?"

"I know the foreman," she said. She edged close to the desk, covered her hand and hit the red recording button.

He didn't look like a killer. And he didn't look half Turkish. But she remembered the legacy of the Ottomans who had promoted intermarriage, and that his father was French. Blond . . . the Afro Coiffeur woman's words . . . "hair like a witch doctor" . . . yellow. And he was tall.

"Aimée, I found Yves's files," Drieu said. "And you won't like it."

Trying until the end. But then he'd been an actor.

"Yves sold out the Kurds."

"More like the other way round." She shook her head. "Your father works for SAHE, you had the connections. Colonel Ehret's your friend. You took the bribes to flush out the Kurds. If anyone sold out the Kurds, you did. Yves realized it and was about to expose you."

Gerard Drieu's face darkened. "I don't know what you mean."

"You overheard Langois arranging to meet me at the Gare du Nord and silenced him, too."

"Calm down, Aimée," he said, "you've got this all wrong."

"You're big pals with Colonel Ehret." She gestured to the blurred fax on the blotter. "Umut Pamluk, that's you, isn't it?"

"What do you want?" Comprehension flickered in his eyes.

"Admit to sabotaging Yves's articles —"

"But why would I?"

This wasn't going the way she'd planned. "The part I don't get is why you thought you had to kill Yves. It was more than hiding bribes, wasn't it?"

The rhythmic pounding of machines thumped dully in the background.

"You come from a prominent Ankara family. With your connections, you could have had his articles suppressed. You could have

435

swung the rest, too, without killing him, *non?* And yet, even in the society columns about your estranged wife, they mentioned her affairs, blaming her. . . ."

Drieu slammed his fist down on the desk, rattling the answering machine. The inkwell spilled, bleeding violet ink onto the blotter.

Wild anger sputtered in his eyes. Green-gray eyes that now were narrowed in hate. "Shut up."

She had struck a nerve.

"Why don't you tell me —"

"I said shut up." He took a step closer. "I tried to reason with him. But he wouldn't listen."

Where was René? She looked for a weapon. Nothing.

"What do you mean?"

"Everyone was gossiping about them. At receptions, at parties. Of course, they were. Yves carried on a blatant affair with my wife, right in my face!"

Did everything boil down to sex?

He pointed to the fax. "It was spread over the gossip columns every day. In the papers I'd written for!"

Chills ran up her spine.

"Yves?"

"Yves denied it. But Ehret showed me photos. He'd caught them together at a villa

436

on the Bosporus."

Was it true?

"No, Gerard, Ehret used you," she said. "Ehret manufactured them, to keep you blinded with rage. He was taking bribes from your father's company. He kept sweeping the Kurds out, flooding the villages, don't you see?"

"So touching, this unshakeable belief you have in Yves." He shook his head. "But you didn't know him, didn't really know him, did you?"

She tried to repress a creeping doubt.

"Do you know what he was doing that morning? Why he left you?" There was a sick smirk on his mouth. "Eh? He liked men, goats, anything, like his friends, the filthy Kurds."

Her hands trembled. Wrong, he was wrong.

"Liar! You followed him from the loft, you knew he was meeting his contact," she said. "Faroum heard rumors about you at the mosque. You couldn't have that. So you wore the chador and slit Yves's throat to make it look like a Yellow Crescent killing."

"No one will believe you."

"And Vatel, who knew your Turkish name —"

"That Kurd . . . a wanted terrorist? An

437

informer on his own people . . . it was just a matter of time."

"So that makes it right?"

"I'm tired of your deluded beliefs," he said, dismissive. "Your simplistic Eurocentric views."

Talk about simplistic: it boiled down to his pride, his jealousy.

Drieu sighed, reached in his pocket.

"And you call yourself a man?" she said. "What man hides as a woman, behind a chador, to kill?"

He lunged over the desk. But she dodged and shot out the office door, past die machines onto the workshop floor. She would have reached the wall alarm if the fire extinguisher hadn't blocked her way. She tripped, felt herself airborne, and reached out. Her hand caught the handle of a metal pressing machine.

Drieu's arm was around her neck. The cold steel tip of a knife was at her throat. He'd kill her like he'd killed Yves.

Clanking metal noises came from the locker.

He pushed her forward, shoved her head near the rows of sharp drill bits of the die machine that were punching holes in rows of flat bronze buckles. Oil fumes and the odor of machine grease filled her nose. She gasped, choking, as perspiration dripped between her shoulder blades.

"Why couldn't you leave it alone? I've had to take care of Georges, too," he said. "All your stupid meddling, your infernal questions."

Her heart raced. She had to stop him. A row of metal die bars, all shapes and sizes, leaned against the machine. She heard shuffling, dragging somewhere.

"My partner's on the way."

"He's a little busy right now. Nice try."

She kicked out, sending the bars clattering to the floor and over the machine. There was a loud grinding noise, and a flurry of metal sparks as a bar caught in the feeder belt. For a moment his grip loosened and she grabbed his hand, twisted the knife away, and saw it fall. But he threw her against the machine and she crumpled. White-hot fire shot through her sore shoulder.

She grabbed the knife and thrust it backward into his leg, hitting muscle and cartilage. He shouted in pain, stumbled. She heard the thump of rapid-fire punches, then an *ouff* as Drieu lost his balance. His head hit the jutting red control lever with a crack. His eyes rolled up in his head. Then she noticed René's white loafers; his feet were scissoring Drieu's ankles in a judo hold.

"About time, René!"

"Sorry, I got held up." He reached a hand to help her to her feet and then pointed to her neck. "You might want to get that seen to."

She rubbed her neck, her shaking fingers coming back covered with blood. A graze. She wiped them on the feather boa she still wore. Her shoulder ached fiercely.

"Thanks, partner," she said. "Nice judo move!"

"And now you'll go home and rest, right?"

She nodded.

"About time, Aimée."

Friday Early Evening

"Ready?" Morbier asked.

In the préfecture's video surveillance control room, Aimée nodded, rubbing her sore shoulder. Ten monitors flicked on, showing videotapes of men being questioned by uniformed members of the DST at plank tables.

"Observe screen three," Morbier said. "They arrested this man in his room near the mosque. In it they found a whole arsenal and enough Semtex to blow up Notre Dame Cathedral. He's the leader of a cell of Algerians, an Iranian, a Turk, and an

Indonesian. A real mix."

Aimée stared at the man. Bearded, dark circles under his eyes, handcuffed and wearing a T-shirt.

"You recognize him?"

"Non." She'd never seen him. But with his beard, he looked like so many who'd stood on rue Faubourg Saint-Denis.

"He's Nadira's activator, a Sorbonne-educated Iranian called Ruhal. Nice, eh?" Morbier exhaled. "Our fault. Remember how we provided the exiled Ayatollah with sanctuary? This *mec* was the thanks we got. They've found links to cells in Lyons and Marseilles. Raided them last night, the last one this morning."

"The DST won't insist on my being held in 'protective custody' now, will they, Morbier?"

"Not that it did any good, did it, Leduc?"

"But now it's safe; they've shut down the network, right?"

Morbier rubbed his chin, saying nothing. Unusual.

Her hands balled in tight fists. "The magistrate listened to Drieu's tape, didn't she?"

"She's re-opening the investigation of Yves's homicide," he said. "The Turkish Consulate refuses to cooperate. But with new evidence coming to light at Agence France-Presse. . . ."

She watched Morbier, sensed something behind his words.

"And that consists of?"

"A laptop containing a disk attributed to Yves." Morbier shrugged. "And there's an Agence France-Presse bank account discovered by their accounting department that contains funds transferred by wire from Ankara. Drieu was the only signatory on that account."

It was more than she'd hoped for. They'd got Drieu and his slush fund of bribes. Most important, they found Yves's work.

"Listen to this." Morbier pushed RE-WIND. Then PLAY. On screen three, Ruhal's eyes shone with fervor. "I'm one of thousands, hundreds of thousands." His hoarse voice cracked. "I fall and another takes my place."

"Big talk," said the officer. "Your cells have been destroyed, everyone is in custody."

"The West invaded our countries, killed our women and children and torched the land. It will reap what it has sown." Ruhal shook his head. "As for you, you know nothing."

"Your network's gone," the officer said.

"It's over."

"Remember 1993, the World Trade Center?" Ruhal leaned back, shaking his head. "That was just the beginning."

Aimée shivered. Morbier was showing this to her for a reason.

"What does it mean, Morbier?"

Morbier leaned forward. "I'm almost afraid to find out," he said.

She checked the time and hitched her bag onto her good shoulder. "Got to go."

"I thought we could have dinner, Leduc."

And she noticed his sagging eyes, how old he'd become. Her godfather, the one constant in her life. The one who tried to protect her in his own way.

"Better than that," she said. "Join me at the Hôtel le Bristol. A reception."

He blinked and recovered. The sly look was back in his eye. "Slumming in the posh quartier, Leduc?"

She pulled out the engraved UNESCO invitation. "I can bring a guest. And since my. . . ." Her throat caught. She couldn't say it.

Morbier stared at the invitation and read. "A reception honoring Roberta Tash's years of service to UNESCO."

He handed back the invitation. "You can't leave the past alone, can you, Leduc?"

Behind that basset-hound look, he never forgot a thing.

"So you knew *Maman* worked at UNESCO and you didn't tell me?"

He looked at his hands, pushed the cuticle back on his nicotine-stained thumbnail.

"No point, Leduc."

She took a deep breath. "I know her name's on the world security watch list."

Her mother was a '70s "terrorist." Branded like Ruhal and these men caught on these monitors.

He sighed. "Ancient history."

PERSONA NON GRATA was stamped next to her name on a world security checklist. Still, she'd give anything to see her. Just once.

"Leduc, she left when you were eight years old," Morbier said. "Time to grow up."

"Maybe you're right, Morbier." She paused at the door, rubbing her shoulder. "Time to move on." Her footsteps echoed down the linoleum hall and she didn't look back.

Mercedes were lined up, letting off guests at the five-star Hôtel le Bristol's entrance. Bellmen in caps and gold-braided jackets scurried from under the glass canopy bordered by a gold frieze. Aimée walked back and forth, debating, on rue du Faubourg Saint Honoré's rain-dampened pavement.

Ridiculous. What could she learn? Time to move on, like she'd told Morbier. To abandon this pipe dream.

But she saw no cafés, only designer boutiques and coiffeurs under flowering linden trees in this exclusive slice of the eighth arrondissement. And she had to pee.

"*Bonsoir,* welcome to Le Bristol," the doorman said.

The scent of perfume and wealth met her. Couples in formal attire clustered in the lobby and perched on the Louis XV chairs in the lounge. A discreet placard read: UNESCO reception, Salle Elysée.

She'd come this far. So she walked down the hall. At the tall, white, carved double doors, she hesitated. The reception hall was filled by men in tuxedos and women in gowns holding champagne flutes, engrossed in conversation, laughing. Everyone talking; they all knew each other.

A fleeting pang hit her. Her life could have been different. But no, it didn't work that way. She turned on her stiletto heel and left.

The white Carrara marble restroom had gold-plated fixtures and crystal vases with lilac sprays. A sharp-eyed *dame de pipi* stood there, a plate of coins by her station. Aimée took refuge in a marble cubicle and closed her eyes, her shoulders heaving, letting herself drift in her pain. No Yves, the illusion of her mother gone. She rocked back and forth until her sobs stopped and the salty tears dried on her cheeks. A tired acceptance came over her. Finally.

She'd been in there a long time. Now she'd have to leave a big tip.

"Mademoiselle?" The henna-haired uniformed woman extended a steaming towel to her. *"Ça va?"*

"Bien, merci." Aimée dropped ten francs in her dish. She didn't envy the woman her job. Even in a plush hotel like the Bristol.

At the mirror over the sink she saw her smudged eyes, the mascara lines running down her cheeks. A mess. She splashed her face with cold water and rubbed it with the steaming towel.

"Pardonnez-moi," said a voice at her elbow. "Don't I know you?"

Aimée opened her eyes. She blinked at the woman staring at her in the mirror. An auburn-haired middle-aged woman, with deep creases in the corners of her eyes.

"You remind me of someone," the woman said, her head cocked. "You look so familiar." Then she laughed. "Forgive me. At my age, everyone looks like someone I know."

Pinned near the shoulder of her cream silk gown was a gardenia corsage and a name tag reading Roberta Tash.

"You're Roberta!"

"Guilty." She smiled. A smile that lit up her face. "I must have met you inside, at the reception. Excuse me for not remembering your name."

Tactful and diplomatic. Nice.

"I'm Aimée Leduc."

"Leduc?"

Aimée bit her cheek. "Sydney's daughter."

It took a nanosecond before Roberta nodded. "No wonder. You look just like your mother."

Aimée's throat caught. "I do?"

"Do you mean no one's ever told you?" Roberta put her hand on Aimée's arm. Squeezed it. "Of course, it's years since I've seen her. She would have been your age . . . but she must be here now! That's right, you RSVP'd."

Aimée couldn't lie to this woman.

She shook her head. "I don't want to spoil your evening. Please understand, I . . . my mother's not coming."

How easy that word mother rolled from her tongue.

"*Maman* left us . . . I was young, I just . . . sorry." Her cheeks reddened. "My mistake,

I wandered into UNESCO hoping to find someone who'd known her . . . more than twenty years ago. . . ." Guilt racked her; this woman should be in the reception honoring her instead of . . . Aimée shook her head. "I'm sorry, gatecrashing your party, the guests. . . ."

"Not at all. I remember her well. Sydney was unique," said Roberta. "She followed a different drummer, you know. A free spirit, so artistic, and she threw herself into everything. Passionate, part of the '60s. Unlike the usual expats who wanted to be posted at UNESCO to live in Paris and snag a husband." Roberta grinned. "I married a Frenchmen too, but Sydney, of all people, married a *flic!* We never figured that out."

Aimée listened, dumbstruck. This woman talked about her mother in a normal, down-to-earth way. None of the subterfuge or secrets she'd grown up with.

Roberta shrugged. Pensive. "Me, I took the conservative way. It's my nature to hold back and try to work within the system. My biggest protest was to wear a pair of wide bell-bottoms." A little smile painted her mouth. "Sometimes I wondered if I'd taken a chance —"

"Roberta!" said an African woman in a

bright-colored headdress. "Hiding in the bathroom of all places. It's time for your toast."

"Just spending time with the daughter of an old friend, Makeba."

She opened her arms and hugged Aimée tightly. Then followed Makeba. She paused at the door, threw her a last look. "I see her spirit in you. Good luck, Aimée."

The pigeons scattered under the stone arcades of rue de Rivoli as Aimée walked there. The flutter of their wings mingled with the peal of a distant church bell. She paused at the corner of rue du Louvre near her office. There was still an hour or so of daylight. She could make a dent in the pile on her desk. Faced with a solitary evening of work, she hesitated. But she told herself she had to accept responsibility. She had a business to run, the Microimage account to maintain.

Bon, she'd fuel up with an espresso at the café. But first she'd check for messages on the office answering machine to see if anything pressing waited.

One message.

"Aimée . . . ?" A hesitant voice. Static on the line. "I'm at the Khartoum airport, catching a flight to Paris. Stupid, I know but . . ." It was Guy's voice. The eye surgeon who'd saved her from blindness, then walked out on her because she couldn't settle down. More static, hesitation. "*A Medécins sans Frontières* conference . . . short notice. You probably don't want to see me but . . . I just wanted to call."

She stared at the rosy sunset spreading over the Louvre's Cour Carrée, bathing the gray-tiled rooftops in a last burst of light. The gray of Guy's eyes. She willed the message to say more. She heard clicking noises. "Arriving Charles de Gaulle . . . 10 p.m. I don't know if you'll get this. Or even listen, but I've thought about you . . . if we could talk. . . ."

Buzz. The line went dead. A taxi slowed down in front of her to turn, its light signaling that it was free. She glanced at her watch. 9 p.m.

ACKNOWLEDGMENTS

Heartfelt thanks go to Jean Satzer, Grace Loh-Prasad, Lauren Haney, Dot Edwards, Barbara, Jan, Max, Carla Bach, Diane Cribbs, and Marion Nowack. To Don Cannon and Andi Vajda on computer patrol and Dr. Terri Haddix for her medical expertise. In the Kurdish community, for many hours spent with the generous Fikret Demirkol, Welat Yuksel, and Kocer Salguta.

In Paris: Reporters Without Borders, Rusen Werdi of the Institut Kurd, and private detectives Madeline Dieudonné and Sylvie Hak. Jean-Damien, Gilles, Patrick Rougelet, Jean-Claude Mulès, retired Brigade Criminelle, Jean-Noel Saniol, retired BRP de la Police, the untiring and knowledgeable Jeanine Christoff, President, Société historique du 10eme arrondissement, Benoît Pastison, Chef de communications of Gare de l'Est, Sarah Gensberger, Donna and Earl Evleth for *les explosifs et toutes,* S.

451

Poursin rue des Vinaigriers, the Anciens Combattants de 10eme, Madame Huguette Malwe for the afternoon on rue Marseilles, Le Londres café and Cristallerie de Paris on rue de Paradis, Demir, *concierge extraordinaire,* the indefatigable Marielle Leteneur, violin maker, Jon Henley of the *Guardian* for tales of his old 'hood,' Pierre-Olivier, and, always, wonderful Sarah Tarille, la petite Zouzou, and brilliant Anne-Françoise Delbegue.

And nothing would happen without James N. Frey, Linda Allen, Laura Hruska, my son Tate or Jun.

ABOUT THE AUTHOR

Cara Black lives with her husband, a bookseller, and their son in San Francisco. She frequently travels to France. This is her eighth mystery in the Aimée Leduc series for which she has twice been nominated for an Anthony Award.

The employees of Thorndike Press hope you have enjoyed this Large Print book. All our Thorndike and Wheeler Large Print titles are designed for easy reading, and all our books are made to last. Other Thorndike Press Large Print books are available at your library, through selected bookstores, or directly from us.

For information about titles, please call:
    (800) 223-1244

or visit our Web site at:
    http://gale.cengage.com/thorndike

To share your comments, please write:
    Publisher
    Thorndike Press
    295 Kennedy Memorial Drive
    Waterville, ME 04901